Edwin Allen Wyman

Ships by Day

A novel

Edwin Allen Wyman

Ships by Day
A novel

ISBN/EAN: 9783337000219

Printed in Europe, USA, Canada, Australia, Japan

Cover: Foto ©Andreas Hilbeck / pixelio.de

More available books at **www.hansebooks.com**

BY

EDWIN A. WYMAN, PH.D., D.D

AUTHOR OF " ACQUAINTANCE WITH GOD," ETC.

WITH ILLUSTRATIONS

BOSTON

JAMES H. EARLE, PUBLISHER

178 WASHINGTON STREET

1896

Press of J. J. Arakelyan,
295 Congress Street, Boston.

TO THE MEMORY

OF MY VERY DEAR FRIEND

George E. Marshall,

TRUE TO THE HEART'S CORE IN FRIENDSHIP

AND IN THE INTEGRITY WITH WHICH

HE TROD THE PATHS OF BUSINESS,

AND, AMONG THE LIVING,

THOUGH WITHOUT HIS KNOWLEDGE OR CONSENT, TO

Hon. E. S. Converse,

MALDEN'S FIRST MAYOR AND FIRST CITIZEN,

WHOSE LIBERALITY OF MIND

AND HEART MERIT ADMIRATION AND ESTEEM,

THIS VOLUME IS

LOVINGLY DEDICATED.

PREFACE.

BELIEVING the book entitled "Ships That Pass in the Night," though containing many good things, is calculated to do harm, offering, as it does, nothing better than a mere guess for a dying pillow, I have written the present volume with the hope, among other things, that the reader may not only be entertained by the story, but finish its pages with the conviction that immortality is something more than a guess, and that the human ship, instead of sailing in the "night," has before it, in spite of occasional clouds and uncertainties, an open sea and the clear light of day.

Aside from the fact that another life is essential to supplement and give meaning to this, no one can rise from the death-bed scene of Dr. Blentwood, which was an actual occurrence, and still doubt existence beyond the grave.

It is the belief of the author that the following pages contain the germs of reform greatly needed, and that must come sooner or later. Though the story may seem to border on the sensational, the great underlying purpose has been to touch the springs of amendment in certain lines of thought and life.

EDWIN A. WYMAN

CONTENTS.

viii CONTENTS.

SHIPS BY DAY.

CHAPTER I.

AFLOAT.

I HAD long pondered the question how to spend a vacation so as to get the most recreation and consequent profit out of it. I at length decided to take a leisurely trip down the Connecticut River with no companion to entertain me or to be entertained by me. Having purchased a light sail-boat and stored it with provisions, I pushed from the shore of what we will call Rocktown one beautiful day in June, full of the glow of bright anticipations and with a sense of freedom which made me hilarious and glad to my fingers' ends.

My mind was preternaturally active—in a sort of poetic frenzy—from overwork. In short, my physician had told me I had reached the incipient limit of nervous prostration, and that very morning had repeated with solemn emphasis, "You must throw up all care at once and let your mind run fallow or you will break down utterly." I was in that peculiar state of mental fervor and bodily exhaustion which will explain the very strange experience through which I was so soon to pass.

"Isn't this jolly?" said I, half to myself and half to my shadow, which nodded to me from the rippling water as I sat in the stern of the boat and glided out into the current. "No more writing or teaching for the present, no anxieties about anybody, no one to look after but myself! Oh! it is glorious to be free upon occasion, indifferent to the world, and careless of everything except to sip the dew of pleasure from the proffered cup of the present.

"Civilization indeed! Poor fools! let them breathe hot steam and dust, and elbow their way through an overcrowded business, and then die in as great a hurry as they lived, with the un-answered question on their tongues or in their hearts, What of it all?

"There is some education in such a life; but beyond that there is no significance in it. Slaves of an unmeaning care! I leave you to your un-necessary burdens. I'll none of it, at least for the present! I am free! Hurrah! Good boat, it is you and I emancipated together from the thralldom of civilized folly! Soul, till now care-ful and troubled about many things, you have nothing to do but to drink in the beautiful pros-pect, the pleasant sunshine, the present joy."

The sun shone brightly on woods, field and river, flooding all my sensibilities and making me in love with life. This and the added sense of freedom from all care filled me with the very

luxury of satisfaction. I did not look to past or
future; I was resting, and that was enough. I
stretched myself back against the stern in a half-
reclining posture. Shading my eyes with my hat
and letting my boat sail itself, I gave myself up
to all the sweetness I could extract from sight
and sound and easy reflection. Houses along
the shores appeared and disappeared; beautiful
forests with opening glades and glens came and
went; merry voices of children and sweet songs
of birds gladdened the ear and then died away;
new scenes, no two alike, constantly coming and
constantly going, and still I rested and glided on,
unmindful of time and of everything else except
the present. Oh, how I enjoyed that sail! Like
a tired child in the lap of a loved mother, I was
contented to lie still and rest, taking in with sweet
satisfaction whatever came to me through the
senses without effort. I was happy. I wanted
nothing. Hours passed. The vertical sun told
of noon, but I hungered not. At last, I lost consciousness and fell asleep. How long I slept I
know not.

Sometime that or the next day, however, I was
aroused by a sudden lurch of my boat which
nearly sent me overboard, and the first thing I
saw was a small white hand on the side of the
boat and a beautiful face earnestly gazing into
mine. I had fallen asleep full of sweet visions,
and was too much at peace with all the world to
be easily startled or afraid, and I looked at this
sudden and unexpected appearance with simple

curiosity, wondering what it could mean, but with
no effort to rise. I had left home resolved not to
let anything disturb me, and I was so happy, so
satisfied with my new-found freedom, that scarcely
a cannon's ball whizzing near my head, would
have made me at all anxious.

The face was very attractive, and the longer I
gazed the more I saw in it of a deeper beauty
and a tenderer pathos, such as belongs only to a
soul richly endowed with the purest and noblest
feeling. The vision, therefore, was pleasant. One
more added to the many with which I was filled,
and I began to hope that it would not disappear
as suddenly as it came. I thought of the old saying, "If you speak to a ghost it will vanish," and
so, proving the force of early impressions, I said
nothing. I had for years wished I might communicate with a real ghost and learn something
more definite of the spirit land, and I longed to
speak, but rationalism came to my rescue and I
said within myself:

"This is all imagination, of course. A snag
tipped my boat and one of the angel thoughts of
my dream stood out embodied before me, and I
am holding the vision of it—that is all! It is
only in our dreams that the angels on Jacob's
ladder descend to us from heaven. When we
awake the angels become mortals or vanish.

"How sweet it would be to go out of the world
in a dream, having heavenly society to start
with! But how real that face is! It is as if an
angel were about to disclose wondrous things.

The Bible speaks of such messengers appearing to men of old and why not to me? The old prophets could not have longed more for direct heavenly instruction than I, and, oh! if this silence could be broken but for a moment, what joy—what relief to a troubled, doubting world!

" But if this were a heavenly visitant it would not have appeared to me submerged all but head and shoulders under water. And again, would a messenger from the spirit world look so exactly like flesh and blood? Possibly. But she has a modern dress and tiny ear-ring and diamond pin ! I must give up the angel theory. But what is it? Not a believer in nymphs, it must be an optical illusion or a real, terrestrial, *bona fide* girl. Of course it is not a spirit, glad as I should be to see one ; for, though there are reasons why God should satisfy my longings for information, there are others why He should not break the silence of ages.

" But the idea of this being a girl is preposterous. First, because swimming girls are not common. Second, where could she come from in this wild region? for not a house is to be seen. Third, what motive could bring her through the water to my side and in so rich a dress? It is no girl— that's settled. By *reductio ad absurdum*, I prove it.

" How glorious is reason! But the image is still there! Like Banquo's ghost, it will not down, reason or no reason! The sense of sight says. that is a girl; reason says it is not.

Evidently I must employ another sense as a corrective."

I felt a pride in settling such questions by reason alone ; but at length I opened my half-closed eyes and raised my head toward the vision, when, to my utter astonishment, the face brightened with a look of relief as she cried :

"Make for the shore or you will be over the rapids!"

CHAPTER II.

RESCUED.

WITH these hurried words ringing in my ears I sat up, still only half conscious from so long a sleep and the reaction of an overtaxed brain and worn-out nerves. It was twilight, fast deepening into shade. I was confused. An overwhelming sense of languor came over me and I sank back into my old place with only one wish in my heart of all the world, and that was rest!

"Oh, how sweet is rest!" I muttered half audibly. A splash in the water and a sudden turn of my boat caused me again to assume the erect posture and to make a great effort to collect myself. I looked for the vision. It was gone! I could see nothing but water and woods, and heard no sound save the rippling waves pattering monotonously against the bow of my boat, which in turn gave an occasional nod as if in recognition of the gentle caress. I will solve this riddle in the morning, said I to myself, and lay down, feeling thankful I could now enjoy much-needed repose.

The gentle god of sleep only waited this opportunity to woo and bear me away to the land of sweet forgetfulness. Never was a visitor more

13

welcome. With a grateful heart I felt his touch upon my limbs, upon my brow, upon my eyes, and quickly yielding up the self-directing will, I floated off into lovely dreamland with angelic companionship, over verdant hills and sweet valleys, and, just as I was softly—oh, so softly !— sinking down, down, down, into utter and blessed obliviousness, I awoke with a choking sensation and with my head partially under water. The shock roused my memory and my first thought was of the rapids. I soon discovered, however, that I was still in the boat with the bow high and dry on a steep bank of the river, while the stern was so low as to bring it for a moment under water.

I had evidently just been placed in that position, for some one was still tugging at the bow. I raised my head, wet and dripping, and stared about. I tried to rise, but found myself too weak to do so. I tried to assure myself of my identity, but could not trace all the incidents connecting me with the morning. Perhaps I am drowned, I thought. Unable to take in the situation, all I could do was to await developments. Presently my angelic visitant approached. Neither of us spoke till her face was near enough to be quite distinctly seen. It was very beautiful, lit up with such a happy commingling of benevolence, strength and loveliness as to disarm all fear ; and when she spoke her voice and words were in harmony with what her face prognosticated.

"You must be very ill," she said, in a tone so

tender and so full of solicitude as to win my confidence at once.

"Beautiful being," said I, "are you mortal or
immortal?"

"Both," she replied, after some hesitation, and
then added with a smile, "We all live in two
worlds, I suppose."

"In two worlds!" I repeated. "I, indeed,
seem to be on the border between a new past and
a new future, and not exactly in either. Have
you come to take me to heaven?"

She again smiled and slowly answered, "I am
here to see that you are taken to a place of
rest."

"Rest," I echoed; "mine ears attend the sound.
There is no sweeter word, good being. When
shall this rest be mine?"

"Now," she replied. "Can you walk? Let
me assist you," and taking me by the arm I was
soon on my feet, and with great effort took two
or three steps and then fell. Looking up into her
sweet face and seeing there a tear of sympathy, I
said:

"You have no wings for me, but I thank you
all the same. I think my old body still clings to
me. Let me lie here a minute and by that time
it may be dead enough for me to get out of it.
It didn't quite drown, did it?"

Without replying to my question, she hurriedly
left me, saying, "I'll be back in a few minutes."

"Gone to give me time to reflect," I mused.
"It is well, perhaps, that the change from earth

to heaven be not too sudden.   It might stun and
dazzle these unaccustomed eyes, and quite con-
found these weak faculties and powers, before
they could adjust themselves to their new relations. I am content. Had I been better and
nobler, I wonder wherein my exit would have
been different. I feel no pain, and Hope, beautiful
and full-orbed, shines over me, and seems to
beckon me on. I begin to thrill with the glorious
knowledge into which I am about to enter. Old
body, I once loved thee, but the sooner now we
are divorced the better. I desire thee no longer.
Thou dost but encumber, enslave and chain me
down. Let me go, and I will be so light!—so
free! I will ascend, up, up, from the circumfer-
ence to the very centre of knowledge! "Fly swift
around, ye wheels of time"—At this moment a
dark figure approached and stood over me. I
looked up and at length said, "I once thought
you ugly, but you are now most welcome."

"I nebber harms nobody," said the figure.

"True," I replied, "death is not a harm.
Thousands suffer because they cannot die. To
the soul prepared death does but open the door
to greater progress. Have you come to help me
shuffle off this mortal coil?"

"Be Model Koll de name ob your boat? I is
not here to shuffle off with dat, sah. I is here to
tote ye to de house."

"The house not made with hands? Do you
live there? I forget, you cannot enter there."

"I does enter dere, for Doctor and Miss Blentwood hab us in de dinin'-room ebery mornin' to hear de Scriptur' and de prayer."

" Then your name is not Death?"

" Lord! no, sah. You look like you could take dat name better'n dis yere nigger. My name Tom."

" Is it simply Tom?"

" No, not Simple Tom; jes' Tom—dat's all."

" I mean, is that all your name?"

" All mine, boss, 'cept what de ole woman owns. Dey all call her Tot, cos she so big one way as tudder!"

" Have you no other name?"

" No udder legally detachin' to me."

" How long have you been here?"

" Nigh on to seberal year, massa. I came wid Miss Ethel after de doctor came, and was mighty tickled to be tuck along, too."

" Ah! I see. You came over the dark river together."

" 'Tain't the fust time we cross de ribber."

" Then you have died the second death. Is that why you are so black?"

" I is jes' as de Lord made me, sah, and I hain't died no second def, nor de fust one nudder."

" I spoke unadvisedly the dull phrase of earth. It is true you did not die; only the body can die. But will you not be made white as wool?"

" 'Spect de Lord like black well as white. Folks am whitest when dey faint, but spect we'll all be well forebber when we put on de

2

high glory ob de Lord. Here come Tot.
Massa Blentwood got home, Tot?"

" No, Tom, and Miss Ethel so anxious. She
say, ' Tot, you can help Tom better'n I, and I'll
get things ready.' So I run all de way here.
Hole out yer arms, Tom, wid dis cushion on,
while I place him into 'em. Dar now, tote him
easy, and when ye get tired jes' gib him to me.
Is you comf'able, sah?"

" Oh, yes, kind friends, you have made my bed
soft as downy pillows are."

" Tank ye, sah; dat'll please missus to know
we does it comf'able for ye. De wust is going up
dis yere bank, but nebber you fear, sah, dese yere
arms nebber fail when on dooty, sah, special for
missus."

" Are you taking me to the Celestial City?"

" We be takin' you to de house where de bright
lady lib what took ye from the drownin' ribber.
You'll be well took keer of, sah; missus am a
angel, sure."

" Shall I see that beautiful being again and
talk with her?"

" Sartin, for sure; we's takin' you dar by her
'spress commands. We be her mos' willin' sar-
vants, sah."

" Servants? I thought heaven a Democratic
land."

" It mount be, sah. Heap 'Publicans roun'
here. Right smart chance of 'em change on
tudder side, but power of 'em coming back."

" Are you permitted to stand in the presence

of the highest company and drink with them at the same fountain?"

"We eats in de kitchen, sah; in de hell."

"Are, then, heaven and hell so near? and do the wicked serve the just?"

"Oh, lors, massa, I dunno. I warn't talkin' 'bout de fiery brimster hell. I mean de hell ob de house."

"Are you happy, good servants?"

"Why shoon we? We sarve a good man and a angel and wants nuffin. I works out, too, when I please. Why shoon we be 'appy?"

"Ah! I see. Yours is a kind of paradise next to heaven, almost heaven, not quite heaven, and yet heaven after all."

"Dat's it, sah. You hit our fix on de cocoa-nut perzakly. Ef heaven mean 'nuff, den to all 'tents and parpuses we lib in dat same place sure."

During all this conversation I had been borne along at a rapid pace for negro feet, and had been transferred several times from one pair of arms to the other; but each change had been made so deftly that I scarcely knew it. Indeed, had I been carried less carefully, my mind was too active to feel bodily pain. I was in that peculiar and happy state of incipient brain-fever which, aided by circumstances, produced and kept up the delusion that I had passed or was passing out of the earthly life and entering upon the sublime surprises of another state. Everything I saw or heard, coming to me through the alembic of a glowing imagination, was transformed and transfigured. There was nothing in my condition akin to insanity; for my mind was clear as crystal and my reasoning faculties unimpaired. It was simply a state of exaltation of mind over body. Thought seemed unconfined and to range at will, and though I seemed

> " Exiled from earth and not yet winged for heaven,
>   Like the edges of a sunset cloud
>   The beatific land before me lay."

I was in an elysium of mingled sweet content and sweet expectancy.

At length, after some silence, and just as we were entering under the shadow of a very high wall, which seemed to cross our path at right angles, I said, " Ah! the outer wall of the New Jerusalem. Will any one be waiting and watching for me at the gate ? "

I had hardly got the words out of my mouth when I felt myself turning short to the left and descending into the earth and into total darkness.

" Purgatory ! " I murmured, shrinking back. " I never believed in it. Is there no other way ? "

" No udder way," replied Tom, " on dis yere side."

I strained my eyes to take in the situation, but could see nothing, not even those who bore me. I was being carried very cautiously and at a much slackened pace, and more and more unsteadily, when, with a suppressed groan from Tom, burden and burden-bearer sank down together. The new motion had hardly ceased when I was comfortably resting in Tom's lap.

"Yer needs rest, sah, jes' a min't, sah," said hard-breathing and self-forgetting Tom.

"Will it last long?" I asked. Either in answer to my question or to encourage their own weary selves, as well as me, the two faithful servants commenced to sing, very softly at first, scarcely above a whisper, but with increasing melody and soothing effect. Among others most frequently repeated were the following lines:

We's mos' dar! we's mos' dar!
Doan' you see dat light shinin' froo de open do'
Cheerly vitin' us come?
Doan' you see dat hand beck'nin' from de lower step?
Oh! we's mos' welcome sure.
And we's comin', comin', comin', yes', we's comin',
And now we's almos' dar."

During all this song, which fell on my ears like a charm, the hand of Tot was passing to and fro across my temples and through my hair. My fevered and over-active brain grew quiet. I felt my nerves relaxing and the will letting go its hold on the mind; my thoughts, unhelmed, drifted out upon a calm sea; past and present were alike forgotten: and so, in the arms of strange but trusted servants, at the bottom of a subterranean passage, in utter darkness and helplessness, I rested from all care, from all responsibility. That is the last I can remember of that day's history. Oh, blessed sleep! "tired nature's sweet restorer."

CHAPTER III.

DR. LIGHTHEART AND TOT.

IT was late in the afternoon of the next day before I awoke, and my awaking was almost like a resurrection from the dead. I had never before been so far down into the depths of utter unconsciousness. The past was for the moment shut out from my memory. I had not gone so far out of myself as to lose my individuality, but still far enough to lose consciousness of my identity. My first thought, therefore, was not, I am somebody, but, Who am I? I am some one in good circumstances, I thought, as I hastily glanced at my surroundings.

I was in a luxurious bed and a richly-furnished room. I arose, and, having turned the faucets, was watching the hot and cold streams, as they mingled together in the marble basin, while my thoughts went off analogically to the warm and cold currents circling through nature and through human hearts, tempering extremes and making the earth habitable and life attractive.

"Well," I mused, "there are no disagreeable currents in this room, a fact which concerns me now more than abstract questions. How beautiful and cozy everything is! not a social icicle any-

where. There is warmth and welcome from floor
to ceiling. Everything is orderly, still not the
smallest thing says, in its stiffness, Don't touch
me, but rather, Enjoy me as you like. The car-
pet, the paper, the bed and canopy over it, the
curtains, the pictures, the little ornaments, all
harmonize beautifully—unity in variety. There
is an air of cheerfulness, contentment and sociability here, which gives me a free-and-easy,
homelike feeling. Wonder if I shall find the
owner as pleasing? If this is not borrowed taste,
hers ought to be a harmonious and lovely character."

At this point of my soliloquy there was a
knock, and, before I could decide what to do with
myself, the door opened and a man of medium
height, dark whiskers and hair well sprinkled with
gray, and a very benevolent countenance, stood
before me. After a searching glance at me he
said, "Ah! excuse me, sir. I was hastily sum-
moned, and thought your need might be urgent."

"You are a physician, I presume," said I.
" Please walk in. I am glad to see you, though
I hope I am not in need of medicine."

"Let me see how the human clock is keeping
time," said he, placing his fingers on my wrist.
"A good time-piece, but a much abused one, sir.
It acts tired and as if inclined to run down. The
machinery must be lubricated or it will stop. I
am glad, however, to find everything favorable. I
left you last night a little in doubt. The danger of
settled fever is over, and what you now need is beef-

steak and rest. You have been running too fast, and, as a compensation, the dry and overheated wheels must move slowly till oiled from nature's own resources, which you have overdrawn. Keep your bed, sir, at least till to-morrow morning, when I will call. . In the meantime think as little as possible, and sleep all you can. I will order breakfast sent up to you as I go out. Good-day, sir."

"But, doctor," said I, as he turned to leave, "I have a great many questions to ask."

"Not now," he replied; and then reading my thoughts before I could speak, he added, "Everything is lovely. You are in hands that delight to minister to the wants of others. In fact you are as near a local heaven as is possible in this world. You are a lucky dog, sir; so let your thoughts lie down with you, quiet and sweet as a June morning, such as I hope to-morrow will be, when I will give you a longer audience."

I stood still, looking at the door until I heard his retreating footsteps on the stairs, and then, feeling weak, I was glad to obey orders, and crawled back into bed. Though among strangers, I could not but feel peaceful and happy; for my surroundings were lovely, and the coming and going of the doctor had only heightened the beauty of the picture. It would have been difficult to experience an unpleasant emotion in that delightful chamber, and I felt for the first time how important to the sick are the impressions made by room, physician and nurse.

"I'SE NO GRAMMY"—page 25.

" I am welcome and not merely tolerated here,"
I said to myself ; " for the hands that made this
room speak so kindly belong to a heart that
loves the whole world."

Here came a tap at my door, and, at my bidding, in walked an apple-dumpling shaped-negress
with a face round as the full moon, black as
coal, and so wrapped about with white cloth as
to suggest the idea of a fly in a pan of milk !

" I's brung up you dinner, sah," said she, placing it on a stand at my bedside.

" Yes," I added, " and a dinner fit for a king,
too. I thank the Lord and all concerned in
getting it up. What a delicious steak ! It is as
soft and juicy and toothsome as the most dainty
connoisseur could wish. Did you cook this steak,
grammy ? "

" Ebery one calls me Tot. I's no grammy. I
got jes' one chile in dis yere born world, and
he's such a ripskeezach sort of a catamount, I
mighty feared he'll nebber make ole Tot any
mor'n a anxious mudder. If he grow up like he
be now, he nebber can stop long nuff ter get
married. He'd wanter stan on 'e head fore dey
got froo de ceremony, or run out de room on
he han's and feet, growlin' and snarlin' like wild
cat. Why, at de funeral ob ole Marmaduke,
when eberybody were cryin' and takin' on, and
in de mos' solemncolly time, just as de min'ster,
obercome wid streamin' tears, brought he fist
kerwhack on de desk, Pomp jump right into de
floor, and scampered out blartin' like scared calf."

" Well, Tot, you'll kill or cure me laughing."

" Nebber knowed nobody die laughin', sah."

" You are right, Tot ; laughing is a good healthful tonic, and I shall want to hear more of Pomp
hereafter, but I fear I shall split my sides with the
vision you have already given of him before I
finish this good meal. Tot, this is the most perfect cooking I ever enjoyed. Did you do this ? "

"Yah, I cook him. I got so I can suit missus
now, tank de Lord ; but it tuck a heap larnin' and
a power o' patience fore I does it. Missus so
good I would bust ober de hot range 'fore I
guvs him up. She say it fine 'complishment as
playin' de pinanna an' 'portant as preach-
in'."

" She is right, Tot ; for both music and preaching are spoiled by vile cooking in its effect on
actor or listener."

" Well, missus say I should cook healthful and
savory too, and she telled me how ter fix ebbery-
thing and jes de color she want in de bakin', and
how dis were skience and dat were art till I gin
ter tink I di'n't know nuffin 'tall scarcely, and
dat it too much for Tot and I coon do 'em nohow, and I say, ' Oh, missus ! you take way my bref
wid so much larnin'. 'Twill take heap more brain
den I got to forstan' all dat.' I was done plum
gone beat. But she courage me 'bout de great
art, and I fort ef I could ony hab one ob missus'
fine 'complishments, I'd be jes' made, and I says,
' Tot, you can't change you leopard spots, but yer
can let missus come into ye and rule ye, and so I jes

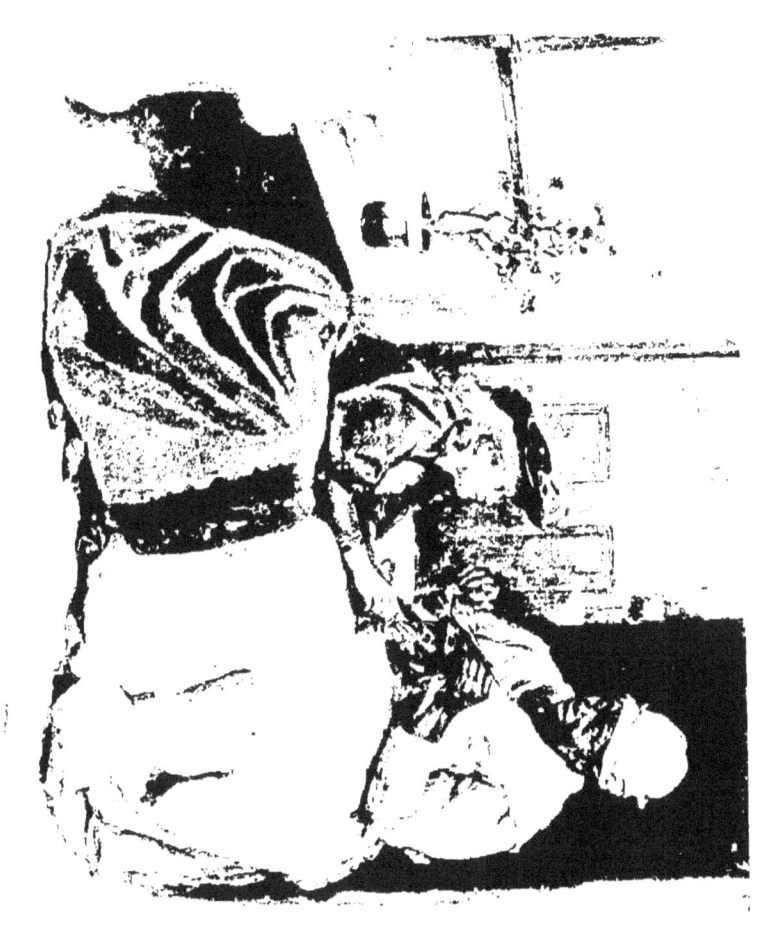

frowed ole Tot away and ony minded missus inside.
I kept forgettin' Tot's 'stakes and minin' missus
till missus inside hab ebberting her own way, and
I shout victory, halleluyah! When missus hear
dat and foun' I cook' em right, she put her dear
purty arms roun' ole Tot's neck and kiss her ole
brack face. Den I coon say nuffin, ony jes bress
de Lord; and I sot right down on de flo' and had
one bressed good cry. I's 'complished cook now,
sah, but missus did it."

"Tot, you are a heroine."

"What's dat?"

"It is a smart, brave woman."

"Tank ye, sah."

"You conquered your ignorance and indisposi-
tion to learn; and to master one's self is the
greatest victory one achieves in this world. According to the Bible, it is a greater act than to
take a city."

"Reckon you and missus am alike."

"Tot, I am thinking you could not pay me a
higher compliment than that. Your mistress must
be a very sensible and excellent lady."

"She be all dat and more too. Oh, my! here
I be talkin' like crazy coot 'ginst doctor's orders.
Ye seemed so peert ye made me forget myself."

Upon this she left the room as fast as her wad-
dling gait could carry her; and for all that day,
when she appeared, as she did occasionally, to see
that I wanted nothing, it was with a look of inquiry and a nod, or a few monosyllables, and that
was all.

CHAPTER IV.

I EARLY fell asleep that night, and slept soundly till morning; and when I awoke my room was flooded with sunshine. I looked out on a world bright and beautiful, as if new-created, and I felt as fresh as the new-born day. I was happy, too, though it would have puzzled me to know exactly why, since I was among strangers, and knew not what a day might bring forth. The secret of my happiness was doubtless largely physical, but much was due to the fact that nothing but pleasing impressions had been made upon me ; and, in addition to gratitude, may there not have been a subtle revelation of a kindred spirit near by, felt and believed in, though mostly below consciousness?

Is there not in every work performed a soul, which is itself a revelation of the author? And is it not as real in so simple a matter as the arrangement of a sick-room as in the greater and more conspicuously heroic deed? May we not, in some advanced period, look back on the so-called trifles of every-day life and read in them our own characters, yes, our very souls, what we were from day to day and year to year? Be that

28

as it may, I was at home with the spirit of the place, felt no loneliness, and was content to await developments. Unconsciously I fell into a semi-poetic mood :

> " Every act has its own spirit,
> Pregnant with immortal fire,
> Kindling in each passing stranger
> Lofty hope or low desire."

I had been awake only a few minutes, when there came a tap at my door, and the benevolent face of Dr. Lightheart appeared.

"Ah! you are as bright as the morning," said he, "and that is saying a good deal. I think you can now do as you have a mind to, provided you keep your mind playful and utterly careless. You must not shoulder a feather's weight of responsibility for months." He added, laughing, "Next autumn, or next year, perhaps, you may break up the fallow ground. But the first breaking now in order will be to break fast ! As it is late, and I am to join you and the family at table, I will at once go below and await your appearance."

I hastily dressed and was soon in the lower hall, where the doctor met me, and, leading me into the sitting-room, introduced me to the family : Rev. Dr. Blentwood, a comfortable invalid of about fifty years, prematurely gray, and some-what careworn, but pleasant and intellectual, and Miss Ethel Blentwood, my rescuer, a remarkably healthy, rosy-cheeked girl of twenty-three sum-mers, blending at once in her mien the intelli-gence of the father and the sweetness, I learned afterwards, of the long-lamented mother. I was heartily congratulated on my recovery, and was as heartily expressing my indebtedness, when Dr. Blentwood took me by the arm, and we all repaired to the dining-room.

I was struck with what is usually termed "the blessing." Dr. Blentwood, looking toward his daughter, who sat opposite, said pleasantly and with touching simplicity, "For this beautiful morning, and the health and happiness of this hour——" Here he paused, and his daughter added with a sweet earnestness, "the Lord make us truly grateful."

"Professor Bloomfield," said Dr. Blentwood, turning to me, "that we did not visit your room on your return to consciousness, was in obedience to the strict orders of our mutual physician, Dr. Lightheart, who would allow no one to attend you but the nurse."

"As a result," broke in Dr. Lightheart, "behold him fresh as the morning, and ready for full rations."

"To Dr. Lightheart's commands as a physician," responded Dr. Blentwood, "we have all learned the unwisdom of disobedience, especially here at Graynoble."

I ventured to ask if Graynoble was the name of the town.

"No, sir," answered Dr. Blentwood; "it is what we call our home."

"Ah!" I said, noting Ethel's downcast eyes, "I was in a dazed condition when I arrived, and thought I was passing from earth to heaven; and, really, though I was mistaken in some respects, I am most fortunate in finding myself in a home so prophetic of that place. The past few days seem still so much a dream, and though I have tried hard to penetrate their history, I do not yet fully know, Miss Blentwood, how much I am indebted to your bravery and self-sacrifice."

"Your indebtedness is very slight certainly," said Miss Ethel, coloring; "for no one used to the water as I am would have done less. Indeed I am indebted to you for lying so still and letting me pull you out of danger so easily. Had you been less manageable, I fear I could not have succeeded."

"I would like very much," I said, "to revisit the scene of my rescue and the route by which I was brought here. It is all a disconnected dream to me, indistinct and visionary, but very pleasant. It is wonderful that I have no recollection of having suffered in the least. I can recall only joyful emotions and bright anticipations. Even now there is a feeling that I may not be quite awake, and that you all may suddenly take angels' wings and fly away, leaving me only the memory of a glorious dream, or vision."

"I fear we are a little too worldly to do that just yet," said Dr. Blentwood, "though I hope, figuratively speaking, our wings are growing. Your experience must have been remarkable. I doubt, from what I myself have been cognizant, that you will ever feel quite clear whether you were in the body or out. Paul in one of his experiences never knew."

"The visions," I responded, "are so satisfying, I would fain hold them as sent from above, whether natural or supernatural."

"Let a physician speak," said Dr. Lightheart. "Mr. Bloomfield enters his boat tired out bodily and mentally, almost exhausted, his mind filled with sweet thoughts of rest, the most blessed boon imaginable in his condition, and, while watching the beautiful scenery along shore, falls, through something like sleep—almost lethargic—into unconsciousness, from which he only partially arouses to see Ethel looking at him, whom by degrees his fevered brain and consequent over-excited imagination places beyond the dark river as an inhabitant of the Celestial City—all explained naturally."

"Because you know that snow is only frozen mist," asked Dr. Blentwood, "does that do away with the fact that there is such a thing as snow?"

"Certainly not," answered Dr. Lightheart.

"Then," continued Dr. Blentwood, "because you think you know the path in which Professor Bloomfield's mind travelled up from the physical to a high spiritual state, does that do away with the possible fact that he did enjoy things beyond the ken of the ordinary working of mind in matter? But the particular point I wish to make is, that God was in his experience, whatever it was. The very fact that it has given him spiritual comfort is proof of this. God is as much in the natural as in the supernatural, in the small as in the great things of life. They are only parts of one grand whole. We are too apt to shut God out from all we can in any measure comprehend. Because we see a little of His method in the natural world, we think we see all.

"Again, what kind of a God would He be who worked without method? That we can calculate beforehand, to a moment, the rising or setting sun and the procession of the seasons or an eclipse, only proves that the God of the universe is a God of order and stability. What we call natural law is only another name for the regularity of God's procedure, a method to be depended upon. It will be well for the human race when men's observation shall be sufficiently broad and deep to bring them back and up to the simplicity of seeing God in all things, in the little gettings-on in life and in the expected as well as unexpected."

"How much comfort and real rest of faith," I here ventured to assert, "one loses who thus fails to see His hand everywhere and in everything!"

"Yes, indeed," answered Dr. Blentwood, "and conscious help, too."

"What!" broke in Dr. Lightheart, "does not God help the man who does not recognize His presence as well as the man who does?"

"He helps all His creatures, sending untold blessings on the just and the unjust alike; but can you not see that they, who recognize, believe in, and are conscious of God's gifts, are the only

3

ones who are really helped spiritually? Belief
draws aside spiritual curtains and opens spiritual
doors, letting God's blessings into the soul. Un-
belief shuts out the light and warmth of His
presence and makes that soul, spiritually, a dun-
geon."

"Then, man can successfully resist God?"

"Yes, by receiving the penalty of that resist-
ance in his own soul."

"Does that penalty relieve God of responsibility? Is He not a father still, with all the
tremendous responsibilities of a father?"

Dr. Blentwood hesitated a moment and then
replied, "I think, Dr. Lightheart, God cannot
and does not rest with the penal consequences of
sin. Though we are on ground where we should
tread lightly and reverently, I cannot answer
otherwise than that He has responsibilities as a
Creator; and I fully believe He cannot fail to
discharge every obligation towards the most way-
ward of His children."

"Very well," continued Dr. Lightheart, "what
I fail to see is, how His obligation can stop short
of the complete blessedness of every human
being."

"Are you not losing sight of the rights of
man?"

"What rights?"

"The right to receive or reject any gift, whether
from God or man."

"It seems to me a man's right to be lost is one
he would willingly forego."

"I think not, Dr. Lightheart; every man prizes his freedom above everything else, and I think I can say with reverence that the infinite God bows in humble recognition of every right with which He has constituted us. If any man is lost it will be because God has respected his rights and not that He has violated them. Jesus recognizes man's right to reject Him when He says, 'How often would I. . . . . but ye would not.'"

"Is it not as much a violation of man's rights to punish him against his will as it would be to save him against his will?"

"What reason have you that God does either?"

"Will a man go to hell willingly?"

"Yes, if he is more fitted for hell than heaven. Why not? He would prefer to go where the society would be most congenial to him, would he not?"

"Certainly," Dr. Lightheart admitted, "I see that. I notice devils prefer devilish companionship here."

"Well, then, if man is wicked and all his tastes and inclinations are low and away from God, he could not feel at home in heaven. He would prefer the society of those who thought and felt as he did."

"Well, admitting that to be true, what are you going to do with the good man of fine taste and high sense of honor, who somehow leaves God out of his thoughts?"

"Can a man be good and not love a good being like God?"

" No ; but the man I wish to bring before you does love the good wherever he finds it and affiliates with it, but not being able to define God, his thoughts do not rest there, but go out practically and helpfully towards those in flesh and blood whom he knows about. What are you going to do with him? Is he not better prepared for heaven than the person who says he loves God, and doubtless thinks so, but shows none of that love towards his fellow-men and, perhaps, is full of unjust criticism and fault-finding towards his neighbors?"

" To answer in the shortest manner, I do not believe God is such a devotee to red tape as to be deceived by a mere technical adherence to outward forms, or that the man himself will always be deceived. It seems to me eminently reasonable that every man will go to his own place, where he is most fitted to go, as naturally and as surely as birds of a feather flock together."

"Are there, then, degrees of misery as well as happiness in the next world?"

" If there are here, why not there? The soul at death does not die ; it is only separated from the coarser body, and is the same soul still. Change of location does not change character."

" Then, Dr. Blentwood, there must be a wide range of misery and happiness, and at the dividing line, those who have the least heaven and those who have the least hell in their hearts, must be pretty near together."

" The dividing line, Dr. Lightheart, will be the

love line. What a man loves determines his character. If he loves God, he acts from the highest motive, loves everything good and beautiful, and his neighbor as himself; and between him and one who does not so love, it seems to me there is a great gulf."

" Precisely, I believe that, for there are gulfs both great and small between men here, though we see them bridged almost constantly, and I believe they will be bridged hereafter. But I would like to know what is to become of the lowest Christian in the next world, according to orthodoxy."

" Well, being on the right side of the love-line, the line of progress, as the corporal in the army once bragged of himself, or as he termed it the line of promotion, though starting from the lowest heaven, having a little love, which is a little life, said Christian may go on to the highest heaven or everlasting bliss."

" And what of the wicked?"

" Many think they will go away waxing worse and worse, till they descend into the lowest hell, or are annihilated."

" And what do you think, Dr. Blentwood?"

" I can only say that the tendency of selfishness is to separate more and more, combining only for selfish ends; and the worst state I can conceive of is that of a soul becoming so selfish as to neither love nor trust anybody, voluntarily shutting himself up to solitary gloom."

" But before he reaches this sad state, if such

a state be possible, which I very much doubt,
may he not repent and receive God's love, and so
pass to the line of progress, or, in Scripture
phrase, from the left to the right hand of the
Father?"

" Never, never," shouted a sharp voice through
the open dining-room door. It was the voice of
Mrs. Lightheart, who had been in the sitting-
room, impatiently awaiting the entrance of the
family, but hearing her creed assailed, could wait
no longer. She continued, " The wicked shall
go away into everlasting misery—into a lake of
fire and brimstone and be tortured with everlasting burning, the smoke of their torment always
ascending with the howls of devils dancing around
and stirring up the fires—that's my belief."

" My wife, you see," said Dr. Lightheart,
ironically, " is much given to the satisfying
delights of sweet reasonableness! The fact is,"
he added laughing, " she is an intense literalist ;
and the way I came to marry her was her mistak-
ing a piece of poetry I quoted as a real, literal
pop of the question ! Being caught, I made the
best of it, and with great fortitude gave myself
up at once as lost to all the comforts of single
blessedness, though I have hankered for them
ever since ! "

This brought down the house, and amid the
general laughter all rose from the table and
entered the sitting-room.

CHAPTER V.

ETHEL BLENTWOOD.

AFTER Dr. and Mrs. Lightheart had left, I said, as best I could, to Dr. and Miss Blentwood, that I was under great and lasting obligation to them for their exceeding kindness, and that I was in much perplexity how to even express, much less discharge, the great debt of gratitude I felt and should always continue to feel. I found it hard to recognize the fact that this place, so full of charming associations was not my rest, my home, but that I must leave it in a few short hours. The pictures here formed in my mind would ever remain to influence my whole life. My voice trembled; for I felt deeply what I said.

Dr. Blentwood approached and took me warmly in both his hands, saying, "My dear sir and brother, we are abundantly paid already for our part in this agreeable episode in our life. So, permit us to feel under obligation to you for your involuntary visit and the unexpected pleasure of an agreeable acquaintance. I assure you, if our meeting has been pleasant to you it has been doubly so to us. We cannot think of your leaving to-day. Besides, it would not be prudent. I must be in my study for an hour, and then, if agreeable to you and Ethel, we will visit the scene of your rescue."

Reading the same cordial welcome in the softly lustrous eyes of Miss Blentwood, I responded, "Dr. Blentwood, I felt that I had trespassed too long already on your generous hospitality. But your cordiality convinces me that you mean what you say, and I gladly remain over till to-morrow.

Playfully patting my shoulder, Dr. Blentwood said, "To-morrow is a doubtful quantity, but if it arrives, and Dr. Lightheart says you may go and you feel that you must, we shall have to yield to the inevitable; but permit us to hope that you will remain and make our home your home as long as it will serve your health and convenience," and so saying he retired.

Miss Blentwood followed him to the next room, and I saw her adjust his necktie, and then, looking up to him with loving admiration, put up her mouth for a kiss, which was mutually given. She immediately returned, and to relieve her from the delicacy of adding anything to her father's welcome, I spoke first, saying that I found myself much in love with her father—that though I had seen him but a few hours, I felt that I already knew him thoroughly,

"I am glad to hear you say that," she replied; "for I do think so much of my father, I want everybody else to appreciate him as well. He is always transparent and true. Never having anything to cover up, he never puts on an exterior different from his inmost feeling."

"He seems to be one who doeth good by stealth, and would blush to find it fame," I said.

"It is but simple justice," she went on, "to say that however many may know of his good deeds, he himself never knows them."

"Ah!" I exclaimed, "right there is the secret of the Scripture injunction to let not your left hand know what your right hand doeth. It will not hurt us if the whole world knows the good we do, provided we keep it from ourselves. It is this making note of our good acts and taking credit for them, which nurtures spiritual pride and spoils us, as it did the Pharisees of old."

"How much that sounds like father!" she said innocently. "He has always taught me that we owe service to our fellow-creatures, and his life has so fully and sweetly illustrated that principle, that it does not seem to be at all like living to sacrifice nothing for the happiness of others. Indeed, I have so grown up in the warm atmosphere of domestic tranquillity and a love which means service, that when I go into a home where the opposite principle predominates, I feel such a chill and shrinking back, as if coming into the house of death! I can almost see the icy fingers clutching the hearts of the inmates and freezing every pulsation, and I ache to say or do something to bring them into the warmth and joy of real life. Perhaps my talk seems strange to you?"

"Not a bit of it," I replied. "If strange it is the strangeness of truth forcibly put, with which I fully sympathize. Whatever one may call the picture of the garden of Eden, whether allegory or fact, there can be nothing truer than that Adam died the moment he selfishly desired to appropriate the only fruit, which did not belong to him, and which God had forbidden him to touch. Selfishness *is* moral death. God asks us then a most reasonable thing when He asks us to deny self; that is, give up selfishness which is death, and become partakers of the divine nature, which is love or self-sacrifice, in other words, life. If physical death is the separation of the soul from the body, or the coarser body (to recognize Swedenborgianism), then it is proper to call the separation of the soul from God—the loss of centrifugal force as a balance—spiritual death."

"You would say, then, that he who is farthest from God is the most selfish, whether called saint or sinner," she half asked and half asserted.

"It seems to me self-evident," I replied. "God is love and love is self-sacrifice, and hence, he, who is farthest from Him, is farthest from sacrificing anything for others, and, therefore, is deepest in selfishness."

"How do you explain the apparent selfishness of so-called Christians, often greater than so-called worldly people?" she asked.

"The name, Christian," I answered, "is often misapplied and sadly abused. But we must bear in mind that selfishness is one thing and its manifestation another, the latter varying with individual ambitions and aims. The most satanic selfishness may put on the garb of pure benevolence for a purpose. One man asks of an action only, How will it affect my social or political standing? Another thinks only of God as the perfect standard and the rectitude of his own conscience. Some spend money freely, because they do not value it, as some squander their honor for the same reason. Others, again, are indifferent to everything except the present, like Esau, very pleasant animals, but incapable of denying themselves or others where pleasure is concerned. We are in a world of mixed motives, and it is very difficult to penetrate to the springs of action; but if we look patiently and long enough, I think we shall generally find the evidence which Jesus meant when he said, 'By their fruits ye shall know them.'

" A further explanation may be found in the fact that some start in the Christian life very low down, and though having a little love, that love has more to contend with in reaching its fruitage than with others. We must admit, I suppose, in view of the Old Testament worthies, that it takes but a very little grace to save a man or to begin in him a work of reformation; and hence, it is not strange in the battle between the new and old life that some of the old selfishness should appear occasionally." I saw that she wished to speak, and I paused.

"Your remarks, Professor Bloomfield," she said, with a pleased countenance, "have cleared away a cloud of difficulties, and I thank you very much. I shall now find it much easier to be charitable towards the lowest and most unattractive Christian. I fear I have not made due allowance for the difference of inherited tendencies and training. I do pity the cross-grained and ill-conditioned, but do I love them? I try to find their good qualities and be drawn to them thereby, but I find it hard work."

"You are not required to do impossibilities, Miss Blentwood. We talk flippantly about love, as if it were something we could control by mere will-power. By no possibility can you love what to you is unlovely. God Himself does not."

"Who, then, can stand? for are we not all unlovely in His pure sight?"

"Only comparatively, I think. He sees in us the embryonic seed as fully developed, which even to Him is lovely, and, so, loves this perfect germ, however small, and the ideal He is working out in each one of His children."

"I see; but does He not love the impenitent sinner, who has not received this divine attractiveness?"

"Not with the love of complacency. He can only love such with the love of pity or benevolence—not cold, but warm, actively helpful, persevering, infinite."

"May not even His benevolence be greater than anything we call love?"

"Undoubtedly it is a thousand-fold more beneficent. Love is a variable quantity, meaning more or less according to the inward state of the individual. How infinite the difference, for example, between what the lowest and the highest man means by it! Again, how much more God puts into the word than the noblest and best of earth! So that when one says, I love, he may mean something almost entirely different from another who says the same thing." I thought I detected a slight blush overspreading her countenance, and the thought flashed upon me that perhaps she had recently had those two words addressed to her. The idea, to my surprise, pained me, and I unconsciously paused.

She broke the silence by saying, " I think we have to know people to understand how much their professions mean, even when sincerely uttered."

I looked up and thought I saw the same blush, as if a double consciousness was going on in her mind, produced by personal experience.

Whether this was so or not, she immediately excused herself, and retired from the room.

Hitherto I had been interested chiefly in her fine mental qualities and her refreshing, open, innocent simplicity. There was an atmosphere about her of winning restfulness and genial warmth, which charmed me from the first; but

now, as she arose to retire, I had time to note her
extreme loveliness of face and figure, her easy
carriage and grace of manner.

She moved

> " As if her body were instinct with thought
> Moulded to motion by music's waves."

As she departed, I involuntarily murmured,
" There goes the most beautiful girl I ever saw,
mentally, morally, spiritually and physically.
What a blessing she will bring to the man to
whom she gives her heart ! If worthy of her, he
will have an ever-present heaven. Her love will
mean so much ! It will be crowded and instinct
with uplifting force and life. If her future husband does not strive with all his might to be, for
her sake, the most appreciative and best possible
man, he will be either a rascal or a fool. Hers,
like divine love, must be transforming, unless it
falls, as sometimes does God's sunshine, on the
flinty rock which can give back no response.
What if, deceived by her own reflected light, her
love does so fall, and she is tied down to a dead
man—dead in all his higher nature, though he
speaks and moves with all the appearance of
life ! "

The thought made me shudder. No, no, I
argued with myself, though innocent and very
sympathetic, she has too much judgment and is
too sensitive to the presence of evil not to be repelled from the selfish and the stony-hearted :

and she will be drawn only to one, who, like herself, is good and true to the heart's core.

Then I began to speculate on the mission of such a pair.

CHAPTER VI.

A WALK WITH ETHEL.

WHAT should the happiest and best couple on earth do? I soon found to be a question which led into infinite depths, and was relieved of it by the entrance of Dr. Blentwood and his winsome, fascinating daughter. I was much struck with the moral beauty of the picture they presented, the quiet, unobtrusive happiness, the implicit trust in each other, the perfect sympathy love so clearly but unconsciously expressed in and every movement, and the grand spirituality which glorified their every feature. The picture was to me, especially winning now, having just come, in the interest of education, from a world of business, which is too much and needlessly a world of diplomacy and deceit.

"Well, Professor Bloomfield," said Dr. Blentwood cheerfully, " I have dropped off the harness of toil, and now shall we take that little outing?"

" If you please," I answered, rising. "I am naturally anxious to see how I came here. I feel as if I had been suddenly let into your restful paradise, and have only a confused and very indefinite idea where I left the world of care and fatigue in which I had been laboring so long."

At the door the doctor was detained by a caller, and so Ethel and I were permitted to walk on " slowly." This permission was very agreeable to me, though I liked the doctor's company; for Miss Ethel's voice had a sweet fascination about it and an accent so soft and tender that I loved to hear her talk. It was one of those rare voices, one hears once in a lifetime, which seems attuned to the melody of a higher order of being, and which, entering the ear, lingers and echoes through all the chambers of the soul like a pleasant memory, a thing of beauty and a joy forever.

I was glad to be out of doors; for the sky was clear except a few fleecy clouds sailing on a sea of blue, and everything was resplendent with that peculiar glory which a June morning alone can give.

"What beautiful scenery!" I was forced to exclaim when we had left the house behind us and I had turned to view it. "You are, indeed, happily situated. This is the first time I have seen your house on the outside."

"Which," asked Miss Blentwood, "do you like the better?"

"The inside," I replied. There is a mingled quaintness and picturesqueness about the exterior, and certain homelike touches in the surroundings which I like very much; but the real spirit and beauty of home is better expressed within. There is a glow of warm heart-welcome in the entire interior arrangement, which seems to say

4

to me as I enter, 'Come in; everything here is yours without reserve.' So, you see there is about as much difference between the exterior and interior of your home, as there is between looking at a luscious cherry and eating it!'"

She looked up for a moment, but long enough for me to see a soft gladness lying in her limpid eyes.

"Well," she said, "I think the interior of a home *should* say that, though I fail to make ours talk as I would like."

"That is because your heart is larger than your expression of it. In other words, you mean more than you say; and, in fact, that is just what your home indicates." She laughed a gentle little laugh.

I went on, "A home should not lie. I have been in homes which had a great deal of money scattered about in costly furnishings, and at first they seemed to say, ' This luxury is for your enjoyment, if you will only stop with us ;' but looking deeper I felt that it was all false, and that at heart they only meant, ' Look, admire, and then go about your business.' "

"Such deception is felt rather than seen, is it not?"

"Yes, one may be intellectually pleased, but feeling the lack of soul he becomes chilled, and before he gets out of the house, sighs for a great-coat and mittens, though in the middle of July."

"How do you account, Professor Bloomfield,

for this feeling—this sensitiveness to the varied moral atmosphere pervading different homes?"

"It is hard to analyze; but I think it comes from the character of the inmates. In one way or another the very walls reflect the spirit of the life there lived."

"Is not something due to skill in making home attractive?"

"Certainly, Miss Blentwood, but it is the skill of the heart rather than the head. An honest and loving heart will find out and apply to the needs of home more comforting things than all the cold intellects that could be brought together."

"Is it the motive, then, revealed behind the arrangement of home, rather than the things contained in it, that give us pleasure or displeasure?"

"Mostly, I think; though, of course, something may be accorded to the mere material. Some homes, like the people occupying them, are heartless, and the motive for their existence lies in selfish pride. Others, on the contrary, in every article and attitude declare themselves wholly for your happiness, and nothing for display."

"I certainly have felt all you say, Professor Bloomfield, but the logical process by which the feeling was produced I may not have clearly detected."

"That is because it was too quick for you. The logic of the heart will always outrun the logic of the head, as the loving John outran the headstrong Peter to the tomb of Jesus."

She was thoughtful for a moment, and then said, " Of course an act, in itself admirable, loses its beauty when prompted by an evil purpose."

" Exactly," I said. " Whatever minor loveliness may be accorded to transactions or things, it is the design which speaks through them, at home or elsewhere, which draws or repels."

" Would you say that a sense of the beautiful everywhere and always comes to us through a similar process ? "

" I think so, even from memory or association. What is it in sculpture, painting, or nature that produces in us an emotion of beauty ? Is it the marble or paint or coloring matter ? What makes this landscape of open fields and sylvan dells, stretching out before us as we walk, glorious? Is it not, as in a work of art, the design, the ideal suggested, the spirit which animates and speaks through it ? "

" Then you would say that all beauty is chiefly immaterial or spiritual ? "

" Chiefly, I think, Miss Blentwood. It is the soul in things, living, breathing, speaking. In other words, it is the ideal or meaning which touches us and makes us say, ' Oh, how beautiful!' To illustrate, you have seen a human face faultless in outline and coloring, which you could not call beautiful, because it meant nothing. Such a face is attractive, if at all, only to another soulless idiot like its owner."

" To branch a little from the subject, though suggested by it, I am reminded of Swedenborg,

who teaches, I think, that every tree and other
natural object is only the material expression of a
soul which shall live hereafter!"

"Whether that be true or not, certainly every
object of nature has in it an idea, a spiritual
meaning—in other words, *is* the expression of a
spiritual thought, the thought God had in making
it; and thus it is, as some one has said, we may
'read God's thoughts after Him.'"

"But, Professor Bloomfield, is there anything
unreasonable in the supposition that these
thoughts of God, expressed in flowers, shrubs,
trees, birds, may be permanent or everlasting thoughts, and that we shall meet them
again hereafter, expressed in more refined form
and as much more beautiful than we now see
them, as we expect our bodies to be?"

"You put that thought very finely, Miss Blentwood, and frankly I see nothing unreasonable
about it. Do you believe it?"

"Oh!" blushing, "it is something one can
hardly believe or disbelieve, I think. It strikes
me as a very pretty and pleasant idea—that's
all."

"How?" I asked, wishing to draw her out.

"Oh, it helps me to think what the other world
is like. If everything pleasant here is the repre-
sentation of a real spiritual life, then the other
better world must be similar to this, only infinitely refined and beautified; and, when I get
there, I shall not feel so far from home or so
much a stranger in a strange land."

At this moment our attention was drawn to a tree about ten feet tall, covered with beautiful blossoms, and approaching us without any visible power to carry it, as if, in proof of some Darwinian theory, it had ambitiously cut loose from the soil, and was trying a life of locomotion! After the first breath of surprise, I said laughingly, Miss Blentwood joining:

"That makes me think of 'Birnam wood,' though it must be on a more peaceful mission."

The tree suddenly stopped, and a black head, followed by a body, emerged from the branches which had completely enveloped him, and, seeing us, he let down his precious burden gently on the grass.

"Our Tom!" said Miss Blentwood with a pleased look, "and a noble old man he is. He has but one fault, an amusing one, quite common I think among recent slaves, and that is a strange pride in using uncommon words and phrases, apparently inventing a word when none comes to hand to suit him. Occasionally he will strike out or stumble upon an original thought which I find worth carrying away, and thinking about."

As we approached Tom took off his hat and put it under his arm, as he used to do when a slave in the presence of a white person, and stood grinning and ducking his head, till we came up. This, I afterwards found was a special mark of politeness, enacted only to those he believed were very respectable. He touched his hat to everybody, took it off to little better people, tucked it under his arm to nicer people still, and when specially pleased to see them, he would in addition grin and duck his head.

"O, Tom!" she exclaimed smiling, "you almost frightened us. Did it not hurt your feelings to cut so beautiful a tree?"

"It did twingle-twinge me some, Miss Ethel, at *fust*," said he, putting great emphasis on the "fust," "it look so lubly enough to grow in de garden ob de Lord; but I say, Booful tree, I want you for de chosen ob de Lord. Is not you willin' to gib youself to happify Miss Ethel? Nuffin' too good for her, be dar? Den, when I mention dat name, de tree seem to smile all ober and say, I's ony too willin' to lib or die for to happify Miss Ethel, and den I cut him down widout any furder obfuscation."

We both had to laugh, but she did not forget to cast an appreciating look upon Tom for his kind efforts to serve her, which made him chuckle with much satisfaction.

As Dr. Blentwood had not overtaken us, we sat down on the grass to await his coming and to engage Tom in conversation. As we did so I managed to sly a greenback into Tom's coat-pocket and said, "Tom, this is the first opportunity I have had to thank you, which I do most heartily, for your kindness on the night of my arrival here."

"You is bery welcome, Massa Boomfield, bery. I is glorified to see you well once mo'. I fort dat night dat de bref ob life were mose clean done gone outer ye, and dat you were sailin' ober to tudder sho' for sure. But in de silent watches ob de night I seen a glory shinin' roun' you boat, and, though de black waves run high and de death winds were drivin' you fast, you boat mistiferously turn roun' and come back to dis yere country; and it come for a purpose, Massa Boomfield. I knowed it; for I seen it. I shall not lib to see de actuality, ony de incipiency, but on tudder side I will climb de golden stair, and witness de bressed consummation. I mun interfere wid de prophetic idee by telling any mo' cept ony jes' this, if ye pray by de dyin' bedside ob ole Tom, ye may know dat de glorious vision will come quick to pass." The ole man bowed his head, much shaken by his emotions; but soon raised it again, smiling through his tears, and simply added, "I is satisfied and happified."

Not knowing what else to say, and to relieve the embarrassment, I said, "Tom, where did you find that beautiful tree?"

"On de hill yonner, sah; dey mos'ly grow on de sidehills. Some ob dem bear white blossom and some pink. Peers like folks dunno what name to give em; but we call em mountain laurel."

"Did that tree really speak to you, Tom?"

"Yes, sah, evything speak to me ob de Lord and his lub."

"Anything more?"

"Sometime a heap. It pends whedder I is equal to de situation. For circumstance, if I and de mountain or de tree or de flower am in de same mood and our hearts beat togedder, den I can open de do' and walk right into de private audience room, and hab a mos' bressed confabulation, sah, a mos' bressed confabulation."

" I am afraid, Tom, you get more out of nature than I do."

" Dat be possible, sah, for dis yere reason dat I find in my own sperience, which am dat larnin' create, sometimes, a cyclogical difficulty discomboberatin' and obfuscatin' de perception. Nature hab a anthromorphic voice only for de chile like and de poetic simpleton, so to speak, sah."

" Well, Tom, can you tell us if there will be flowers in Heaven ? "

" I is sure of it, sah."

" How ? "

" I may not be able to splain de location ob my faculties on dat ar' pint, but i shall sartin see 'em up dar."

" What makes you think so ? "

" Well, Massa Boomfield, am de Lord goin' to take back any good thing he make for us, as if he made a 'stake, specially de flowers, which am de smile ob de Lord—de expression ob His heart ? Am de Lord not goin' to smile in de nex' world ?·'

" But you may be so changed as not to need the flowers in Heaven."

" Den, sah, I shall not be Tom, and, to all tense and purposes I shall not be dar. Where shall I be ? "

" If there is not continuity enough to preserve your identity and keep you still Tom, I admit it will be practical annihilation. But you will know yourself, Tom, and I have no doubt there will be something in the next life to correspond with flowers—something to meet the want they supply here."

"You say somethin' to correspond wid 'em, Massa Boomfield; dat may be clear nuff to de larned lik yousef', but to me—member I say to me, Massa Boomfield—dat lack definization, and be too immaticular and scatterin' for my poor heart to seize on. I wants de flowers, sah, deir bery selves."

" You will be willing to see something much more beautiful, will you not ? "

" Dey good nuff for me as dey is; but if de Lord please to make 'em finer I is willin', as I hope to be finer up dar mysef ; but I want to cognize 'em as de same, so when I meet de peony, de violet, de rose, de pink, et cetra, I shall know 'em as a ole acquaintance, and not find 'em so stuck up as to gib me de shivers ober a friend lost forebber."

"Oh, Tom," cried Miss Blentwood, " do sing for us, ' Should old acquaintance be forgot.' "

" Yes, do," I added, " it will cap the climax to your very fine argument. I am delighted that you can sing it—the very song for the occasion."

Tom was evidently pleased and readily commenced a negro version of the above-mentioned song. He was in the mood, and soon forgot all about us, so lost was he in his own deep and powerful emotions. There was little or nothing of the familiar song after the first line except its repetition. His voice, or as it seemed voices, so quickly did it change from far to near, rose and fell unbroken, like the waves of mid-ocean after a storm, descending at times to a mere whisper, when I could distinguish only disconnected words such as "gwine away . . , good-bye . . , nebber forget." Then all sound would cease for an instant, and commence again far off, and, as if imitating a return of the tide of life, slowly swell louder and louder in volume and power, but never so high as to break the melody.

All this time there was so much action of hands, feet, and whole body, that I was at first amused, then charmed, and finally carried away on the swelling tide of the old man's feelings. The waves flowed in upon me so hard, they had to be bailed out at the eyes, and I began to question my ability to reach dry land gracefully! I felt rather foolish till, looking up, I saw another bark had been floundering in the same pathetic sea, but now looking all the more beautiful from the washing of the tide. I sprang to my feet and grasped her hand before I thought what I was doing, and said, "You look as if you were going right up into heaven, Miss Blentwood. Please don't leave us yet."

She smiled and blushed; Tom chuckled, and then we all laughed—laughed ourselves back to the hillside, whence we had been swept away by the musical flood.

CHAPTER VII.

WE were thanking Tom when Miss Blentwood exclaimed, " Why, there is father at last." And, sure enough, he was right upon us.

" I hope you will excuse my long delay," said he, " for I got away as soon as I could from a parishioner who had pressing business."

Tom, with his flowery burden, resumed his journey homeward, while the doctor, his daughter and myself started on our circuitous way to the river. We passed up a little higher to the brow of the hill to get a more extended view of the country, which disclosed a beautiful valley of cultivated fields, orchards, woods, and the suburbs of the town, on the outskirts of which nestled the lovely home of Dr. Blentwood, with its trees, walks, lawns and grapery, and the river, not too far off, smiling in the sunshine. We descended to a round clump of pitch-pine trees, which loaded the air with a grateful fragrance, and sat down on some rustic seats the doctor had placed there.

" I sometimes think," said the doctor, " if I could live here continuously, I should get well and strong. Before the sun has drunk up the dew, I have found the air under these trees so laden with healing balm as to produce in me a grateful sensation at every breath. I occasionally prepare a sermon here; but by the force of habit I can think and write easier in my study surrounded by my books and pictures, which create around me a sort of literary and religious atmosphere. The law of association is strong with me."

After filling our lungs with long, deep breaths of this aromatic air, suggesting to Miss Blentwood the lines of Milton: Here

> " Gentle gales,
> Fanning their odoriferous wings, dispense
> Native perfumes,"

we descended to the river and out to a projecting point of land, the right arm of a bay, within which I recognized my boat at anchor near the shore. I looked at it and then at Miss Blentwood, and asked, " Where was I when — when you first saw me ? "

" About there," she answered, pointing her finger. " At first I thought the boat empty, but soon discovered a person, apparently asleep, lying in the stern. You were so far inland that I saw you would be dashed on the rocks and overturned, and I tried to awaken you by singing, and finally shouted as loud as I could ; but you did not move, and, not daring to wait longer, I plunged in, and reached you in season to tow you into this little harbor. It was not much of a feat, but was opportune."

I gazed long at the rapids, and saw clearly that
my boat could not have lived in them, and that
in my then helpless condition I must have been
drowned had I entered them, and, not daring to
look upon her beautiful face, yet feeling the
magnetism of her presence, I continued my gaze
towards the whirling, tumbling waters till, mas-
tering my emotions, I said :

" Miss Blentwood, you saved my life. Whether
it was worth saving the future alone can reveal ;
but, whatever its value, I owe it to your providential presence, to your noble courage, to——"

" Please don't," she interrupted, evidently wishing to blunt the edge of my sense of obligation ;
it was a very simple thing to do, and no one
whose cowardice was not of the meanest type
would have done less. I was glad, however, that
my father had taught me how to swim when a
child."

I was thinking of my own recent experiences,
but roused myself to add, " If the laws of nature
were more reverently and obediently studied as
the laws of God, accidents on land or sea might
become almost unknown."

" Why are we put into a world of such unyielding laws and dire penalties?" asked Miss
Blentwood.

" To prevent us, by learning the nobility of
obedience, from being self-centered and wilful,"
replied her father, and then added solemnly, " It
is amazing, when we come to think of it sanely,
how many have to be bruised by repeated punish-

ments, before they will obey the behests of their highest interests!"

We had been retracing our steps, and were now standing on the semicircular shore near my boat and the place of my landing. For a few moments I wished I were alone that I might think; but at length I said meditatingly, "It seems that I left home only a few days ago, and how much—yea, how long I have lived in that time!"

"You are right," said the doctor; "for length of time is not in itself length of life. One person may live as long in a few days as another in as many years. Not clock time but experiences, ideas, deeds, mark real life and tell how old we are. Rightly speaking, Ethel, the youngest of us, has already lived longer than Methuselah."

"What! I older than 969 years, father?' said Miss Blentwood, laughing. "It is rather hard to reveal a lady's age that way."

The doctor smiled good-naturedly, and, patting his daughter on the shoulder, he said, "I must hold to the truth that you have lived longer than Methuselah, but you are much better preserved!"

"How apt we are to think of age in the sense of decay instead of maturity, breadth of experience and knowledge!" I remarked.

"Swedenborg has a very pretty idea on that point," said Miss Ethel. "In his vision, or entrance into the other world, he found that the oldest person in heaven was the youngest.'

The doctor, looking at his watch, declared it was time to be moving towards dinner.

We clambered up the bank, where Tom had borne me in my helplessness, and walked leisurely along a winding path, occasionally stopping to admire a beautiful view of the river and other scenery, or to inspect a peculiar growth of wood, when we came to a high wall, which recalled, as from a dream, my thoughts of purgatory and descent where Tom, exhausted, sank with me in his arms to the ground, and he and Tot had sung me to sleep so self-forgetfully. Turning to the left, descending a flight of stone steps, we entered a subterranean passage of ancient construction, thought to have been used by early settlers as a refuge from the Indians. This, by the aid of a little masonry, vines and climbing roses, the doctor and his daughter had converted into a thing of picturesque beauty as well as convenient passage-way from that side of their house.

CHAPTER VIII.

A SURPRISE.

AS we emerged from this umbrageous cavern I was charmed and delighted by the unexpected scene spread out before me. Over the mouth of the grotto and along the wall on my right hung vines and flowers in beautiful festoons. A path straight ahead, lined on either side by a low hedge and occasionally overarched by trellised vines, led directly to a sort of Irving porch connecting with the house; while another path wound to the left between shrubbery and flower-beds to a clump of maple trees, amply provided with seats, on the bank of the river. Between this and another clump, and parallel with the river, were two rows of elms within which was tastefully spread a table, from the centre of which rose, with delightful effect, the top of the very tree whose loveliness I had enjoyed a few hours previous. Tom and Tot had been diligently at work all the forenoon to make the table and accessories attractive, and they certainly had succeeded.

The grotto, flower-garden, trees, table and river formed a lovely picture, and I exclaimed, " Are we in paradise? This is the best visible suggestion of it I have ever seen."

5

"I am glad the grounds please you," said Miss Blentwood frankly; "have you nothing to criticise?"

"Nothing," I replied. "My ideal is satisfied. I shall have to grow before I can suggest anything that will not mar rather than help the general effect, which is indeed charming. Is this your work, Miss Blentwood?"

"Partly," she answered. "Father calls this my outdoor school, and I have had full power to do anything I liked in it; and, really, I think I have received an education here, which the schools alone could not have given me. I have had to think and plan for myself—try the effect of different combinations, and study successes and failures—until I have acquired some little independence of thought and critical judgment, which, though small, are of incalculable value to me."

"Miss Blentwood," I said, with an earnestness born of admiration, "I hardly know which to congratulate most, your father for his wisdom and great good sense in providing this school, or you in the almost marvelous manner you have wrought with the materials and opportunities at your disposal. You are an artist, Miss Blentwood, with the added imagination of a poet. The picture you have drawn here with organic and inorganic matter, is exceedingly beautiful, and more crowded with suggestion and the seeds of thought than any I know by paint or brush. Your success makes me wonder why landscape gardening is not made more of a study."

"Why is it," I asked Dr. Blentwood, who that moment came up, having lagged behind studying the peculiar construction of a leaf and doubtless drawing therefrom an illustration for next Sunday's sermon, "Why is it, there is not as much enthusiastic study and artistic devotion given to the creation of the beautiful in nature as in marble or on canvas? Is not landscape gardening worthy of a place among the professions and as closely allied to the elevation and happiness of the human race."

"I think," answered Dr. Blentwood, "as a study and a lifelong calling it should take high rank. It ought to be taught too in some of our higher institutions of learning, but how to teach it practically as well as theoretically? and where? are puzzles to me."

"Might it not be added very conveniently to the curriculum of our agricultural colleges? The future farmers of our land could study it with perhaps as great a profit as any other class, and though none of them might follow it as a separate profession, it would be of incalculable advantage in making farm life attractive and rural homes more desirable, and secure to the country cultured people and the very best society."

"Very good, Professor Bloomfield; but what are you going to do with the young ladies and especially the future wives of these farmers, who need the uplift and refinement which comes from this æsthetic culture?"

"I would admit them also to the same classes

and privileges with these possible farmers, and
these two movements or innovations would boom
the agricultural college and make it a blessing
indeed."

"I believe in your ideas, Professor Bloomfield,
and if carried out somehow and somewhere, one
result would be a better adornment of home surroundings which are so often wickedly, because
needlessly, neglected. Our homes need not be
more expensive, but they could and should be more
attractive. Especially is this true in the country,
where there is plenty of land to make the sur-
soundings delightful. If the reform you have
suggested could be properly and successfully
inaugurated young men and women would not, as
now, be educated away from the country, but
towards the country."

"Were education what it should be, so that
money-getting would let go its present grip, and
men would ascend into their higher natures, and
take time to live there, and learn what sources of
enjoyment they have, how much more happiness
there would be in the world!"

"Yes, yes, Brother Bloomfield, I was coming to
that. Our schools and colleges really touch only
a part of the man or woman they essay to
educate. To be complete, education must reach
and vivify the moral, æsthetical and spiritual faculties as well as the intellectual and social.
Could this be thoroughly accomplished, as it must
before the perfect society is reached, crime,
insanity, suicide, oppression and strikes would

gradually disappear, and as you say, happiness would abound."

" I cannot see," said Miss Blentwood, who had been a most attentive listener, " what we are in this world for, if not to make others as well as ourselves better and happier."

" Well," said I, " as the first step towards this consummation so devoutly to be wished, if I had abundance of means I would purchase a hundred acres of land and materialize my idea of Paradise. I would consult the highest ideals and build a home in the midst of grounds so lovely, so full of spiritual suggestion, that no one would say, How expensive! how magnificent! but, on the contrary, every one would exclaim, How lovely! how heavenly! The buildings and grounds should speak not a word of ostentation, but volumes of æsthetic, moral, social and spiritual thought. They should appeal to the entire higher nature— to all that is noblest and best in the beholder. I would then open the doors, and make this home a source of spiritual education to thousands.

" The schools separate men by making them unequal, thereby creating divisions in families and society, which religion itself finds it hard to reunite. What we need is a system of culture which shall draw mankind together by developing the whole higher manhood and womanhood, and it should be my aim to meet this felt want by daily practical instruction in landscape gardening, the laws of health, food, clothing, economics, and in mental, moral and spiritual philosophy. I would take special care that there should be as much heart as head culture. A person is but half educated, who has only an intellectual education. A true education should increase a man's resources for happiness as well as for action ; and happiness rests on right conditions of heart, on character, rather than on head-culture. It seems strange that in this nineteenth century we have gone no farther in our ideas of education. It is true our schools and colleges are giving attention to physical culture ; but the body and intellect are only parts of what we mean by manhood and womanhood. The better part would be left to starve were it not for the instruction of homes and churches. There is not a school that comprehends in its system of education the development of the whole individual."

"So far as common schools are concerned," said Dr. Blentwood, "I suppose it is the theory of the state that it has no right to carry instruction to the highest, the religious faculties."

"Why not if the stability of our government and the happiness of our citizens rest more on the character thereby secured than upon mere intellectual and physical culture ? Has not the state the rights of self-preservation ?"

"Certainly ; but the fear is that it would infringe on the legitimate work of the church and the liberty of the individual."

"But would it necessarily, Dr. Blentwood ?"

"I think not. I think there is such a thing as

spiritual science, which may be taught so as to draw out and enlarge and enrich the higher faculties of the soul, without touching denominational or sectarian lines, and without any union of church and state.''

CHAPTER IX.

TURNING to me, Miss Blentwood said, "Thinking it would be a pleasure for you to meet our esteemed friend and physician, Dr. Lightheart, once more before departing, we have invited him and Mrs. Lightheart to dine with us."

Although I was hoping to have Ethel's society more exclusively, I appreciated the motive prompting the invitation, and made my acknowledgments accordingly. I had hardly finished before she was hurrying to welcome the newcomers, and we all met at the table at the same time.

Dr. Lightheart, with a cordial grasp of the hand, expressed gladness at seeing me so well.

"You could not have been laid up for repairs in a more delightful spot or in better society," said he, borrowing a phrase from the ship-yard and looking at me quizzically.

I felt the blood rushing to my cheeks, and, without daring to look at Miss Ethel, or even to look up, I answered, "True, Dr. Lightheart, but had this been a dreary place it would be so much easier to leave it."

Tom, as spokesman for Tot, who was evidently

72

afraid the quality of her meal might suffer from further delay, bowing his most graceful bow, said, " De dinner am waitin' you immediate consideration, and de sooner de deglutition take place de better you will esteem de cook."

Tom grinned as if he had got off a good speech, and we all with smiling faces gathered around the table, and while standing Dr. Blentwood repeated the following passage of Scripture: " Bless the Lord, O my soul, and forget not all His benefits."

Miss Blentwood added, " They that seek the Lord shall not want any good thing."

The outdoor air so soft and balmy, the beautiful table, delightful scenery, pleasant company, cheerful conversation, and the rebound of my physical nature towards health, filled me at once with pleasure.

I was not at that time aware that a new life was already springing up within me, like the seed in the warm earth before its tiny blade is observed unfolding above the surface.

" People are differently constituted," said Dr. Lightheart, after we were seated, " and all rules have their exceptions, I suppose ; but it is evidently God's law that we should eat in company, and I don't think it safe to break it. He has set the race in families, and I believe families also should mingle together oftener than they do at the festive board on occasions like this for the sake of good cheer and good digestion. One thing is certain, a dyspeptic should rarely dine alone or in dull company."

I ventured to look at Miss Blentwood, hoping she would speak, not so much, perhaps, for the sake of her ideas as for the soft tones and varied inflection of her utterances, which had come to fall on my ears with all the charm of musical notes. Whether there was an electrical communication or not, our eyes met, and I said:

" Agreeable emotions, I infer, not only promote good digestion and longevity, but have a moral mission as well."

" And, therefore," Miss Blentwood responded, " housekeeping should be studied as an art, and good food, like fine jewels, should have attractive settings."

" Amen!" almost shouted Dr. Lightheart. " The future reformer will begin back of penal institutions and rescue missions in the home."

" Exactly," said Dr. Blentwood, " every human being has or should have the right of being well born, and then the right to healthy food and clean air and sunlight, and an occasional view, at least, of nature dressed in her most lovely apparel."

" On this account," said Miss Blentwood, " the outing given to the poor children every summer must be a duty as well as an inspiration and blessing to them."

" Yes," responded her father, " but the older poor should be included in these outings. The change from foul basements to the verdant hill: and sweet valleys and native woods would give them a new lease of life, physically and morally.·

and this, followed by improvement of home environment and wise Christian instruction, would do
much towards emptying police stations, jails and
prisons."

" I think," said Mrs. Lightheart, who had hitherto said but little, " low people are foreordained
to be the coarse, ill-bred, reprobate creatures they
are, and so good for nothing except as hewers of
wood and drawers of water and a warning to others,
and your puny efforts can't change them."

" God can," said Dr. Blentwood.

" True, but why don't He ? "

" Perhaps it is because you and I and others
haven't done our duty."

" Are we necessary to His work, Dr. Blentwood ? "

" Perhaps not, but work for others is a necessary schooling for us, and if we neglect it we may
be no better than those we affect to despise."

" How can that be ? "

" Well, Mrs. Lightheart, you and I may daily
grow better without effort."

Dr. Lightheart interrupted, " my wife can't."

This was laughed off as a joke, and Dr. Blentwood resumed : " The idea I was after is simply
that one may grow better without effort, because
the currents of his being run towards the good,
while another may be carried towards the bad,
though he struggle hard, because inherited tendencies are too strong for him. Now the question is, which person in the sight of God has the
most merit ? And this question is intensified if

the person of good tendencies does not go to the relief of the other. Jesus denounced the Phari- see, not for lack of outward good conduct, but because of his spiritual pride and want of sympa- thetic helpfulness towards those below him."

" Well, I see nothing to admire in a man who is growing worse, anyway."

" That, Mrs. Lightheart, may be because you and I cannot look into the heart. If we could we might see something heroic and even beautiful, though he is defeated at every stand he makes, as we see something to admire in the soldiers who fought so bravely at Bunker Hill, though they were defeated."

" But that defeat was a virtual victory, wasn't it?"

" Yes, and so every struggle in the human heart is a partial victory, though an apparent defeat. All goodness is the result of struggle in ourselves or our ancestors; and I believe God cannot afford and will not allow a single struggle towards the good to be lost on the character of him who makes it."

Dr. Lightheart clapped his hands and said, " That is why publicans and harlots may go into the kingdom of heaven before Pharisees. If my wife would make one struggle to allow me a little peace in my home I should have more hopes of her. I think I ought to go to heaven for relieving her folks of the plague of their lives, and yet I don't want to go if she goes there; I have seen enough of her here!"

"You ought to be thankful," replied his wife, that you have somebody to train you and make you decent; but I don't hang my hopes of salvation on my good works."

"If you did," said her husband, with a comical face and gesture, "your poor hopes would have to fall for want of a hook, like a man's clothes in a woman's closet."

After a little more good-natured sparring, in which Mrs. Lightheart took refuge in God's sovereignty, Dr. Blentwood said, "It is evidently not God's plan to drive people into the kingdom of His love and service; He calls for volunteers. We know nothing of goodness by force. By close espionage and prison walls we may make a man outwardly and negatively blameless, but unless there is created within him an aspiration and longing after the good, he becomes the same man when restraint is removed, as before."

"Our work, then, is to lead him by precept and example into good influences and to awaken conscience, is it not, father?" asked Miss Blentwood.

"Precisely," was the reply. "Man's freedom allows him to put himself under either of two sets of laws, and here lies the opportunity of the Christian."

"Ethel," asked Dr. Lightheart, "where will a true Christian woman commence her service, especially by example?"

With a significant smile she replied, "The Christian spirit of forbearance, gentleness and love in man or woman will necessarily appear first and always at home, I think."

"Like the mission of the apostles," I added, "it will necessarily commence at Jerusalem, or at home, but not end there."

Mrs. Lightheart evidently did not like this kind of Christian evidence; for she went back to the subject from which we diverged and said, "If God meant to save the degraded classes He would have made them worth saving, and not made it so repulsive for us to do anything for them."

"Better let some folks, who call themselves saved," said her husband, with a merry twinkle in his eye, "ask whether there is sweetness enough in them to keep. Just think of a sour, crabbed, little soul living forever, and in heaven! If she attempted to sing, all the angels would stop their harps and ask, What is that?—Is it a crow?"

"Better be a crow in heaven than a turtle in brimstone," retorted his wife.

"Oh, what a talking couple!" exclaimed Dr. Blentwood, laughing in spite of himself. He added, "Whether one is worth saving is not for us to judge. According to Darwin we were all very unpromising specimens of humanity once, lower than the degraded classes you referred to are now."

"The development theory is contrary to the Bible, doctor."

"No, not contrary; it is simply a question of method—whether God was one minute or thousands of years in creating man. The latter, even more than the other method, harmonizes with

God's known plans, and better shows His purpose to have been eternal rather than a sudden impulse."

" Then you believe in a theory which has been called one of infidelity, Dr. Blentwood?"

" I neither believe nor disbelieve it. The scientific facts seem to lean that way, and I am in a teachable attitude, as all lovers of truth should be. There are too many indocile, intractable Christians who find it easier to cry heresy than to search honestly for the truth, and so reveal only their own weakness of faith."

" Oh, these riders on the coat-tails of progress!" broke out Dr. Lightheart. " They once affirmed it to be rank infidelity to believe the world moved instead of the sun in producing day and night, and the phenomena of a rising and setting sun!"

" Independent of the Darwinian theory," I here asserted, " we need not go very far back in history to find our Saxon ancestors clothed in bear-skins, and living in huts; and if God had not watched over and tenderly taught them, and lifted them and succeeding generations higher and higher, where would we, their proud Anglo-American descendants, be to-day?"

" I would like to hear some good possible reasons why God started the human race so low down," said Miss Blentwood.

" Aside from His apparent love of progress and the evidence it gives of His eternal working purpose," her father answered, " it may be for man's everlasting happiness to be able to trace his ascension from the lowest depths to the highest attainable good—from the hell of ignorance and selfish passion to the heaven of intelligence and righteous peace. This conscious progress may also be essential to man's permanency and freedom in goodness, when goodness is acquired. This experience was wanting in the first man, and that explains his fall, as it does why so many children, grown up in ignorance of sin and how to meet it, yield to the very first temptation presenting itself. Like a weed grown up in the shade, they have no resisting power. They are simply moral infants."

"Like back-yard toadstools and slaves of majorities in politics and theology, you step on them and they acquiesce!" said Dr. Lightheart laughing. He added, "But, Dr. Blentwood, granting Darwinianism to be substantially true, is not Beecher's remark, that the race fell up instead of down, correct?"

"We must not get our notion of Adam or the first man from Milton, as many do. He was simply innocent, like a child, with no positive holiness, and when he took possession of himself, so to speak, to think for himself and guide himself, he lost even his negative innocence, and so had to go down before he could rise again, as a man climbing a mountain has sometimes to go down into a depression before he can go up. As the mountain-climber goes higher by means of his descent, so man rises from his fall, through the inborn spirit of Christ, infinitely higher than before; he rises into positive and permanent freedom in goodness."

"Is that the only sense in which he fell up?"

"I think, Dr. Lightheart, no one can rise into the highest manhood or womanhood, who has not the spirit or disposition of Christ. I care not for mere technicalities or sect, or however loud the profession or non-profession; no one who has not the love exhibited by Jesus of Nazareth, and creates no social warmth and no sunshine in the home and society, can rightfully be called a Christian or a real true man or woman. The man who has this serving, helpful, glorious love-lit disposition, whatever his creed or want of creed, is the highest style of man."

"Amen," said I, in approval. "How much better it would be for the good name of Christianity and the progress of the world in all that goes to make heaven here and hereafter, if manifesting the spirit of Christ should become the chief creed subscribed to by the churches!"

"If I was a young man," said Dr. Blentwood, with tears in his voice, "I would start a church with a creed something like that. I should feel that I was working for Christ indeed, and for the glory of God, because for the glory of man; but my work is about done, and my opportunity is passed."

Tears stood in the good man's eyes, and I silently prayed that health might be given him and his life be prolonged; and, as I looked into

6

Ethel's sympathetic face, tears sprang into my own eyes also.

"Well," spoke up Mrs. Lightheart, in a voice as dry as summer dust and about as comforting as the hottest sirocco that ever blew, "I believe the church is composed of the elect, and a pastor's duty is to encourage the church and not the non-elect by any twaddle about disposition. Don't you believe in election, Professor Bloomfield?"

I answered, that I believed the elect are whosoever will, and the non-elect are whosoever will not.

"It isn't a question of will or will not, but one of election of the Lord," she replied hotly. "And, furthermore, I think the more silly notions you put into the heads of the non-elect, especially of the degraded classes, the more they will suffer in this world and the next. All they are fit for is to serve the elect and as a warning."

"You see the use she has for me; and may imagine the solid comfort she takes in that belief!" said her husband, with a mixture of irony and an expression I could not understand.

"Have you," asked Dr. Blentwood, with pitying pathos, "ever looked teachably with Peter into the sheet of creeping things let down to him from heaven, and which convinced him that he should labor for the lowest as well as the highest?"

Before she could answer, Miss Blentwood exclaimed, "Excuse me, but do see that beautiful cloud! How peculiarly white and fleecy it is!"

All looked, and all admired. " Was anything ever finer?" asked Mrs. Lightheart, with as near approach to ecstasy as she was probably capable.

" That cloud," I asserted, " has risen for Mrs. Lightheart's benefit."

" How so?" she asked.

" Well, as the first step to an answer, let me ask Dr. Lightheart, as a scientific man, where that cloud came from?"

" Very likely," he replied, "from the filthy pools and miasmatic swamps, in the vicinity of which I have dealt out so much quinine."

" Now, Mrs. Lightheart," I said, "the same power that raised that cloud from filth to purity, can raise, and does raise, the ignorant, sinful soul, and make it clean and beautiful, fit for the society of angels."

" I don't dispute God's power," responded Mrs. Lightheart, "but I don't think He requires refined people to soil their pure feelings by laboring among such characters; it is so shocking to one of elegant taste and delicate sensibilities, you know. I think the coarse should labor for the coarse."

" I agree with so much of homœopathy as is contained in the last sentence," said her husband laughing. " I am always glad when I can agree with my wife. As a rule the morally degraded can be more successfully reached by those of like ways of thinking."

" Very likely," said Dr. Blentwood, " but does that relieve the refined classes of responsibility?"

"Certainly not. They can set the wheels of benevolence in motion, superintend their operation, and work where they can fit in."

"Do your remarks find any confirmation in the fact that the heathen prefer native preachers, and that negroes of the South prefer teachers of their own race?" asked Miss Blentwood.

"The question of refinement does not come in there so much as race prejudice," said her father; "but there may be force in the argument of adaptability of kind to kind, and the feeling expressed in the phrase, He is one of us."

"But," I asked, "cannot men and women of true refinement do successful work among the lower classes?"

"Oh! that would shock their nerves," answered Dr. Lightheart laughing.

"Jesus of Nazareth," I went on, "was our highest ideal of a perfect man, and therefore must have had the finest, keenest sensibilities—no soul ever recoiling with such tremendous repulsion from contact with sin as did His—and yet He drew the degraded classes to Him, and won their confidence—their joyful, unstinted, exuberant love. Does not this prove that a man of real, true culture, and not a dilettante—a man of roundabout, sanctified common-sense—can bring himself down into sympathetic and effectual work for any class of society?'

"It would seem so," Dr. Lightheart answered, with a squint towards his wife; "but the trouble with over-refined people is that they haven't

sanctified common sense, or much of any other
kind of sense. Their culture, instead of improv-
ing and properly embellishing the quality, has
only worn away the substance, and left them
more useless than before."

Whether his wife took this remark as having
any reference to herself, I could not tell, for, at
this juncture, a messenger came announcing company and a patient for the Lighthearts. Our
repast was over. Mrs. Lightheart, rising, addressed Miss Blentwood petulantly, but with a
voice thinly sugar-coated by an affected smile and
grace of attitude and gesture, " My company always come inopportunely ; I hope you are more
fortunate."

" My friends never come inopportunely for
me," Miss Blentwood responded, smiling, " but
perhaps they often do for themselves, as I cannot
always serve them as I would like. I think, however, that sensible people, whose opinions we
value, can make allowances for circumstances over
which we have no control."

"Well," continued Mrs. Lightheart, with vexa-
tion clearly marked beneath the smirk of her thin
lips, " my company never come when I want
them. As sure as I set out for a good time by
myself or with others, company or something else
is sure to come and spoil all my plans."

Here, I thought, is a great gulf between these
two women, as " fixed " as that between Lazarus
and the rich man : for no thought or feeling in
common can pass over from one to the other.

Ethel's remark had contained an implied, but unconscious rebuke—unconscious, because her limpid eyes told of a heart too tender to offend. Her evident frankness, purity of motive, gentle, unselfish spirit and sweet thoughtfulness for others opened to me more and more as I gazed admiringly upon her. I was so entranced I almost forgot my manners, and scarcely rose in time to wave my hand in farewell as the Lighthearts departed, and Dr. Blentwood with them, the latter communicating something confidential to his physician.

CHAPTER X.

A PHILOSOPHICAL DIALOGUE.

ETHEL BLENTWOOD and I were alone, standing on nearly opposite sides of the table, she
watching the retiring guests and I watching her.
Whether there is such a thing as silent communication of mind with mind or not the blood
mounted to her cheeks, and, though she was
looking away from me, I felt conscious of the
touch of a kindred spirit. The thrill was so
marked, I thought of one, who, in merely touching the hem of Jesus' garment, touched Him also.
In a transport of ecstasy, I thought, half audibly
I fear, "Beautiful! beautiful!"

She turned towards me with an inquiring but
softening look in her long-lashed blue eyes full
of magnetic scintillations. With some confusion
I asked, "Do you believe in visions, Miss Blentwood?"

"In a limited sense," she answered, smiling.

"To be more definite," I continued, modifying
my intended statement a little, "I think there
are times which come to us all, when there opens
to us the best thing possible for us to be and to
pursue; and if we accept nothing lower, but can

87

say in after years, like Paul, 'I was not disobedi-
ent to the heavenly vision,' glorious will it be for
us."

" I believe that," she said earnestly, " but the
trouble is worldly ambition leads so very many
to accept something lower than the best possible."

" Precisely," I assented, " and since there are so
many, you will not consider me uncharitable,
when I say we have had a case in point this afternoon. Mrs. Lightheart likes to go to church in
rich attire, with nice, genteel people, and, though
she hears the Christ preached, is very careful to
be as unlike Him as possible."

" She is called a very elegant and stylish lady,"
said Ethel, with a troubled look in her eyes.

" Undoubtedly," I responded, " and therein lies
her ambition, which not only perverts and dwarfs
her own higher impulses, but the impulses of
those who have placed in her their confidence and
love. When a beautiful face and an elegant form
inspire in others only a love for elegance and
fashion, then, indeed, are those gifts pernicious.
On the other hand, what a force for good a
woman can exert whose mind is as beautiful as
her face and figure, and can inspire in man a
passion which shall flow in the same general
direction with the noblest aims and possibilities!
Such a woman can make a great life-task easier,
carrying, as she does, a benediction in her very
presence."

" Is not the converse of this also true? " asked

Ethel. " Are not the nobler aspirations of woman kindled or depressed in the same way ? "

" True," I admitted, " but where is the beautiful woman who chooses a mission for herself to be helped or depressed ? She is apt to rest satisfied with her beauty and to have no higher ambition than to be mistress of a fine home, live in luxury, with everything at her command, and enjoy a sort of lavender-water existence! Nothing but the smallpox, leaving the pits deep in her face, can save her from utter worthlessness."

" You do not believe much in beautiful women," she said, with a faint smile.

" There are noble exceptions," I responded ; " in them I believe. But as a general rule, it is the plainer girl that stores her mind with useful thoughts, and is willing and ready to make sacrifices for the sake of truth and righteousness. She is the one capable of seeing something higher than personal adornment —of choosing or accepting the harder tasks of life for the good she can do."

" Do you not think it a duty, Professor Bloomfield, to make one's self as attractive as possible, consistent with other duties? "

" Certainly, Miss Blentwood."

" Do you not also think it proper to get as much enjoyment out of life as possible, consistent with the faithful discharge of duty to God and mankind ? "

" Most assuredly ; I am no stoic. I quarrel with no delight which is not base. I love the

innocent pleasures and comforts of life, and resist
their blandishments only when they would step
between me and duty to myself and others. But
it is not well to live altogether in one class of society however enjoyable. We must have the low
tones as well as the high. Life's tenor, some one
has said, has its bass, and its soprano has its alto,
in a full-choired humanity. Mine shall not be a
chained and bent and visionless life, but it must be
one of comparative poverty."

"How so?" she asked, with agitation.

"Well, to begin with, my taste would be satisfied only with elegant surroundings, and all the
privileges of art and travel; and, indeed, I am so
full of hungry passions, it would take so many
things to satisfy me that I dare not seek them. I
should want to win, and in elbowing my way among
other seekers, there might be great temptation to
wink at the wrongly-held notions of commercial
honesty, and pocket the proceeds, thereby losing
that fine conscientiousness which is essential to
true manhood and real life."

"Do you think the temptations you refer to
are found in the ministry? Why would not a
pastorate be the very place, and most congenial
too, where a person of your talent, culture and
taste could be the most useful?"

"I have great respect for the true pastor; but
even in the ministry there is too much sanctified
selfishness, too much unholy ambition for place
and power, too much temptation to nurse denominational pride, and the pride of oratorical dis-

play to meet the demand for mere entertainment from the pulpit, rather than self-forgetfulness in seeking the good of others. In short, there is a temptation to wire-pulling and to put one's unworldly aspirations in pawn for the sake of a rich pastorate, big salary and all the refined comforts of a worldly life. I prefer to work where I know I am actuated only by the purest motives."

She was looking sweetly thoughtful, and, as I paused, said with a gratified smile, "You are much like my father.

> "'He would not flatter Neptune for his trident,
> Or Jove for his power to thunder. His heart's his mouth.'

You implied there were other reasons, for self-renunciation, I think."

"Yes, we are debtors to the ignorant and debased as well as to the wise and the good ; for we all belong to one common humanity. Those below me have the right to ask me to let down my hand and lift them up to where I stand, as I have the right to ask those above me to help me to their better footing. Now the church is not doing this work as it might and ought. Christianity encamps in costly church edifices, and says to the poor, Come and be converted ; whereas Jesus, its author, went about doing good, carrying Christianity to the very homes and hearts of the needy. He mingled with the neglected classes, ate with them, talked with them, slept in their humble abodes, and, by precept and example, taught them the way of life. The poorly clothed say they cannot feel at home in fine churches and among the well-dressed. They need a living gospel brought to them by warm hearts full of the blood and nerve of human sympathy to help them out of their low environment and wretched state of body and mind. Not feeling the need of a physician, they will not call one, or come to your office to be healed. Somebody must go and convince them. Who will go? Why not I? I fear necessity is laid upon me."

I suppose I spoke with some enthusiasm, for she said, with glowing cheeks, "You seem inspired. I feel the force of your words. Somebody should go, certainly, but at first thought it seems rather hard that one of fine abilities and culture, to whom beautiful surroundings constitute a native element, should forego these to come in contact with harsh people and harsher surroundings, that act upon one like a rasp lascerating the tender flesh and often wounding still deeper the tender spirit."

"Do you think one need be necessarily unhappy in such a work?" I asked.

"No," she said thoughtfully, "but the work will require great patience, a noble self-poise and constant rill-like out-flowings of goodness; and where the soul of the worker is large, fed by deep. springs of love, fired by passionate devotion, and sustained by an abiding, unwavering faith in the beneficent purposes of God, I can see not only satisfaction but even happiness—not the noisy, light-hearted happiness of an easier life, perhaps, but possibly deeper, sweeter, more abiding and comforting. I believe a luminous, all-submerging joy flows back upon the soul in divine compensation for every truly beneficent expenditure; and, on the other hand, the poor happiness that hovers around self, like the foolish moth fluttering about the blaze of a lamp, soon dies from its own suicidal folly. Indeed, a life with no sacrifice in it has no beauty, no nobleness, no attractions in it that I can see."

As she paused her face was all aglow with spiritual light. I had not seen her look so beautiful. It was not the beauty of color and well-formed features, though she had these, that charmed me; it was something deeper -the all-animating almost divine expression, the heaven-born spirit speaking through her physical loveliness, giving it meaning and power, as if an angel were looking through her eyes and angelic light radiating from her countenance. I felt an inward uplift, a heart-drawing, the kindling of a new strange feeling.

Here, I thought, is one instance, at least, of a woman combining remarkable intellectual strength with great beauty of face and disposition. Unlike many also, her large mental powers do not absorb her womanly nature. She preserves all the charm of girlhood with its transparent frankness, its tender, innocent, unstudied ways, so attractive to a man who sees so many calculating eyes and hears so many measured utterances. What charm of child-like simplicity linked to depth of soul, nobil-

ity of purpose and correctness of judgment, all
glorified by a true Christian culture and the discipline of domestic love! With her as my other
self, my needed better half, my life would become
completely rounded. I longed to express my inmost feelings. But no, I thought, she does not
know me as I know her; for her whole nature is
so guileless, so generous, so true, that there is
nothing covered to be unpleasantly revealed by
any future experience, whereas I may not be so
clearly read. Besides, what have I to offer her
except a loving heart, a fair amount of brains and
a life of service to others? No, no, that will never
do. Oh! if I could devote my talents to surround
her with the beauties and comforts of life; but I
cannot live for wealth. I must do my life-work,
and it would be mean to seek to link her life with
mine for the sake of my own happiness. But, I
argued with myself, she would make my life a
fuller and more useful one. Yes, but at an awful
sacrifice to her. Would she feel it a sacrifice?
Perhaps not, for she will live nobly whoever she
marries; but there are so many paths it would not
be right to divert her steps into the hardest one,
when she might be even more useful in the
easiest.

She looked up, and I had to cut short these
reflections, which had run much more rapidly
through my mind than I have portrayed them.
It seemed to me that a heaven of purity and
peace was looking out of the calm depths of those
liquid eyes. I said, rather tremulously, " Miss

Blentwood, if I believed in the transmigration of souls, I should think I had been acquainted with you in some other sphere a thousand years!"

" It does seem impossible," she said smiling, " that we have known each other so short a time. Can you tell why it is that we become acquainted with some persons more thoroughly in a few hours than with others in as many years, the latter perhaps never being known to us?"

" Some souls," I replied, " are printed in minion type, and others in capitals, some on blurred paper and others on clean."

" Yes," she assented, " but there are some excellent people with whom it is hard to get acquainted."

" Very true," I said, " but the closed human volumes, that open only a page at a time, may be very judicious and very correct and proper; but I like an open book, as I do an open Bible, which seems to say, Read the whole story at once or a portion anywhere you wish."

" I like that kind too," she said, with a pleased look, " but may not some keep the volume closed from self-depreciation, thinking they have nothing a stranger would be interested in?"

" Perhaps," I admitted ; " but more because they dare not reveal themselves. The experience which has turned the leaves of their souls has been wholly selfish. And that reminds me of the many whose pages are so blotted by sin that they themselves do not know what is in the volume of their own souls."

" How can they," she asked in Scripture phrase,
" unless they be taught ? "

" And how can they be taught," I added,
" without a teacher ? "

" And how can one teach," she smiling asked
again, " unless sent ? "

This gave me a good chance to say, " You are
qualified for the work ; how do you know that
you are not sent ? "

She looked a little surprised, and then replied,
" You have too high an opinion of me ; but, admitting for the moment, that I have the requisite
qualifications, is that an evidence that I am
called ? "

" So far as it goes," I answered.

" And how far is that ? "

" It holds good, I think, Miss Blentwood, till
you discover that you have other qualifications
better fitting you for another sphere of usefulness. Have you never felt drawn towards some
such work ? "

She merely quoted, in answer, Dr. Holland :

> " I count this thing to be grandly true,
> That a noble deed is a step towards God."

" I felt sure, Miss Blentwood, you had a clear
perception of what it is to live sublimely ; but, if
you will allow me the question, can you imagine
yourself deliberately choosing a hard lot, in pref-
erence to an easy one, for the sake of so living ? "

" I can imagine it," she answered gravely. " A
life of elegant ease in the absence of high demand

would seem both monotonous and wasteful to me.
It would cheapen life and take away its elixir, its
deeper relish. I should feel that an atmosphere
of moral mediocrity was settling down over all
my prospects, nullifying my better ambition, sti-
fling my highest aspirations, and preventing me
from fulfilling the obligations of my existence.
But, while I should not like a silken bondage,
which arrests all motive, I have no love for a hard
lot and contact with sordid vulgarity in themselves considered ; and the only relief to such a
dark picture, would be the keeping my eye fixed
on the moral beauty to spring up beneath this
harsh contact, under the sanction of the Master,
whose example I followed, and the consciousness
that, however slow it might show itself in spiritual
refinement, the leaven would go on under God's
eye blessing individuals and their homes."

Her words drew me by a power I could not
clearly define, something beyond the resources of
expression. I only knew she was perfectly lovely
to me, with a glorified human light shining forth
from every feature. When a woman first gives
embodiment and life to our day-dreams and
shadowy conceptions of all that is truest and
best, she fills a void in our spiritual nature, till
then, perhaps, unknown, because we realize the
fulfilment in her of our prophetic longings.

She raised her truthful, innocent, blue eyes to
mine ; I felt their magnetism, and dared not speak
for a moment, lest I should forget the proprieties
belonging to a short acquaintance, and was glad

7

to avail myself of the sight of Pomp to refer to
him. Ethel laughed so brightly, that it seemed
a part of the very sunlight which at that moment
shimmered and rippled through the leaves of the
trees upon her fair face.

"You ought to have seen him," she said, "after
he had tumbled downstairs on his return from
your room, where he had been sent to see if you
were awake. He rushed into the farthest corner
of the kitchen and crouched there with his hands
held tightly over his face, trembling and speech-
less. After being questioned repeatedly he looked
through his fingers, and finally withdrew his
hands from his eyes, which stared wildly about,
and asked his mother, 'Is I here in de same ole
kitchen?'

"'Ob cose you is,' replied Tot, 'what de matter wid ye?'

"'Dey killin' dat man up dar.'

"'Who killin' him, you pickaninny?'

"'De debbels, marm. Dey were shakin' and
burnin' him inside; for he eyes were all ablaze,
an' fire an' smoke an' brimster were pourin' out
he mouf. When de debbels spied me froo de
crack ob de do', dey yell an' grab for me, and
knock me down sta'r, an' shake me an' poun' me
all de way to de bottom.'

"'More like de fall shake ye an' de sta'r pound
ye, ye wild-cat chile!'

"Pomp looked at his hands and felt of his face
to satisfy himself that he was all there, and then
looked up with such a relieved and droll expres-

sion that our laughter became uncontrollable, in which we were joined by father and Dr. Lightheart, who had just entered the room."

Tom and Tot now came to rearrange the table for another meal, to which they had been permitted to invite their special colored friends, including their children. We passed to a seat under the row of maples next the river, where was an unobstructed view of that broad sheet of water and an extensive landscape of varied surface and color.

As we seated ourselves we were a little startled by a noise which sounded like the mingled cry of all the animal creation. I rose to my feet. I could see nothing explaining the sounds. They came again, and on the side-hill just emerging from the woods I beheld a dozen black children, all capering on their hands and feet, each with a different style of action and cry in imitation of some particular animal. Pomp, as might be expected, was the leader, and excelled all the others in his grotesque feats. He would spring forward, then sideways, then upwards, as if thrown by his hands as well as feet, and, before coming down, would spring again as from an invisible foothold, precisely as I had seen deer on a western prairie. He would no sooner strike the ground than he would go up again like a rubber ball. This remarkable feat he continued till apparently exhausted, when he would creep slowly and stealthily, and then, rounding up his back, strike out with his hands, snarling and crying like a cat, and then he would run and twitter and sit up in exact imitation of a squirrel while peeling a beech-nut or eating an apple. He was metamorphosed into various other creatures, the last and most ludicrous being the ape. Here he was more at home than ever, playing tricks with the others, and acting so preposterously absurd that laugh we had to in spite of ourselves, even after re-suming our seats.

" It would seem," I remarked, " that Darwin's chimpanzee has reasserted itself in that boy Pomp."

" What an attraction he would be for ' Barnum's greatest show on earth ' ! " she responded.

" Out de way, ye brack bars, ye wild-cats, ye draggle-tailed monkeys ! What if de Lord trans-mogrify ye into dem ar' animals yer imitatin' ? What would be de consequentiality den ? "

It was the voice of Tom, and I looked round in season to see the children, who had surrounded him, scampering away on all fours towards Tot, who was puffing under a load of fried cakes fresh from the house-kitchen, her round, fat face, look-ing more like the full moon than ever, for there was Indian blood in her veins, which asserted itself when overheated. Placing her burden safely on the table, she broke out :

" Doan' you know dat missus and Perfessor Boomfield are jes' on tudder side dat sugar-maple ? Now go way wid ye, ebery brat of ye, and 'have you'selves, ef ye want any dinner." With this admonition and a mouthful of cake for each, they scurried away like so many rabbits, and Ethel and I resumed our conversation.

She quoted Paul, "Not first which is spiritual, but that which is natural, and afterward that which is spiritual."

As much for the sake of listening to the melody of her voice and enjoying the charm of her varying expression as to draw out her views, I asked, "How much do you mean by that Scripture quotation?"

"Simply that no one is born spiritually, but only naturally."

"Do you mean there is no spiritual capacity or germ, or depraved spiritual nature or——"

"I mean no more than this—that the animal alone manifests itself, and wholly predominates at first, and the lower you descend the human scale the more you find of the animal."

"What advantage has the most favorably-born child over Pomp, for instance?"

"Many generations the better start."

"But Pomp has more of the animal than his parents."

"And he dates back. As you yourself intimated, the ape has reasserted itself in him. We are talking of appearances, I suppose, and not necessarily of facts."

"You will admit, will you not, Miss Blentwood, that even Pomp, buried as he is in the animal, may be converted?"

"Certainly, but from conversation with missionaries and others of large experience, I infer

that in such cases the spiritual life rarely gets
entire control, though giving evidence of its
presence in the soul and struggling for the mastery."

"Are animalism and selfishness synonymous
with sin?"

"That is too deep a question for me. I only
know that selfishness in us is sin, and that the
animal life is essentially selfish. Is it not so,
Professor Bloomfield?"

"Most assuredly. No one who has ever fed
animals but must have found that out."

"Your admission leads me to strike a horrid
blow at the poetic sentiment, which calls a babe
an angel!" she said, blushing behind her smiles.

"So long as you don't hit the babe I'll risk the
sentiment," said I. "Proceed, please."

"It seems harsh, but isn't it true that children
at first are only little animals?"

"'Only,' do you mean?"

"Hyperbolically speaking, and they want their
way just like other little animals."

"The poor dears," with mock seriousness.
"What sweet, winning ways they have!"

"Yes, and so have all young animals."

"But the animal does not ascend, whereas the
babe becomes angelic, it may be."

"Yes, *becomes*, but is not now."

'Well, but how good little children are—sometimes!"

"And so are cats when you stroke the fur the
right way, and they are in the mood; but look

out for scratches! the claws are there, depend upon it."

We had been talking only half seriously, interlarding our conversation with much laughter; but I now asked somewhat earnestly, " Why is it that children come to your house, and you are so fond of them, and do so much for them, if they are not angelic ? "

" I love them in spite of their wants, as I believe the Creator loves me in spite of mine."

" But, Miss Blentwood, you cannot love a nonentity. You must see something to love. What is it ? "

" Well, one thing, children have cunning, innocent ways, and are attractive on that account, as pet animals are ; and that is about as far as the love of many silly people goes who blanket their dogs and take them out for an airing to the neglect of poor children by the wayside, who would be immensely benefited by taking the dog's place."

I clapped my hands in approval. She continued : " I love them for the same reason these people do, but for something, I hope higher and nobler. I see within each child, however rough externally, a possible angel, somewhat, perhaps, as the sculptor sees one in his block of marble ; and as he with inspiration chips away that which surrounds his ideal that it may, unimprisoned, stand out to view, so I am seized with enthusiasm, whenever I see a child, to do what I can to make the possible angel a reality, before the angelic capability is imprisoned by habits of stone so hard that they cannot be cut away except by the heavy blows of a stern experience—stern, though directed by the love of the divine Architect Himself."

How my heart sang, as I sat with my back against the tree watching her, and wishing that the sweet now-and-now would last, and wondering if there would or could be any higher bliss for me with her in the sweet by-and-by!

There was silence for a few moments which I did not care to break, content, as I was, with the joy of seeing and being. I wondered whether she could feel the touch of my sympathy, my love, my happiness, as I felt the touch of her holy innocence and supreme loveliness—whether the communion of our spirits was as real and certain to her as to me. But I felt sure that, while my mind to commune with hers must ascend, hers to meet mine must descend; and therefore my happiness was the more exalted. It looked up— had in it the element of worship. I had watched and worked and prayed that I might possess the Master's disposition; but hers was a beauty of soul, to the dizzy height of which I had never climbed. I could climb, I thought, with the uplift which her constant society would give me.

I had often hoped, if the time ever came for me to marry, I might find some such girl as Ethel, and not, like so many educated men, fall in love with one of empty head, drawn by her apparent large-heartedness and femininity, and discover when too late that her supposed affectionate disposition was as shallow as her brains. But the time had not come, I reasoned with myself, for me to fall in love, and, furthermore, this girl was too good for me—too good for anybody, except to be her father's daughter. He must be exceedingly vain and self-opinionated who thinks he can make her happier by asking her to become his wife.

She lifted her soft blue eyes so kindly and so full upon me, mirroring in their calm, clear depths a soul so pure and peaceful, and withal so full of beauty and noble purpose that, for an instant, I felt that I was looking into the spirit land. Forgetting for the moment where our conversation left off, I said, " Miss Blentwood, I wish you had as good company as I have."

She laughingly rejoined, " Oh, that will do for a joke, Professor Bloomfield ! but the truth is I am the more fortunate ; for there is much of society I can enjoy as a recreation only, beyond which it is a waste of time, and it is a treat to have some one, in addition to father and Dr. Lightheart, to converse with to my mental profit as well as pleasure. Don't misunderstand me ; I like fun and can talk nonsense, but am not satisfied with it as a steady diet ! I like a helpful guide, who can and will look with me beneath the surface and into the philosophy of things a little. It makes life seem more worth living." As she said this a slight tinge of color suffused her cheeks.

" I think I understand you, Miss Blentwood, and it is largely because I understand you that I

have enjoyed your society beyond all measure.
It stands out unique among all my experiences as
the greatest feast of my life. You possess that
rare combination which satisfies me intellectually
and socially, and satisfies me as no other lady I
ever met."

I suddenly became aware that I was putting
the case strongly, and revealing my heart inopportunely, and in explanation added, "You are
aware that I leave to-morrow morning, and Providence only knows when we shall meet again, or
whether at all, and you will please consider these
words spoken—when I may not have an oppor-
nitunity of speaking them—at parting. It is in
simple justice to you and the truth in my own
heart that I have said what I have."

She looked up with more color, yet pleased and
trustful, showing that deception played no part in
her composition. The transparent purity and
frankness of her character struck me with new
force, and won me with tremendous and unwonted
energy. I felt myself drawing dangerously near
to that ancient precipice of avowal, which stands
high above and beyond the highest peak in the
whole mountain range of admiration, down which
I might any moment plunge. Almost over-
powered by the forces drawing me on, I struggled
against them, at last conquered, and was ready to
listen.

"I have implicit confidence in your conscientiousness, Professor Bloomfield, and, therefore,
though you are too generous in your opinion of

my abilities, I am comforted by the thought that
I am not altogether stupid to a person of large
intelligence and Christian culture like yourself.
I am sorry you must leave, and not be near us
where we could all meet occasionally and discuss
the great questions of life so interesting to me.
I think I could grow under your tuition. You
awaken thought, and stir that which is best and
deepest in me."

"I am very grateful," I answered, "if I have
been able to compensate in the slightest degree
for the pleasure I have enjoyed in your society.
Mutual helpfulness is one of the divinest of joys,
but whatever my society has been to you, I am
and shall ever remain greatly your debtor."

"Well," she said playfully, "if the indebtedness is mutual, that ought to square the books.
To return to the question we were discussing, I
inferred you had something more to say on the
possible angel in every child."

"Yes, I would like to ask what in your opinion
is that possible angel? Is it only a capacity, a
capability? Or does it exist in embryo, in the
seed form, germinally? Or is it a fallen angel,
with powers all there, only perverted, overborne,
clubbed down? or, stronger still, so corrupted by
inheritance as not only to be inclined toward sin,
but to be sin in its very essence?"

"Oh, Professor Bloomfield! these are deep, hard
questions. I only know which view satisfies my
mind; but if not Scriptural I must of course give
it up; for where the Bible speaks clearly, it is the

clue by which to thread our way through the labyrinthine uncertainties of this life."

" Very true, Miss Blentwood ; we agree in our loyalty to the Book ; but I am interested to know which theory satisfies you intellectually."

" I would like to think man is created with all his faculties in germ, spiritually as well as morally, intellectually, æsthetically, socially, physically— in other words, that every power, from foundation to superstructure comes with us in our birth into this world. This view seems to harmonize with the plan of creation as one of development and progress ; but is it Scriptural ? "

" That depends. Present orthodoxy requires a belief in corruption or a tendency to sin from some source. Believers in the development theory locate that tendency back of Adam in the brute creation whence we sprung ; and the brute instincts men exhibit would seem to favor that theory. The Biblical account of Adam's disobedience does not, I think, necessarily militate against this view, and some would say that it explained it. If Adam developed from the animal kingdom, inheriting instincts centering only in self, it is easy to see how he might go astray, however innocent he might be. But until science speaks clearly, we are not called upon to adopt its guesses, though shrewd and may prove to be true. One thing is certain, that all have this tendency to sin, however it got into our composition and wherever it may be located ; but your theory harmonizes with all the known facts of science, and I see no reason why it may not be made to harmonize with the Bible. But all this may be profitable only as a sort of intellectual gymnastics; the great fact remains, which no theory can dissipate, that the spiritual faculty of the child may be born into life and power by the quickening influence of Divine love. You have something to appeal to in every child—something higher than matter, higher than intellect. All the possibilities of the best man or woman lie enfolded in the little child. Christ is in it, waiting to be born."

"That takes me out of the woods into light," exclaimed Miss Blentwood with animation. "The different theories threw me into the jungles."

"Doubtless I have passed through the same difficulty," I said.

"Please state it, Professor Bloomfield; it will make my way still clearer."

"Well, Miss Blentwood, in your search for a scientific method of procedure with the little child, you have said, All its body wants is food and training, and the same is true of the intellectual, social, affectional, æsthetical and moral natures; but is the spiritual germinal and to be fed and trained in the same way? If so, where comes in the new birth? If the new birth is the creation of a new faculty, then my possible angel is not a whole being to start with, and I have nothing here to feed—no real foundation on which to build. However I may develop all the other faculties and powers, for that which crowns, over-

tops, and beautifies all the rest, and makes the
child at all angelic, I must fold my arms and await
the creative fiat.   But when you said that no new
faculty is added by conversion, it was clear to you
that whether this spiritual faculty is simply germinal or essentially wicked, it is there, and you had
something to appeal to.   If feeble, or, in Scripture
phrase, dead, it is so because starved, and needs
food.   On what shall it feed?   On God.   It must
have the life-giving or the life-restoring impact of
God through inspiration of the Holy Spirit.

"To sum up, you reasoned that every human
faculty and power is a feeding creature, each on
its kind.   The body must have material food, the
intellect intellectual food or truth, the moral nature moral truth, and the spiritual nature spiritual
truth, or Divine truth—the Truth, as Jesus declared Himself to be.   Here, then, is as plain a
work for me to do for the spiritual as for the intellectual nature.   I am to feed it with the bread
of life.   Here is a ground for spiritual instruction
in Sunday-Schools and elsewhere."

Miss Blentwood brought her pretty hands together in a most expressive manner and with
charming emphasis said, "Professor Bloomfield, I
thank you very, very much; for you have stated
my case a thousand-fold better than I could, and
let in a flood of light where before it was dark, and
I can see so far!"

I was surprised at her enthusiasm, but——Oh!
how beautiful she looked, with her heightened
color and joyful animation!   Her right hand was

resting carelessly on the seat near mine, and, before I realized what I was doing, my toying fingers went slowly towards hers till they touched. I drew back my hand quickly, but not till that touch had gone through me like an electric shock, minus the pain. I managed to regain my normal condition and to say, " You looked so ethereal I began to doubt almost whether you belonged to this mundane sphere, till I touched your hand."

" You are hitting my enthusiasm," she said, with a look and gesture of playful warning.

" Not in the least," I replied. " On the contrary, it is a joy to find one who can take so much pleasure in ideas as you seem to. There cannot be too much enthusiasm in that direction. Indeed, I feel a strong sympathy for that Greek philosopher who, discovering a new idea, forgot all about the fashions, as he ran through the streets crying, Eureka! If Columbus was laudably enthusiastic in the discovery of America, why should not we be as enthusiastic in exploring for new worlds of thought, which have so close a relation to human happiness and well-being? "

" I am thankful," she said, " there are Columbuses in the mental world, who go on voyages of discovery, and bring back trophies of rare interest and value, and hints of still greater things. I only wish there were more explorers spiritual as well as intellectual."

" There would be more, Miss Blentwood, if more people knew the happiness of living in the upper

rooms of their many-storied nature. The trouble
is, so many get no higher than the basement for
a better view, a purer air, and a more glorious
sunshine. Having experienced nothing higher,
they are content with material things. It only
proves that their lower nature predominates over
their higher."

"This brings us back to our former discussion,
Professor Bloomfield. It is evident that the first
step in the higher education of such persons is to
be taken on the basement floor, where they are
living. It is of no use to teach them from the
attic ; we must go down where they are, enter
into sympathy with their thoughts and views,
and lead them step by step to the upper
stories."

"You have the true theory of education, Miss
Blentwood, scholastic and Christian. You cannot
teach seven leagues off. Jesus did not do it.
He took people as he found them and where
he found them. He taught them with evident
sympathy by illustrations familiar to them, the
spiritual meaning of which dawned upon their
dull minds at last."

CHAPTER XI.

A NEGRO WEDDING.

AT this moment Miss Blentwood excused herself, and went to the assistance of Tot, who was seating the children at the table in evident perplexity. With a merry and cheerful countenance she soon lifted all signs of burden from Tot's full round face, causing her to say, "You knows how to do ebery ting, Miss Ethel; no need hab no trouble where you is. Your hubban wont break his back staggerin' under de burdens ob life; for when he comes home and looks at you cheery face and gentle ways, 'fore he know it, de burdens will roll clean off'n him, done gone forebber."

She did look lovely enough to scatter the darkest clouds that ever gathered on a human face. Pink roses bestarred her fair cheeks, and her lustrous blue-eyes spoke so winningly of inward joy and harmony, it was like listening to glad music to look at her, making the very pulse of my blood beat a strange rhythmic tune, as if in step with the melodies of her nature. My heart went up in silent thanksgiving for the existence of this ideal of young womanhood, whose presence in society would be like the welcome sunshine of early summer, which gladdens and glorifies everything it touches. I thought of the separation which must come in the morning, and of the many places, which had acquired, and would henceforth ever possess, a charm from association with this delightful creature.

Ethel returned with a pleased expression, and said, "Professor Bloomfield, there is to be a wedding of two colored people, here in the grove immediately after the children get through dinner. The ceremony is to be performed by father, assisted by the somewhat noted Father Taylor right from the South. Indeed, all Tom and Tot's guests were former slaves and they are to have a kind of jubilee supper. We are invited to witness the ceremony. Would you like to?"

I assured her it would be a great treat, when our attention was called to the road whence the guests were coming almost in a body, and numbering when arrived twelve to fifteen, of all complexions from coal black to pale yellow. There was a general shaking of hands, and hearty welcomes from Tom and Tot, who performed the part of host and hostess with genuine, old-time, plantation hospitality. Fine rows of ivory were to be seen in almost every mouth, stretched from ear to ear, and, while their "pump-handle grip," odd atttitudes and droll expressions were very amusing, their simple, whole-hearted, unrestained greeting was very touching, and, indeed, a refreshing relief from the cold, calculating manners of an overcultured society.

Dr. Blentwood and Father Taylor, as he was called, whose snow-white head and tall form gave him a most venerable appearance, approached, followed by the bride and bridegroom, and a circle was formed, which we joined, and the ceremony commenced. Dr. Blentwood was very happy in the mingling of instruction with his portrayal of wedded life and its responsibilities, evidently intended to help the new pair in the establishment of their united home. Father Taylor offered prayer, which was so original, I will give it as near as I can.

"O, Lord," he said, "when here you did attend a wedding you'sef, and added to de joy of it by supplying good, safe wine when dat fell short, and we knows you is interested in dis yere occasion. Darefore wid confidence we ask you to bless dis yere married pair—not wid wine which dey don't need, but wid Christian honesty and squar common sense, so dat dey perform deir vows, and raise up a family to de Lord. Dey hab gibben demselves away to each udder, and may dey nebber take back what dey hab gibben. When de fancy and all de moonshine of lub go, may de true, steady sunshine of lub remain, and stay wid em. May dey trust one anudder, and be true to dat trust. May dey walk togedder on de heights ob mutual confidence and placid joy during de heat and burden ob de day, and at night cuddle down togedder in lub, like two turtle doves in one nest. And when de time come for dem to cross de dark ribber, may dey turn up deir faces for de Lord to wipe away all tears from deir eyes, and den jump into de ole ferry-boat, like chillens goin' to a picnic, and sail shoutin' in de spirit to de udder sho', where is de white robes and de married supper ob de Lamb dat last forcber. Glory dat it last forcber! May we all be dar; but not yet, for we hab a little more work to do. Abundantly bless Brudder Blentwood in his home and work of mercy and his Christian daughter, who is de angel of his heart and de image of his soul, and dese udder godly ones sheltered under deir roof—under all whose kindness we are to partake of one more jubilee feast protected by wide-branching trees, God's first temples. May holy doves of gratitude fly up through de branches from all our hearts whom you did bring out of bondage, as you did the children of Israel, wid a high hand and a outstretch arm; and, unlike dem, may we know how to, have ourselves, now we got out. Here, Lord, we say, amen! So mote it be! Amen and amen!"

The prayer was uttered with so much touching pathos, that I found myself alternately weeping and shaking with suppressed laughter.

Father Taylor was the first in his congratulations. Placing one hand on the head of the bride and the other on that of the bridegroom, he looked down benevolently upon them from his towering height and said, "An undershepherd's blessing go wid ye, young folks." Then taking a hand of each he added, " Keep de boat of

wedded life right side up. When de storm come,
stop paddlin' and spend your time preservin' de
balance, so dat she don't topple ober. If a squall
come up from de wife side of de cabin, neber you
mind you'sef, Mr. Jenkins, how de squall come,
but keep you' eye on de boat till de storm pass
and dar be a calm. Den examin' de craft, and
see if she leak, and at de fitting time and place
administer de proper repairs. Remember, Mr.
Jenkins, I put de emphasis on de word proper.
And Mrs. Jenkins, if a hurricane strike you widout
any warnin' from de male quarter ob de heavens,
de very fust question you must ax you'sef is,
What can I do to keep de boat from tippin' wid
de wind? Keep dat interrogation travelin' round
in you head by de Lord's aid, and you may be
sartin for sure dat dar will be no sufficient cyclone
to swamp you domestic felicity."

This advice was greatly enhanced by Father
Taylor's dramatic action, fine voice and expressive features, his tall form now erect and firm, and
now swaying in convulsive good-will, and gentle
laughter.

As he turned aside, Dr. Blentwood, Ethel and
myself shook hands with the newly-married couple,
and wished them a happy future. The darkies
followed our example, timidly at first, till one
fellow, bolder than the rest, with a dandy air,
droll step and comical expression, shook both of
the bride's hands, saying, as he did so, " You got
anudder name, but you looks 'mazing natural,"
and then he gave her a smack, which sounded

like the collapse of a main-topsail in a storm.
This was the signal for general hilarity, and after
that the smiling couple each received kisses fast
and hearty, till the supply was exhausted.

As they were being seated at table, Miss Blentwood said to me, " I think they will enjoy themselves better now in our absence." I was glad to
think so too, since Dr. Blentwood had gone to
his study, and I could be alone with Ethel !

CHAPTER XII.

A STROLL BY THE RIVER.

WE moved towards the river, and strolled leisurely on its pleasant banks, chatting familiarly, giving and receiving information on various topics, and drinking in whatever enjoyment we could easily extract from the present, as befitted the closing and languid beauty of a hot June day.

It was one of those hours, when the passing moments are all sufficient,—when we do not need to make excursions into the past or future, but are content to live wholly in the present, making the most of what it has to give, gathering into our nature all its sweet delights, and helpful comforts, in storage for future expenditure, when there is call for outgo and no income of joy.

The sky had a mellow look, the air was soft and balmy, sweet with the perfume of the new-mown hay and blossoms both near and far off. The oriole, the yellow-bird, and bobolink attracted our notice here and there, mostly quiet, uttering only an occasional note or half-note, as if too lazy or too contented to sing. There was not breeze enough to stir the foliage except the ever trembling aspen leaves, which glistened and shimmered in the rays of the declining sun. We did not wander far, for there was no occasion to hurry, and we examined everything, and enjoyed everything, sometimes sitting down, now to analyze a flower, now to break a stone in pieces and look at its particles through a pocket microscope, which I always carried, and now to watch a sailboat anchored near the opposite shore, the two occupants preferring to lounge and read, rather than use their oars.

When we thought of retracing our steps, the red edge of the sun was scarcely visible above a western hill, and the sky was rapidly changing her robes to a more brilliant hue. The city spires glistened in the red fire of the setting sun, and the gable windows looked as if all ablaze with an internal raging flame, ready to burst out into a conflagration, suggestive of fire-alarms and fire-engines. Yet the hour was so sweet and congenial nothing unpleasant could enter my mind. Happy and grateful as I was, the moments seemed to come and go only to bring me unmerited blessings, and all I had to do was to drink and be filled.

We walked homeward for some time in silence. We did not need to speak. I at least enjoyed a higher communion ; for there are passages in our life when speech pulls down, rather than lifts up, and jars on the melody going on in our souls. Words are material, and there are thoughts sweeter, nobler, purer than any form in which they may be materialized.

So we walked on quietly, observant, yet seeing only sweet design enfolded in every created thing. It was the loveliest twilight I had ever experienced, or else it was my own happy state, which threw a halo of glory upon everything around me.

Did I think of the companion at my side? I thought of everything good and must have thought of her. I seemed to be moving with her in a new and beautiful world, all our own, of which she was the creator, though had I stopped to reason, my title-deed to it would have been utterly wanting. I had received no intimation that I could remain in that world.

We had now reached a bend in the river, where suddenly the music of a guitar fell softly and sweetly on our ears, with the accompaniment of alternating male and female voices. The distance and atmosphere were such as to strain out all harshness, if any there were, and produce the finest effect. We stopped instinctively, and listened without a word of comment. To me it was only an added charm to an already charmed life. Had I caught a glimpse of heaven's landscape, or a breath of its fragrant air, and seen the flitting of an angel's wing, I could not have been much surprised, for I was in heaven, and why should not all loveliest things come to me?

When an interval in the music occurred, Ethel said softly, as if not to disturb the happy illu-

sions of the hour, " One of them is the voice of
Charley, I think—Charley Lightheart."

" A connection of the doctor's ? " I asked.

" A younger brother," she replied.

The music flowed on, and we listened again,
seating ourselves on a rustic seat, encircling a
huge elm, whose branches spread out over the
water's edge, and cast a somber shadow in the
light of the moon, which had come out to take
the place of the now departing sun. I quoted the
lines of the grand old poet :

> " How sweet the moonlight sleeps upon this bank !
> Here will we sit, and let the sounds of music
> Creep to our ears ; soft stillness and the night
> Become the touches of sweet harmony."

" Most befitting the place and the hour ! " she
said, with a pleased look. " You are very happy
in your poetic memories, Professor Bloomfield."

Her face was a study. Blessed memories,
noble impulses, and pure aspirations were the
divine artists there at work. There was, too, a
wealth of love, without which no woman is
beautiful, a wealth, however, which showed itself
only as a possession held in reserve, except as I
had seen it flow out in little delicate and helpful ways to her father, for whom she displayed
great admiration and devoted attachment.

The music increased in volume by the added
strains of a banjo and mandolin, borne to us now,
however, in fitful gusts, by a slightly rising and
changeful breeze. Then broke upon our ears a

melody which could have had its birth only on a
negro plantation. It would heave and swell like
an ocean wave, and then as gradually subside, or
sweep by us, and break with an echo on the opposite shore of the river. The negro voices sub-
siding, the stringed instruments could be heard,
producing by contrast a charming effect. Again,
instruments and voices, blending together, be-
sieged our ears with augmenting force, as if to
take them by storm, and then receded with even
sweeter footsteps of harmony, that they might
advance upon us separately, like different skir-
mish lines in battle.

"What does that   sic remind you of, Miss
Blentwood?" I asked.

She turned towards me with a little surprise,
looking out at me between the long-fringed curtains of her expressive eyes, as if I had divined
her thoughts.

"I was thinking," she answered, "how all the
discords of the world would be done away, if
every soul could find and strike the keynote—
divine love."

"Your thought is more beautiful than mine," I
said slowly. "I was thinking what a sublime
coquette music is!"

"Ah!" she questioned, "when can a coquette
be sublime?"

"When," I answered, "she unconsciously in-
spires in a man a longing and love for the morally
beautiful, and at the same time stands so far
above him, so unattainable, that all he can do is

to gaze and adore, yet glad that he has seen his ideal, and can worship even afar off."

She displayed no consciousness that I meant her, wearing only a more thoughtful look, and I said rather impulsively and too abruptly, I feared: "Miss Blentwood, I wish to ask a favor."

She raised to me questioning eyes, and waited. She was so pretty I had to look at her, and the longer I looked the lovelier she grew, and I must have quite forgotten myself; for, before I knew it, she was really blushing. The sky, which a few moments before, had colored so resplendently in the rays of the setting sun, could not be compared, in richness and brilliancy of tone, to her rosy cheeks and ripened lips.

"The favor I wish to ask," I stammered, in confusion at my own awkwardness, "is the privilege, if you will grant it, of calling you—Ethel."

"Oh, is that all?" she asked with receding color, and a smile breaking into a gentle laugh. "That is a favor easily granted, Professor Bloomfield. Ethel is my name."

"Yes, I know," I said, slowly recovering myself, "and a very pretty name it is, and, liking it, I wish to use it unadorned by prefix or suffix, as a friend, who believes that 'Beauty when unadorned is adorned the most.'"

"As you please," she said, "but you will use your privilege only for a short time, Professor Bloomfield, if you leave us to-morrow morning, as you say. However, you will visit us on your return trip—will you not?"

" Will Ethel please be just a little bit sorry that I am going away, so as to help me come back ? " I asked, with poorly-concealed earnestness.

" I shall be sorry to have you go, and glad to have you return, and I know father will say the same." She spoke with all the simplicity of her truthful nature, and I saw in her eyes that she meant it, and I was satisfied. Satisfied? Yes, as to my judgment ; no, as to my heart. Friendship was all I had any reason to expect, and it was a great comfort to have the friendly esteem of so noble a girl. When I reflected that it would be months, and perhaps years, before we might meet again, my heart knocked loudly for the privilege of correspondence, but my wiser judgment told me that would be too much to ask on so short acquaintance, though I had to appeal to facts to assure myself that I had not always known her.

Some spirits are indeed so fitly strung as to blend at once, like naturally attuned voices, and without preliminary practice or rehearsal, into sweetest melody. Ethel supplemented my poor half and imperfect notes and satisfied the longings of my heart, and I knew that I knew her ; but, as I reflected that that knowledge did not necessarily prove that she knew me, I tried to hush the loud beating of my impatient heart, and to convince myself that I must prove my worth before asking the privilege of even a friendly correspondence with this idol of her father's house.

But the thought of separation on the early morrow from this bright, pure being at my side, grew more and more painful as it forced itself on my mind, and brought home the conviction that I was thinking too much of her—too much for my own happiness. Hitherto in life I had kept my heart with all diligence, determined never to love till my head said where and when. My head approved of the where, but not of the when, if I was loving her now, unless my love asked only friendship in return. I tried to convince myself that that was all that I did ask or expect, and called upon my common sense to witness how absurd it would be to think, at present at least, of anything beyond friendship, or strong friendship at most.

And thus I battled silently in the intervals of conversation, not quite realizing that love had got as quietly, and yet as irretrievably, into my heart, and was at work as effectively as a sunbeam gets into a bud, steadily pushing it wide open to the full rays and complete influence of the sun. Strange to say, in the midst of this tumult of emotions, I was happy, proving that moments of greatest pain may not be entirely inconsistent with the highest heaven.

CHAPTER XIII.

WE rose to go, and I was anticipating the supreme happiness of Ethel's exclusive companionship home, when we were almost startled by the splash of oars and the appearance of a boat drawing near propelled by one man, and the jumping ashore of the other occupant, who had been lying lazily in the bow. Leaving his companion to row alone up the river, he approached, and, feigning surprise, saluted Ethel and apologized for intruding on our company. Well, I thought, there is no paradise without a serpent, or something to interfere with its blessedness.

Ethel introduced this metaphorical serpent as Mr. Stockmire, a young merchant, who had recently started business in this growing suburb of the city, and a member of her church. He had a dark complexion, large Roman nose bent a little to one side, and the whole shading and cast of countenance partaking somewhat of the Jewish type, and yet, in view of the unmistakable marks of intelligence which illumined his face, he was what might be called good-looking. In addition

127

he had an innocent way which, though studied, had all the appearance of having been born with him, and this deception was enforced by a seeming humility and a drawling tone of voice, which, as I afterwards learned, led almost everybody to say, " Stockmire is as honest as the day is long." The state of my heart gave sharpness to my mind, and I read him through as if he had been an open book, although afterwards I began to think I had been mistaken.

" Glad to make your acquaintance," said he, extending his hand in a semi-shy and semi-assertive style. I could not honestly return his compliment. The fact is I was not glad to make his acquaintance. On the contrary, I could have parted with him at that moment with enthusiastic resignation and even signed a petition for his promotion to a consulship in Patagonia or Algiers, or yielded with extreme fortitude to his immediate translation in a whirlwind to heaven ; that is, if prepared and it was all the same to him ! I had no wish to hurt .him, not even his feelings, and so I answered his expressed gladness to see me by saying :

" Thank you, Mr. Stockmire, I hope you had a pleasant sail or row on the river." I knew instinctively he had not rowed any, and I waited to see how this Uriah Heep would answer.

"O, yes," he replied, " we had a lovely sail down stream ; but on our return the sails were of no use, and we had hard work rowing against the current."

I felt sure that the " we," who had done the

work, was the other fellow, and I asked, "'Did you blister your hands badly, Mr. Stockmire?'"

"Oh! no," he said, doubtless fearing I would look at his hands, "my friend was too generous, knowing my wrists were still weak from a sprain, to allow me to do my share of the work. It was very humiliating, and so I landed to relieve him of my weight."

After telling this whopper, which I could see Ethel received as literal truth, he moved from me with a sinuous, twisting, sidelong movement, as if he was accustomed to get through narrow places, and to do it easily without hurting him, however hard it might rub the truth.

Turning to Ethel, he continued, "It did make me feel mighty mean to lie there in the bow like a great lubber, and let that little fellow pull me up the river. If he had been as large as I am, it would have helped my feelings some, but being so much smaller, it was really excruciating."

He spoke so shamefacedly and with such pathetic tones long-drawn out, sounding so very honest, that I did not much wonder that Ethel, in her kindness of heart, wished to relieve him of his apparent mortification, which she did undoubtedly according to his wishes, by saying, "It is a credit to your generosity, Mr. Stockmire, that you take the situation so much to heart; but really I cannot see that it was in the least your fault."

Ah! I thought, this man deceives the very elect. I wonder I do not believe in him. I wanted to say something very ironical, but fear-

9

ing I might be prejudiced, and, not wishing to disturb the pleasant relations between this parishioner of Dr. Blentwood and Ethel, to whose friends I ought certainly to be polite, I simply said, " I think I saw you and your friend about an hour ago becalmed and reading on the opposite shore ? "

" Yes," he answered, " we waited there several hours, hoping there would be wind enough to fill our sail ; and so we spent the time over some of Mark Twain's jokes."

We were now ascending a little rise of land commanding a larger sweep of country, from which, however, the light was slowly stealing away before the approaching darkness, which was gently settling down about us, a thin cloud veiling the moon, and dimming the light of an occasional star, narrowing the circle of our vision, but bringing with the change a refreshing coolness, and giving a weird beauty to the landscape. The darkening river lay coiled at our feet like a monster Python asleep, with its scales glistening here and there in the shifting rays of the moonlight, and the maples, which stood guard on its bank, frowned down upon it in deeper shadows, while the soft, sweet, distant sounds of the guitar and mandolin rang out upon the air about us with a subdued and musical echo.

We quickened our pace. The conversation was mostly carried on by Mr. Stockmire, with an occasional comment or question from Ethel, just sufficient to keep his smooth, slow-moving tongue in steady occupation. I was glad to have it so, as it gave me an excuse to be silent, which I considered my safest course, now that the serpent had got into my garden ; for I felt an occasional righteous impulse to make him describe a semicircle in the air, and come down into more fitting companionship with the slippery eels and water snakes of the river. This impulse I, of course, checked, and with the thought, Can I be right in my hastily conceived prejudice, and Ethel, who has known him longer, and can judge more dispassionately, wrong? It was not my nature to think evil of any one, and I tried to explain my present mood on Bacon's theory that,

> Suspicions among thoughts are like bats among birds;
> They ever fly by twilight."

When we reached the place where we had taken our late dinner, and where we expected to find the musicians, who had filled the air with so much melody, lamps were appearing in windows here and there, though it was still light except under the trees, and even there the shadow was sufficiently luminous to make the place and the hour only the more romantic ; for the moon had laid aside her cloudy veil, and was smiling down upon us in every feature of her bright-shining face.

CHAPTER XIV

A PLANTATION DANCE.

THE music had ceased, and while we were wondering where the authors of it could be, a lurid light flamed up through the trees skirting the edge of an embankment just ahead of us, and going there, we discovered on a low flat, hemmed in on three sides by an almost perpendicular ledge with wooded summits, a pile of pitch-pine knots just kindled, and about a dozen colored men and women, old and young, preparing for a dance, and three musicians, two of them white.

"O, what a Charley Lightheart!" said Ethel in a low breath; "he is in his element though, having his fill of enjoyment in the rough, uncouth, untrained, and unrestrained happiness of this recently liberated people. Nothing delights Charley so much as to contribute to the happiness of others, high or low."

The musicians were seated on a log. Charley Lightheart with a mandolin; a young man, whom neither Ethel nor Stockmire recognized, with a guitar; and Tom with a banjo.

The music struck up, and almost simultaneously the whole company was in the air, with arms and

feet flying out in all directions, yet with such
good time and ease as to make their movements
a mixture of wonderful grace and oddity. From
the centre of the plot of ground, where they were
grouped, they backed in couples in all directions,
advanced, twisted, whirled on one foot, swayed
backward and forward, clapped their hands,
jumped with both feet and then on one, bowed
low, threw kisses, turned their backs on their
partners, danced away from them, whirled, advanced, shook hands, laughed, took each other by
the arm, whirled together, then separately, placed
both hands on each other's shoulders, face to face,
then side by side, advanced, retreated, and so on,
in almost endless maneuvers, all the while keeping admirable time. It was a plantation-dance,
very amusing, and, at the same time, very interesting, as an exhibition of the survival of instincts
and characteristics, which in their short stay in
the North they had not outgrown.

I was much amused in watching Tom, who
seemed the very incarnation of the banjo he was
thumbing, so animated was he from head to foot
and from shoulder to finger-tips. He appeared
wholly lost in, and swayed by, the spirit of the
occasion ; and if he had any consciousness at all,
he must have thought himself on the old home
plantation in Mississippi, where his young feelings grew, and where ties were formed and broken,
where loved ones lived and died, but where there
were bright spots, as there are in all our lives,
which we love to look back upon, and live over

again. His feet kept up a constant clatter on a board beneath them, his body swayed to and fro, sometimes lifting himself entirely from the log on which he sat, his shoulders rose and fell, his head wagged, and his elbows flopped, as if he could not keep himself down on the earth, and was ready to fly off into space. Though constantly humming, he occasionally raised a shout as a sort of safety-valve to his overwhelming enthusiasm, while his face wore a strange, wild expression in the lurid light of the pitch-pine knots.

We rose to go, thinking we would steal away and not let the merrymakers know we had seen them ; but accidentally or purposely (I never felt quite sure which) a stone, on which Mr. Stockmire had been seated, was loosed from its position, and rolled down over the ledge. I shouted an alarm to the dancers, and then held my breath in mortal fear that one or more would be fatally injured by the large and swift-rolling stone, but the latter buried itself among the burning knots, and spent its force scattering the firebrands, and doing no other damage. The dancers stopped as suddenly as if struck by a thunderbolt, and stood with mouths wide open, transfixed with fear ; and poor Tom, so suddenly brought down from his ecstatic flight, was looking round and rubbing his head in great bewilderment.

" Let's slip away, and not let them know what did it," whispered Stockmire. I looked at Ethel, and saw that she, no more than myself, approved of leaving these simple-hearted, but superstitious,

people without an explanation ; and so, clamber-
ing down to a small sapling, which, rooted firmly
in the crevices of the ledge, leaned out over the
little plateau below, and, catching hold of it, I
swung myself off, and was let gently down by it
within two or three feet of the ground, when I
dropped easily, and exclaimed at the same time,
" I am glad, good friends, nobody is hurt." I explained the accident as briefly as I could, and,
after expressing the hope that it would not
interrupt their enjoyment, I turned to thank the
musicians for their excellent music.

" Is dat you, Perfessor Boomfield ! " cried Tom
in great astonishment, holding his banjo in one
hand and his hat in the other. " I mose fort de
debble come arter me for sure, when de noise came
and de fire busted and went flyin' ebery way. I
fort maybe my time come. De fac' is, Perfessor
Boomfield, I oughtenter be cotched givin' my influence in favor ob de dance. Dr. Blentwood doan,
prove of it ; nudder do I in de abstrac', and generally speakin'. But you see all de dancers here
are religious folks, and my ole banjo has been in
a powerful number ob revival meetin's, and is
converted to de Lord togedder wid myself, and
dese facs make it big dif' from a unregenerate
dance. It transmogrifies it tetotlum, seems to
me. Why, Perfessor Boomfield, when de dancers
am pious and de music am pious, too, what is de
dance but a pious meetin' — de piety spressin' it-
se'f froo de graceful action and de stringed instrument, rudder dan froo de vocal utterance ? I hope

you cotch de sentiment, and foster my meaning, Perfessor Boomfield."

"I think so, Tom," I answered, controlling my risibilities as best I could; "but I fear the distinction you make is too metaphysical to convince the worldly-minded."

"Jes' so, persacly, it may be, Perfessor Boomfield, and dat is because dey is obfuscated by sin, and want to make demselves out as good as pious folks. Two pussons may do de same act, peers to me, and one of dem be justified befo' de Lord and de udder condemn. But I'se not gwine to stan' on mootable ground. Dis yere is de las' dance wid me. It is de farewell plantation-dance, de good-bye to de ole times and scenes ob childhood and youth. Wid dis yere dance I shut de do' to de bygone life, sah, and look to de future, and lib in it, sah, as a free citizen ob Massachusetts in de Lord. I jes' wanted to open de ole cabin do', and shake hands wid de ole inmates once mo', and look into deir faces a spell, and den come away foreber."

Tom could say no more; his voice choked, and he turned away. I confess I was touched by the simple pathos of his closing words and manner. For a moment I could not control my voice from sympathy for the old man, who stood between a past and a future so essentially different, with all his habits formed in harmony with a past civilization, and yet trying with all his might to bring himself into fellowship with a life and a civilization almost entirely new. Do we not expect too much sometimes from those born low down in life? and would not a little thought enable us to cease wondering why such unusual means as those adopted by the "Salvation Army" reach them where our more refined methods—so refined as to be out of sympathy with them—fail?

Putting a hand on Tom's shoulder, I said almost in a whisper, "God and heaven and progress are forward and not backward, Tom; but this does not imply that you have done any wrong. Go ahead steadily, trusting in the great, patient Teacher, who does not expect you to jump clean out of your past self with one bound.

" Ah ! dat is comfortin' sah," said Tom wiping his eyes, " I is glad He can wait for me to creep a little."

Charley Lightheart and his friend joined us on our way to the house, which we reached in a few minutes.

CHAPTER XV.

WE all went into the parlor, which was already
lighted and occupied by two young ladies
waiting to see Ethel. The mandolin being a new
instrument to me, and having enjoyed it so much,
I prevailed on Mr. Lightheart to accompany Ethel
with it on the piano. They played together with
fine effect, to the great pleasure and satisfaction
of all. Charley Lightheart sung a college song,
and then we all sang together, both songs and
hymns, chatting and laughing in the preludes, in-
terludes, and postludes, till we had chatted, sung
and played the evening pleasantly away. The only
drawback to me was the lack of opportunity for a
secret dialogue with Ethel. I had so many things
to say to her, of which I had said nothing as yet,
and the thought of going away without saying
them, and feeling the inspiration and comfort of
her exclusive presence, was relieved only by the
privilege of standing beside her and turning the
leaves of her music, and by the hope that we
might meet again.

Before the party dispersed, Charley Lightheart,
with whom I had become rapidly acquainted, and

for whom I felt a strong liking on account of his frank, open nature and cheerful, sunny disposition, had hinted that it would be a pleasure to accompany me down the river, and I had invited him to do so, and he was to be on hand early the next morning.

When I retired that night, I found it difficult to sleep, so many thoughts were crowding my brain, and so many questions asking for a solution. I arose, lifted the curtain of the open window, and looked out upon the night. The stars were shining brilliantly, and the moon was walking the heavens in all her queenly majesty, making strange contrasts of shadow and sheen with the trees and open spaces. The river was flowing smoothly, taking on fantastic shapes under the varied, marginal foliage of the opposite shore, and my eyes followed its course to where it was shadowed by the tall elm on its hither bank, under which Ethel and I had sat and passed the early twilight so pleasantly.

I thought of all she had said in her sweetly accented speech, every mark and turn of her kindly disposition, every grace of manner and expression of her beautiful eyes, and I said almost aloud, " What a treasure she will be for somebody ! What a pity if she should be deceived into marrying some one unworthy of her ; one who could not appreciate her, and would cause her warm, generous heart to recoil on itself, and wither instead of blossoming like the rose ! "

Like every other young man in love, I thought

nobody could make her so happy as I could, nobody appreciate her so thoroughly, care for her
so tenderly, or watch so faithfully for the smallest
as well as the greatest opportunity to please her,
and make her life full of satisfaction.

It did not occur to me that her good father had
had years of experience in taking care of her
where I had only hours, and knew better than I
what her wants were and how to meet them.   If I
had thought of this, I doubt if it would have
made any difference.   Her home was the nearest
perfection I had ever seen ; but it lacked one
thing, a certain something more than father, in fact
an acknowledged lover or husband, and that lover
or husband should be—well, of course, who could
fill either place with such absolute devotion to
her interests as myself ?   It would be really too
bad, horrid, for her to call herself the wife of any
other, and thus fall short of the happiness, she
was so worthy of, and so capable of experiencing !
It was my duty to shield her from anything less
than perfect happiness.

These thoughts did not arise from any over-
weening notion or self-esteem ; for, in fact, I was
very humble and self-depreciating.   The idea
possessing me was, that nobody could love her
and anticipate and supply every want, before it
was felt, as I could.   Like many another in the
glow of youth, I felt that no home on this earth
was quite up to the home I would have.   Mine
was to be the ideal home, a paradise, a heaven
below, where the strings of its harmony should

never give forth a discordant note, touched, as they always would be, by the gentle fingers of loving thoughtfulness.

But, I asked myself, will she be able to see how happy I can make her? Is there anything in me she can love, so as to suggest that idea to her mind? Was there only friendliness in her eyes when they looked into mine under that elm tree? I could not tell. It was so easy to love her; but it seemed too good to be true, that she, the possessor of such grace and beauty, such wealth of mind and heart, could ever be mine. Then I thought of Stockmire. What if that snake in the grass keeps on deceiving her, as he does everybody else, till she believes him an angel of light! With a sharp pang I crept back into bed, and went to sleep praying that she might be protected from all deception and from all harm, and that God would forgive me if there was any selfish motive in my heart.

CHAPTER XVI.

THE MORNING OF DEPARTURE.

WHEN I awoke from my fitful slumber, the morning was already looking at me through the window with a bright and smiling face, and the birds were twittering their good-morrows from Ethel's favorite maple, whose branches reached my windows as well as hers. Thus sweetly called, I hastily dressed, and sat down, looking out through a screened window at the clear sky, and breathed the fragrant air wafted to me from thousands of blossoms. One or two fleecy clouds in the horizon were blushing in crimson, as if ashamed of their feeble attempts to keep down the day, while the last traces of night, that had taken refuge in a distant and wooded ravine, were being quickly routed by the resistless invasion of light.

I remained a considerable time looking at objects now familiar and dear to me from very pleasant associations. Would I ever look on them again? What influence would this strange adventure of mine have on my future? I had unintentionally invaded this loved home of Dr. Blentwood and his daughter, and we had come into each other's lives, and who, save One, could foretell the result? With one more look at the big elm on the river bank and the rustic seat encircling it, which seemed to have a peculiar fascination for me, now that the best girl in the world had sat there, and looked at me so kindly, and told me I might call her Ethel, and, with a good-bye to my beautiful room, I took my satchel and went down to the parlor.

Dr. Blentwood, coming in at that moment extended his hand, bidding me a cordial good-morning, and was soon followed by Ethel, whose soft, white hand, I could not help holding a little longer than mere politeness required.

" I hope you rested well, Professor Bloomfield, the last night before your departure," said Ethel, looking at me with her usual bright smile, though with a little touch of sadness, as she spoke the last word.

" Ah! yes," broke in the father, " this is the morning in which you are determined to tear yourself from us."

" That is just the word to express my feelings, doctor," I replied. " It will tear me pretty hard to leave this beautiful home, where I have been so kindly treated and been made to feel so much at home.'

" I assure you,' responded the doctor, placing a hand on my shoulder in a friendly way, " the tearing is not all on your side. Your coming has brought only brightness and cheer, and we feel indebted to you for getting ill at the right time."

Dr. Blentwood spoke so warmly and with such

evident sincerity beneath his smile, and Ethel
looked at me with so much sympathetic approval
of what her father had said, I was glad to have
breakfast announced, as it gave me time to
recover my self-control before I should need to
speak again.

We had an extra-fine and royally good breakfast, which I attributed in part to Tom and Tot,
who, I was sure, felt a special interest in me, perhaps because they had borne me home in their
arms on the night of my insensible arrival; for I
have noticed this, that to do a person a kindness
is a long step towards loving him, while to do
one an injury is a still longer stride towards
hating him.

The table-manners, in recognition of God's
bounty, I had been pleased to notice, never
degenerated, at Dr. Blentwood's, into a formal-
ity; but always varied with each meal in harmony with the occasion; and so there was no
stiffness after it, requiring a joke to put the
guests at their ease by implying that the service, though necessary, didn't mean anything.
The doctor and Ethel seemed always to enjoy
this service, whether it was the giving of thanks,
silent or verbal, the recital of Scripture passages,
or loving comment on some phase of Providence.
Whatever form the service took, it was so natural
and so delightful, that it was a preparation for
good digestion, and, therefore, being in harmony
with a law of the body, must have been in harmony with its Maker.

This morning the doctor asked me if I had any particular Scripture on my mind, and I repeated the passage most comforting to me at that time, which was, " All things work together for good to them that love God."

" That passage," said the doctor, " is as full of blessed encouragement as this beautiful June morning is of sunshine, and ought to keep every Christian beaming with smiles and ready to take up every apparent burden with gladness of heart. We are too often ungrateful and sad when we cannot see the good, whereas we should always know that the good is somewhere, though we may not at the moment find it. For instance, it is easy to see the working for good of your coming among us; for we have made a valued acquaintance and have been permitted to be of some service to you, and therefore, are thankful and glad, but it is not so easy to see the good of your going, and, therefore, a shade of sadness gathers over us; and yet, while we cannot escape the shadow, we may rejoice at the light streaming down to us from the text you quoted, that all things, without exception, work together for a beneficent end, if accepted in love. Could we look far enough, we might see opportunities for personal help to one or more of us depending on this very departure. God moves in mysterious ways His wonders to perform."

Should I look back on these words as true prophecy?

We ate our last morning meal together with

10

considerable cheerfulness, which good Dr. Blentwood held to be a Christian duty as well as privilege. He had not much faith in the giving of
thanks at table and then proving by our sadness
that we are not grateful.

" We need never to be utterly cast down," he
said, " if we always remember not *some* things
shall work together for good, but *all* things, and
that means everything."

" You would not then," I asked, " regard the
providential dealings of God with the Israelites
and with individuals in the Bible as exceptional?"

" The Bible," he answered, " gives us a little
history to show us that God is in all history. It
gives us a touch of biography here and there to
show us that God is in all biography, and is ready
to direct and control every one's life. Tom and
Tot, as well as we three, are each moving under
a divine archway of love, which watches and
anticipates every want."

" Sometimes we have to wait long," Ethel
asserted, " before we can see that love, especially
when clothed in disappointments and afflictions."

" Waiting," I responded, " is the hardest trial
of faith. Washington waiting at Valley Forge
required a truer courage than when facing the
enemy in active battle. There is a kindling of
enthusiasm, a feeling of heroism, a consciousness
of doing something, in an advance, even upon the
enemy's guns, which buoys up and bears one on
in hope of victory."

" Therein lies the advantage of youth and health

over old age and weakness," said Dr. Blentwood
with a smile of resignation ; "for the former can
act, when the latter may only wait."

"And yet what a blessing," I interposed, "that
when there is no more active service for us in this
world, hope is not cut off, but still beckons joyfully to a future of immortal activity, as bright
as anything that fills the mind of youth!"

"Yes, and how gloriously the ripening spirit,
in the midst of approaching disease and old age,
may reflect, for the benefit of others, like the setting sun upon the clouds, the rosiest and most
resplendent hues!" said Ethel, as she looked
lovingly towards her father.

This delicate tribute of daughter to parent I
felt to be as sweet as it was poetic and as beautiful as it was real.

When the meal was over, the servants were
called in, and we had singing. I read the Scrip-
tures, and the doctor's prayer was so appropriate
and touching, remembering me in it so fully and
tenderly, I was much moved, and when he closed,
we all, even to Tom and Tot, murmured a responsive Amen in unison.

We were entering the hall from the dining-
room, when, through the open outer door river-
ward, Charley Lightheart appeared, swinging his
hat at us, and singing out, "All aboard for downstream ; land lubbers will go ashore."

"Are you ready so soon?" Ethel asked, as he
came up.

"Completely equipped," he replied, with a

military salute, " and awaiting the captain's orders.
All my plunder is down there in the boat, surrounded by fish standing up perpendicular in the
water, and looking with strained eyes at the good
victuals, which they smell! It is only a proof
what tempting morsels my Dolly can cook."

" Who is Dolly, you naughty boy?" asked
Ethel, more than suspecting that he referred ironically to his sister-in-law.

Putting his hand on his heart and groaning, he
replied, " It is too early in my career to tell you
who Dolly is."

Tom had got my boat down below the rapids
the night before, and we were to embark nearly
opposite the house. I took my hat, and was
extending my hand to say good-bye, when the
doctor said, " We will accompany you to the
boat." I went to the kitchen to say farewell to
Tot, who, as I shook her hand, exclaimed, " Is
you 'deed guine, sah? God bress you bery much,
all de time. You mus' come back; for de good
doctor and dear Miss Ethel will want to see ye, I
knows for sure. We filled de box 'fore ye was
up, and Tom, who made de box, is done gone wid
it to de boat. Miss Ethel were mighty tickler
what went into de box for ye, sah. She dotes on
ye, I rekon, and ye oughter come back and seen
her and the res' of us, as we all sets heaps on ye
too. De Lord be wid ye, honey, and hab marcy
on you soul and body. Dat's Tot's prayer, and
de prayer is white, if poor ole Tot's face be brack.
It's de innards God looks at, I reckon."

Though amused at her expressions, I assured her of the truth, that I had as much confidence in her prayers as if she was white, and the finest lady in the land, and with this assurance, after putting a piece of money in her hand, I left the kind, simple-hearted, old woman, and rejoined the party, who were waiting for me on the lawn.

There was no chance to talk with Ethel alone, but I managed to walk between her and her father, and took the liberty I fear, scarcely knowing what I did in this parting hour, of taking her arm as well as his and holding both till we reached the shore. Every step was a step towards separation, perhaps forever, and this thought revealed to me that I was loving this girl tenfold more than I had hitherto been conscious.

I had always intended to be wise, and not allow myself to love where there was no hope; but here I was without a particle of heart left in me, and no assurance of Ethel's in return. I had been imprudent, but what could I do about it now? I did not know. I was greatly perplexed what to do. It was not clear that I could do anything. I felt keenly that I was on the borders of Paradise, the Paradise of all my hopes of earthly happiness, and might never be so near again, and if I took her arm in the fear of losing her, what wonder? How could I help it, I should like to know? What need was there of trying? I don't believe I did try. Trying would not make the Connecticut River flow up stream!

CHAPTER XVII.

CHARLEY LIGHTHEART TAKES THE HELM.

BUT, as before intimated, I do not know what I did. I only know that, when I left her side, and jumped into the boat, I felt as if I had fallen down out of heaven, and the door was closed against me, perhaps forever. I was so agitated, so dazed, I do not recall what I said to any of them, as I shook hands, and bade them good-bye That I was a fool for falling so hopelessly in love was clear ; but, having lost my wits, I might as well remain a fool, I thought, and would anyway, persuading myself that the pain of being a fool of that kind was sweeter than the rewards of being wise.

Though I cannot recall words, I remember the strange thrill which ran through me as I took Ethel's pretty white hand, and pressed it, I don't know how hard, and looked into her tender, liquid eyes, so deep and yet so full of light ineffable ; and I remember also how they all looked as we left them—Tom with his cap under his arm sitting on the empty wheelbarrow, on which he had trundled my things, looking a little disconsolate, and Dr. Blentwood and his beloved daughter standing erect and waving their handkerchiefs in affectionate farewell. Never shall I forget the beautiful picture they presented, especially Ethel, with her wind-tossed ringlets, fair face, and superb form clothed in a white morning dress symbolic of the purity of her spirit.

When we passed the point of land where Ethel and I had sat under the wide-spreading elm, and while I was waving back my adieus, and watching Ethel with longing eyes, Charley purposely hugged the shore, shutting her and her father off from view. I begged him to point the bow out towards the centre of the river, that I might see them once more, "just once more"; but he was inexorable.

"You must save your eyes, friend Bloomfield," said he, "they are sore now from over-straining."

"Oh, bother my eyes, if I cannot see them again!" I exclaimed.

"Remember, my dear brother," he replied with mock gravity, "you have need of eyes going down the river; indeed, everywhere eyes are an important adjunct to the genus homo. As the son and brother of a physician, I really cannot allow you to strain them by looking again, at long range against the wind, at the Blentwoods. Indeed, I must be firm, as a wise custodian, where the health of your eyes is concerned."

"Have it your own way," I said, half petulantly and yet with a lugubrious smile at his drollery, as I lay down in the bow of the boat, and gave myself up to reflection. What if I should never see Ethel again? I queried, or see her only too late

after her engagement or marriage to another?
Too late!—what an awful thought! And then
Stockmire came into my mind. What if this
hypocrite should gain the hand of that angel!

"Lightheart," I exclaimed, rousing up—

"Call me Charley," he interrupted. "When in
company you may address me by the more digni-
fied title; but here, between you and me, I prefer
the great condescension of allowing you to call
me Charley. The feeling of humility, which this
permission begets, does me good, and I enjoy it.
Call me simply Charley; that and nothing more."

"Well," I resumed, "simple Charley——"

"Omit the adjective," he interrupted again,
bowing low and removing his cap. "It ill
becomes me to listen to flattery, after I have
decided to humble myself."

"Charley," I resumed once more, "do people
believe in Stockmire?"

"He is held to be an honest, respectable, indus-
trious, and successful business man," he replied.

"But is he sincere, conscientious, and always
what he pretends to be?"

"He is so accepted generally, I think."

"Do the Blentwoods think highly of him?"

"I have no reason to suspect otherwise."

"Is he after Ethel—in love with her?"

"I should not wonder; everybody is, unless you
are an exception."

This did not comfort me much, and I exclaimed,
"Depend upon it, Stockmire is a wolf in sheep's
clothing."

"Ah!" said he with a wise look, "you may flatter Stockmire as much as you please. But didn't you notice how very honest he talks? That drawl of his proclaims him genuine to most of folks without any further recommendation.

"I know it, and therein lies his dangerous power ; but I could not trust him. I have a feeling, I can't tell why, that he works his way underhandedly, and will carry a point apologeti cally, under cover of humility and the pretended pressure of other people's opinions, which he is not above forging to suit his purpose."

"Well, well! for an extemporaneous judgment, you hew pretty close to the line, methinks," murmured Charley half to himself.

"Watch him, study him, and if my judgment proves true, warn Ethel in time."

"Yes, yes ; but why are you so desperately in earnest and solemn about it?"

"Because that girl is innocent-hearted, unsus- pecting, and worthy of the best man that ever lived, and it would be monstrous, murderous, an awful criminal blunder in her friends, to permit her to go unwarned into the sacred bands of wedlock with a heartless man capable of developing into— I dare not say what."

After a pause Charley raised his eyes to me and said abruptly, "Elbert Bloomfield——"

I stopped him with, "Simply Elbert, if you please; just that and nothing more."

He waved his hand in deprecation, and went on, "Elbert, my son, you are in love."

"In love," I exclaimed; "do you know anything about love? Were you ever in love,
Charley?"

He dropped the paddle with which he was toying,
stood up as straight as an arrow, and, with head
erect, smote on his breast, and said, looking down
on me with well-feigned superiority, "I am a free
man, free in body, free in mind, free in heart."

"You ought to pose for some comic almanac,"
said I, laughing for the first time.

He went on unheeding. "Young man, I am sorry
for you. Falling in love, as has been well said,
implies that love is beneath one. The girls, I
admit, are winsome—very pretty to look at, but
my dear fellow, beware! Love is a snare; at last it
biteth like a serpent, and stingeth like an adder!"

He then went off into an eloquent peroration,
exhorting me to flee from love as from a pestilence.
Seeing that he was about to resume his seat, and
wishing to be entertained further, I asked, "What
makes you think I am in love?"

Turning away his head he thrust back his hands
with a repellent gesture, very dramatically, as
much as to say, some things are too obvious to be
discussed.

"Well," I said, "if you will have it so, it can
only elevate and ennoble a man to love a person
like Ethel Blentwood."

"Ah!" he replied with a pitying look, "I
perceive that the chains of love's sophistry are
already about your neck. That you esteem Ethel
very highly is an honor to you, but I conjure you,

as you value your massive brain, to love no
woman; for it will make a fool of you. Fasten
your affections on me."

" No, Charley, I claim my right to be a fool."

" No man, Elbert, has a right to *make* a fool of
himself."

" What reasons have you for that, Charley?"

" Well, my boy, as I must make a Dombey
effort to save you, I will give them. In the first
place, there are born fools enough without the
making of any out of sensible people; and,
secondly, a man should make the most of himself, and—and to be a fool is not the best thing
one can become."

" How do you know that?"

" Oh, Elbert! thou art already hopelessly en-
tangled in the subtile meshes of metaphysics,
poor love-lost boy!"

" No, Charley, the question has been seriously
raised by German philosophers, who, in their
despair of explaining the problems of life, have
recently declared it preferable to be a flat-headed
Indian and a fool than to be wise. A fool has no
such anxiety, and has no need to commit suicide,
as some wise ones have done, to escape the misery
of thinking on the awful and inexplicable mys-
teries of life."

I saw I had puzzled him, and it amused me to
see him rack his brain, and run his fingers through
his hair, as if to open spaces for ideas to enter,
looking wise all the while, and pretending he was
only halting to show his contempt for such

reasoning. At last he ventured the following :

" Every blessing has its penalty attached to it, and the penalty of having nerves is pain, but would you become an oyster for the sake of freedom from pain ? "

" Your implied argument, Charley, does not quite meet the case. The question is not who would or who wouldn't, but which is the happier state, that of the wise man who thinks and suffers, or that of the fool who has no care. The only escape from this philosophy of despair for a worldly wise man is, I think, to become a Christian. Jesus of Nazareth casts a light upon earth's path, and the light and love revealed by Him can alone give rest to the overburdened brain, and make thinking a painless pleasure. Education out of Christ may bring misery and despair, as the mere worldling has experienced ; but in Christ the more one knows the nobler and deeper his joys."

Charley dropped his head, the fun all gone out of his face, for he was not a professed Christian ; but rallying, that he might not appear too serious, he took up his assumed dignity again and said, " My brother, I am glad to find your mind has not all gone down into the jelly-pot of love. You have answered well. I could not have done better myself. There is great hope of you yet. I am more encouraged than ever to do my best to rescue you from the morass of love into which you have fallen, and where the more you struggle alone, the deeper you will sink into the mire."

" Stockmire ? " I asked.

" Ah ! " he said, " the clutches of Stockmire are no comparison to——"

He never finished that sentence.

CHAPTER XVIII.

CHARLEY was standing with both feet close to the side of the boat, and so had no room to enlarge his base of support in that direction, and, the sail striking him in the midst of his sentence, his efforts to regain the perpendicular only made matters worse, and over he went into the water, and shut the door behind him. When he saw he must go, however, the ludicrousness of his situation struck him, and he said, as he went down, "Will see you later." I watched him, and when he came up I could just reach him astern, and, hauling him to me, I assisted him into the boat.

"As I was saying," he went on as soon as he got seated, and as if nothing had happened, the water still running down his face, and his hair and clothes clinging to him like the fur to a drowned rat, "as I was saying, when my attention was called to the river bottom——"

"Oh, don't!" I interrupted, laughing so heartily that I could scarcely speak. "I am more interested now in another question."

He looked at me with quiet dignity, more pleased to see me laugh, I know, than anything I

158

could do, and with his imperturbable good-nature
beaming in every feature, he said bowing, " I am
bound to respect your curiosity, my boy. Please
state your question, as I shall only be too gratified to impart to you any desired information."

" Well," said I, between gasps for breath and
repeated outbursts of unmanageable laughter,
" what in the world were you diving after beneath
the surface of the river? Tell me that, will you?"

" Don't you know?" said he, with well-assumed
and grave surprise. " I thought my conduct perfectly clear. But I forget that you are not a
paleontologist, nor an antiquarian of any sort.
To answer your question, then, categorically,
Elbert, I was diving after the buried treasures of
experience. I have learned not to let opportunities to gain information slip by me unused. In
fact, I watch for them, and seeing one of these I
went for it, suddenly, it is true, for it was then
or never. It may have seemed impolite to leave
you in the middle of a sentence; but the sentence
could wait, while a lost opportunity is lost forever.
Are you satisfied? Is the wisdom of my conduct
clear to you now?"

" Clear as daylight," I shouted, as soon as I
could command my vocal organs; "and now, for
the future welfare of the paleontologist, I suggest
that we seize upon the opportunity of going
ashore in that sheltered nook or bay, just ahead
of us, where you can change your clothes, and
have them drying in the sun, while we eat dinner."

" A capital idea, Elbert, I think your mind

gives evidence of being fully restored now to its former state of health."

We landed, and after drawing our boat well up on the beach and looking about, we were both agreed that a better place for our purpose could not have been found. Charley rapidly disrobed, wrung out his clothes and hung them on poles stuck in the sand, and with plenty of underclothing in his satchel he was soon dressed in dry, white linen. The weather was warm, and he was more comfortable without than with his outer garments, and as he stood in bright slippers combing his hair by the aid of a pocket mirror, I could not but admire his neat and comfortable appearance.

He was a fine-looking fellow, well built, of a rather florid complexion, dark auburn hair, that made me think of Ethel's; full, blue-gray eyes, that twinkled and snapped, and told beforehand almost what he was going to say, and a face broad at top, and narrowing down to a rather small chin.

"White becomes you, Charley," I said.

"That is what my mother used to say," he replied, putting his mobile features into one of those fun-provoking expressions, which he seemed to possess in almost infinite variety, "and it reminds me to say to you as the result of my ample experience, the treasures of which you have seen me ready to dive after, even at the risk of being impolite, that it is the duty of every man to look attractive in his night clothes."

" Ancient and sapient sir, how long have you lived, pray ? "

" Thousands of years longer than the centenarian, who counts his age by clock-time ; for I have travelled faithfully over the varied fields of imagination and research till my tread has become heavy under the staggering weight of accumulated knowledge ! "

" That is as much as I can stand," I said, " until after dinner, and I adjourn the meeting."

We found a very pleasant dining-spot, grassy, and provided with a log for a seat, and shaded by an oak, near the edge of the bluff forming a part of the little bay in which our small craft was sheltered, and reached therefrom by a gradual ascent. Here we tugged our boxes containing our food. I confess I had some curiosity to see what Ethel and Tot had provided for me. Anything, I thought, which Ethel had cooked, or ordered, or smiled upon, even a crust from her hands, I could eat with a relish.

Tom had made a very convenient box, with pockets, shelves and all needed partitions to prevent the food from being jammed or mixed, doubtless under the superintendence of Ethel ; and, as I lifted the cover, and looked in, and took out dish after dish, and saw how much thought had been expended for my comfort, I exclaimed, unaware I was thinking aloud, " The dear girl ! "

Charley either did not hear, or pretended not to, being busy with his own " cupboard," as he called it, and, much relieved, I could let my

11

thoughts flow back to Ethel once more as I examined my bill of fare. There were pies, cakes, tarts, turnovers, hard-boiled eggs, pickles, pepper, salt, sandwiches, chicken-pie, strawberry shortcake, and a tin box labeled, " Pour this over the short-cake." There were other delicacies and creature comforts, but I could not examine further just then, and, turning to Charley, I asked with enthusiasm, " Do you know what is the prime, essential quality of an angel ? "

" Of course I do," Charley quickly answered ; " it lies in the wings."

" Hens have wings, child, and hens are not angels," I remonstrated. " We associate wings with angels merely to symbolize their swiftness."

" True," he responded with diplomatic shrewdness, " but what is swifter than love ? Love and wings are synonymous, almost identical ; for love is so full of wings within and without, that you cannot cut away the smallest portion without clipping its wings also. A wingless love is a misnomer in man or angel. What is it that wings the early bird with a worm in its mouth to its patient mate or young ? Is it not love ? What is it that has just now winged the soul of Elbert Bloomfield back to Graynoble with the swiftness of lightning, and made his face all aglow with the vision of Ethel Blentwood ? Could the vision have been possible without wings of love ? "

" Who now," I asked with some embarrassment, " is floundering in the sophistries of metaphysics ? "

"Ah!" said he with mouth agape, as if astounded at my question; and then relaxing and blinking, quietly asked, "Please give us your definition of the highest angelic quality."

"Well, Charley, I think it is that kind of love known as thoughtfulness for the welfare of others."

Promptly straightening himself, he asseverated, "I accept your terminology with great joy. It shows you quite out of the bog and quicksands and standing on solid granite. Thoughtfulness for others, I freely admit, will make a present heaven anywhere, everywhere." And he took off his hat in profound respect to his own remark.

"Charley," said I, "you must dine with me to day. This short-cake will never be so good again as now, and here is enough for us both."

He looked longingly at the tempting dish and replied, "Out of pure regard to you, my dear friend, and for the sake of the economics of life, I accept your pressing invitation."

We sat down on the grass resting our backs against the log we had proposed for a seat, and, with a wooden plate in each lap containing half of my strawberry short-cake covered with delicious cream, ate, with ancient fork and tin-spoon and with many blessings on Ethel and Tot, a very hearty meal. For drink we had a bottle of cold coffee diluted to our taste by " oirnon catholicon " or the universal wine, which bubbled up pure and fresh from a spring in the bay below.

" Charley," said I holding up a mica cup of this sparkling water, " thousands upon thousands not only waste their twenty years, like Rip Van Winkle, but desolate their whole lives and the lives of others, because they reject this wine of Nature for the fire-water of Satan."

" Truth, every word truth," responded Charley, holding up another cup of the same cool, clear beverage; "you do speak forth the words of truth and soberness, and, therefore, in the language of poor deluded Winkle, may you live long and prosper." He drank the last drop in his cup, and set it down with a complaisant nod, adding, as he did so, " Thus endeth our first dinner together after leaving the classic shades of Graynoble."

CHAPTER XIX.

AFTER-DINNER EXERCISE

"WHAT say for a walk, Charley?"

"My lord, thou speakest mine own thoughts," he replied. "A gentle stroll will be a friendly act towards the short-cake I am outside of, and may prevent the employees in the great laboratory of my stomach from striking ere their work of mysterious chemistry be complete."

"Were not our Creator a benevolent being," I said, "this process, which we think so little about, might be very painful instead of the pleasant thing it is."

"That's so," said Charley, stopping a moment as if struck with a new idea; "I never thought of that before. Good! How He could rack and torture us with every mouthful digested, if so minded!"

"And what conclusion do you draw from this, Charley?"

"This clearly, that a malevolent Creator would put an end to all pleasure in eating strawberry short-cake though direct from the hands of so lovely a creature as Ethel Blentwood. Factum

165

factorum! what would become of all the fine
suppers and the sociability of the world, if guests
at table knew, that for every pleasurable sensation
in the palate, they must pay tenfold in pains of
the stomach? Glad 'tisn't so, chum."

"Towards whom are you glad, Charley?"

"My dear Elbert, I am glad first for myself; and
then my gratitude goes on to the inventors of
agricultural tools; to the farmer who ploughs and
sows and reaps and thrashes and winnows; to the
miller who grinds; to the inventor of yeast cake,
though I would rather bread be raised without it;
to the purveyors of condiments; and especially
to the good cook, black, white or yellow. I should
not omit to add, however, that I eat with a keener
relish when a pretty girl, like Ethel, prepares the
viands. If you ever get married, my boy, stip-
ulate that your wife do the cooking. How
much happier the world would be, if wives took
as much pride in cooking as in piano-playing,
or painting or any other accomplishment! Why
don't they? Ah! my dear Elbert, therein lies
the weakness of the female mind."

"Why do you leave out, in your gratitude, the
very Being whom you have virtually admitted to
be the source of all the pleasure of eating?" I
asked, determined not to be led from my main
point.

"If I am grateful," he replied soberly, "to the
creatures who serve me, am I not thereby grateful
to the Creator?"

"Not necessarily, although you cannot be truly

thankful to the Creator with no gratitude to the creature. If a man love not his brother whom he has seen, how can he love God whom he has not seen? The greater includes the less, but the converse of this may not be true."

"But why need I declare gratitude to Deity?"

"For your own good, and the fitness of things."

"How for my good?"

"Gratitude unexpressed soon dies."

"But I do express it towards men."

"And that keeps it alive towards men."

"Is not that practically enough?"

"No, not enough. The man, who fails to put himself into direct communication with God Himself, suffers a great loss."

"How?"

"To refuse is in itself hardening to all the better feelings; besides, not being linked to Him by personal sympathy, there is a lack of inward inspiration and the helpful influence of God's Spirit."

"Does not that Spirit shine upon all?"

"Certainly, and so does the sun shine upon that ledge yonder as well as on this green turf we are treading, and what a difference! The ledge gives back no visible token, while the responsive turf throws up towards heaven a beautiful vegetation, as if in grateful acknowledgment of blessings received."

Charley Lightheart was silent for some moments and seriously thinking.

"Elbert," he asked slowly, "are not the ledges

doing all they are capable of doing in return for the sun's rays?"

" I suppose so," I answered, anticipating his point; " but are you doing all you can to prove your appreciation of the Divine Benevolence, whose rays have been falling on you every moment of your life?"

A long silence followed, which I would not break, knowing it to be well employed. At length he stopped me, and, putting a hand on each of my shoulders, and looking me directly in the eye, said, " You are the most sensible on religious subjects of any one I ever met. Now, I ask in all candor, do you really believe any change can take place in me, through faith in God, corresponding in the slightest degree to the difference between that ledge towards which we are travelling, and the springing vegetation beneath our feet?"

" We must remember Charley, that all physical illustrations are imperfect, and are used as aids to the imagination and not as literal correspondence. You may be very near the kingdom (and I wish you would step into it at once), and may only need to recognize God's personal love to bring your whole heart into joyful union with Him. The change in you would be chiefly within; for outwardly you are already moral, thoughtful for others, and upright in all your dealings, pretty good evidence, one might say, that you are a Christian already in spirit without knowing it. An acknowledged conscious love for God would give you a deeper peace, increased joy, sweeter views of life, and a nobler charity; but to the on-looker you could not have a marked change, like the conversion of the outwardly wicked."

"But, Bloomfield, do you think church members are really any better than the so-called world's people?"

"On the whole, yes; although there are many and grave exceptions."

"Don't the exceptions spoil the rule?"

"No, the counterfeit coin proves the genuine. People do not counterfeit that which is worthless. Besides, are not all the best people you know either in the church or respectful attendants on its service?"

"Yes, that I think is so; but there are so many church members, who exhibit anything save a Christian spirit, to say nothing of square dealing!"

"Too true, Charley, but it is not the fault of Christianity. Some people have a great deal of piety, but not a particle of religion! They talk gushingly, or are great sticklers for forms and ceremonies and the avoidance of amusements, but their conduct shows their piety to have no moral fibre, and that Christianity never got any intelligent hold on them."

"I have seen so many of that class, whose talk has been the merest cant, or the most drivelling nonsense, when not the most outrageous blasphemy, that I have been disgusted and repelled from the very thought of publicly professing Chris-

tianity. To profess more than what is possessed
is a crime against decency and humanity, and for
one I prefer not to profess, but in secret to possess,
and to walk honestly and manfully before God and
man. To live truly is my desire, but to put on
the forms of piety, save in my own closet, is, in
view of what I see around me, repugnant to all
my notions of real manliness."

He spoke warmly.

" What, to be more specific, have you observed,
Charley ? " I asked, wishing to get at his difficulty.

" I have observed churches exhibiting as much
selfishness as any worldlings. I have seen members full of religion on Sundays and in prayer-
meetings, but never carrying any of it into their
business. I know of women who talk pious
twang, profess the severest creed, bow their
heads on entering church, sorrow over their unconverted husbands, and yet, by their very peevish, snappish, fretful, uncontrolled temper, drive
those same husbands from their homes, and then
complain because they are not more at home.
You must have noted that my pious sister-in-law
would make a hell where her husband would make
a heaven, and does not God know the honest good
heart of my brother as surely as he knows the
mere technical religion of his wife ? "

" Anything else, Charley ? "

" Yes, I heard a native Missouri preacher, who
had been a " bushwhacker " in the civil war, killing
our boys individually in irregular, murderous warfare, say from the pulpit, that failing to join a

church was a sin big enough to damn a world, and yet, the audience swallowed him metaphorically, and let the drivelling rascal preach on!

"Near literary Boston I heard an intelligent-looking man say in prayer-meeting, that to go to a theatre was sin enough to send a man to hell forever, and yet that pious twaddle went unrebuked, when some, at least, who heard him, knew that in business he cheated and lied shamefully. Only think of his knocking at heaven's gate, and offering as his only qualification for admittance, that he never went to a theatre! When I see men vaporing against mere technical sins of their own construction, I always suspect that they are trying to erect a platform on which they can stand."

"Have you finished?"

"No, one thing more burns in my heart, and I must open the safety-valve and let it out. I know a preacher who, for fifteen years has, like his Master, been going about doing good, visiting and praying with the sick and the sorrowing, preaching to the poor and the imprisoned, feeding the hungry, and clothing the naked! More than a hundred otherwise unprotected children, whom he has adopted and cared for, are growing up to call him blessed. And yet, this devoted, godly man, solely because he is a Universalist, and believes that all will finally repent and be made fit to be saved, was refused admittance at a funeral into a so-called evangelical pulpit, though requested to officiate with the pastor! Where is the evangel in such conduct as that? Where is the sweet gospel principle, which would lead a man to stalk so ruthlessly into the presence of death, and wound afresh hearts already lacerated and bleeding under the heavy loss of a near and dear one gone?"

"Was it a matter of conscience with the pastor?" I asked almost in a whisper.

"He so claims; but that is the kind of conscience, which, in the early Romish church, blessed the knife that was to drink the blood of a Protestant. I freely accord liberty of opinion to a narrow mind as well as to a broad one, when that liberty is not accompanied with a blow. Had it been on any other occasion, I would not mention it here as an objection to a Christian profession, but when in the presence of death, where all ranks are levelled and all distinctions are done away, where the war drums cease to throb and the battle flags are furled, what shall we say of a conscience which leads a man to clang his iron-bound creed, as a Goliath might his heavy armor, displaying its sharp points over the dead body of one of his own church members, a wife and mother in Israel, in utter disregard of her dying wish, and, too, when everybody else is weeping tears of sympathetic sorrow! When a creed takes the heart out of a man, like that, it savors more of the satanic than of the Godlike. Think of the awful sacredness of a dying request! Professor Bloomfield, could you, would you have refused that request?"

He trembled with emotion, and almost equally moved I answered, " Oh! Charley, you know I would burn at the stake rather than do such a thing. But we must soften our judgment of this pastor with the thought that men's minds and consciences often play strange tricks with them. He doubtless reasoned that to admit a Universalist into his pulpit, even at a funeral and for the sake of a dying request, would be wickedly countenancing a grave error; and, perhaps, he took credit to himself for suppressing his sympathies in accordance with his own ideas of loyalty to the dead and living ! "

"On that ground you may lessen the guilt of the Spanish Inquisition."

" Perhaps so, Charley, for its supporters reasoned, or pretended to reason, that it was better to kill a heretic than to let him ruin himself and others too ! "

"That only proves a conscientious devil the worst kind of a devil, and, also, that a human heart may be, as the Bible says, deceitful and desperately wicked. The pastor referred to, it seems to me, and the Spanish Inquisitors reasoned in the same way, both moved by denominational selfishness, assuming that no one but themselves had a conscience, and both willing to inflict suffering, physical or mental, not on themselves, indeed, but upon others, to maintain the supremacy of their creed and of themselves. I tell you, Elbert, the modern Pharisee, had he the power of the State behind him, could no more be trusted

with our liberties than the ancient Pharisee, or
the slayer of the Huguenots."

"Well, Charley, admitting all you would imply
against these men, would you present them as
representatives of real Christianity?"

"They are allowed to represent it."

"Too much so, I admit, but the Author of
Christianity does not allow them to represent it;
for He calls them hypocrites, who strain at a gnat
and swallow a camel. His severest denunciations
were against church members of their class, who
were so puffed up with spiritual pride that they
could not learn anything outside of their own circle
of ideas; and hence it was that publicans and
harlots, who were more teachable, would go into
the kingdom of heaven before them. It is the
heart, the spirit, or the love, which is of prime
importance according to Jesus. Paul tells us that
love is the greatest of Christian virtues. That
man is to be pitied, therefore, whose sympathies,
whose humanity, and whose higher and holier
instincts are swallowed up by the faulty logic of
an inhuman, self-glorifying creed, or, if you will,
by a faulty deduction from a faultless belief; for
a man may have an infinite creed and, at the
same time an infinitesimal heart! But, Charley,
there are large-hearted, straightforward, thorough-
going, high-toned Christians, and I very much
wish to see their number augmented by your
public enrollment among them. They need you,
and true Christianity needs you."

CHAPTER XX.

A NARROW ESCAPE.

WE had now reached the elevated ledge, which was our objective aim, and ceased our conversation to look about us and enjoy the view. Below us a sun-lit valley stretched away to the north, and, winding through it, lay the smooth waters of the Connecticut, apparently as motionless as if fast asleep and unruffled by a dream. On either side were beautiful intervals and cultivated fields, from which rose hills of more or less grandeur, some with wooded summits, and all prophetic of warmth and food for man and beast. Over our heads the branch of an elm, rooted in the soil far below us, spread itself out like an umbrella to shield us from the hot sun. In it hung, half-concealed, a long oriole's nest, swaying in the gentle breeze, and revealed to us by the appearance of the male bird of bright plumage, the most beautiful our country affords, impelled by a God-given instinct, carrying in his beak a worm with which to feed his housewifely mate.

I was dilating on the footsteps of God and man, brought out in such pleasing contrast in the panorama before us, when Charley stepped for-

ward towards the edge of the bluff to get another
view, but delayed midway to pluck a tiny flower
growing in a crevice of the rock, and during that
momentary delay, and just as he was about to
step over the fissure, the great rock there parted
beneath his very feet, leaving one foot projecting
over the dizzy height, and fell with a tremendous,
reverberating crash, imbedding half its size in the
earth below, the upper half breaking off and rolling and bounding with a fearful velocity down a
steep ravine towards the river, carrying everything before it.   Charley wavered on the brink of
the fearful precipice from vertigo or the draft
of air set in motion by the rock-slide ; but as I
sprang to grasp him, he rallied to a safe footing,
and we looked at each other in silence, and took
a long breath of relief.

"What a narrow escape!" I exclaimed, trembling with mingled excitement and thanksgiving
for his safety.

"A pretty close call!" said Charley, trying to
smile.   "Had I not stopped to pluck that flower,
I should have been on the wrong side of that
fissure, and gone down with the falling rock to
my death."

"God has saved you," I said warmly, grasping
one of his arms in both of my hands, as if to
make sure of him.   "Give Him the praise."

"Was it not the flower, and my love for it,
that kept me from taking the fatal step?" he
asked.

"Yes," I answered, "they were the tangible

instruments; but God caused that flower to grow, and gave you the impulse to enjoy it."

" Do you mean to say God worked a miracle to save my life ? "

" Certainly not ; but is it too much for you to believe that an infinite Being of unlimited knowledge must have seen you on this rock when He created this world, and, therefore, must have taken your perilous condition into account ? The laws of disintegration and gravitation, which carried away that rock, are laws of God, and so also are the laws of germination and growth which produced that flower. No law has been violated, and yet you have been saved by Divine Providence as surely as if God had stretched out a visible hand to draw you back from that brink of death."

" If God at creation arranged to save me from violent death to-day, it seems an ice-cold, long time ago that he took an interest in me! Does He care for me now ? That is what I want to know."

" Remember, Charley, that I said, 'took you into account,' which, of course, must be true, else the Creator was not omniscient when arranging and unfolding his plans ; and bear in mind, too, that God *is* in all his works—not *was* in them at creation merely. He is the same yesterday, to-day, and forever, and the past and future are not separated in His mind, as in ours. We think one thought, and then drop it before we can think another; but with God all times and all thoughts

12

are ever and always present. All things with
Him are as one eternal now. This faulty expression is, perhaps, the best hint I can give you of
what I mean. 'And when I say, He took your
life into account at creation, I mean that He
made room for you, and made His plans large
enough to provide for every circumstance in
your life without breaking any of His own laws,
or interfering with the established order of
things."

"You mean to say, then, that He was just now
actively employed in keeping me from that one
step, which would have proved my probable
death?"

"I do. Because God acts continuously and
methodically, and so uniformly that we can count
on it, is no proof that He does not act at all, but
is, on the contrary, the very best proof of His all-
wise and all-powerful management. A finite and
unwise mind may have to change his plans to
meet every new case; but with God there are no
new cases, and no need of afterthoughts to provide for them. Jesus says, ' My Father worketh
hitherto and I work.' The world is full of His
life-giving and active presence. He is in the
Providence that hovers over the robin's nest
swinging above our heads. He is in all this
springing life of field and forest before us. He
is mirrored in the heavens above us, and in the
calm depths of the river below us. He is in
every flower, as well as the one you hold in
your hand. I think flowers, especially, must

speak to you hereafter more forcefully of God than they ever have done before."

" Yes," he answered, holding up the tiny flower, " I realize the truth of Mary Ainge De Vere's words :

> ' Sometimes a little flower will tell us more
> Of God's good wisdom than the grandest words
> That ever preacher preached or organ chords
> Thundered within the temple's sacred door!
> A flying seed wafted on busy wind,
> A bird-nest hiding where the branches lean,
> A glimpse of sunlit valley, left behind,
> With sweet homes nestled in the living green,
> Some friendly voice that greets us on the road
> In common salutation brief and kind,
> A gentle glance by stranger eyes bestowed,
> The dear face of a child with tender meaning lined,
> A lonely grave where violet buds have blown—
> These are the presents by which God is known.' "

" Where did you learn that ? " I asked.

" In the church one Sunday when the sermon was dull. I found it on a slip of paper between the leaves of a hymn-book, and I learned it to repeat to my mother the following Sunday in expiation of my purpose to take a walk into the woods instead of the meeting-house."

" Well, your time was not wasted, to say the least, whatever you may have lost in not listening to the sermon. Did you take to the woods the next Sunday because you disliked the church ? "

" In part, I suppose, but I always loved the woods and fields, and always felt better after roaming in them. They seem to have a personality all their own, and to speak to me without affectation or deceit, telling just what they think of me frankly, truthfully, and with a sweet confidence that won me in childhood, and wins me to-day and makes me feel that in them I can ever find faithful friendship."

"Your enjoyment of nature does not come from flattered self-esteem."

"On the contrary, nature never flatters me. She tells me my faults, and I go from her communion with aspirations for a purer and better life—aspirations, however, which have in them no sting, no bitter self-reproaches, only a noble discontent and a strong yearning to be something finer in quality every way than I am."

"Do you see clearly anything except stern, unrelenting law in nature?"

"Yes, sir, I do. I know theologians picture her as cold, unyielding, and merciless, and she is in some of her aspects when she shakes the heavens with lightning and the solid ground with earthquake, and we hear the crash of land-slides, and witness the destruction by wind and flood; but the verdant hills and sweet valleys, the varied flowers, the singing birds and laughing waters, and the glad sunshine have each a fellow-feeling for me, which bids me hope. While they tell me to be perfect, they say it so benevolently, so gently, and with so much tender sympathy, that there is implied in it the fact of a path leading to perfection, and that my business is to seek

and find it. In other words, I see the Creator in
nature, something more than law, even personality and mercy. It is true, that rock-slide we
so narrowly escaped, said pretty plainly, 'Get
in the way of my broken law and you shall be
crushed;' but that tiny flower growing in the
fissure mercifully said, 'Stay here and you will
not break that law; stop here and be saved.'"

"My dear brother," I ejaculated in surprise,
"I am very glad you look so deeply into nature.
You will take hold of the Great Teacher's hand
and come out right in the end, I trust."

"With your help, Elbert. I confess I have
read her to-day more clearly than before."

"What, then, is the creed of nature, so far as
you have read?"

"It lies in four lines of poetry, which I recently quoted to my sister-in-law, Mrs. Lightheart, in reply to some of her unreasoning views
of religion, and runs thus:

> 'Not enjoyment and not sorrow
>   Is our destined end or way;
> But to act that each to-morrow
>   Finds us better than to-day.'"

"A very good creed; but how can you live it?
—that is the question. I grant you that God in
nature beckons you to a higher life, but it is like
a man calling you to come ashore when you are
struggling in the waves. What you want is a
life-boat. To rise out of the surging tides and
from the strugglings and buffetings of sin may be

the very thing you are trying to do, and you need
something more than a beckon; you need help,
and help personal and immediate. Nature is full
of the thought and the life of God; but to know
His real love, to feel His all-embracing tenderness
and helpful, heart-beating sympathy, you must
come, I think, to Jesus Christ."

"You may be right, Elbert, but I cannot quite
see why Christ is the only way to a helpful knowledge of God. To me there is something more
than a beckon in nature. There is inspiration
and sympathy, and consequently help. Nature
is fresher and more direct from the hand of God
than even the Bible; for the latter may have
suffered in transcribing from interpolations and
changes, while the former comes to me at first-
hand—not second-hand."

"My dear Charley, that you see so much in
nature is because you read through the revelations
of Jesus Christ. Had Christ not come and interpreted God to the world, you would not see in
nature what you now see. He having come, you
were borne into His views of God, as expressed in
His life and words; and, whether you have read
the Bible or not, being in literature and in the
common speech of the people, and forming a
necessary part of your inherited ideas, you cannot look at nature except through the glass of
Christianity."

"Reasonable words, Elbert, but look! Is it
possible time has rushed so rapidly? The whole
western sky is aglow with the bright coloring

of the declining sun! It has no frown. It is one broad benignant smile divine, full of benediction, and makes one thirst for something of its beauty in his own life."

"Yes, Charley, it should lead us to pray with Moses, the beauty of the Lord our God be upon us. Christ revealed that beauty, and through Him it can descend into the human heart."

Perhaps anticipating what I was about to add, he startled me by saying, "I am full, and must digest the large amount of thought-food you have already given me before receiving any more. Mental indigestion is the bane of the world. If people digested what they heard before accepting or rejecting it, there would not be the slow progress, the waste of words, or the irritating nonsense so extensively uttered for solemn truth. Why, there are crowds of so-called Christians, who are only spiritual dyspeptics. They have never mastered, really and fully, one clean, spiritual idea, and, so never assimilating truth, never making it a part of their life, they say one thing and act another, and drive away sensible people by stripping Christianity and its Author of every semblance of reason and even common sense.

"My sister-in-law is one of these, though it would not be a graceful thing to say, were I not sure that you know it already. If I ever accept Christianity, it will not be her Christianity. She would make my brother the rankest infidel, did he not see Christianity sensibly and attractively interpreted in such lives as the Blentwoods.

" This conflict of hateful and attractive views of Christianity may serve the purpose of making me more careful and sure of my ground in my step-by-step investigation of its claims. However thoughtless I may be in other things, I shall not be thoughtless in accepting or rejecting Christianity." He extended his hand, and I took it as a pledge of his sincerity and warm friendship.

CHAPTER XXI.

A GHOSTLY RIDE.

WE returned to our landing-place in quiet, each busy with his own thoughts. I could not keep Ethel out of my mind. " Where is she?" I asked myself. " Not in the house at an hour like this. She must be in the maple grove, enjoying this beautiful sunset; or is she under that elm tree, where we sat last together? Is she thinking of me? How much I would give to know! What a dear good girl she is! How devoted to her father! It must take a more transcendent love than I can hope to inspire to win her away from such a father. Would it not be selfish in the best man living to ask her to leave a home where she is so needed and so happy? But she is worth waiting for a thousand years. " Yes," I repeated and this time aloud and with emphasis, " a thousand years!"

" What!" broke out Charley with a comical expression, " are you computing the probable duration of the earth? or some other planet? or are you trying to locate and realize the millennium?"

185

" Call it the last," I answered a little confused,
" and you will come near enough to the truth."

We were now in sight of the landing, and, pointing to something nearly white in close proximity
to our dinner-box, Charley asked, " What is that?
—a polar bear strayed from a menagerie and
robbing us of our food? If it is, I'll capture him
if it takes a thousand years," quoting my words,
and imitating my voice and gesture. And off he
ran with the speed of the wind, and soon had by
the tail an animal which proved to be a mule,
which he mounted, as it was getting up, declaring that Long-ears should give him a ride as a
penalty for coming into our kitchen unbidden.

Assuming the dignity of a lecturer on his white
rostrum, he said, " Whether the donkey, or any
of his near relations, is the crude result of
Nature's feeling after her idea of a horse or not,
the mule is certainly peculiar. I put emphasis on
peculiar! Note the sanctimonious physiognomy,
the deacon-like, lawyer-like, and mother-in-law
contour of the brain! He is a born diplomat.
You never know what his intentions are. He
suppresses his emotions, and carries his point by
concealment. His long ears indicate that he
hears everything, though you would not believe
it by the look of his eye, which says nothing."

After going on in this style of harangue for a
few moments, he raised his hat, and, bowing with
lordly dignity, concluded by saying:

" And now, friend Elbert, I must commence
my evening's ride. Grieve not at my absence,

for I shall soon return with increased knowledge
of the country to enhance our happiness in squat-
ter sovereignty, as we gather round the evening
meal." Whereupon he began bowing and tap-
ping the mule in a laugh-provoking way. The
taps became blows, and still the mule did not
stir. He now put on an irresistibly droll expression, which doubled me up in continued outbursts of laughter.

Finally controlling myself, I raised my hat in
mock dignity, and said apologetically, "I hope
your lordship will not think me rude. I was not
laughing at your departure, but rather at the prospect of not being separated from your valuable
company, even by a short exploring expedition."

At this, with an indescribable expression of distress, he raised both hands, and exclaimed, with
King Richard, "A horse! a horse! My kingdom
for a horse!"

"Since you are so earnest to depart, perhaps I
can assist you," I said, cutting a stick, and presenting it to him with uncovered head and a low
bow.

Up to this time the mule had not even winked
in recognition of our existence, but with a vigor-
ous application of the stick there began a slow
rounding up of the back, rising higher and higher
with every blow, till at last from its summit
Charley cried out, "This is not a mule ; this is a
dromedary!"

"It is simply a mule acting in his diplomatic
capacity," I said. "He has an idea in his head,

depend upon it, although it expresses itself only in his back!"

"Then diplomacy must be met by diplomacy," said Charley, applying the sharp end of his stick to the dromedary hump till it slowly descended and became the back of a mule again.

The whiteness of the mule and its rider suggested the idea of a ship, and, tying a long withe to the mule's tail, and standing off at a safe distance, I vociferated with as much pride of service as possible, "My lord admiral, the pilot is at the helm, and awaits your orders."

"Starboard and port the helm in quick succession," came back the command from Charley in nautical tone.

I obeyed orders by jerking the tail from left to right, and then from right to left, and Charley, seizing a long ear in each hand, shouted some nautical commands into one, as through a trumpet, pushing the other forward, as if to inflate it for a jib-sail, and then, drumming with all his might against the mule's sides, and gesticulating with monomaniacal enthusiasm, he almost screamed:

"In prophetic vision already methinks

"She starts ; she moves ; she seems to feel
The thrill of life along her keel."

This was too much for the mule's equanimity. He dropped all diplomacy, and revealed his mulish spirit by kicking and trying to throw his rider; and failing in this, he soon disappeared with him behind a clump of firs on a dead run, Charley

waving his hand, as he went out of sight, and
shouting back, " Au revoir !"

Though weak with laughter, I managed to run
to the point of dissolving view, and saw the run-
aways, with unslackened speed, pressing towards
a farmyard not far away, the long withe bounding
into the air with every leap of the mule, and
Charley's white robes fluttering in the wind like a
scare-crow eloped from a corn-field. When they
reached the fence, the mule stopped so suddenly,
Charley had to travel on a few paces beyond, and
lit on top of a post, I trembled, fearing he might
be hurt, but he raised his hat so politely to some
one in the yard, that I concluded, since the fun
had not been knocked out of him, he must be
unharmed.

"The holy Vargin preserve us," said a voice
near me, and an Irish woman, emerged from the
grass where she had evidently fallen in a faint ;
for her dish of berries she had been picking was
bottom side up, and she was trembling with fear.

" And did ye see the vision, meester ? " she
asked in great trepidation.

" What was it ? " said I.

" Sure it was a ghost, sir, flying on a white
baste, and I could not tell whether from the clouds
of hiven, or up from the pit, it came so sudden
loike ; and before I knew it my sinses left me, and
the vision was gone."

" What you saw," I said, " was my friend riding
a white mule."

" A mule ! was it ? " she exclaimed in evident

disgust. "Ah! bad luck to ye. It was the angel of death come to warn us of the eend of the world."

Seeing Charley coming, I said, "Well, perhaps the ghost will be here to speak for himself. In the meantime let me help you pick up your berries."

It was a slow process, but the task was finally accomplished, and the berries all replaced in the tin dish apparently as good as before.

"Would you like to sell these berries?" I asked.

"Indade I would," she replied.

Taking a paper from my pocket, I emptied her dish, and returned it with a quarter in it.

"You are very ginerous," she said as she saw the coin. "May the mither of God bless ye."

"Mother of God!" broke in Charley, who had just come up in season to overhear these words. "Has God a mother?"

"Ter be sure."

"I hope she was a fine woman."

"Indade, she was that," answered the berry woman eying him doubtfully.

"I am glad to know God comes from a good family," said Charley with a queer facial expression; "but why not ask God Himself to bless my friend here?"

"It is all the same, indade, sir. The holy mither has more influence than a poor woman like meself. Indade, indade she has, Ah! yes, indade, ter be sure. The holy saints preserve us!"

With these words she went off, evidently glad to get away from such a heretic to the Romish faith.

" Why is it," asked Charley, as we started for the landing, " that Roman Catholics worship the Virgin Mary ? "

" It arose originally in part, I presume, from a failure to see mother-heart, or motherhood, as well as fatherhood in God, and the craving for a divine womanly nature. It is strange they cannot see that Jesus, who reveals the Father, is a complete Being, exhibiting in perfection the highest traits of both man and woman ; for where can you find female tenderness and sympathy so beautifully illustrated as in the life of Christ ? "

" There you are again full of the seeds of thought ! " exclaimed Charley. " I must think this all out some time, but not now. My head aches from the large overdoses you have given it ; but supper and a little more fun will bring me all right. Food and fun, like the Siamese twins, should not be separated. When one of those twins died, the death of the other followed ; and it is just as true that when fun dies the stomach dies. Fun is just as necessary for good digestion as fresh air is for the lungs."

" Well," said I, as we reached our lunch-box and opened it, " here is food. Mix it with gratitude, and as much judicious fun as seemeth to thee good, and let thy heart rejoice in the Giver to thee of so much super-abounding health and happy good-nature ; and, if thou hast a little more fun than thou needest for thine own digestion, spill a little over for thy less fortunate comrade."

"Amen!" responded Charley seriously accepting my words as sufficient grace before meat, and, taking up a chicken-bone, remarked, "I suppose Christianity, as interpreted by you and the Blentwoods, requires that I pass you the breast meat and retain the wing for myself; but as there is some doubt about the keeping, I think we better make sure of the best first, and if anything spoils, let it be the wing."

"You are right, Charley, and, furthermore, I forego all parts of the chicken to-night, since farinaceous suppers, unless I am to sit up late, are best for me,—most conducive to sleep. So eat breast meat, my brother, eat all the breast meat."

"You are as generous, Elbert, as a duck might be in refusing an umbrella."

'Just about, Charley; and I am glad you have no need to coddle yourself, or restrain your appetite. You are a perfect rhythm of bone and muscle and tissue and nerve, and when food, at any time of day, gets into your stomach, it sets in motion the whole symphonic machinery from your crown to your toes, till digestion is completed and its results appropriated."

"My digestion is good, I admit, but I fear it would not last long, if I moped." Do you not regard laughing as a Christian duty?"

"Yes, Charley, I do; and if I saw nothing to laugh at, I would laugh occasionally anyway, mechanically, until I could laugh heartily. It is a historical fact long ago supported by Quack-enbos and others, that one can put himself into almost any mood by putting on the externals of that mood. Actors do this. To feel blue, draw down the muscles of the face, and put on a woebe. gone look. On the other hand, smile, look bright and cheerful, and you will soon feel so."

"Suppose we test your theory," said Charley, as he took the last mouthful, "and, so, send my big supper on its beneficent mission rejoicing?" Suiting the action to the word, he threw back his head, and exploded with a loud, "Ha, ha, ha!" I joined in, and very soon we were both laughing because we had to, and as heartily, as if we had started with something to excite our risibles.

"There!" I said, as soon as the paroxysm was over, "the theory is proved, and we must repeat this after each meal."

"Some such practice as that," said Charley, "would brighten up many a dining-room, and be better than medicine for feeble stomachs."

Our next business was to erect our tent, and place in it as soft a bed of boughs as we could make, first scorching them in a fire made for the purpose. During this process, which consumed considerable time, Charley entertained me with the following description of the *finale* of his ride:

"The mule stopped so suddenly at the farm-yard bars, I found it convenient to pass on a few feet, not wishing the mule's company any longer, and so slid over the animal's head, and alighted on

13

some blankets, hanging over a post, as neatly and easily as if placed there by a fairy. A man in the yard looked up half-scared to death, as if he expected every minute would be—the next! I raised my hat, and putting on all the urbanity at my command, I said, ' Good evening, neighbor.' Finding I was no apparition, but real flesh and blood, though clothed in white linen, he at length broke out, ' Neighbor! Who in the devil are you anyway ? '

" I replied, ' Friend, you make a slight mistake ; I am not in the devil.'

" ' Well,' he essayed again, ' where in the devil did you come from ? "

" ' You still mistake me,' I said, ' I did not come in the devil, I came on a mule, this one,' pointing to the panting beast standing at the bars quite subdued and docile. ' I had a very fine ride ; and as this animal is probably your property, I am very much obliged to you, sir, and will make any pecuniary compensation you desire.'

" ' The devil, you will,' said he, his muscles beginning to relax and twitch about the mouth.

" ' Friend,' said I, ' I insist that the devil and I have no business relations whatever.'

" ' Don't eh ? ' he asked, beginning to shake. ' That's good. He, he, he ! No business with the devil, eh ? Guess you don't do business round here, then,—he, he, he ! Most of folks round here takes him in partner, and the devil runs pretty much the whole concern. But ye don't say, do ye, stranger, that ye rode that devil—I mean that vicious mule without bridle or saddle ? '

" ' Certainly,' I answered.

He began to slap his knees in ecstasy. ' That's too good for anything. He, he, he ! ho, ho, ho— oh! That's worth big money to me, stranger. Why, that mule is the terror of the neighbor- hood, and I couldn't sell it for a song ; but if you have rode it bareback and without reins, Jehosephat! that'll bring it into market, don't ye see? I'm obliged to ye, stranger, though when I first saw ye, I thought ye'd come from that warm country where they have to wear summer clothes the year round ! Let me git ye a glass of cider.'

I excused myself, and came away ; and the last I heard from him was the raucous sound of ' He, he, he ! ho, ho, ho—oh ! ' "

Having finished our task, I began to read silently from my New Testament, when, to my relief, Charley asked that I read aloud, which I did, and after gratefully commending ourselves and others to the watchful care of the Supreme Ruler, we lay down on our fresh-made bed, and slept soundly.

CHAPTER XXII.

A BRISK MORNING SAIL

WHEN we awoke, the tops of the trees, lit up by the rising sun, were smiling down upon us a seeming benediction for the day. The rays of light, as they crept towards us, played hide and seek with the moving foliage, now skulking behind the leaves, and now darting at us long shafts of bright light, till, at length, the shadows all fled away, and the whole landscape seemed to wake up, and become conscious that it was day.

We ate our breakfast with a good appetite, folded our tent, put all our luggage into our boat, and in reluctance to leave a spot now become a part of life's pleasing associations, we reclined for a while on our primitive bed delectable with the fragrance of balsam and pine. We lay so quiet, a bird came picking crumbs close to our feet, and then wiped its bill, and preened its feathers in glad satiety. A squirrel followed, its tail actually brushing Charley's boot, and, after getting its fill, scampered away with many antics. At a little distance a rabbit was seen making short detours, approaching in zig-zag lines, and taking observa-

tions at every turn. It would raise its head
slowly and very cautiously, and then stand on its
hind legs for several moments without a motion,
except in the erect ears, which seemed almost to
quiver in the eagerness of listening, and then,
coming a little nearer, repeat its observations and
listening attitudes.

"There is a meat dinner for us," whispered Charley passing me a pistol he had brought with him
for game, which I took, and slowly covered the
breast of the little fellow, as it was again exposed
to view, but did not fire. I was so interested in
the creature's movements, especially its extreme
precaution against danger, proving thereby its
love of life, I concluded that I did not want to
eat it, and silently passed the pistol back to Charley, who as silently raised it in position ; and when
the cunning little creature exposed its head again,
I feared to see it drop, but Charley laid down his
pistol, saying, "I think I'll take fish for dinner ! "
We both laughed, and, the spell being broken,
there was no further advance in sociability on
the part of our dumb companions.

Taking long sniffs of the balsamic air, I said, as
we rose up, "We may not have so soft and healthful a bed to-night, unless we take it along with
us."

"We'll trust in Providence, Elbert."

"Ah! Charley, Providence does not encourage
any slackening in the exercise of forethought.
There is a great deal of educating power in being
called upon, as we are in this world, to look fore

and aft. It would be an unkind Providence to relieve us from the necessity of thinking."

" Did not Jesus say, 'Take no thought for to-morrow'?"

"No, that is the language of King James' translation of what he said. His words in Greek, in which they were recorded, contain the idea of anxiety, and a better rendering is, 'Be not anxious for the morrow, etc.'"

" When, then, may one expect Providential help?"

"When he has exhausted his utmost resources, and can do nothing more, he can then look up with implicit confidence for Divine aid."

"Well, I likes de horn you blow, brudder, as Tom said to Dr. Blentwood, when he first heard him preach, and if you say so, I'll tote the whole bed aboard in a jiffy."

" Remember, Charley, I have no anxiety in the matter; indeed, I am somewhat in the condition of the hypothetical donkey, which the medieval metaphysicians said, if placed exactly half way between two bundles of hay, would not, between the two equal motives, go to either bundle, but remain in his tracks till starvation relieved him of all perplexity."

"Ah!" Charley exclaimed, the fun beginning to bubble up through his eyes, "those much-abused and nobly employed hair-splitters were right. Behold yesterday's mule! Was it not held fast in its tracks by two opposing motives? Where would have been my ride, had we not added a preponderance of motive in my favor? The very moment he had a little more motive for yielding to our will than to have his own, he scooted, and streaked it for home, bearing me with him, flying over the fields in gleesome, blood-dancing exhilaration."

Here he branched off into an eulogium on metaphysics, waxing more and more grandiloquent, until, pretending to be overcome by his eloquence, I threw up my arms, falling back on the boughs, staring at him with mouth wide open, when he began to congratulate himself on this demonstration of his power to sway an audience. Halting, his countenance at the same time falling into the most lugubrious expression, he continued:

"But alas! my joy is touched with sadness as I reflect, that I must leave my friend here as a footstool for the ever-watchful partridge to drum on, and the cunning squirrel to peal his beechnuts on, the crow to peck at, and, indeed, for the whole animal creation to prey upon! Were he the metaphysicians' donkey, I would not mind; for I am not much on donkeys; but it overcomes me to lose my friend, whose majestic dome of thought, whose beetling brow, and whose eagle eye plainly indicate how he could startle the world with the brilliant movement of his mental artillery, lighting up the very heavens with the flash of his lightning-like thought, and shaking the earth itself with the ponderosity of his intellectual cannonading."

Pausing to take breath, and looking at me pathetically, he suddenly changed aspect, and, clapping his hands, ejaculated, "A salvation thought occurs to me. I am a third power, and may break up this equilibrium of forces," and, so saying, he pulled the boughs from under me, and carried them off to the boat, placing them in the bow so carefully as to make an attractive couch to recline on. He came back with sparkling eyes, prophetic of a frolic, and, putting himself into fantastic shapes, exclaimed:

"You still linger, O great philosopher! I perceive by the molecular motions in your orbs of light that you are now up to mischief!"

" No, not mischief, but *bou*chief," I replied, and, holding up one remaining bough, added, " Here is the only link left in the motive force which would chain me to this spot."

He tried to get it, and, failing, picked me up, and tugged me to the bed of boughs in the boat amid much hilarious mirth, which is the best antidote to the blues, hypochondria, dyspepsia, and kindred diseases, as well as the best restorative yet discovered for jaded nerves.

A brisk wind was blowing directly astern, and we hoisted sail merely for the sensation of riding fast, and not that we cared to get along; for we had no object in view except to obtain the most change and recreation possible, and were ready to abandon the river any moment it became monotonous.

"What is the best method of spending a vacation?" Charley asked, as we began to get under way.

"With Charley Lightheart," I answered emphatically.

"I call for a philosophical answer, and put the emphasis on *method*," he insisted.

"My answer was philosophical so far as it went," I replied, "but to go a step farther, it should be spent as free as the air, which has periods of great energy and periods of absolute quiet. Those of soft muscles, especially, should imitate the air at rest, and become magnificent loafers like me, for example, stretched out at full length on this sweet-smelling couch, making no more exertion than what is necessary to breathe, and feeling little or no more weight of care than an infant. And now, if you please, we will hear your opinion."

"My opinion," said he, bending backward and running his thumbs, with fingers spread wide apart, up and down the armholes of his vest in a ludicrously pompous manner, "my opinion is that a man should spend his vacation as he chooses, provided he chooses to spend it right."

"A very safe remark, Charley."

"Yes, dear Elbert, safety is my strong point. There is nothing like being safe. When my father caught me tying a tin pail to a young cow's tail, I illustrated my genius for safety by saying, 'Father, I am some afraid this will frighten the heifer, and I guess I won't do it.' Safety, you see, was my controlling motive even at that early period."

"Was it safety for the heifer, or for you?" I interjected.

He looked at me in well-feigned bewilderment. "How could I be as well versed in the safety of cows as in my own? Self-preservation is the first law of nature. I knew that my pantaloons were thin, and my flesh tender, and that I could not bear pain very well, and to fortify my position with safe breastworks was a wise discretion, which, we are told, is the better part of valor. I was going to give you other strategic movements for safety in my early life, but I fear you do not appreciate this beautiful trait in my character!"

"Oh, yes I do," I replied. "To keep on the safe side of the road always, and not run the risk of trying how near you can come to the precipice and not topple over; to keep on the safe side of temperance by never running the risk of taking the first glass of intoxicating liquor; to keep on the safe side of virtue by never trying to see how far you can come to doing wrong, and not doing it; to keep on the safe side of honesty by never borrowing so much as a penny from a trust fund, or employer unconsulted; to keep on the safe side of truth by never entertaining as a guest the slightest approach to falsehood;—these and other pursuits of safety cannot be too highly commended."

"Amen! in my end of the boat," said Charley in approval; "but don't you think a more worldly pursuit of safety desirable, if secured by pure strategy? Mark, I say pure strategy with no moral obliquity."

"I highly commend the strategy by which you escaped a whipping."

"That is all I can ask of a man, who is such a stickler for small points of equity. I cannot expect you to approve of my tying the pail to the cow's tail; you would sympathize with the cow, and not with my boyish love of fun!"

"I should keenly sympathize with your fun-loving nature, Charley, but my sense of justice and fair play would not allow me to enjoy fun created for one party by the suffering of another, except, it may be, in the line of duty. I am a great lover of innocent sport in boy or man, and hope I shall always be."

"Was I right in attaching the pail?" Charley asked, jumping up, and raising his arm with a most energetic gesture. "That is what I want to know, uncovered of rhetoric, and in plain English."

"Not if it would have frightened and injured the cow," I made answer, as soon as my laughter would permit.

"Now I have got you!" said he, still more eloquent of gesture, and looking down on me with a droll mixture of haughty pride and benevolence. He paused a moment to enjoy his advantage, and to give weight to his words, and then, with both arms sawing the air, he asked, almost in a scream, "Was it right to attach a withe to a mule's tail, and treat it as if it were the helm of a senseless ship? Tell me that!"

"That is a very different matter," I answered, as soon as I could speak, holding my sides. "The cow is useful only in giving milk, and, to that end, needs to be kept very quiet; but the mule is only useful in going, and he would not go, from pure stubbornness; and so we took the least painful, and, at the same time, the most enjoyable, method of conquering his rebellious spirit, and making him of some worth in the world. This is a case, Charley, where duty and fun kissed each other."

He threw down his hat, and sat down, saying, "It is no use to exhaust myself in eloquence; you will not see through even an old boy's eyes. The most sublime oratory, I perceive, has its limit!"

"That reminds me to ask, 'What profession, or occupation, do you intend to follow?'"

"I don't know," he answered, a little more seriously. "I am somewhat in the condition of your hypothetical donkey; several callings in life draw me about equally, and I cannot decide. I hope I shall learn what I am fitted for in season to be prepared for it."

"Glad the question of self-ease does not come in to bother you."

"Perhaps it does though. Should not one choose that profession which he would enjoy the best?"

"He will be most likely to succeed, if in love with his work"

"Is not happiness a legitimate object of pursuit in life?"

"Not according to the higher law."

"What! isn't it right to be happy?"

"Certainly, and desirable, too, though it is better to be happy in being right."

"Why not seek happiness?"

"Because it is an unworthy object, as an end in itself, and to live for it is the surest way not to reach it, at least in highest measure."

"Make that clear to me, Elbert, and I'll give you half a dollar."

"Well, to begin at the first parallel, is there anything noble in self-seeking?"

"Probably not; but is there anything noble in seeking misery?"

"Certainly not. To seek happiness or misery, as an end, is a kind of selfishness, and has no merit in it. To be worthily heroic we must go out of self, and the farther we leave self behind the grander we are. As Emerson says:

'The hero is not fed on sweets,
Daily his own heart he eats.'

"Self or service is the question before every man, and on his choice pivots both character and destiny; yes, and the truest happiness also."

"But can I not serve others and my own happiness too?"

"Real service may lead directly in the line of self-sacrifice and personal discomfort, not to say hardship and suffering. There can be no noble daring for truth and the right, where personal happiness must be consulted at every step. Whoever in the struggle of existence thinks first of his own happiness is out of place in life ; for there is no true work for him to do. On the other hand, he who aims at noble service may find joy even in self-sacrifice."

" But, Elbert, I do not see why I cannot find happiness by seeking it."

" Well, Charley, it is simply a matter of fact that happiness is a coy maiden that will not be caught that way. To win substantial happiness you must forget self in your unselfish devotion to others' welfare, or to some good and worthy cause ; and then, indeed, it may come in all its richness, a thousand-fold more desirable than that enjoyed by the mere pleasure-seeker. The highest happiness comes to us obliquely and incidentally, and not when sought directly."

" But, Elbert, doesn't a man wholly seek his own happiness when he marries ? "

" He is liable not to find it if he does. Many a couple find the bonds of wedlock grievous, because in marrying each expected to be made happy by the other. On the contrary, if a man marries with the hope of giving happiness to the woman he loves by his unselfish devotion, he is not only likely to succeed, but to receive in addition the happiness which comes unsought ; and the woman who marries to be happy rather than to dispense happiness, as wife and mistress of a home, by working for the good of others, will, in all probability, fail, because her love is selfish and downward, craving everything, and not genuine love, which prefers to give everything."

A long-drawn sigh came from Charley, who presently said, "You have pretty high ideals, Elbert. I fear you breathe fairer air than I do, and feed on invisible substances, and that incipient wings are already emerging from your shoulder-blades."

" Oh ! no, Charley, I am wholly mundane in body, and too much so in mind. I wish I had more wings within."

" Don't go too fast, Elbert, and leave me so far behind as to take away my courage, for I am really striving to come up to you, and have a great deal to think over and incorporate into my moral corporosity."

" In some respects, at least, you leave *me* behind, Charley."

" In what, pray ? "

" In a certain natural gift you have, and the disposition to use it, of making people forget themselves. It is a grand power, Charley, one which will make you a welcome guest everywhere, and a needed presence in the sick-room. To you and Ethel I owe a large share of my speedy recovery and continued improvement. You both have the same power in effect, though dissimilar in operation. Yours is more like nature in her varied, frolicsome moods; hers like the steady, gentle rays of the sun, scattering the dews of unwelcome thoughts and drawing all the richer life to the surface. What E. R. Champlin said of another might be expressly said of Ethel, and the last two lines apply to you as well; and how much brighter the world would be were there more Ethel Blentwoods and Charley Lighthearts in it:

> 'She took her lesson from the sun—
> That gave her wealth ere she beheld it—
> And gave a smile to every one,
> And, if she saw a cloud, dispelled it.'"

During all this conversation we were not un-mindful of the panoramic views along shore, which, however, we enjoyed mostly in silence, only occasionally interjecting a remark paren-thetically to call attention to some particular fea-ture. The wind was now blowing with increasing force, and our little craft sped on at a rapid rate, throwing up an occasional spray, which we had to dodge or get wet. This furnished us with considerable pastime.

" There ! " Charley would remark as he failed to escape a spirt of water, " my starboard eye is drowned ; " and, perhaps, before he had that wiped dry, he would cry out, " My port ear has shipped a cargo of liquid ! " and so on, using sailor terms only to describe his condition.

At length, the fun beginning to wane, I asked, "Isn't this getting a little monotonous, Char-ley ? "

" Yes," he replied, " I think I don't like a

douche-bath in spots any more. Suppose we drop sail?"

"That will suit me exactly," I said, but had scarcely finished before the wind lulled, and then died quickly away.

14

CHAPTER XXIII.

DINNER WITH DELIGHTFUL STRANGERS.

THE ruffled face of the river smoothed down all its wrinkles, and looked as innocent as if it had never known anything but eternal calm. The now almost vertical sun poured out his hot rays upon us, until we were glad to dip our hands in the water to cool our pulses. Not a tree moved, and the river's surface, like a flawless mirror, reflected everything in matchless perfection. The sky beneath was an exact counterpart of that above us, and we seemed in the centre of a hollow sphere, with no visible support to hold us up. Occasionally, it is true, this liquid reflector would be slightly disturbed by a fish lazily swimming to the surface for a fly, and then as lazily sinking down again, as if the morsel did not pay for the exertion.

No one could feel energetic in such an atmosphere; and if we had any thoughts we kept them to ourselves. It was a time for day-dreams, and we gave ourselves up to pleasant revery.

At length I asked Charley if he was in the body; and, rubbing his forehead, he answered

slowly, " I was out somewhere, but am all here
now. Any news?"

Looking at my watch, I answered, " It is one
o'clock ! "

" Factorum ! " he exclaimed in surprise. " I
thought I was hungry, and now I know it.
Where shall we dine—on shore? or on ship-
board ? "

" There," said I, pointing to a tree on the right
bank with a grassy slope, " is an attractive spot ;
let us go there for a change, and dine more like
monarchs of all we survey."

We had not reached the shore before a gay
party, about ten in number, appeared under that
very tree with lunch-baskets, and saluted us with
the waving of handkerchiefs. We returned the
salute, and, having landed and secured our boat,
we marched boldly up to our proposed dining-
place, lunch-box in hand. We took off our hats,
and Charley, being a little in advance, thus addressed them : —

" Ladies and gentlemen, we seem to demon-
strate the truth of the saying, that great minds
agree, in our selection of this pretty spot as a desirable place to dine ; and the fact, that we choose
it is a proof that we are in love with delightful
things, and, therefore, must be in love with each
other, as kindred spirits ; though this latter fact
may not yet have come up into consciousness, because we imagine we have not had that experience which small minds call getting acquainted.
What does it signify that we may not have met

before outwardly, when inwardly we touch one another in all those superior qualities, which make acquaintance worth having and friendship abiding ? Great minds, like ours, know each other intuitively, and at once, without the preliminary necessity of being put into quarantine for fear some latent poison may be developed. It is as plain as the sunshine that we are all very congenial, and very delightful people, and, therefore, should consider ourselves as the oldest and best of friends.

" Besides, we have met by providential appointment, which is another argument that we know each other, and should feel thoroughly at home. Ladies and gentlemen, my name is Charley, and this is my excellent friend, Elbert, in search of recreation and health. We both felt a double yearning for this attractive place, and now we know why. It was because you, our old, valued, and long-separated friends, were here to greet us. I congratulate you and ourselves on this happy meeting. We are dying to take all of you by the hand, as, of course, you are dying to take us by the hand, and, therefore, I will waste no more time in words."

This unique speech was greeted during its delivery, and at its close, with abundant smiles, laughter, and clapping of hands. There was a slight pause, when one of their number stepped forward in reply :

" Gentlemen, Charley and Elbert, your admirable speech finds a responsive echo in all our hearts. Your argument is most convincing that we are old and true friends. We will be your brothers and sisters and cousins and aunts (pointing to a young lady, which, having some special application, produced a laugh). It gives us unspeakable pleasure to meet you after so long a separation. My name is John."

"How do you do, John?" said Charley, and they both shook hands cordially. Then John and I shook hands as old friends. After that each one was introduced by his or her Christian name, and the handshaking, from first to last, was more or less demonstrative according to disposition, and the ability of each to meet the demands of the occasion.

There was a good deal of laughter during the process, and an evident desire on the part of each to throw off all needless reserve, and we at once felt at home with them. Charley's spirit was so thoroughly caught that there was no place for an apology.

The ladies spread tablecloths, and covered them with the contents of their baskets, and we added those of our box, which, in the line of frosted cakes, tarts, turnovers, and meat pies, made a good showing. There was an abundance of everything, and we all ate as heartily, and with as much freedom from anything like stiffness, as if we had always known each other. The ladies were profuse in their compliments of our cake, and we as truthfully, as well as gallantly, praised the choice things they passed to us.

"We are exceedingly glad you came," said an intelligent, and pretty-voiced lady to me, after dinner, as we stood a little apart from the rest. "I assure you we have had a much better time than we otherwise could have had. You and your friend have given zest to the occasion. It does not seem possible we were strangers only two hours ago."

"I suppose we owe our rapid acquaintance in part," I replied, "to the skilful speech and captivating manner of my friend Charley, but more, I think, to the delightful congeniality and intelligent good sense of your party."

"That was, indeed, a phenomenal speech, and so remarkably winning in its delivery that it broke down all barriers, and we were ready to capitulate even before he got half through. He must be a delightful companion. There is much truth in what he said about kindred spirits."

"Undoubtedly such need only the slightest contact to awaken knowledge and friendship. Indeed, kindred minds are the only ones, who ever really know each other. Between opaque and unrelated minds there will always be more or less ignorance of each other, and consequent misunders ndings, though they may live under the same roof forever."

"How far do you think all trouble between friends may be referable to want of knowledge?"

"It would be difficult to say, owing to different moral states and dispositions; but this much I think is true, that two persons cannot know

each other truly, until all misunderstandings
cease."

" Is such knowledge possible in this world? "

' It certainly cannot exist without love as an
interpreter. Where we cannot love, we cannot
see and cannot know. Even the beauties of
nature and art must be loved before they can be
really seen and felt. To illustrate more fully what
I mean, take that quality of self-denial, or self-
sacrifice, which characterizes a true Christian; can
a selfish person see it, understand it, and appreciate it at its full value? "

" Only so far as it pleased and benefited himself."

" Precisely, and even then he would take it
chiefly as his due, and that others, who failed to
do as much, defrauded him to that extent. Again,
a man who stands up for the right against his own
interest, and, incidentally perhaps, that of some
others, will necessarily be misunderstood by all
who lack his true sympathy, moral courage and
sound integrity."

" I could never have interpreted my own sentiments so admirably as you have done, Mr. Elbert,"
she said, smiling at the handle she attached to my
Christian name. " You make me feel more keenly
than ever the hungerings and cravings I have long
felt for intellectual associations. I hope you will
excuse the frankness which leads me to express a
simple matter of fact."

" Oh, certainly ! " I said, a little embarassed.
" I will be equally frank, and say that I greatly

enjoy meeting a lady of your cast of mind, who can talk upon subjects other than gossip and the latest style of bonnet, and can stimulate thought in others, as well as think herself. There are so many who never acquire, and never strive to acquire, any taste for profound study, and who never inform themselves on any of the great questions of the day, or, and more especially, on any of the deeper problems of human life, that it is a treat to find delightful exceptions."

She thanked me, and said, " I have books at my command, and an intelligent brother, who, however, is away a large part of the time, and intelligent friends, of course ; but what I most need is to have some one, or ones, with whom to talk up more frequently the suggestions, which come to me from reading and experience."

"That is certainly helpful and satisfactory to us all."

"Yes, and what is peculiar is the fact, in my case, at least, that it is only the very few who can tell us just what we want, to know," and then with a little blush, she added, " I should be pleased to exchange full names and addresses, if agreeable to you, with the hope that we may meet again."

" With pleasure," I responded, finding a blank card in my diary, on which I wrote, and handed her.

"Elbert Bloomfield !" she read aloud in surprise, as she handed me her card. " Why, did you not speak, last Spring, on Salvation and Character, in Springfield ?"

" I did."

" Well, I thought I must have met you some-where, but could not place you. My brother Thede and I heard you, and that one address of yours saved him from going wholly over to infi-delity, and cleared up so many difficulties that were troubling my mind also. We never before got such a reasonable and common-sense view of what is meant, or should be meant, by Christian salvation. You made it something real and tan-gible, and something no intelligent mind could carelessly lay aside, or fail to make a subject of profound study. My brother would be delighted to see you. Cannot you and your friend dine with us to-morrow? It will be hardly out of your way, as we live down the river, and not far from the shore. I suppose you will stop at ——?"

" We intend to."

" Well, ours is the first large, square, and some-what old-fashioned house on the hill beyond, and you will know it by the clump of trees on its north-ern side provided with hammocks and patent swings. I can assure you nothing would please brother Thede better than a talk with you. I hope you can come."

At this moment Charley came up, and she re-peated her invitation, which he at once accepted, supposing I had done the same. I had, practi-cally, but added, "It will certainly be a very pleas-ant change for us, and we are exceedingly obliged to you."

"Then we shall expect you," she said, as we took our leave.

I bowed, and Charley said, " Nothing less than a cannon-ball will prevent us."

Raising our hats, we bade the company adieu and started for the boat.

CHAPTER XXV.

TWO JOLLY FELLOWS IN A BOAT.

WE were ready to push off, when two young ladies came rushing down the bank, and one of them, whom Charley introduced as Carrie Horton, exclaimed, "We shall miss you awfully," a remark meant for Charley.

"I hope we shall not be long separated," Charley replied; "for I shall simply exist till we meet again."

"Oh, you'll forget us," said Carrie Horton, "as soon as you are out of sight."

"Forget!" ejaculated Charley with a sigh of distress. "Can a wounded eagle forget the dart that pierced its flesh?"

The girls giggled. "You don't look much wounded," remarked Miss Horton's companion.

"Ah!" Charley replied, placing his hand over his heart, "how much, then, my looks belie me! for my wound is deep, and can never be healed except by the sweet, soothing, mollifying salve of —I leave you to supply what my timid tongue dares not utter."

The girls giggled again, and, as we pushed off from the shore, I thought I detected Miss Horton throwing a kiss at Charley, and his movements bore out the idea; for he opened his mouth as if to catch something, and then swallowed with every manifestation of delight, patting his throat and stomach as if it tasted good all the way down. His acts and facial expression were so comical I could not help shaking with pent-up laughter, though I managed to work hard at the oars, and we were soon out in full view of the party on the bluff, who saluted us handsomely, and then sung " Should old acquaintance be forgot." We lifted our hats, and waved them in acknowledgment till they were hid from our view. I then broke the silence with hearty and continuous laughter.

" Where are you hurt ? " Charley asked, looking up with a face of solemn aspect and feigned alarm.

" What outrageous thing are you going to do next, Charley ? "

"Outrageous? Don't use such strong, Biblical terms—I mean Eastern-country terms, where the Bible was writ."

" You are a brick ! " I said, falling into a college expression, with which I knew him to be familiar.

" A brick," he retorted, " is a parallelogram ; I am not a parallelogram, and therefore not a brick, though of clay and burnt—by the sun." Rising, and striking an attitude, he continued, " Behold these graceful proportions, and this exalted mien, and then belittle my mighty aspect by calling me a brick ! "

He sat down with the air of one who had annihilated his opponent.

"Charley Lightheart, you paralogize."

"No, Elbert Bloomfield, I syllogize; but I will
condescend to hear you state the paralogism,
though it hurts my dignity to have my great reasoning faculties called in question."

"Well, because you are not a parallelogram,
you draw an unwarrantable conclusion."

"Listen then," said he, counting his fingers;
"a brick is hard, and coarse, and stiff, and rough,
and insensible, sharp-cornered, unchangeable, and
generally red in color; whereas I am soft, and lim-
ber, and fine, and smooth, and sensitive, round,
changeable, and generally pinkish in color, when
not wrought up to the white heat of indignation
by your obfuscations of my sparkling, intellectual
ratiocinations. Listen again, I am conscious;
a brick is not conscious: therefore I am not a
brick. Is there any paralogism about that? Is
it not a perfect syllogism? Have I not touched
the nadir depths of logical profundity? Let the
contents of your cranium be still. Silence is
golden at an hour like this!"

Of course, there was nothing to do but laugh;
for the soberest Jew, even a weeping, wailing Jer-
emiah, could not look upon Charley Lightheart
in his droll moods without convulsive laughter.
Charley saw the grotesque side of everything, and
no one enjoyed a laugh better than he, especially
after getting me to laughing, because, I suspect,
he was under orders from both Dr. Lightheart

and himself to keep me in good spirits. At any rate, we laughed much on this vacation trip and always felt the better for it. Better than medicine, clarifying the brain, it made me more in love with nature and nature's God.

"Charley," I said, as soon as there was sufficient calm, "you have a mission."

"State it, my Lord Elbert."

"It is to take out overtaxed brain-workers and convalescents on easy excursions, and cure them by making them forget themselves. Do you know I have a theory, that the salvation of the body may, in part, hinge on the same principle as the salvation of the soul, at least, in one important consideration. In either case self must be buried out of sight. We find our higher selves by losing our lower selves. If we seek Christ, and think only of ourselves, we shall not find Him; and so, if we walk, or ride, or exercise, and continually think, This is for my health, we shall not find the health we seek. What we want, for health of body or mind, is to get out of self, and stay out, and live in the glad sunshine, the fresh air, the songs of birds, the beauties of nature, the thought of God, and the welfare of man."

"I am afraid," said Charley, "I should not always find so appreciative an invalid as you are. Many people, you know, receive our best efforts to cheer them with about as much response as the mud receives the pebble."

"Too true, Charley, but there are enough of the other kind, who, I believe, are actually dying, not from any cause recognizable by medical science, but because they are living in the sultry atmosphere of self-consciousness breathed over and over, till it has become poisoned and suffocating, and they need some one like you to drag them out of it."

"What if they prefer their lethargic air to the free breath of heaven?"

"Well, if anybody can send into their miasmatic world a shaft of social lightning to drive them out, where God's free winds can blow upon them, and fill their lungs with healthful, life-giving oxygen, that person is yourself."

"You overestimate my ability, friend Elbert; besides, I am a very retiring, shrinking, timid young man."

"It looks so by the way you met and spoke to a whole company of ladies and gentlemen you never saw before, this very day noon."

"That was a case of necessity, where, like the children of Israel at the Red Sea, I must go forward or perish. I might have slunk away like a fool, and thereby revealed just what I was, but I resolved to put the best polish on the fool I could, and so waded in, as the phrase goes, though with palpitating heart and smiting knees."

"Well, I don't see but you got through your Red Sea as triumphantly as the Israelites did through theirs."

"Not quite, I think; my knees are rather sore, and my heart may be wounded just a little."

"Who could have wounded you?"

"Oh! there were so many pretty girls, I felt the prick of Cupid's darts in several quarters. Perhaps Miss Horton wounded me deepest. I got the most acquainted with her. She is in for a good time, and isn't afraid to push for it. She is good style too. How were you struck with her, Elbert?"

"Oh, not specially."

"Bah! you want a woman to be a theologian."

"No, Charley, what I want to find in a woman is some depth of mind, and great depth and steadiness of heart, and, having these, she may boil over with fun, the more the better."

"Isn't Miss Horton all that?"

"She seemed rather shallow, though bright, what there was of her, and fairly quick-witted."

"Well, she skims the surface pretty lively, and perhaps, after all, gets most of the cream of things."

"There is something in that, perhaps, but I like to see a love for the solid, and a disposition to look into the heart of things, together with some moral purpose in life. A shallow-brained and shallow-hearted girl is no fit companion for an intelligent fellow like you. In the hour of trial and in times of small disturbances and petty disappointments, instead of helping you by uncomplaining cheerfulness, she would add to your burdens by her peevish fretfulness. Without brains or heart enough for self-control, unconsciously to herself, perhaps, she would be more thoughtful for her cat than for you. But this in general as a warning, and not that I read it in Carrie Horton."

" I thank thee for that saving sentence. Really, now, don't you think her chatty and pleasant ? "

" Apparently, yes. She could assent to what you said very prettily, but seemed to have few ideas of her own beyond dress and gossip."

" You must have observed her very closely."

" Oh, no! only what I was forced to by her making herself somewhat conspicuous at one time, while I was conversing with Miss —— Oh ! I have her card ; here it is, and her name is Theodocia Willmette Thornton. She called her brother Thede, short for Theodore, I suppose. Their parents, who, she told me, are dead, must have had a taste for alliteration, though Willmette would seem to militate against that theory. It was an afterthought probably, put in on account of its originality and prettiness. She doubtless is known by the name of Theo."

" She seemed a trifle too serious," said Charley, " but whether appropriately named or not, she was mighty good to invite us to dine to-morrow. I expect a fine spread, and you know my heart is very tender towards the author of fine spreads. I almost love her already in anticipation of the good, square meal she will set before us."

" You are of the earth earthy, Charley."

" No, I am firmly planted on the earth, that's all. Jacob's ladder, I believe, rested on the earth."

" Yes, but its top reached to heaven."

15

" Well, I may top out there sometime, but I'd like to frisk around the base awhile first."

" The longer you stay at the base of the ladder, the harder it will be to climb. The spiritual limbs get stiffened and fixed in a measure by non-use."

" Perhaps so, but I have an idea that, after having a full experience of what there is in this world, I can start on more understandingly towards the spiritual world."

" That seems to be the common idea, or inclination, but it is wrong. To say nothing of the waste of time in chasing after mere worldly pleasures, which like, soap-bubbles, look beautiful in the sunlight of anticipation, but when realized leave, in the hand that grasps them, only a cold, damp spot of disappointment ; to say nothing of the formation of habits hard to break ; to say nothing of the weakening of the will from self-indulgence in its power to turn toward the better way, you need the spiritual as an every-day interpreter of the natural world, to throw light on a thousand questions which otherwise have no meaning. The lower cannot explain the higher ; but the higher can supplement and make plain the lower. To form a clear and correct idea of even a worldly life, you need the spiritual qualification first and always. Man here is buried in flesh and blood, and the only true Light reaching him is from above, and it is only by following that Light and climbing by the steps of faith, and hope, and memory, and patience, and love, that he can rise free and clear above what is merely physical, and look off with extended and correct view on all below him."

" Now, Elbert, don't you see you are making my position uncomfortable by knocking the pins out from under me, and letting me fall flat as a flounder?"

" There are foundations which cannot be shaken; but the folly of living for this world has been demonstrated over and over again."

" Well, the fact is, I want to see the folly of it myself, and then I shall know from experience."

" Oh, the strange perversity of human nature! Why not learn from the experience of others?"

" Do we really know what we have not experienced?"

" I suppose not fully."

" Why then complain of me?"

" Because there are some things not desirable to know—for instance, how a man feels when suffering from remorse over the committal of a crime, or wasted faculties and opportunities."

" There you have me again! I see what you are coming at. Suppose we adjourn the meeting till early candle-lighting?"

" I fear we might as well, Charley."

" Oh! I will think this over sometime."

The silence, which followed, was broken by Charley.

" Elbert, do you know much about the Thorntons?"

" I know they are very nice people. I learned

incidentally of them once, though I had forgotten about it till my memory was refreshed."

" I was told to-day that they were rather aristocratic."

" Wealthy people are apt to have that reputation, and not always justly ; but I like a little aristocracy of the right kind. Mark, I mean the genuine, not the codfish."

" Will my brother Elbert just explain a little, so I can get his idea ? "

" Well, I like a certain amount of agreeable and polite formalities, since there must be forms, or methods of some kind. For example, I like to see a well-set table, the food in nice, pretty dishes, on a nice, pretty tablecloth, with flowers, if convenient, and other table adornments, such as a little forethought and taste may supply. Then I like to have the coarser food removed before the dessert is brought on, and to see no one rise from the table without a well-expressed excuse, until all are through eating. In short, Charley, I like to see an air of refinement in the home and outside of it, and an orderly procedure and politeness in the household affairs and family intercourse, free from all stiffness, because originating in a genuine respect and thoughtfulness for each and all."

" That is not a bad kind of aristocracy, Elbert ; but the unnatural, uneasy, uncomfortable, put-on airs are a stench in my nostrils. Deliver me from codfish, anyway. I want none of that in mine. But, oh, Elbert ! the height of earthly happiness, the concentrated sweetness of life's most delectable joys, lie in an abundance of luxurious food, and in sufficient variety, with plenty of elbow-room (aristocratically speaking, you know!), and no hypercritical eyes to watch the rapid disappearance of the goodies. Every nerve in me thrills at the thought, and my gastric juices begin to bubble and boil, as if it would be a pleasure to them to tackle all I could put in my stomach. I wish I could portray to you the material glories of the day coming, when I shall sit down with my wide-awake Carrie at one end of the table, and myself at the other, and I am expected not to stand too much on the ceremony of going in, but to go in! That last clause is a hint from Shakespeare, or some other elegant fellow."

"All poetic thought with you, I see, must be a dance of the blood, like that of Saxe, and not of the spirit, like that of Tennyson. If you get a spiritual idea, you straightway clothe it in flesh and blood, and give it something to eat, and so your perversion of poetic sentiment is to be expected. Just think of your highest earthly paradise—stuffing the hole in your face with meats, and fowl, and pastry, and using your chin as a mill with which to grind it! Noble, isn't it?"

"Elbert Bloomfield! are you trying to flatter me?"

"Perhaps."

"Well, sir, I find it difficult to so construe your words. I will not sit—I will rise and stand so long as there is a doubt of your appreciation of

my superlative grandeur as a man every way.
Behold this noble dome of thought, jutting out
over eyes that look down on you like balls of
fire, in very wonderment over your stupid lack
of insight into the capabilities and powers of my
ponderous brain! But I will condescend to dem-
onstrate, even to your apprehension, that I am
not only some pumpkins, but great pumpkins.
Even now, at the slightest bidding, the proof of
my high position in the niche of literary fame
comes bubbling up from the wells of genius.
Listen to my poetic soul, and be dumb as the
rocks on yonder shore; listen with confusion of
face, and be confounded."

Throwing back his head and shoulders, and
folding his arms on his breast, and rolling his
eyes as if nearly bursting with self-esteem, he re-
cited the following lines:

> "' From the billowy green beneath me,
>   To the fathomless blue above,
> The Creatures of God are happy
>   In the warmth of their summer love.
> The infinite bliss of Nature
>   I feel in every vein;
> The light and the life of summer
>   Blossom in heart and brain.'

"I wonder," he continued, looking down on
me very pompously, "how you can hear me
without shrinking away withered, and blighted,
and blasted by the scorching thought of my overwhelming greatness!"

"How long were you in composing that fine poem?" I asked.

"How long? Did it not come forth at once, and spontaneously from my overflowing and superabundant thought?"

"Then it did not cost you as much labor as it did Bayard Taylor?"

"Bayard Taylor! Do you mean to insinuate that that poem is not mine? I want you to understand I bought the book containing it a long time ago, and it is my property. Besides, did not the poem pass through the alembic of my own memory, voice, and dramatic attitude? Bayard Taylor indeed! I think he preferred the money to the book, and thought it a fair exchange, or he would not have sold it."

"Of course," said I, continuing the serio-comic conversation; "but do you think you bought all the rights of authorship, when you bought that book?"

"No, sir, he had a perfect right to commence another book the next moment without consulting me in the least."

"You are a generous fellow!"

"I know it, Elbert, and yet I am not puffed up by it. It is my nature to be fair-minded and manly. I do not even now glory overmuch in your discomfiture in claiming that the poem I gave was not mine. Having proved that the front chair in the literary universe belongs to me, I will now resume my seat."

Here he put his thumbs in the arm-holes of

his vest, and spreading out his fingers, sat down with such an air of preposterous assumption of superiority that he was simple irresistible. If I did not have more lung capacity that night, and more muscle and nerve force from better circulation, it was not Charley's fault.

CHAPTER XXV.

AN UGLY VISITOR.

REACTION came at last, as of course it should and will in all healthy minds, and we became quiet and reflective till we reached a good place for camping. That Ethel became mysteriously involved in some of these reflections it is not my purpose to affirm nor deny ; but I tried to school myself to the thought that her happiness was the first and only thing to be considered, and not mine. If I could do nothing as a lover to make her life round and full and sweet, I would keep from her all knowledge of my great love ; but I would always be a friend, and watch for opportunities to bring blessings down upon her, though no eye saw me but the eye of Him who is the source of all creature comforts.

We went early to bed under our little tent, pitched on the highest bluff we could find. Our bed was made soft by using the boughs in our boat, and, thanks to plenty of exercise in the open air, and the hearty enjoyments of the day, we slept well, and were awakened the next morning by the singing of the thrush and the oriole. There was a slight rain, and then the clouds scud

away, as if frightened at the approaching sun,
which suddenly burst forth in glorious light, sending its bright and cheering rays along the valley,
and among the trees, till every raindrop became
illumined, and the face of nature wore an aspect
of pensive beauty, like a beautiful woman smiling
through her tears.

We got what we failed to get the night before,
a view of the town we were to visit, with its
suburbs of fine residences looking beautiful and
attractive in the glamour of the dawn.

We had breakfasted, and Charley was standing
outside the tent, while I was within, replacing
food in our lunch-box, and rolling up our rubber
blankets, when I heard a strange footstep, and
looking out through a small hole in the tent, I
saw a very ugly-looking tramp with a devil-may-
care air, who immediately asked Charley where
his companions were.

" My companions," Charley answered, " are the
birds of the air, the fishes of the river, and the
rabbits, squirrels, et cetera, of the woods." Infer-
ring from this that .Charley was alone, he demanded money, and received the following reply,·

" What are your principles, man, to demand
all a fellow has ? "

" I hain't no principles what won't take money,
which I must have," said the tramp.

" Don't you know that a man without principles
is like a ship without a rudder ? "

" I want yer money, and not yer gab."

" It is a great blessing to be poor, my little yonker," said Charley, very coolly and provokingly, scanning the tall, bony tramp from head to foot. "People who have money worry lest they lose it; whereas you don't have to hide your wallet when there is nothing in it."

"Are ye goin' ter hand over?" demanded the tramp savagely, taking a step forward.

"You must not hurry me," Charley replied, still calm and fearless. "Besides, I have a few remarks to make to you."

"Darn yer remarks," growled the tramp grinding his teeth.

"My remarks need no darning, but I'm afraid your character does. Those ugly holes in your soul should be mended at once."

"Your money or I'll——"

"One question, please; why not labor and earn money, if you want it?"

"That's my business," hissed the now exasperated tramp. "Fork over, or I'll smash yer mug fer ye."

"Call my face a mug!" exclaimed Charley, in well-feigned anger. "Money is trash; but defame my transcendentally lustrous countenance, and you defame me. Oh, you dry-boned villain! shall I rend you as the tiger rends its prey? I cannot restrain myself."

I was watching the tramp, who seemed bewildered at this sudden change of front; but thinking I saw a knife in his hand, I jumped out, and exclaimed, "What is the matter?"

"Oh! Elbert, hold me! hold me!" Charley

almost shrieked, " or I shall light on this vile blackleg, and tear him into a thousand shoe-strings."

" Hold me!", he yelled again, as I clasped him round the waist, while he jumped, and snapped his jaws, and clawed the air like a wild man.

" Run," said I to the tramp, "if you value your life, run; for I cannot hold him a minute longer."

The tramp edged off, and then took to his heels, his long, fiery-red hair flying behind him, and his loose garments bagging and flapping about his skeleton frame, as if he had just escaped from some graveyard, with avenging flames prematurely in hot pursuit. He was scarcely out of sight when we exploded with laughter, uncontrolled and uncontrollable, till we fell to the ground in sheer weakness. We made several attempts to rise, when something would be said to set us off again in another paroxysm of merriment. The picture of the flying tramp was so absurd we could not get it out of our minds, and it was a long time before we felt sufficiently sure of ourselves to strike tent and carry our luggage into the boat.

CHAPTER XXVI.

THE sail was uneventful to—, where we landed, and looked over the town; and then,
laying in a fresh supply of canned meats and other
imperishable articles of food, we dropped a little
farther down the river, and secured our boat in a
safe and obscure place. Here we used each other's
eyes as looking-glasses, and made ourselves as
presentable as possible, and then started in search
of the Thornton establishment, where we were to
dine. We found it with no great difficulty, and
Miss Thornton herself met us at the door, and
received us so pleasantly and cordially, that we at
once felt both at home and glad we had come.
We were ushered into a large parlor with open
fireplace and brass andirons, and roomy, old-fashioned furniture, made for comfort rather than
elegance, and in perfect keeping with the solid,
substantial appearance of the house outside.
When she excused herself for a few minutes,
Charley said, as she disappeared,

"There is no codfish about her."

"She is above that," I answered, "and has too
much brain to care for empty formalities."

"One of the aping kind," added Charley,
"would have let a servant give us our first intro-
duction to the interior of the home, even though
she might have been ready, waiting and watching,
with nothing to hinder her from opening the door
herself."

Miss Thornton returned with a rather short,
thickset, round-faced man, and introduced him as
her brother. He had not the easy grace of his
sister, but was as intellectual, and as frank and
hearty in his greetings, and we were at once on
very easy terms with him as well as with his sister.
Addressing me, he said :

" I feel somewhat acquainted with you, Professor
Bloomfield ; for I was one of a favored audience
that listened to you on a subject which interested
Theo, here, and myself very much indeed. I remember your face very distinctly and the general
drift of thought, and even some of the sentences
you favored us with that day."

"A few listeners like you, Mr. Thornton," I
said, " would be invaluable to any speaker."

" Perhaps I am not always a good listener,
Professor, but your subject, and the views you
presented, were just the kind of food I was hungry for; though I did not know I was so hungry
till you began to feed me, and then I saw I had
been starving for precisely that nourishment.
Had not the supply come as it did, and when it
did, I should have gone over into open and avowed
scepticism. And yet," he added, striking his fat
knee with waxing earnestness, " if you will believe

it. I heard church-members criticising you for
making Christianity so comprehensive and simple!
To come out into the sunlight of practical common
sense seemed to blind their unaccustomed eyes,
and their bantam religion fainted at the idea of
going into the struggles of every-day life, especially business. It left them no cloak of mystery to
shield them from the responsibilities which light
and knowledge bring. Like the Romish Church,
they would put out the light which loving and
profound research throws on the most important
subject engaging the human mind. Such persons
do an incalculable amount of injury. They repel
sensible men by misinterpreting Christianity.
They came near preventing me, by their imbecile
twaddle, from seeing any beauty, or nobility, or
helpfulness, in the religion of Jesus Christ. Can
such be Christians, Professor Bloomfield?"

"If you mean representative Christians, or
mature Christians, or intelligent, desirable Christians, I should answer in the negative."

"Can they be Christians in any sense?"

"I think we must admit the possibility, as there
are infantile Christians and mature Christians, the
intellectually wise and the intellectually foolish.
A person may have a little grace covered up under
a great amount of ignorance and superstition.
Unless we believe that, what shall we call some
of the Old Testament worthies,—to say nothing
of some New Testament professors of religion,—
and how shall we account for the salvation of **any**
dark-minded, present-day heathen?"

"Is there any sliding scale in the holiness of God to accommodate the low-down Christian?"

"Certainly not. God is perfect, immutably so, and needs not become less holy to reach the low-down ; for He comes to them by His compassion with instruction and help, and in the person of Jesus Christ, but the sliding scale must be with us, and must be upwards. We must be holy as He is holy, but it must be that a little grace will make us so ; for if the seed is in us it is holy and must do its work, though it be as small as a mustard seed."

"That will take time, and if Christians die in all stages of progress, how can they all go to one heaven?"

"So far as heaven is a state, they will not in my opinion."

"Do you believe in an intermediate state?"

"I do ; it is a matter of every-day experience."

"I don't think I understand you."

"I mean only that every progressive person is always in an intermediate state between what he leaves behind and what he is approaching."

"Oh! yes, certainly—ha! ha! There is no getting round that good sense. And you believe that will hold true of the next world?"

"Yes, in all worlds where there is progress."

"Will there be as many heavenly states, then, as there are individuals?"

"That seems to be about the way it is here, to state it strongly, and Jesus himself says, In My Father's house are many mansions."

"Will not differing degrees of perfection interfere with companionship?"

"It does not here, unless the difference is too marked. It is the good and bad that will not mix. Goodness everywhere tends to unite. There is such a thing as a perfect babe, as well as a perfect man, and the two are not inharmonious, but are rather drawn, the one to the other in love. Every one, it seems to me, will be happy in his own place, just where he is fitted to be, and for the time prefers to be, not to remain stationary, but to advance through all eternity, and it will be His delight to help every one else to advance. There can be no such thing as envy, because there will be nothing to envy, unless it be the love which each will feel towards one and all."

"The growth will be intellectual, will it not?"

"Every way that can enlarge and ennoble the personality; otherwise it could not be heaven, it seems to me."

"Then, to come back pretty close to my first question, Brother Bloomfield, is there any excuse for a Christian remaining in ignorance and superstition, and a consequent unprogressive state, where the advantages for study are so great as in a country like ours?"

"It would seem not."

"Is it not a too common fault among church-members that they do not sufficiently feel the inducements and urgency of growth in all spiritual knowledge for their own good and the acceptance of Christian principles by others? If they love

16

Christianity as they profess, they should try so to interpret it as to commend it to the intelligent judgment of mankind, and thereby extend its sway."

"Alas! I have to admit that likewise."

"It seems to me, Professor Bloomfield, that Christian knowledge lags behind every other knowledge."

"How about medicine, Mr. Thornton?"

"Medicine, I admit, is a little uncertain; physicians often have to strike at the disease in the dark, and many times hit the patient instead of the disease, owing to the fact that diseases are constantly being modified by heredity and complications with other diseases."

"Diseases are nearly as subtle and deceptive as sin with which Christianity has to contend."

There was a general laugh at this.

"Well," resumed Mr. Thornton, "if physicians sometimes kill the bodies of men, ignorant and shallow interpreters of Christianity do what is worse, they mangle, if they do not kill, the soul. In some things even medicine has reached the rock-bed of truth, and can be relied upon; and surgery and dentistry have each been reduced to a positive science. The natural sciences, too, are marching on with no uncertain tread, sweeping the fields clean of doubt so far as they go, relieving human labor and want, facilitating international and other communication, promoting social intercourse, and ameliorating the condition of mankind generally. Indeed, all knowledge is becoming more and more clear and positive except religion, which is taught as vaguely as ever. It has no clear, well-defined steps out of sin into holiness. Nowhere has it been reduced to a science in its methods of growth. If it had it would have done more for the world. Why has not Christianity produced more and grander specimens of manhood and womanhood?"

"Theological teachers are, perhaps, some at fault, and then it may arise in part from the fact that ministers are more intent on the conversion of their congregations than on their progress after conversion. Better Christians, however, would make preaching easier and more effectual."

"Yes, indeed, and in preaching to the unconverted they might improve vastly. They tell us to come to Jesus, and their converts get up in prayer-meeting and tell us to come to Jesus, but what they mean by it is not so clear, and they give the impression that they don't know themselves. The whole question of conversion, and especially how to overcome sin, and grow in all the graces belonging to a beautiful life, are too much, and it seems to me needlessly, in the fog. You are the only one who ever gave me any clear, steady light on these things. If men have felt certain things, and know they have, why can't they speak of their experience in that plain, candid way they would speak of their business? Why so loose and vague in religious matters, and so clear and definite in their ideas on other subjects? Is it because in the latter case they know what they

are talking about, and in the former they do
not?"

"As I intimated, I think preachers may be a
little at fault. Like priest, like people."

" If I could have my way, Professor Bloomfield,
I would wipe out every theological seminary in the
land."

" Why so, Mr. Thornton ? "

" Because I believe they turn out preachers with
their backs to the future and their faces to the
past. They mould them all, too, after one pattern, despoiling them of every original and natural
aptitude for the illustrative enforcement of their
ideas, and reducing them so nearly to machines
that they will run in denominational grooves, and
never get out unless thrown out by an earthquake, or some intellectual convulsion, and then
they scarcely get awake enough to see over
ancient and sectarian lines."

" Our theological seminaries may not encourage
independent thought and original methods as
much as they might safely, and doubtless might
give more time to the science of Christian living ;
but they are useful, I think, in their way, with all
their faults, and their destruction would not
remedy the defects you so strongly deprecate."

" I can only judge the seminaries by their
preachers, who come forth with their eyes either
turned inwards or reset in the back or their heads,
so that they are neither independent nor varied,
and can tell us nothing new how to make Christianity helpful in everyday life."

"That reminds me, Mr. Thornton, of what I have long felt would be a great step towards a much needed reform; and that is the establishment by wealthy laymen in our theological seminaries, of professorships on applied Christianity, especially on the science of character-building."

Miss Thornton here exchanged looks with her brother, and though interested before, appeared doubly so now, her dark eyes sparkling with delight, as if she was entertaining a new and welcome thought.

"The aim," I went on, "should be to make the process of reformation and development, by statement, argument and illustration, as clear and practical in all its steps as the building of a house, so that the dullest could see the way and walk therein. In short, the best and deepest thinking of the age should be turned to this most important of all subjects and, so, as far as possible, reduce to a science the method of building up the Christian character, or enlarging and ennobling Christian manhood and womanhood."

"It seems to me, Professor Bloomfield, you are just the one to give the first course of lectures on that subject," said Miss Thornton, looking at me a little timidly but eagerly.

"Yes," assented Mr. Thornton, "and if you will give such a course here next winter, we will relieve you of all care in the expense of publication."

"You are very kind indeed!" I exclaimed in surprise, "and I thank you very much; but I am comparatively a mere stripling, and not equal to the task. Older and abler men should lead off in a matter so momentous."

"Older men are not so well qualified to speak on such a subject as you are," Mr. Thornton asserted emphatically; "for you have thought of it, and they have not."

"Do not refuse," pleaded Miss Thornton shyly, and blushing in her earnestness. Not heeding my plea, they went on urging, till I could only look from one to the other, bewildered for a moment at their earnest persistency. At length, fearing their pressing desire might be a cry from their own hearts for help, I said:

"I find myself unable at present to refuse what is so cordially and generously asked, lest I be found closing my eyes and ears to a plain call of the Master. I can do nothing in preparation at present, but in the autumn, or as soon as I take up work again, I will consider it."

"The more you consider it, the more you must feel that duty calls you to this work, and I shall regard the matter as settled," said Mr. Thornton confidently.

"You will make our house your home during the lectures," said Miss Thornton, "and we shall look forward to your coming with a great deal of satisfaction, determined to be very unreconciled if you disappoint us;" and so saying she left the room, returning with Miss Horton, whom we met at the picnic the previous day.

We at once repaired to the dining-room under

the leadership of Mr. Thornton, Miss Thornton passing us along and following in the rear. A tiny wood-fire was burning in the fireplace, more for ornament than use, and the table was richly set with old-fashioned china and solid silver, and adorned with cut flowers in beautiful antique vases, and a button-hole bouquet tastefully arranged with each napkin. Miss Thornton presided with that easy grace which natural endowment and custom give, and did her full share in anticipating and filling any gap in the conversation by her ready wit, and suggestive questions. Charley was happy. It was just the meal he liked, and there was plenty of time to eat it; for it progressed with that delicate leisure which is the mark of good breeding and true culture.

Between courses we told some of our adventures down the river, Charley touching them off in high-comedy style, which produced much merriment. Mr. and Miss Thornton entertained us with vivid descriptions of neighboring scenery and incidents of travel, and Miss Horton confined herself mostly to giving queer and unexpected meanings to what was said.

We all ate heartily, but the slowness with which we ate, the good cheer with which we swallowed our food, and the laughter with which we pursued it, and finally the stroll we took in the flower-garden in the open air, at the suggestion of Miss Thornton, immediately after dinner, were the best guarantee against indigestion and the horrors of dyspepsia.

CHAPTER XXVII.

AFTER exploring the garden, the Thorntons and myself entered a pretty little summerhouse provided with comfortable rockers, and sat down, while Charley and Miss Horton were at the other end of the garden apparently satisfied with each other's company.

" Professor Bloomfield," asked Mr. Thornton, " to renew one point in the conversation we had before dinner, how do you account for the fact that so many so-called Christians exhibit nothing of the disposition of Christ ? "

" If they have not the spirit of Christ, they are none of His, according to Scripture. They are deceived by superstitious forms and technicalities empty of anything real. They are in the condition of the fellow I heard of in our civil war, who, as an answer to the question what company he belonged to, was boasting that Jesus Christ was the Captain of his salvation, when a soldier spoke up, ' Well, sir, all I have to say is, you are a long ways from headquarters ! ' "

" Pretty good ! pretty good ! ha, ha ! That soldier hit the case of a large proportion of

church-members, I'm thinking. Why, I have seen
them in their business meetings display as much
selfishness, and even bad temper, as any body of
worldly sinners."

" It is sadly true, Mr. Thornton, that too many
have so little of the love of God, as manifested in
Jesus Christ, that it does not control them steadily, and they drop down too easily out of the
love-life into their old, selfish, animal life."

" Many of them do not seem to have any love-
life except in prayer-meetings ; and that is what
kills the evidence, to many worldly-wise, that
Christianity has any power to make men better."

" Too true. Christians, and especially Christian
teachers, forget that it is perhaps just as important that the good be made better, as it is
that the bad be made good. If this be not true,
there is no explanation of the discipline of sorrow
that good men receive at the hand of Providence.
Besides, Jesus seems to urge the feeding of His
flock as strongly as their conversion. I have long
felt that the Christian world has waked up to only
half its duty ; and the neglected half is the study
of Christ. To know Him crucified is to have His
disposition, His self-sacrificing, charitable, and
loving spirit ; and the fruit of the Spirit, we are
told, is ' love, joy, peace, long-suffering (there is
a good deal of suffering in the world, but not
much long-suffering), gentleness, goodness, faith,
meekness, self-control,' or the government of all
the desires."

" How many Christians exhibit such fruit as that, Professor Bloomfield ? "

" Alas ! it might be difficult to find one, Mr. Thornton. If I had ten such to support me in Christian influence and service, I could build up a church without much urging of the gospel upon people. Those ten persons would make the gospel so attractive by their lives that the church-doors would be thronged by eager seekers."

" Yes, indeed ! and now if Christians are in earnest and can have this most effective way of drawing us by exhibiting the disposition of Christ in its beauty, why don't they have it and exercise it ? "

" It is owing partly to a want of knowledge how to proceed, this subject being little studied, and because conversion is held practically to be the only important thing. A person at conversion is said to be saved, and he looks upon himself as saved, and therefore does not feel the urgent need of anything more as he ought and would, if taught that, at conversion, he has only entered the school of Christ, and has everything to learn.

" I believe we are progressing towards the day when the whole gospel will be preached and practiced, as much as a part of it is now. The importance of growing up into the fulness of the stature of Christ must, and will be, explained and enforced, as well as conversion. Why, conversion is only the beginning of correct living ! When I send a ball into the air, the point where it turns to come back is the point of conversion, but how slow it moves at first ! and how fast it increases

in force till it strikes the earth! So a Christian,
once started in the divine life, should advance
with accelerated speed till the end comes here,
and then the angels will sing, Lift up your heads,
O, ye gates! and let this child of glory in. It is
indeed sad that the Master has no better representatives on the earth, but, slow as the progress is,
there has been progress, and the times are ripening, I believe, for a decided impetus to be given
in the right direction. There is a great yearning,
growing more and more widespread, for something
deeper and grander and more glorious than what
Christianity has thus far produced; and this
yearning is a prophecy that will have its fulfilment. It only needs, perhaps, some new Luther,
fired with an unquenchable zeal and an invincible
faith, to bring about a new and great reformation
hardly second in importance to the first. There
may be reformers before this reformation, as there
were before the first; but each apparent failure
will only help ripen the times, and prepare the
way for the appointed and successful Luther,
when he comes.

" The time has gone by, or is fast going by, when
a mere historical Christianity can satisfy. We
cannot rest upon the past. We crave and need a
present Christ, and a living, forceful Christianity.
What can Christianity do *now*? is the great test
question, and it must be answered by living examples. Will the examples be forthcoming? I
have not the least doubt of it. Christianity, to-
day even, is better taught and better lived than

ever before, however discouraging some things
may appear ; and a higher, broader, deeper, truer
kingdom of heaven is at hand. The creed of the
future will be a pledge to prayerfully pattern
after the loving disposition of Christ, and to
strive everywhere and always to exemplify the
fruit of the Spirit."

"Professor Bloomfield, the fact that you see
all the defects I see, and perhaps more, and still
have confidence in Christianity, gives me encouragement to hope and believe ; but another
difficulty stands in my way. Could not the
ordinary prayer-meeting be made more sensible
and helpful?"

" Undoubtedly, Mr. Thornton."

" I ask because at the last one I attended, the
whole meeting was nothing but sentimental brag
from beginning to end, and it was no great exception to the others I have attended. One said, I
love Jesus ; and another, Jesus loves me ; and
another, I am pressing on towards the kingdom ;
another, I am washed and made clean ; another, I
am saved—come, poor sinner, and be saved too,
and so on ; not one helpful idea for the conflicts
of life ; and I came away feeling that I had been
feeding on husks ! Can God be pleased with such
unseemly self-assertion? If they had told their
experience in the battle with sin, I might have
carried away something from the meeting. I like
emotion, but not pumped-up emotion. Why
should not the best thought be put into worship,
Professor Bloomfield?"

" Religious subjects are certainly worthy of all the thought we can put into them, whether in the prayer and conference meeting, or elsewhere ; but we must bear in mind that all Christians are not capable of much thought, and the weak ones should not be discouraged from expressing, as best they may, the religious life that is in them ; for life without expression, like the tree which puts forth no new shoots, soon dies. By full and free expression the weak Christian may grow and become strong ; but, while the little ones should be fostered and cheered on their way, the high aim of the prayer-meeting need not and should not be sacrificed. The leader should not confine the meeting to babes.

" Those of experience, who have something to say, and know how to say it, are needed for the instruction and help of all, and should be the controlling spirits, the younger and more emotional coming in to give freshness and variety and impetus to the meeting. Every class of gifts, however halting, has its uses, and will help somebody, and should be encouraged ; but, as before intimated, the thoughtful should see to it that they contribute something helpful and inspiring, so that the people may go away with their emotions distended with ideas to think about during the week.

" The trouble is, one talks without thinking, another thinks without talking, and those who both think and talk, are few. Persons who do not think, have little or no appreciation of the

value of thought ; and yet, there is nothing more
substantial, and lasting, more fraught with the
possibilities of germinative and procreative power
than a live thought, especially a Christian thought
We are not making the best use of the prayer-
meeting ; it should be more of an experience
meeting, more of a school for study of the means
of grace, for comparing Christian exercises and,
methods of overcoming the world, or selfish tendencies,—a meeting of mutually helpful sympathy,
and prayerful yearning to be made worthy of
being useful to others, as we have opportunity."

" How would it do to give out subjects beforehand, such as, how to conquer a bad temper, to
resist temptation and overcome sin in the heart,
to become conscious of acceptance with God and
of His constant indwelling, etc.?"

" I think the giving out of such very important
subjects occasionally would be an admirable plan,
tending to spiritual growth, if Christians would
give them hard, earnest, prayerful study, and then
come to meeting in a teachable mood, and compare
their varied views and experiences of the matter
in hand, the pastor, perhaps, at the close, summing
up the different helpful thoughts and suggestions,
so that the members could easily grasp and carry
them away. Our church covenant meetings, especially, might be made more of a school for the
study of Christian experiences, both successes and
failures; more of a waiting on God, and learning
of Him, and so be more helpful, uplifting, and inspiring means of grace. At any rate, something

must be done to lead the church into higher
Christian living, so that it can preach the gospel
more effectually than it does now ; for the first
step in reforming others is to reform ourselves,
whether it be Christian reformation or any other."

Mr. Thornton here spoke slowly, thoughtfully,
and with a good deal of feeling :—

" I should like to be a member of a real school
of Christ ; for that is what I deeply need. I could
not join as an ornament, but merely as a learner.
My great desire is not so much to be saved as to
be fit to be saved, to be accounted worthy, not
merely by men, but by God, who sees down into
the centre and core of the heart. I wish to be of
use in the world by partaking of the character and
manhood of Jesus of Nazareth."

" My dear Thornton," I said, warmly clasping
him by the hand, " you are just the kind of man
God wants in His service to-day. Men are needed
who seek Christianity, not as a screen from eternal
fire, but as a transforming power that shall make
them so pure that fire will find nothing in them to
burn. How much you would help Dr. Blentwood,
if a member of his church ! You strengthen my
belief that God is moving in the direction in which
I think and feel so much, and that some time I shall
have the sympathy of the best Christian minds."

" I do not see how any Christian can fail to feel
the desirability of having your views prevail."

" Ah ! you little know how hard it is to move
the Christian world in any new direction, and how
suspicious even good men are of any change.

Why, even Dr. Blentwood has been accused of Unitarianism because he presses the importance of Christian character!"

" What! are they so narrow as to reject a truth because held by another denomination? I wonder they do not go barefoot because infidels wear shoes!"

" The fact, I suspect, is that Dr. Blentwood disturbs the self-complacency of church-members by preaching to them; whereas the gospel, in their view, means preaching to sinners. This is another proof that the church is not wholly sanctified, and therefore needs preaching to. And then, there is such a thing as a depressing, repressing fear of getting out of old lines of thought and action, which deprive men of that breadth of judgment and teachableness of spirit so essential to the appreciation of anything at all new, though it be but an old truth in a new light.

" But, to recur to what you said, there is, undoubtedly, an unreasoning prejudice in most minds against any truth held by an opposing denomination, perhaps because they think it is in bad company. If the early Protestants did not go barefoot because Roman Catholics wore shoes, they rejected almost everything else practised by them. They would not even have Scripture quotations on the walls back of their pulpits because, they said, it savored of popery. But, ever since, Protestantism has been going back after truths left behind in the Romish Church. Dr. Robinson used to say that, to stand alone, a bag must have something in it, at least straw or stubble; and so every sect, however heterodox, must have some truth in it or it would collapse."

"Professor Bloomfield, if church-members were all like you, I could not stay out of the church."

"Dear Brother Thornton, I am grateful for your appreciation; but remember, if the church were all to your liking, it would not need you so much as it does now. Isn't it a part of your mission to help the church up to the true standard? And, moreover, is it not your imperative duty to put your influence where it will tell for the right? If God has been working on your heart, is it not your privilege as well as duty to proclaim it before the world, and buckle on the armor in His cause?"

"I have not thought of it in just that way, but, as much as I dislike to come in contact with bigoted people, if I knew I was a Christian, I would not hesitate."

"Do you desire with your whole being to have the kingdom of heaven set up within you?"

"I do, and would do anything to secure it."

"Then you will be willing to pray with me; and you, Miss Thornton, I know, will join us, for you are only waiting, like your brother. There is enough here to claim the promise, the special one, I mean. Let us unite our hearts on the one thing at hand."

We then and there knelt down in the little summer-house, and my prayer, with choking utterance, was followed by touching petitions, with a

17

full surrender of their hearts, from both brother and sister; and when we arose a new light was shining in their eyes, for their tears were tears of joy. They had become conscious that they loved God and were members of His spiritual family; and, when seated again, we clasped hands in our mutual gladness, and sang with overflowing hearts, " Praise God from whom all blessings flow."

CHAPTER XXVIII.

THE DYING TRAMP.

AT the first pause in our singing a ragged, unkempt, barefooted boy looked in upon us very much out of breath, and in a scared manner said, looking at Mr. Thornton, " Please, sir, paup is killed and wants ter see ye, and have ye bring a man what knows what God thinks."

" Who are you ? " asked Thornton.

" I am paup's boy."

" Well, who is paup ? "

" Paup is the ole man, my dad, what struck marm this mornin', and then got struck his own se'f with er derrick, an'—an' he's awful sorry, sir, he is."

" What is your name ? "

" My name's Bill Durgin, and paup tole me ter come fer ye, 'cause you'd been kind ter 'im."

" Oh ! you live over in the hollow, near the brook ? "

" Yeah, and paup and marm's in a awful hurry fer ye ter come."

Mr. Thornton jumped up, saying, " Will you go with me, Brother Bloomfield ? "

" Certainly," said I, and we were off im-

mediately in a direct line across field, and were
soon at the door of a rough-looking shanty. We
entered without knocking, and saw lying on a
clean, but scanty bed, a large, coarse-featured
man, whom I recognized as Charley's would-be
robber! Remorse had evidently sunk both beak
and talons deep into his soul. He had a wild,
untamed, out-door look, like that of an eagle
brought down suddenly to earth, and deprived
for the first time of its freedom. Animal-like and
uncouth as he was, there was something all the
more pathetic in his look, as the first sorrow,
probably, of his life, went hotly surging through
all the range of his meditations. As we approached, he looked up, and Mr. Thornton asked :

"What is the matter, Durgin ?"

"Oh, Mr. Thornton, I'm killed, and a darn
fool—that's what's the matter."

"Have you had a physician?"

"Yas, where I got hurt; but what I want ter
know, Mr. Thornton, is, what God does with darn
fools. He don't want 'em foolin' round Him, I
s'pose, and if He puts 'em in kettles over the
fire, and biles 'em, as I've seen the picter of, and
has the devil's dance round 'em with sharp pitch-
forks ter keep 'em in, I don't see what good'll
that do—do you, Mr. Thornton ? 'Twon't bile the
fool out of um, will it ?"

"No, that is not the way God makes men
wise ; but why do you call yourself a fool ?"

"'Cause I *is* one, worse'n wicked, fer I tried
ter rob a man this mornin', and 'cause I couldn't,

I came hum mad, and knocked Polly down, and then went ter Jones's, and hadn't been ter work five minutes afore God'lmighty knocked me down for my cussedness; and Polly says they brought me hum, and here I is killed! I'd been drinking a leetle too much. Oh! O—h!"

" When you struck your wife, Durgin, you struck the best friend you have, and without reason, too."

" Reason! does a darn fool want a reason fer doin' anythin'?"

" Perhaps not."

" No p'raps 'bout it. Look at that air Polly, and see ef ye can find any reason fer hittin' her, 'cept the reason of a fool what's got no reason."

Polly began to cry.

" Gods' agin me, Pol! ef ye'll hit me with ther poker, it'll do me a heap o' good."

" Yer didn't mean ter, Jim."

" Yer too good! Pol, don't say that. Why don't yer throw ther tongs at me, and maul me with the mop and fire-shovel? That'd make things more kinder squar', and I'd feel better. Oh, Pol! Oh, Mr. Thornton! I've been the plaguetakest fool ye ever laid eyes on, and what's God goin' ter do with me? What's ther use o' fools, anyway? All ther devil can use me fer is ter make fun of, and I'm 'fraid he'll carry his fun too fer. Nobody wants me fer any good."

" I want ye, paup."

" Pol! Pol! ef ye'd broomstick me hard on the face, ye'd comfort me some. Yer goodness is what leaves me without underpinin'. Oh, Jim Durgin!"—addressing himself in great agony—"yer fool you! yer empty-headed numbskull! yer never got any sense till God'lmighty knocked it inter ye with ther derrick. Yer debts are mountain high, and ye've nothin' ter pay with, yer tarnal idyut! Oh! Mr. Thornton, what shall I do?"

"Mr. Durgin," Thornton replied, "I have brought you Professor Bloomfield, a wise and good Christian, who will advise you better than I can."

"Wise and good, eh?" said the injured man, turning his eyes upon me. "Yer must feel mighty tickled not ter be a fool like me."

"A wise man once said," I answered "'If all fools wore white caps, we should seem a flock of geese.'"

"He thought 'em pooty thick, did he? None of um such fools 's I've been though, and ef they be, I don't want none o' their comp'ny, for I'm sick of myself. Ugh! ef my soul should bust, what a mess! What can God do with a man, what ain't satisfied ter be what he is?"

"He can make him wise unto salvation."

"What d'yer say?"—trying to rise on his elbow, and his face brightening.

"If you are truly sorry for your past life, and with all your heart wish to be a good man, God can convert you, and make you fit for the company even of angels."

"I'd be too mighty big a job for that, wouldn't I?"

"He has declared through His Prophets, and through His Son, Jesus Christ, who revealed Him

more clearly still, that whosoever will may come
and have real, true, divine life like that of God
Himself ; and ' whosoever ' means you, wicked as
you have been."

" Me ! " His whole frame shook with eagerness
as he added, " Kin yer 'splain how 't could be
done ? "

" Before Molly bakes her bread, she puts something into the dough to make it rise, does she
not ? "

" Yas, emptin's."

" Well, God can put His love, His divine life
into your soul, and make it rise into likeness with
Him, eventually killing out all the weeds of sin."

" How'll I squar' the 'count for ther ole fool I've
been ? "

" Your folly will be remembered no more
against you ; for you will become a new creature,
old things passing away, and all things becoming
new, and you will have nothing but love for God
and everybody, and everybody nothing but love
for you."

" I ain't it too late when a man's killed ? "

" He will take you now, just as you are, if you
sincerely repent, and crave forgiveness, and give
yourself wholly to Him."

" Oh, there's nothin' but ther fag-end of me left !
and ain't it mean ter give Him that ? "

" It is mean not to have given Him all your
life ; but it is meaner still, if that be possible, not
to give Him what little life you have left.   God, as
revealed in Jesus Christ, is full of tenderness, self-

sacrifice, and compassionate, helpful love, and is waiting to begin a new life within you, to save you; and you ought not to lose a moment of time in giving Him all your gratitude and all your love."

" That's so, whatever He does ter me, hain't it, Mr. Thornton ? "

" Certainly," Mr. Thornton replied, "you owe everything to Him."

" And ther way I've been payin' Him is actin' like a pesky, tarnation fool all my born days ! "

" Please don't use such harsh language."

" Why, good man, shouldn't I be hash' on myself? fer I hain't hit myself half hard 'nough yet. Why not call things what they is ? "

" Well, I would rather hear you say you are very, very sorry for your past wicked life, and that you would give everything you have and are to become a good Christian man, such as God would have you."

" Good man alive ! sorry ain't no name for it ; it's too dogonned tame !"

" Then, do you not desire above all things to get rid of all that past life that you now so hate ? "

" Hang it, good man ! I'd get inter one o' them air devil's kittles and be biled, if they could bile ther dang stuff outer me; but they can't, can they ? "

" No, punishment cannot make a new man of you; God alone can do that through your repentance."

"Wall, I wanter do what'll make ther 'count square."

"The account is square already," said Miss Thornton, coming in from the open door, where she had hesitated a moment, and overheard the last words of the dying man.

"Oh, Lady Thornton! you've helped us out many times, and given Molly fine things, and paid her too fer workin', and so you're all right; but how can ther 'count be square with me?"

"Jesus died," she replied, "and paid every debt you owe, and all you have to do is to believe, and give your heart to Jesus."

"Then I've got ter pay Him, and what's ther dif?"

"He asks no pay but your love. He paid the debt, because He knew you could not."

"I will though; fer I've skinned my way long 'nough from other folks, and I'm goin' it squar now, ef it kills me. Ef He won't let me work out my tax fer Him, I'll go down and squirm it out with t'other chap, till He says it's square."

Miss Thornton, perplexed, looked at me beseechingly, and then went over to comfort Molly.

"Mr. Durgin," I resumed, "the only way for you to pay your debts is by obedience to God's commands, and He commands you to give Him your heart that He may love it into life. He pities you with an infinite pity, and has declared in Jesus, His Son, that He will forgive and forget all your past sins, and let you begin life anew, making you His child by giving you of his Spirit,

iove and wisdom, if you will only give yourself
entirely into His hands, and submit wholly to
Him, who knows just what you need, and better
than you can ask or think. Remember, Mr.
Durgin, it is the one you owe God Himself, who
is waiting to forgive the debt."

" Oh, I thought Lady Thornton said Jesus paid
it."

" Jesus revealed God's willingness to forgive ;
it is God, in Jesus Christ, who accepts you, and
declares the debt off the moment you sincerely
ask it. If you could make the past and yourself
right before God, you would not need Him as a
Helper and Saviour."

" That's so, tru's yer live, by hokey ! My ole tough
skull begins ter crack open a bit, and let in ther
light. I see God's got ter take me as I be, ef He
takes me at all, and Oh ! Oh ! what a mess o' poor
stuff He'll find in me !"

" I think I see your difficulty," said Mr. Thornton. " You find it hard to believe that God can
forgive so bad a man as you have been."

" That's it, Mr. Thornton ; I've been worse'n
pusley."

" And yet God sees something in you to love."

" Somethin' in me ter love ! Did yer say that,
Mr. Thornton ?"

" Yes, and has proved that He loves you by
sending His Son into the world to reveal it. He
has a heart large enough, and loving enough, to
take you just as you are, with all your selfishness,
and, adopting you into the family of His Son,

make you a worthy child in the great household
of the good, and a partaker of His glory."

" Oh ! this is all too good ter be true, hain't it,
Mr. Bl—Bloomfield?" said the trembling man,
with all the eagerness and half joy of a struggling
hope.

" It is God's truth," I replied.

" Oh ! is God so good as that? That is the
God I want. Oh, talk with Him, Mr. Bloomfield !
and tell Him I want Him ter make me good
right off. Tell Him I'm good fer nothin', but
want ter be forgiven, and do jest as He says. I
want ter be a little child agin, His child, and
mind Him in everything. Oh ! do try mighty
hard fer me, wont yer, Mr. Bloomfield, right off
now ? "

We all knelt down by his bed in united prayer.
He interrupted me by saying, " Tell Him how
sorry I am fer everything, and want Him ter take
care o' Polly." Afterwards, he placed his hand
on mine saying, " Put my hand inter His, and
ask Him ter lead me, 'cause I don't know, much,
and ter hole on tight, and I'll foller Him
anywhere," soon adding, " There ! that's it. Now
I've got safe holt. Thank Him, and tell Him
Jim Durgin's all His—all His."

When we arose, he opened his eyes, and the
tears for the first time rolled down his bony
cheek ; but they were tears we were glad to see,
for his face had lost not only the hunted, wild
look of an animal at bay, but all its painful expression, and soon it was all aglow with happy

resignation, and the joy of a mind at peace, while we sung at his request :

"I am so glad that my Father in Heaven
Tells of His love in the Book He has given."

At the close he said, " It's growin' dark. Polly, come and take holt my tother hand. There, you must be glad ther derrick hit me Pol, fer I never had no sense afore, and might never seen ye on t'other side. Don't cry, good Pol. Mr. and Lady Thornton, will ye look arter Polly a little?"

" She shall go home with us, if she will," both replied in a breath.

" Do yer hear that, Pol? And by-and-bye I'll come fer ye over there, where the light is, and where ther white ones are walkin' in the mist by ther river, and we'll be tergether agin, and happy, 'cause I won't be bad ter ye any more. I'll make it all square then. Don't cry, Pol; fer ye'll be better off now. How dark 'tis! Polly! I can't see yer, Pol. Speak ter me. Did yer speak, Pol? Good Pol, I'll come back fer ye. I'll do my best fer ye. Happy days comin,' Pol. Ther waves are comin' in! There! I'm driftin' out. Good-bye, Pol. I'm driftin' out—driftin—out."

The voice had died down to a whisper, and now naught was heard save the sobbing of poor Polly on the pulseless hand clasped in hers. James Durgin, let us trust, had "drifted" away to a safe harbor on the other side, though his body lay wrecked and dead on this shore.

The forgiving Polly could not be induced to leave her sad home until after the funeral, when she took up her permanent abode, as servant, in the home of the Thorntons.

CHAPTER XXIX.

IN THE THORNTON PARLORS.

WHEN we returned the setting sun was sending along the surface of the ground long shafts of dull fire, causing the shadows to dart grotesquely in and out among the trees, and, seeing no one in or about the summer-house, we repaired to the parlors, where we found Charley was being highly entertained by Miss Horton at the piano— to whom we explained our unceremonious absence, an absence, barring the cause, apparently very gratifying to them.

It was too late to renew our journey, and Charley and I were easily persuaded to spend the night with the Thorntons. Besides, Mr. Thornton wished to have further conversation with me on certain subjects lying near his heart.

After tea we gathered in a circle for serious talk.

"That man," said Thornton, referring to James Durgin, "just began to live as he began to die ; and he furnishes an apt illustration of what we were talking about before dinner. As your remarks implied, something more than place is requisite for perfect happiness, and as this is corroborated by experience, which teaches that two persons may live in one room, the one happy and the other miserable, and, therefore, since the man who just begins to live on his death-bed cannot go straight, or immediately, to the same heaven or state of bliss with the man who has lived all his life a growing Christian, and ripened into the very spirit and disposition of Christ, and consequently, since he must commence somewhere at the foot of the ascending scale the question arises, Is his happiness complete?"

"To the limit of his capacity, I should say; but that he must suffer loss, in comparison with one who has an abundant entrance into heaven, is clear, not only from such passages as 1 Cor. 3 : 15, and 2 Pet. 1 : 11, but from reason as well. Jesus' 'many mansions' and Paul's 'seventh heaven' plainly indicate a diversity, and a gradation of blissful conditions. Whoever puts off beginning to live, as Christ explained life, loses ground with every day's delay. Does this view disturb you, Mr. Thornton?"

"On the contrary, it strengthens my faith, because it appeals to my reason and sense of justice. To preach the opposite, that all Christians, when they die, go at once to exactly the same state of bliss, seems to me a most immoral and pernicious doctrine. It makes salvation a mere technical, red-tape affair, in no way dependent on character, or a living, transforming faith. If a death-bed Christian is as good as a lifelong Christian, there is no such thing as growth."

" And we know, Brother Thornton, that growth is as much a law of spiritual life as of natural life. God does not make a great saint out of a great sinner all at once by any sudden, almighty stroke ; He converts and grows him, if I may use a southern expression, though we must bear in mind, that with some the conversion is deeper, broader, fuller than with others, and may be so pervasive and all-controlling as to bring about a more wondrous change in a shorter space of time. One person may experience in a day more of the love of God, as manifested in Jesus Christ, than another in a year, simply because of greater thoroughness of consecration. To illustrate, it takes the master of a vineyard a whole season to ' grow ' his grapes before he can express the juice, ferment, and convert it into wine, and even then it requires age to make good wine ; but at the marriage feast Jesus compressed the whole process into a few moments. So it is not for us to say how much may be done towards changing a man's character even on a death-bed ; but this does not annul the great fact, that every day's delay in beginning a true life is so much time wasted, and whoever wastes time that way commits the most stupendous folly, both as regards happiness here and hereafter."

" Brother Bloomfield, you have helped me so much ! and now for another point ; for I am greedy for ideas. I believe in Jesus Christ, but not in everything proclaimed as Christianity. I wish to be an honest, unprejudiced searcher after truth, avoiding both credulity and scepticism. Now I wish to ask on which side does the most danger lie—on that of believing too much, or doubting too much?"

"It is more dangerous, I think, friend Thornton, to doubt than to believe. The darkest state a man can be in, is to doubt everything, and suspect everybody. We must believe in many things we cannot absolutely know."

"Why must we?"

"Because much truth rests on the authority of persons better informed than ourselves."

"Please name one."

"Well, your parents knew you to be their child; but how do you know it?"

"It never occurred to me to doubt it."

"Just so, friend Thornton; you accepted the truth handed down to you, and that acceptance has been a great blessing both to you and your parents. In loving them as your parents when alive, and their memory as such since death, you have proved that the heart is a better guide in matters of the heart than the head. The heart has its own proofs, which are more satisfactory than those which appeal mainly to the head."

"You would say that the head or intellect is chiefly to be relied upon in searching for truth, would you not?"

"Yes, in searching, perhaps; but it takes the heart to see it when found, and to feel it, appreciate it, and apply it. Belief in spiritual truth does not rest so much on demonstration as on that intuition which comes from sympathy and

18

kinship with the truth, its inner harmony and beauty. Jesus said what we know to be true, when He said, Blessed are they who have not seen and yet have believed. Many reject the truth, because they do not wish it to be true, having no affinity for it, no inner appreciation and spiritual insight into it, and therefore are wanting in the highest attainment of the soul."

" Should anything be accepted as truth, which cannot stand the test of reason?"

" I think not, though some things are beyond our reason at present, as, for example, how trees grow. We only know that they grow. But I think the deepest truths of God make their appeal directly to the spirit of man."

" Without credentials?"

" Without external credentials; they carry conviction in themselves."

" But you would say, would you not, Professor Bloomfield, that every faculty and power of the mind should be exercised to its utmost in the search after truth?"

" Most assuredly. It is a sacred duty, God-given, and if obeyed there would be less opinionated and uncharitable men in the world ; for then they would see that their opinions are worth just as much as their reasons for them, and no more. The proper spirit is to be ever willing to go over to the side of truth, the moment the truth is found not to be with you. The honest searcher will seek to know things just as they are. It is a most salutary thing to commit one's self to the truth, and follow it regardless of consequences, never fearing that truth is in danger, but that he alone is in danger, who clings to his *opinions* with an unsubmissive, unteachable spirit. It is that utter *abandon* to the truth, whether it leads to, or from, one's creed, which gives inspiration and a true uplift to the soul, and is the test of loyalty to God and one's own faculties or personality."

"Then, there are a good many disloyal ones, I fear," said Charley, who had been an attentive listener; "for the most I talk with seem to think as much, at least, of their opinions or creed as they do of the truth."

"Of course," I continued, "a revelation from God presupposes something to be revealed, and, with our utmost study, there will always be mystery enough, even after we have studied thousands and thousands of years in heaven; for the more we know the more we shall see that we do not know; but the man who fails to search with all his might for truth, that he may be able to give a reason for the hope that is within him, is either sinfully negligent of duty, or is too weak-minded to know what duty is."

"Yes, and the man who does not endeavor, concientiously and prayerfully of course, to clear his sky of the fog of mystery and let in the sunshine of knowledge, has no right to decry or criticise the creed of the man who has so endeavored, in my opinion," said Thornton.

Charley clapped his hands, and Miss Thornton asked :

" Do you not think the spirit of denunciation in the war of creeds arises largely from the tendency to identify truth with one's opinions, thereby precluding that teachableness so essential both to charity of judgment and to advancement ? "

"Undoubtedly most people find it one of the hardest and most humiliating tasks of their lives to feel obliged to give up their cherished opinions, and we all know that without teachableness no one can learn. This is why Jesus told His disciples, if they would be great, they must become as a little child. Mary, you remember, who sat teachable at the feet of her Lord, pleased Him more than Martha, who, more assertive, thought she knew what Jesus wanted without asking Him."

" That reminds me of a dispute I once heard, over the respective merits of these two sisters," Charley remarked.

"Which do you think most of, Mr. Lightheart?" asked Miss Horton, laughing to conceal her eagerness.

" As my friend Bloomfield knows, I am very fond of a big feed, and so I should prefer Martha before dinner, and then Mary after dinner," Charley replied, trying to look sober, casting, at the same time, a quizzical glance towards Carrie Horton.

" That's just like a man ! " exclaimed Miss Horton with a demure little pout.

Charley drew a long breath with a face expressing such an odd mixture of drollery and mystification that a general laugh ensued.

"Which," asked Mr. Thornton, looking at me, "do you think is the leading motive to study, doubt or belief?"

"I should say, belief; for, though we doubt when the foundations of a supposed truth begin to crumble, we still believe there are real foundations somewhere, or we would not study to find them. The sailor drops the lead of inquiry only when he believes himself in hopeful soundings. Belief, also, is courageous and steady, while doubt is uncertain and wavering."

"Yes, but I was thinking of those who believe a dogma to be true merely because old, but I fear even there doubt would not lead them to study; for they are so wed to custom, that they prefer to hug the shore of their own little harbor, though reeking with the polluted waters of tradition, rather than strike out for an independent voyage of discovery on the great ocean of Truth."

"Independent thinkers are few, friend Thornton. That men prefer to be led, rather than lead, you will notice at church, when the congregation sometimes does not rise until the singing of the hymn commences, because waiting one for another. This love of conformity is a good thing where it does not enslave the heart and brain, and shut up one's sympathies and thinking within certain ruts, as it did the Jews."

"But there the trouble lies," said Miss Thornton thoughtfully. "The moment you question inherited ideas the unprogressives assume an antagonistic attitude, and so render themselves incapable of learning. Only a few days ago a person in my hearing expressed a fear that modern investigations might undermine some of the great truths of Christianity, proving that it was not truth that he loved, but what he had been accustomed to regard as truth, or his version of it. If he loved the truth, he should be glad to see error uprooted and sloughed off, however hard to give up traditional forms."

"Such people are too comfortably settled in their ideas," added Charley, "to like to be disturbed. They are like the sluggard, who lies abed till the sun is high in the heavens, because it requires a little sacrifice to get out of a warm nest."

"Like me for instance," said Miss Horton giggling, and Charley, from sympathy or politeness or some stronger motive, added a remark, which made us all merry for a few minutes, but the discussion was continued a few minutes longer.

"I suppose," said Miss Thornton, "we must hold that bigoted people are conscientious, and though that does not make their views right, is not their conscience their guide as well as ours?"

"Yes," I replied, but there is a question back of that—how came they by their unenlightened conscience? A dark conscience may justify dark deeds."

"Should not a person obey his conscience, good or bad?" she asked again.

"What else can he do? His guilt lies not in obeying his conscience, but perhaps in not obeying it in previous years. His prime duty is to be teachable and learn."

"Is it not enough to be conscientious?" Miss Horton ventured to ask.

"No, not enough. We need to be intelligent, keenly sensitive to truth and goodness, and quick to discern them, and those who will not learn assume a fearful responsibility."

"I suppose," Mr. Thornton remarked, "it is because religious truth is of so grand a character, so highly important, and so sacred, that gross and belittling conceptions of it appear so repulsive. Only think of the hideous religious bigotry that would kill a man to save his soul, so often exhibited towards early Protestantism!"

"Why do you think," Charley asked, "that these perverted consciences have not always been followed studiously and faithfully?"

"There is nothing," I answered, "that shrivels and warps the conscience like disobedience to its still, small voice. Some minds, by continued faithlessness, have became so crooked that no truth can get into them without being twisted beyond recognition; and others are conscientious only in spots and on occasion, and therefore exhibit Quixotic notions of truth and transcendental behavior."

"Goethe tells us," said Miss Thornton, "'tis much easier to meet with error than to find truth; error is on the surface, truth is hidden in great depths; and the way to seek does not appear to all the world."

"True, Miss Thornton, but people lose their way, because they do not wait and watch for truth in a teachable attitude of mind; it is so easy to dismiss an objectionable or uncomfortable idea without patiently and prayerfully listening to what it has to say. Jesus says, in John 7 : 17, If any man will (desires to) do His will, he shall know of the doctrine. It is faithful, persistent, unprejudiced, actual seeking that finds."

CHAPTER XXX.

THE large, old-fashioned, cuckoo clock, which stood in a corner of the rear parlor in which we were sitting, struck the hour of eight, and Mr. Thornton said :—

"It is hard to leave this feast of fat things, but I hope you will excuse me for an hour's absence to look after the interests of poor Polly Durgin. Her husband was of little worth to her while living, but she doubtless feels now, that if he could be restored to her, he would be all that her early imagination had pictured."

With these words he left, and I remarked to Miss Thornton, "You have an excellent and true-hearted brother, and I find myself much drawn to him."

"Yes," she replied, "he is generous, kind, and true. His roughness is all external, like the outside of a bird's nest, which, you know, explains its meaning and beauty to those only who look inside."

"Your beautiful illustration, Miss Thornton, reminds me that life in general is not specially attractive, until we find its meaning."

"That will account, perhaps, for the fact that my life is not very attractive to me."

"Why, Miss Thornton! have you not found the meaning of your life yet?"

She dropped her eyes, and then, as Charley and Miss Horton, who had retired to the front parlor, commenced a duet on the piano, she looked up and answered pensively:

"I am afraid not, but I would like so much to find it."

"I both hope and believe you will; for, as a writer has well said, Life is so beautiful and symmetrical when you only get hold of the right clue. To quarrel with one's fate is not to understand it; and it seems to me you have so much to be thankful for, so much to live for!"

"I certainly have no reason to quarrel with mine, so far as money and friends are concerned, and yet I am not content, not happy as I should be, if I knew I was doing the work assigned me to do. Don't you think" (and this she asked with much earnestness) "that it is the privilege of every one to know he or she is fulfilling a mission?"

"I think one can feel sure of trying to do it. Perhaps you are looking too far off for your mission, not near enough to your home and surroundings. A mission does not necessarily imply some great, or exceptional thing. If it did, how few of us could have a mission!"

"I have done but little more than manage a household."

"If you have done that so well that you have

made home happy, as I know you have, and inspired your servants to lift up their minds and hearts towards a better life, you have had a mission."

" Do you mean to say, Professor Bloomfield, that there is a God-given mission in doing necessary, every-day duties?"

" I do. There is, or should be, a heavenward end to even the commonest, secular duties. Whether a mission is noble or not depends on the spirit one puts into it. In God's eyes it is not so much what we do, as how we do it."

" Yes, but my work is so transient, so ephemeral!"

" Even a cup of cold water, given to the thirsty with a loving spirit, is an act that can never die. On the other hand, the greatest deed done without soul, without love, perishes, so far as the doer of the deed is concerned. So, Miss Thornton, your work may outlive that of those you now feel inclined to envy."

" How can I do the commonplace things of a housekeeper, Professor Bloomfield, and feel that I am doing an immortal work?"

" Well, you can dignify, and even glorify, housekeeping by looking upon it with the eye of a Christian artist, and love it so much that you cannot but be cheerful and happy, and make others cheerful and happy also. You may turn even the humdrum of every-day life into poetry, though you cannot write it, and feel that you are sweetening life, your own and others, and doing something towards character-building, which shall last forever. The drudge and slave is one who does her work mechanically, without heart, and thus brings discomfort to herself and those with whom she comes in contact."

"I feel deeply the force and beauty of your words, Professor Bloomfield, and can see the great amount of self-victory required to fill even the humblest sphere aright; but I feel the weight of other and new responsibilities, the responsibilities which accompany the possession of a fair amount of wealth. I wish to do the best possible service with it; and yet I have had the control of my property nearly a year without learning what my mission with it is."

There was a tremor in her voice, and I saw she was feeling more than her words indicated. Too self-depreciating, I thought, and tried to reassure her.

"You have done more good, Miss Thornton, than you think; for I know you have not failed to do the nearest duties, and the little charities, as they have been made known to you, to say nothing of the delightful home you have made for all dwellers under your roof, transient or permanent."

"I have done all these so far as I know, and helped make up deficiencies, and replenish empty treasuries; but I would like to do a more special and distinctive work, where I could see the good effects springing up about me, and know it to be a needed work."

"Have you an idea, Miss Thornton, of the kind of work you feel called upon to do?"

"Only in a nebulous way. I need some one to draw pictures for me. When the right one is portrayed, I should recognize it, I think. What would you do with wealth, Professor Bloomfield?"

"That is a puzzling question, Miss Thornton, for no one really knows what he would do in certain circumstances, until actually placed there; but I have thought, for the past year, especially, if I had wealth, I would do something in the spirit of Robert Falconer. It might not resemble his work very closely, in fact might differ largely from it; but I would do something wherein I could be certain I was doing a practical and needed work neglected by others, and doing it not from worldly ambition. It would be so sweet to know, by demonstration, that it was pure Christian benevolence with no selfish motive in it. Have you read Robert Falconer?"

"I have, and, strange to say, I have been thinking about the book to-day in connection with your suggestion of endowing a professorship of Christian Living, or Character-building, and have queried if the two ideas could not be combined; but I am not able to formulate just what is proper and right for me, as a woman, to do."

"Some one has said that all things come round to him who will but wait."

"Yes, come round to *him*, but will they come round to *her*? It seems to be woman's part to wait and to watch, in the tragedy of life, till it is too late to do, perhaps, and then die broken-hearted, when she might have been so happy in inaugurating, or helping to inaugurate, and carry forward, the work she felt inwardly called upon to do!"

She spoke almost pathetically, and stopped suddenly, blushing deeply as if having betrayed a secret. I quoted the following lines:

> "'Nothing is late
> In the light that shines forever.'

"Waiting may be a necessary preparation, and, therefore, an essential part of your mission, and, whether you enter on your actual work or not, will count on the credit side of your character in the light that shines forever. Work intended, if hindered by no fault of ours, is work done."

"That is some comfort certainly, yes, everything to one cut off in the midst of preparation; and, yet, how hard it is to be deprived of the happiness, as well as the privilege, which comes from having all the energies of mind and heart employed in a loved and longed-for service!"

"True, but think of the grateful woman, who, not knowing what else she could do, brought simply a box of costly ointment to one she loved. She did what she could, and that was enough in her Lord's eyes. Her holy purpose magnified the little act, and glorified her spirit for time and eternity."

"Yes, Professor Bloomfield, but I am not doing

what I might, what I very much desired, and what I could and would do, if——"

She trembled as she spoke, and left the sentence incomplete, and I noticed, as I had not before, how tender and delicate was the flesh which enwrapt her spirit—so delicate that the latter seemed to shine through it.

" May I ask," I said, with genuine sympathy, " what hinders you from commencing where the light is clear, and letting the work grow on your hands, as the way opens and duty is revealed to you ? "

She hesitated, blushed, and looked for her fan, and rose, and went towards the front parlor as if in search for it, but really, I thought, to make sure what I already knew, that Charley and Miss Horton were not there, but out on the veranda, wholly engrossed in each other's company. As she came back, the following lines came involuntarily into my mind :

> " Such harmony in motion, speech and air,
> That without fairness she was more than fair."

She sat down in great agitation, covering her face as much as possible with her fan, which she had picked up, and which she used somewhat vigorously.

" In answer to your question," she said, at length, " the work seems unsuitable for a woman alone and too rough, especially for me. I need a guide and helper."

" I should think, Miss Thornton, many men

could be found, who would be only too glad to help carry out your ideas."

" Perhaps so," she said, with downcast eyes, "but the more I have thought of employing a missionary, the more difficulties I have found, because I wish to engage in the work myself."

" Could you not do that?" I asked innocently.

" I do not see my way clear," she answered slowly. " Whoever enters upon the work must be closely identified with it, and—and—with me."

" Yes?" said I, not yet seeing the obstacle in her way. She must have thought me dull; for she raised her dark eyes to mine inquiringly, and then looked down, twirled her fan nervously, and, as I thought, looked beautiful in her perplexity; or was it because, as the poet puts it,—

> " All tihngs are beautiful,
> Because of something lovelier than themselves,
> Which breathes within them, and will never die?"

What that something was, which had transformed and transfigured her, was not apparent to me, unless it was the all-animating mind exalted by a noble purpose struggling anew towards the light, and fast gaining the supreme mastery. She looked almost ethereal as she sat there, the flesh scarcely veiling the sensitive soul, which seemed ready to break through every feature and lineament of her countenance.

" If I were differently constituted," she presently said, "the matter might be more easily arranged. The person I need must not only be

adapted to the work, but to my purpose and ways.
He must be more like the sun than the north
wind. A rough, steam-engine sort of a person,
however good and useful in his place, would not
do. The energy I enjoy and believe in, is that
which comes through gentleness and refinement,
and great elevation of mind. Besides, I want to
feel that this person's heart is as deeply in the
work, at least, as mine, and so identified with it
and with me that what he does I do, my better
self sanctioning every movement of his. I want
to have so much confidence, and something akin
to pride in him, as my spiritual interpreter and
representative, that, whether I am in this world or
the next, I shall know that the work is going on
better than I could execute or devise myself. In
fact, I want to feel that I, in my better moods,
and most exalted ideals of love and duty, am
working through him and by him—in short, that
we are one in mind and heart, in thought and purpose, so that I could take more comfort in his
receiving even heavenly honors, as the better
expression of my personality, than I could in
ecciving them myself."

As she ceased speaking, her face was almost
glorious to behold, having evidently been carried
beyond herself by her mental pictures, and as she
came back to self-consciousness, her face became
covered with blushes.

"Do you expect to find such a person in this
imperfect world?" I asked, with mingled perplexity and deep interest.

19

"Not again," she answered with a little unconscious sigh.

"Then you have met him?" I asked with as much of an exclamation-point in my voice, perhaps, as of interrogation.

The color came and went in her fair cheeks before the reply came, slowly, modestly, but earnestly :

"Yes, I have met one, and only one, in all my life, who comes up to my ideal, and he goes just enough beyond it to make it round, full, complete."

"Is it possible?" I said in great astonishment. "And does he know of your great esteem?"

"I think not," she replied softly and with downcast eyes.

"Why do you not tell him?" was my next question.

"Because," she answered with a faint smile, "it is not the custom for a lady to tell a gentleman what she thinks of him before she knows what he thinks of her."

"True, it is not the custom, but your position, wealth, and noble life-plan give you an advantage over custom, to say nothing of the right of mere custom to seal the lips and blast the life of any woman."

Her eyes had a new light in them as she looked up and asked :

"Would a man respect a woman who laid bare her mind and heart to him unasked?"

"Respect! If he failed to, he certainly would

not be entitled to your respect, much less anything more."

"I have heard," she said, "that Dr. ——, a noted preacher of Boston, sent this sharp answer to a lady, who had offered him her money with her hand and heart : ' Give your heart to the Lord, your money to the church, and your hand to the man who asks it.' "

" Yes, Miss Thornton, I have heard that story, and I confess I have never thought so well of him since, though it may be claimed, in apology, that he belonged to the old school of ideas on that point, and, further, that she really had no heart to give, or that the circumstances might have been provoking ; but I cannot conceive how a real gentleman can treat harshly the admiration or devotion of a true woman. He is certainly not my idea of a man who could be otherwise than considerate and kindly compassionate, even where unable to reciprocate either affection or admiration."

" Your words only confirm what I believed before, that you could not be otherwise than appreciative and thoughtful for others ; but even you, Professor Bloomfield, do not know what effect a declaration of love would have on you."

She looked at me inquiringly, with a sweet, pathetic smile, and then continued :

" While it may be the custom of queens to propose to their intended consorts, and while it may be proper for ladies of lower stations in life, the question of love is so vital, so awfully sacred,

I dare not say what may be a fatal word to all my plans."

"You have perfect confidence in him?"

"Yes," she answered with cheeks aglow, " but I fear to break the charm of uncertainty. So long as I do not break the secret, I may hope, with whatever is not wrongly akin to silent worship, that if we cannot devise and plan together, I may induce him to take my work upon himself and carry it forward alone or with some more fitting companion. If he is happy, I shall try to be content. If I knew the telling would not substitute self-consciousness in place of freedom in our social and, I hope, future business relations, or in any way mar the pleasure of true friendship, and thus the success of my life-plan, there should not be a corner of my mind or heart that I would not reveal to him, though I have not known him long by clock-time—years, however, by heart-throbs."

That last expression recalled vividly the wonderful similarity of my own experience in the society of Ethel Blentwood, and my sympathies were much moved. She went on :

"You have my confidence so thoroughly, Prof. Bloomfield, it will lighten the burden of tumultuous feeling, which has become oppressive for want of expression, if I tell you more. The first time I met this man he impressed me as thoroughly honest, true and good, on whom one could lean without the shadow of a doubt or misgiving, and all I learned of him through friends only con-

firmed my faith and increased my admiration, and
lately, having been thrown more into his company,
his lovable disposition and congenial ways have
won me, and won me until I have waked up to the
consciousness that I love him with all the intensity of my being. I should not have allowed my
heart to go out to one who had not asked my
love, but, fight against it as I might, I could not
help it ; and my mission waits. Every man who
has sought me has disclosed some coarseness or
narrowness of mind, which has made me uncomfortable. Though it is said that the tough rind
may cover something soft within, such a rind
gives me too much pain to enjoy the softness.
But this man, who has not sought me, soothes
and comforts me by his very presence, flooding
all my sensibilities like a congenial sunshine ush-
ering in a sweet June morning. Besides, he draws
all my goodness to the top and puts me at my
best, and I am sure, in his presence, I should be
kept there, growing better and nobler as time
wore away. And then, again, his conversation is
so helpful! I could listen to him without a
thought of food, as Mary did at the feet of One
she also loved."

"Miss Thornton!" I exclaimed, half rising in
my astonishment, "such love as yours is worth
more to any true man than all the gold and silver
in the world! It is not difficult to find a wife
who may give an easy-going affection, but such
fervid, all-controlling, worshipful devotion is a rare
and priceless gift, for which any man would do well

to sacrifice everything except loyalty to God and his own conscience. Let two persons mutually qualified give each to the other such a love as that, and what a heaven! I can only wonder who can be so fortunate as to command such devotion, and from one so noble as yourself. I have never met but one person heretofore worthy of so great admiration and love, and that person is a woman, and to be frank with you as you have been with me, do you know that you have almost exactly described my estimate of her and my present attitude towards her. I cannot but think what an infinite blessing it would be to have all the treasures of hope and reverence and love lying in her great and pure soul, given to me as freely and fully as you give those lying in you to the man of your choice! But I am unworthy of so great a love from so great a source. She is too good for me to hope, and yet, strange to say, I do hope—— Miss Thornton! what is the matter?" I exclaimed in the midst of my sentence, springing towards her, as her head fell back, pale and lifeless.

"Are you faint? What can I do for you?"

A low murmur was all the response I got, and, placing her quickly on a sofa, and snatching a goblet of water near at hand, I bathed her face and temples, and was on the point of rushing out to find a servant, who might know better than I what to do, when she revived somewhat and opened her eyes with a half-conscious smile, so feeble, yet so sweet and winsome, that, had I been a girl, I should have kissed her, and came very near it as it was! That pathetic look! I shall never forget it.

"You dear girl! Am I doing all that is necessary?" I asked anxiously.

"Yes," she faintly whispered, almost inarticulately, and closed her eyes, like one in the peaceful enjoyment of needed rest, satisfied that she was being cared for. Sensitive soul! I thought, needing a very delicate, protecting love to shield her from the rough contact of a blustering world.

When able to sit up, she apologized by saying,

"I hope you will excuse this episode; I find I am not strong lately, and then again," she added, trying bravely to smile, as if she would jest, "it may have been a little too hard for me to look into the happiness you were picturing, as lost to me."

"No, not lost," I said, hopefully. "You will find it, if that man, you delight to honor, ever learns, as learn he must, if you will give me any clue with which to identify him, what an appreciative, loyal prize he has in you."

"Impossible!" she said, her eyes moistening.

"Impossible?" I repeated. "That is a harsh word."

"Yes," she answered, with a suppressed sigh, "but, strange as it may appear to you, the truth has suddenly flashed upon me like a revelation, that his heart belongs to another. While you were speaking, a sentence, uttered by him, came into my mind, revealing that fact but too plainly. Until that moment, I had a floating, glimmering hope of an active, personal mission for good ; but from this hour dates the death of all that."

She covered her eyes with her handkerchief, and sobbed convulsively. My sympathies were so aroused I could not speak for a moment, and could only express them by pressing her unemployed hand. As soon as the lump in my throat would allow, I said :

" I am glad you can cry, Miss Thornton; you will feel better for it. The pent-up heart can only find relief by expression. Let not my presence restrain in the least the flow of tears ; for there is, perhaps, no one, not even the one you love, who is in just the condition to sympathize with you so thoroughly as I am. I hope, however," I added, as she grew calm, and her thankful eyes met mine, " that your revelation is not final. His love for another may be a mere fancy, and when he knows of the wealth of affection he has in you, his heart may fly from that other to you in spite of himself, and with the other's consent."

" That cannot be," she replied, gravely ; " for his judgment is too correct to mistake, and his heart too loyal to forsake the nest it has made and warmed in the breast of another ; and I cannot believe any girl, good enough to command his love, can fail to cling to him till death. Let your own experience convince you, Professor Bloomfield. You could not withdraw your heart from the one you love, although not quite certain that your feelings are reciprocated."

" Too true, Miss Thornton, my affections must go on without wavering, steady to the home they seek, unless they find the door shut against them, and are turned away homeless."

" That is what I knew you would say, Professor Bloomfield, and I esteem you for the frankness with which you assert it."

I had no suspicion who the loved one was, and asked, " Am I to infer, then, that you have given up all expectations of having your affections met ? "

" Yes, completely."

" Does the thought make you miserable ? "

" Not now. The pang from loss of hope was sharp, cutting like a knife until all selfishness died within me, and now I am beginning to find a pleasure in giving up ; and I shall be happy in his happiness and usefulness, to both of which I hope to contribute, and that will be a great comfort to me."

" Yours is a generous and noble nature, Miss Thornton, and I cannot but feel that that man's loss, whoever he is, is greater than yours. You are worthy of the best man living, and if the one you love is lost to you, there must be another somewhere as good and true, and probably better calculated to meet your wants, and when Providence sends him, you will love again."

" Can the full-blown rose shut up and be a bud again ? "

"No, Miss Thornton, but the water-lily shuts up, when the day leaves it to darkness and sleep, and when another new day comes, it is won open again to gladden the beholder with a loveliness all its own, fresh and beautiful as before."

"I know what you say comes from the kindness of your heart, Professor Bloomfield, but the thought is distasteful to me. I have not the slightest hope, or wish, to love again."

"Forgive my blundering. All I can say, then, is, that it is better to be a rose than always a bud —in other words, better to have loved and lost than not to have loved at all."

"I think I understand your meaning, and am content, though, loving the good, my love is not lost. I am richer and better for having found, esteemed, and loved a perfect human ideal; it makes heaven seem nearer, and the ultimate triumph of good more possible. When it flashed upon me that we could never work side by side as one, I felt that death, in its worst form, had come to me; but in the past hour I have lived years! and God has shown me that it is even better as it is. If I am not to last long, it will be easier, and interfere less with his mission, to part as we are, than if our relations were something nearer and dearer than friendship. Now, all I ask is, that I may live long enough to discharge my obligations for the property at my disposal, and then I will go willingly, satisfied that he will be happy in the love of another, and probably more useful; and the thought that I may be of some secret service to him and the great Over-Soul, gives me unspeakable delight. It is so much more happiness than I deserve!"

"Miss Thornton," I said, with much feeling, "there is a heavenly light in your countenance, which convinces me that you have found the joy that lies in self-sacrifice."

"Yes," she answered, with sweet, tender pathos, and a depth of holy peace looking out from under her eyelashes, "I am unexpectedly and greatly blest in giving up. I see now, clearly, that is what life means to me, and I know that it is not only blessed to give, but blessed to give up. Truly, all things work together for good to them that love God."

"How about your life-plan?"

"I am convinced God will permit me to so leave it, that it will be carried out better by another than by myself."

"Would you not love to see your work growing up under your own eyes?"

"That would be very pleasant in certain circumstances; but God knows His own business best, and I am content to see at last what my mission is, and to do it."

"You have already accomplished a mission of good to me, Miss Thornton, and if the occasion comes to require it, as it may, I shall try hard to imitate your beautiful example of Christian resignation. But really, Miss Thornton, is there any clear foundation for your belief in a short life?"

" It is a case of sudden intuition, or revelation, better felt than explained, and I see the hand of Providence quite plainly making the way easy for me." She spoke with an expression of rapturous enthusiasm softened by a pathetic sweetness of voice.

" The world can illy afford to lose you, and now that we have become so well acquainted, and I am so much interested in you, I cannot bear the thought. Do you know that you remind me in many ways of one I have thought the very best in the world?"

" By way of contrast?" she asked, smiling.

" No, by similarity. Spiritually and in frankness and transparency of motive you are both at one. There is also, in common with you both, a timidity, a sensitive delicacy, a clinging tenderness, and yet, a practical common-sense, coupled with a depth and strength of principle, which would not slacken the performance of any clear duty, however disagreeable."

" You do me great honor, and I am very, very grateful for your appreciation. I have talked freely beyond my intention, because—because— well, one thing, because you are one of the few men with whom a woman can feel perfectly free, and confidential, without the least admixture of doubt, or fear of being misunderstood." And then she added, with a touch of girlish animation, " I am glad I have talked, and now shall we not be strong friends as long as we live?"

She extended her lily-white hand rather playfully for my pledge, and, grasping it in both hands, I answered cordially :   ·

" If it rests with me, we will most certainly, and I shall count it one of the greatest privilege· of my life."

CHAPTER XXXI.

CARRIE HORTON AND CHARLEY.

AT this point in our conversation, Mr. Thornton entered the room, and was soon followed by Charley Lightheart and Carrie Horton. The latter saucy-eyed, full of mirthful exuberance, filled the room with the noisy effervescence of her pleasure, and put an end to all seriousness. Charley, too, with his explosive warmth of heart and love of fun, was soon aroused, and filled the social air, now with fleecy crystals of wit, and now with irridescent sparkles of mock sentiment, till every one was shaking with irrepressible laughter.

It was late before Miss Horton arose to go, and, when she did, I noticed she had a lithe figure and a buoyant step, and I tried to fathom the mystery of Charley's liking for her. She was not handsome, or possessed of much depth of mind, but she had a fairly attractive face, that could look very good and innocent, and a vivacity of expression, and piquant gesture and snap of the eyes, which were stimulating to a mind like Charley's, freeing him from that natural restraint he felt in the presence of quiet, reserved ladies.

302

Although she could not talk on any subject requiring more than superficial thought, she was quick to catch any occult meaning, in conversation, which she could turn into her familiar line of favorite topics, where she felt at home; and, while she was waiting and watching to do this, she gave the impression of listening intelligently, and that she only turned the conversation from an irrepressible love of the unexpected and ridiculous.

Charley accompanied her home, only a short distance away, which, however, he made long by either walking very slow, or taking a good deal of time in saying good-bye on the door-step. When he returned, after a few jests at his expense, we retired for the night.

CHAPTER XXXII.

BREAKFAST.

THE next morning was cloudy and cold for the season, and the open fire in the dining-room was a cheering and welcome sight.

"An open fire is a means of grace in weather like this," I said, after table manners were over, preliminary to our morning meal. "It not only takes the chill from the nerves, but imparts its warmth and glow to the spirit."

"A hint for good housekeeping, and domestic tranquillity," Charley remarked, looking up slyly.

"You think it might often prevent domestic quarrels, I suppose, Mr. Lightheart," observed Miss Thornton, and then added archly, "The responsibility in such matters rests wholly with the lady, of course, and not at all with the lord!"

"Certainly," Charley answered soberly; "if I am ever a domestic bear, it will be because of my wife's mismanagement of me. If she allows the damp weather to get into my disposition by neglecting the fire-place, *et cetera*, it, of course, will be her fault, for it will be her duty to see that I am always kept serene and in a blissful mood."

I was glad to see Miss Thornton laugh, and

therefore asked, "When there is no one to build the fire except yourself, Charley, what will prevent the appearance of the domestic bear?"

"That question," answered Charley, trying to blush, "puts me into the warm weather; for it is a calorific reflection on my docility and native loveliness of disposition. Of course, if my wife has no servant to order, she must order me to build the fire. I shall always be obedient where I see that she is weatherwise, and watching to provide against thermal disturbances likely to eventuate in a storm!"

He heaved a long-drawn sigh, and added, "To build a fire would be pretty work, were it not for the incongruous ashes! Why the Creator should give to the beautiful flame so disagreeable a concomitant is beyond me! Going to war, and sacrificing one's self for one's country is nothing to the sacrifice of the finer and more delicate feelings required in emptying ashes! In the former case the body is patriotically, and beautifully, killed, but, in the latter, the tender sensibilities are murdered! And yet, so long as my wife manages me properly, my manly bosom will never entertain a thought of rebellion, and I hope this fact will inspire you all with some appreciation of my wondrous docility."

"You need give us no other proof," asserted Thornton. "Ashes are a nuisance, from which we hope electricity may sometime free us."

"Nuisance is no word for them," Charley declared scornfully. "To illustrate, you turn down

20

the ash-pan and run, but the ashes go for you and
pass by, and when you think you have escaped, a
gust of wind brings them back in your face, eddy-
ing and whirling about you, and when at last
you can see and breathe, you extend your arms
diagonally, stoop over and look at yourself, and
then you want to say Gorry, but you will not
belittle yourself by giving way to uneducated
temper. You try to feel amiable, but there you
are with your neat appearance all gone, and your
dignity utterly squelched! Now, whether there
is any home happiness for the rest of that day
depends on the sensitive thoughtfulness and
affectionate skill of the wife. This is her supreme
moment!"

"Do tell us particularly just what she should
do," said Miss Thornton much entertained.

"Well," replied Charley sedately, " I am
always glad to impart my superior knowledge,
and will say, if she meets her lord with loving
gladness, as if he had been gone months instead
of minutes, dances about him, calling him pet
names, and kisses him, and then comes back for
one more as she starts off for her work again,
domestic felicity is made secure; but if she is
thoughtless, and does nothing to revive his droop-
ing spirits, the dying embers go on dying, and
marital felicity perishes."

"I hope you will excuse me, Professor Bloomfield," said Mr. Thornton at the first lull in the
conversation, " if I ask the clearing up of a Biblical difficulty?"

"Certainly," I replied, "I shall be only too glad to assist you as far as I myself have got out of the woods."

"What! you have difficulties?"

"Many of them."

"Well," continued Mr. Thornton both surprised and relieved, "it is some comfort to know that. Coming home from poor Polly Durgin's last night I got to thinking of the raising of the widow's son, and it struck me as a hardship, instead of a kindness, to call him back to life, after he had got through with the suffering attendant upon sickness and death, to pass through it all again."

"It never occurred to me that he must die again," Miss Thornton exclaimed.

"Strange I had not thought of that either," added Charley.

"We can conceive," I said, as they all looked to me, "that the object-lesson might be worth all the pains of another death, and that the extension of preparatory time might be of inestimable value to others, as well as to the son ; but I like to think of it as a mark of sympathy not only for our sorrowing humanity in the breaking up of family ties (as when Jesus wept with Mary and Martha at the tomb of their brother), but for the holier tears of a mother widowed and lonely, and, therefore, as a divine tribute to motherhood—a declaration in action of the service due from child to parent."

"I thank you for that thought ; I like it," said

Thornton emphatically. His voice trembled a little as he added, " A mother's tears are sacred if anything is in this world."

" Your remark," I continued, " finds a responsive echo in all our hearts, and gives emphasis to what I was about to add, that Jesus reached the higher nature of man through some benefit to the lower, bringing the truth into direct contact with the mind by first getting body and mind into the right condition to receive it."

" That reminds me," Miss Thornton said, " to ask how you would apply the Christ idea to the lower classes ? "

" I would live among them, at least part of the time, dress neatly but plainly, be interested in all their little gettings-on in life, and, if they were suffering in body, mind, or estate, relieve them, and then bring home the truth."

" That would require great self-denial in one who loves nice surroundings," said Mr. Thornton, thoughtfully.

" Yes, but what is a Christian good for who cannot practice self-denial ? Besides, nothing valuable can be accomplished without it. And yet, again, in self-denial, with the right motive, lies the purest and most abiding joy."

" I fear I should find it too hard to give up a fine home, and go down and live among rough, unappreciating people, even for the sake of helping them."

" It may not be your duty, Mr. Thornton, personally, but it is somebody's duty; and if I had the means, I should burn to undertake a work where I could walk so clearly in the footsteps of One whose moral heroism and loveliness of spirit fill me at times with the profoundest enthusiasm." A wistful look was in the eyes of Miss Thornton, as they met mine, and tears were starting from their fountains; and I hastened to add, " This idea of commencing with people where you find them is suggestive also of the proper method of instruction anywhere, even of sermonizing to a cultured people.'

" That's right," said Charley, " give us a course on homiletics, so I may know how to supply the defects of dull sermons when I have to listen to them."

" Please go on, Professor Bloomfield," urged Thornton.

" I was only thinking that the common method, and perhaps the most logical, too, is to commence inward with principle, and work outward to conduct, and, therefore, too far off from the auditors to get their immediate attention, leaving some without sufficient interest to get aboard the train of thought ; whereas, Jesus commenced outward with what was familiar and interesting to his hearers, and worked inward, thereby easily carrying them with him, and letting them go away with their last thoughts on the springs of conduct or convictions of duty, which is a great point gained."

" That recalls the pictures we have," said Miss Thornton, " of Jesus drawing the attention of his hearers to the lilies of the field and the sparrows before their very eyes, and, by means of them, inward to a conviction of God's providential care over all his creatures."

"In all his parables, and even in his miracles," I added, "he led them from the outside fact to the inside fact—from the material and familiar to the immaterial and spiritual."

"If homiletical professors and all who run the theological mills taught the Nazarene method, I think we should have more interesting preachers," said Charley with the sparkle of mingled merriment and earnestness in his eyes.

"Better still," added Thornton with some spirit, "if the gospel mills, as you call them, were abolished altogether."

"Why so, Thede?" asked his sister.

"Because, Theo, the pulpit might then say something new and interesting, and the religious world be relieved of its present unprogressive, dull monotony. Theological seminaries are denominational, and both create and perpetuate ruts, and, so, pervert the divine plan of original, independent, individual thinking and method. They lead men to look at truth for the sake of party or sect, and not from the love of it. There is no encouragement to think, and every inducement not to think, except along denominational lines. Is not that so, Professor?"

"It is true," I responded, "that our theological seminaries are in a measure open to the objection you mention. Some preachers are undoubtedly

injured by a theological course, being spoiled for
what they might have been, and not made into
what the seminaries would build them; and
yet

"But just think, Mr. Bloomfield, (When excited it was simply " Mr.", at most other times
" Professor "), these seminaries are sectarian, and
all the teachers are chosen to think one way, with
little or no latitude; and if one is independent
enough to take a broader view, and, in his larger
sweep finds new ideas outside of the prescribed
limits, and teaches them, he is at once bounced,
as the phrase is. How can there be any progress
under such a system? It is high time people
stopped thinking in platoons and phalanxes, or
denominations, and began to think as individuals,
standing alone in the glory and power of a personal responsibility."

The last sentence was spoken with much
warmth, and I thought it best to simply ask:—

"Mr. Thornton, how would you remedy the
defects of the present system of theological instruction?"

"I would either dump these schools into the
Back Bay, Mr. Bloomfield, or introduce into them
untrammelled teachers of every denomination,
and, perhaps, one good, honest, common-sense
sceptic to sharpen their wits, and keep their heads
clear of all nonsense, and, by broad, healthy discussion, free them from the stagnation and death
of partisan and antiquated knowledge sealed and
delivered in iron-bound creeds."

"A good idea, Mr. Thornton, but before it can be materialized men must need be better, and larger every way than now."

"You believe, then, in denominations and creeds?"

"I think at present our religious liberties are safer with many denominations than with one. Unless Protestant human nature is different from Roman Catholic human nature, I would not dare to trust even my own church without the check of opposing denominations and beliefs."

"There is something in that, I admit ; but my objection to creeds is, that those who subscribe to them take a partisan view of truth, and keep their minds set in a defensive, instead of a teachable attitude."

"There, indeed, is where the great danger of all parties and creeds lies. But of course every one has a creed, something he believes, or he would have nothing on which to stand, no fulcrum over which to pry, and give his thoughts a higher range."

"Very true, Mr. Bloomfield, but how is one to get out of an iron-bound creed? He might as well try to lift himself over a fence by his boot-straps."

"I believe, Brother Thornton, that a man who imprisons his mind in an iron-bound creed is verily guilty before God and man."

"What, then, can the subscriber to a written creed do?"

"He should be just as conscientiously free as the man with only an unwritten creed, and enlarge it as he outgrows it ; as the written constitution of the United States has been enlarged by being pulled here, and patched there, till, like a country-boy's coat, the original is nearly out of sight."

" Well, Professor Bloomfield," with a laugh which went round the table, " I could manage to get along with your interpretation and use of creeds ; but the trouble is, so many make a nest of their creed, and lie in it as a finality, and only snarl at you if you attempt to show them something not in their nest."

" Too true, and, if they do not snarl, they pity you that you are not tucked in as warmly as they ; but might not such persons settle down into something as stationary without, as with, a written creed ? "

" Possibly ; but it is the ministry, and those who ought to know better, who are to blame for the immobility of church creeds. Oh! it is a crime to deprive men of the necessity of thinking ; and shame on the man who, for the sake of denominational standing, or for his bread and butter, even will sell his birthright to receive and proclaim all the truth God gives him ! "

" Amen to that, friend Thornton, but are you not fighting a man of straw ? "

" God knows I wish I were ! " He spoke sorrowfully, pausing, and then with increasing indignation went on. " Why, only recently a well-known theological professor admitted, to friends of mine, that there should be a restatement of theological doctrine. The times, he said, required it, and the interests of truth demanded it. He went so far as to give his approval of such a statement drawn up by a conscientious and rising pastor of his own faith. Other religious teachers and leaders gave their unqualified approval, and there was a great scramble among certain religious editors for the privilege of first publishing it to the world. When published, however, a cry went up everywhere from the babes in the woods, that they had the faith once delivered to the saints, and wanted no new theology! Then the frightened theological Professor went to the author, and said that on further reflection he could not approve of the restatement, many of the other original adherents saying about the same, leaving the honest author to fight for truth almost single-handed. Oh! this quailing before men, fearing the loss of position more than dishonesty before God, is not leaving all to follow the truth!"

"All I can say is, brother Thornton, if there are such craven religious teachers, so cowardly, so recreant to their trusts, as to teach, in part even, what they do not believe, it is one of the saddest thoughts in the religious history of this hopeful nineteenth century. It makes me sick to think such a thing possible!"

"Possible! Why—Excuse me." He disappeared, bringing back copies of a religious paper published in Boston. "Here is something nearer home, which shows that some ministers, at least, don't want the truth proclaimed, and that religious teachers and editors can be frightened from the duty of giving it to them. A series of interpolated Scripture texts has appeared from week to week by a professor in a theological seminary, until, at length, communications poured in, crying, 'Save the Bible! It is time to cry a halt!' Since then I have looked in vain for any more interpolated Scripture texts in that paper. Are these people afraid of the truth?"

"They are timid, brother Thornton, and, perhaps, afraid to trust the people."

"Then they ought not to blame the Romish priests for not trusting the Bible in the hands of the ignorant. I tell you, good brother, this lack of confidence in the truth, and in the people, is more than a mistake, it is a crime! This resting on a perhaps, instead of digging for the rock-bottom truth, is unaccountable to me."

"I am heartily with you, brother Thornton, but we must remember that Christianity has to deal with pretty poor material, some of it low-down, weak, and awfully twisted, and it takes time to lift it up and straighten it. To some people whatever is old and familiar becomes sacred, and they prefer to be deceived, almost, than to be deprived of it. And then, again, many are apparently controlled wholly by their surroundings—kept out of the Church by them, and swept in by them, and take their faith from them, it is so much easier to be borne along by forces outside of them, and not have to lift their heads and breast the popular current!"

"Delightfully happy persons!" broke in Charley, filling his goblet with fresh milk from a pitcher by his side. "They have accommodating consciences like this liquid, which always takes the shape of the vessel holding it. I find a pliable conscience a very convenient thing to have about one, it is so delicious to do wrong semi-occasionally!" This turned the conversation into lighter channels, which was what Charley desired.

CHAPTER XXXIII.

A TEARFUL FAREWELL.

AFTER breakfast we read from three different translations, and one Greek Testament which I always carried with me, the twentieth chapter of Acts, descriptive of the touching separation of Paul from the elders of the Ephesian Church, that chapter occurring as a coincident, and not by design, in the regular course of my Scripture reading. As we read in turn each voice had a note of tenderness; and, when Charley read how "They all wept sore, and fell on Paul's neck and kissed him, sorrowing most of all for the words which he spake, that they should see his face no more," his utterance became choked, Thornton cleared his throat, and Miss Thornton covered her eyes with her handkerchief. I, too, was deeply moved, and found it difficult to go on with the service.

Why we should have so much feeling on this separation morn is not easily explained. Was it prophetic that we should not all meet again? Or is there a subtle cord of sympathy communicating with kindred spirits, as by an electric wire, whatever of keen emotion there may be in one loving heart, though outwardly unindexed? One thing was certain, that, next to the Blentwoods, this

home of Theodore and Theodocia Thornton was
the pleasantest I ever enjoyed—Theodore a little
brusque in his manner, but kind and honest, and
Theodocia every inch a woman of refinement,
great delicacy, and yet, great strength of feeling,
frank, confiding, modest without prudery, tender,
unconventional, and innocent as a child. I had
in my heart of hearts a very strong friendship for
both of them.

Theodocia reminded me of Ethel Blentwood
in that they had similar rallying points of faith
and courage, the same conscientious love of truth,
the same frank, loving disposition and purity of
purpose, were similar in height, and in the deep,
luminous expression of their eyes. Both were
graceful in movement and figure, but Ethel had
more roundness of contour, a more elastic step,
more vivacity and varied expression of countenance, a more aggressive warmth and joyousness
of temperament, at the same time more of self-
reliance, self-poise and self-control.

One appealed to you from her sweet, childlike
dependence, the other from her more positive and
winning cordiality. One roused your manliness
and devotion, the other inspired you with the
noblest impulses and activities. Both were
lovely and lovable, and, in some circumstances,
it might have been hard to choose between them.
Theodocia had that vine-like, twining disposition,
which appeals so strongly to every man, and it
seemed a pity that her great affection could not
have the sunshine of encouragement to grow up

about the man she loved. What oak, I thought, would not be improved by such a vine!

But whatever the cause, when we arose from our devotions, mine, I knew, was not the only face suffused with tears. Thornton looked out of the window, Charley fumbled a book, and Theodocia went, deeply agitated, from the room. I found her afterwards half reclining in a large easy-chair, screened behind the ample draperies of the bay-window. Her hands hung limp by her side, from one of which her handkerchief was slipping away, and from her half-closed eyes there were traces of fallen tears.

The whole picture was so touching, so pathetic, that, without knowing what I did, but wishing to do something, I raised her head upon my left arm and passed the other hand over her temples. It was entirely the impulse of unstudied sympathy. She did not move, however; but a slight thrill went through her frame, the color came to her cheeks, and, as I began to feel alarmed, she opened her eyes, and smiled at me through her recurring tears. It was like the breaking out of a rainbow through the drops of a clearing shower.

"Oh!" she said, "I have had such a beautiful vision, and must have been asleep when you came to me. I was in heaven, and, seeing you coming, I hurried back, but think you got here first."

"It was too bad in me to bring you down out of heaven, but I didn't wish you to go there to stay just yet," I said, trying to laugh.

"Oh, I was glad to come," she explained, "for

I thought I wanted to say something to you. It was all so wonderful! and so very real! Such bright and glorious spirits! and they, the few near me, seemed to know by sympathetic intuition, what my errand was, and to enjoy with me my sanguine hopes. You will promise? I know you will."

"Am I to promise without knowing what?"

"It is a sacred trust, which I commission you to perform, the details of which I will leave under seal to be opened immediately after my burial."

"Oh, don't talk of burial! Miss Thornton; you may outlive me many years."

"If I do, you will be released from your promise. If within your power, will you accept the trust?"

"Must I promise without further light?"

"Yes, if your confidence in me is sufficient."

I hesitated from a natural repugnance to a step so utterly in the dark, where a thousand contingencies might change the whole aspect of things, and render the fulfilment of a promise a very delicate and difficult matter of conscience, but I said :—

"I can trust you, Miss Thornton, to give me no unjust task, and, therefore, I promise to do what you wish, limited only by my ability."

"I knew you would; the angels whispered it, and looked glad as I left them; and now let us seal the compact." Placing a Bible in my hands, and clasping it in hers also, she added, "We will consider _her_ hands on this book, if you like, so as to make this a possible tripartite agreement; and now, in the circumstances, with our hands on the Bible, and in the presence of two worlds, I think we are capable of sealing it with a—a—holy—"

There was an unworldly, spiritual look and a question in her eyes, as she hesitated, and to save her the embarrassing word I bowed my head, and the strange compact, or possible tripartite agreement, as she called it, was solemnly and sacredly sealed. She looked at me as if she saw into my very soul, and then, with a smile more angelic than earthly, said:

"I shall not die untimely, and I am very grateful, and very happy."

She gave me her hand, and I asked, "Shall we say good-bye now?"

"It might as well be here," she answered, "if you will excuse the seeming impoliteness; for I am exceedingly weak this morning."

I pressed her hand, and, with thanks for her friendly hospitality, and a God bless you, together with a few comforting words, cut short by a lump in my throat, I rushed out upon the piazza, where I was soon joined by Charley and Mr. Thornton, the latter with a well-filled lunch-basket in his hand.

We had scarcely started for the shore before a message came for Mr. Thornton, and Charley and I went on alone. When we turned for a last look at the house, Thornton waved his hat from the piazza, and a white handkerchief fluttered from the open bay window, where I had left Theodocia.

21

CHAPTER XXXIV.

WE were soon moving downstream in the middle of the current, each occupied with his own reflections. What I thought of my strange experience may better be imagined than expressed. I naturally queried whether Theodocia would select Ethel as my ideal of a woman, or I the man of Theodocia's choice, and why our affections should pass each other, when, with a common object and her ample means, we could do the glorious work I longed for; and I wondered whether love had any common-sense in it anyway. But Ethel held the throne in my heart, and God, I thought, would solve the problem some way; and in sheer reaction from the too serious strain I began to rally Charley from his revery on his attachment to Carrie Horton.

"Physician, heal thyself," he remonstrated.

"Good medical advice," I acknowledged, "which I fear you cannot take, because you exhausted all your little pills on me when we were leaving the Blentwood shore, but which I will now proceed to pay back to you, in lieu of coin, for your professional services:

"Charley Lightheart, my boy, snap the chains

322

of enslavement which Carrie Horton has wound about your too willing neck. Be free! Stand up with St. Paul and me on the sublime heights of female disenchantment! Wash away the films which girlish blandishments have cast over your eyes! Give your affections a little fresh air! Ensmall not yourself, my boy! Allow not your sympathies to be hedged about by matrimonial intentions! Be enlarged, and love the whole world! Soar, my boy, soar on the wings of a boundless aspiration!"

This harangue had its effect, and Charley, raising himself and his hat with great and solemn dignity, said :—

"Allow me to inform your highness that to love Carrie Horton enlarges a man, and does not hedge in his sympathies. She is a cosmos, and, therefore, whoever loves her loves the world! She sparkles with all the brilliancy of a Kohinoor, more beautiful is she than the rose, sweeter than the pink, lovelier than the lily. In short, she is Carrie Horton, and in these words I exhaust the English language!"

He sat down with the air of one who felt supremely satisfied with himself. To help on his self-complacency, which I enjoyed immensely, especially the manner of it, I said :

"Your weighty arguments have silenced the guns of opposition. I confess myself squelched."

Charley smote upon his breast, and, bowing slowly, as if agitated by his emotions, gravely responded:

"Your magnanimity touches my heart! I, too, am conquered; but neither you nor I, great souls that we are, can take advantage of our victory! I confess that Carrie Horton is not so great intellectually as Ethel Blentwood, and may not have so high a purpose in life—which fact will enable me to commit any little sins, which are sweet to me, unmolested, and that is an inestimable boon! I need, you know, just the tiniest little devil in my wife to keep up a happy equilibrium, or balance, of marital forces, and Carrie has one, I think, about the right size. She is deliciously lively. In fact I may say, without qualification, she is lively. She plays lively, sings lively, talks lively, laughs lively, and loves lively. She is not the girl to get into the dumps, and sit against the north side of a tombstone on a cold moonlight night. She likes the warmth and the sunshine, and the buttered side of the world's bread, and knows which side that is; and we shall unitedly seek, not for the first seats in the universe, but for the softest and pleasantest, where we shall be fanned by the balmiest breezes, and the fragrance of life is sweetest. In a word, we shall live on the very mountain-top of wedded felicity equally delicious every day in the week!"

"But suppose an unlooked-for domestic breeze blow you off your pinnacle of glory?"

"Then I will scramble up again."

"Good! but suppose the next breeze proves a squall, and it is repeated faster than you can scramble up, and you become so sore you find it difficult to climb, and discover when too late (O, the horrors of such a discovery!) that your confidence was grounded in ignorance of the new forces and changed thermal conditions of married life?"

"Do you mean to say that my Carrie can become a nimbiferous cyclone, perpetual or intermittent? my Carrie, who is always as balmy, and as bright, and as sweet as a June morning!"

"A June morning she may be in the halcyon days of courtship, with nothing but sunshine between her and you, but——"

"Are you insinuating (interrupting, and pounding the boat with his fist) that I can ever exhibit any other than a sunny side to the woman of my choice? or that I have any other side to exhibit, in fact?"

"You can never be other than a dear good fellow, Charley; but suppose adversity should make your pocket-book lean, and the clouds should gather thick and fast in your sky, will your personal sunshine keep the damp and chill from your home, and prevent the tempest? or even the little whirlwinds, which disturb domestic tranquility?"

"Prevent it? Of course it will! How can there be any storm, where the domestic air is kept full of such warm and luminous sentiments as these flying about,—my joy! my sweet-scented orange blossom! my delectable juice of pine-apple! my luscious essence of figs! Eh? my veteran, of long and varied experience!"

"I speak only as a student and close observer."

"Well, my Carrie is necessary to my happiness, squalls and chills notwithstanding, O, great philosopher!"

"If you marry only to make yourself happy, your selfishness will deserve defeat, and Carrie will prove more of an angel than I think she is, or you will wake up some dark morning and lament with the Dutchman :—

> 'When I tinks of what I is
> And what I used to vas,
> I tinks I frowed myself away
> Mitout sufficient cause!'"

"Poor Dutchman! Mine will be a good cause anyway. But if she, too, marries to be happy, are not the conditions of mutual happiness met?"

"Only till the glamour passes off, my untutored boy. Selfishness is a non-unionist, pulls apart, and never goes beyond itself, except to get something not its own."

"Yes, but you leave out the factor, love!"

"You left it out, and I took you at your word. Marrying to make yourself happy is a selfish motive. Love does not think of self, but of the object loved, and finds its highest happiness in the happiness of that object."

"Ah! I see I am a neophite, and surrender to your erudite and more comprehensive interpretation. Carrie Horton is a necessity to me, because I can only be happy in serving her happiness. How does that terminology strike your judicial sense?"

"Much better, Sir Charles. If you know you are the one to make her happy, and seek to marry her for that purpose, your motive is genuine."

"Of course it's genuine. Don't you think her an angel?

"No."

"Isn't she seraphic?"

"No."

Charley rose up, threw his hat violently into the bottom of the boat, clawed the air with his spread-out fingers, run them through his hair till every spear stood on end like the quills of a fretful porcupine, rolled his eyes, and, looking like a madman, exclaimed:

"O, for something to quench the flame of my righteous indignation!"

"You might try a little river water," I suggested.

"River water!" he roared; "nothing but the waters of a better judgment on your part can abate this rage."

"Rage? I thought you had only a sunny disposition, which could not rage!"

"Ah! It is the good in me that boils. It is because I have too much sun that I am become a withering, blighting, blasting furnace. O, for breath! I gasp for breath. Tell me, ere I become a cinder, is Ethel Blentwood an angel? Is she a seraph?"

"No, dear fellow. If she were, what man of lesser glory could hope to increase her happiness?

It is enough for the Lighthearts of earth to win seraphs and marry mortals ! "

Charley dropped into the boat collapsed, declaring in an exhausted tone of voice, " You have saved me on the very brink of the ashpit ! But have you no praise for Carrie as a mortal ? "

" Carrie," I answered, in his own language, " is a lively girl. Yes, I may say without qualification, she is lively."

" That is reviving—talismanic," he said, sitting up.

> " I start, I move, I seem to feel
> The thrill of life from head to heel ! " .

which is partly Longfellow and partly Lightheart, the one risen to the zenith of poetic glory, and the other just rising above the horizon."

Saying this, he put on his hat, and began to whistle.

CHAPTER XXXV.

THE STONE WALL.

WE took dinner that day on a little island, and found the Thornton box well filled with toothsome and nourishing food. We ate heartily, and as we replaced the remaining eatables, Charley gleefully exclaimed, "Two square meals more, before we are reduced to hard tack and dried cheese!"

We re-embarked, two as free and happy fellows as ever sailed down the Connecticut, I imagine, pleasing ourselves by being now chatty and now silent and observant, enjoying to the full the beautiful visions and glorious suggestions, which came to us from shore and sky and water in blissful ignorance of any reverse of good fortune.

All went well till past five p. m., when our craft rose at the bow, quivered, and stopped so suddenly that Charley, at that moment standing, was laid out handsomely at full length. Staring at me with a queer facial expression, he called, "Why don't you put me in the arms of my mother?" Then, looking over the boat's edge, he muttered, " A blow on the head has made me see stars sometimes, but never a stone wall before ! "

" That is what it looks like," I interjected.

" What ! a stone wall across the bottom of the river ? A likely story ! "

" Tell an unlikely one, then ! "

Rubbing his eyes he looked again, asking, as if communing with himself, " Is this nigrescent air playing a trick with my senses ? or have we both lost our wits ? " He tried to push the boat. It stuck fast. Rolling up his sleeve he reached down and felt with his hand the rock on which the bow rested. " Sight and touch agree," he murmured, and then aloud,—" Say, Bloomfield, there wasn't brandy enough in that pie to fuddle us ? "

" Nonsense ! There was no brandy in it. Aren't you well ? "

" Never better, but the idea of a stone wall across the river is preposterous ! You are Bloom field, aren't you ? "

" Yes."

"And I am Lightheart ? "

" Yes."

" And we are in a boat together on the Connecticut River ? "

" We are supposed to be."

" There is no mistake in our identity ? "

" None."

"And still you say with me that we are aground on a stone wall ? "

" Yes."

"Then I see no logical escape from the conclusion that drivelling idiocy is staring us in the
face, do you?"

"No escape, unless there is a stone wall!"

"That is absurd on the face of it." And he
pounded his head, closed and opened his eyes,
tried various experiments to test his mental
acumen; but the wall, like Banquo's ghost, would
not down; neither would the boat move. He
mumbled something about the "absurdest,
blankest blank situation!" and then, as if giving
up the problem in despair, he lay back in the
boat with his fingers interlocked behind his head,
and with the most comical expression of perplexity imaginable, said:

"Chum, the next thing we know, if we ever
know anything again, we shall be in the 'Greatest Show on Earth!' as curios of mental delusion."

At that moment the thump of paddle-wheels
fell on our ears, and soon a steamboat, some distance off, went steaming unobstructed up the
river.

"There!" exclaimed Charley, that proves the
falsity of our stone wall craze. But what puzzles
me is why our senses should deceive us."

"Our senses may tell the truth, Charley; they
only say it looks and feels like a wall, and the
fault, if any, may lie in the inference we draw,
that it is one."

"I enjoy your metaphysics; please go on a
bit."

"Well, to illustrate, suppose I see something in a tree which looks like a crow, and at once call it a crow, when on investigation I find it a black knot shaped like a crow, which was at fault, my eyes or my mind?"

"Your mind in its hasty inference, of course. A prudent mind will reflect that things are not always what they seem."

"Precisely. Now the only question is, are we correct in the inference, that our boat rests on a stone wall, because appearances so indicate?"

"That's it. Well, Elbert Bloomfield, I say there is no stone wall here. What do you say?"

"I say just what pleases you. Excuse my laugh, which is one of great admiration. I am proud to be under your leadership. You have entire command henceforth."

"There is no reason, then, why we should not go on," he said demurely, and, putting down the long pole, pushed with all his strength, and the next moment we were struggling in the water amid boughs and boxes and satchels and oars and our boat bottom upwards, upon each end of which we managed, after much difficulty, to mount and balance ourselves by lying face downward. A dense fog enveloped the banks, and we could not estimate the distance, or know whether the shore at this point was accessible. A precarious predicament, and yet the irrepressible buoyancy of Charley's spirits soon asserted itself, and he asked :

" How do you like my leadership ? "

" The way you took us over that—that—obstruction," I answered, my teeth beginning to chatter, " was something more than skilful navigation, it was splendid strategy, it was brilliant pyrotechnics, and had it imparted its warmth to this bath it would have filled me with admiration ! "

" As it is, it only filled you with river water," Charley added, raising his wet face to mine.

" Merely as to my clothes," I asserted, " my spirit is untouched, it is not even damp. But what is the next move, Captain ? "

" Put this youngling into his little bed, and accept his resignation as skipper," he answered ruefully.

" I cannot, unless your resignation is in writing," I said firmly.

He raised a pitiful look, and shook his picturesque head, and dolefully exclaimed, " Then, indeed, is my chagrin inconsolable, for all my office material is floating off—hatefully floating off ! There goes the Thornton box and the two square meals ! I'm glad I ate that piece of pie, I hesitated about. Some things are safe, after all, in this uncertain world ! "

" You are not on land yet, Charley."

" I know, but you forget that I'm fat, and it's a long way the fish would have to eat to reach that pie ! Besides, unless you object, I think I'll pull for the shore, and for reasons I will state."

" How can a subordinate object ? Remember

you are captain of this crew till your written
resignation is received. But go on with your
logic. That you can preserve the logician in these
untoward circumstances, proves your fitness for
your high command."

"Well, my first reason is that I can swim :
second, I find it hard to maintain an equilibrium
on this slippery boat's back ; third, to remain here
endangers my health, which is of some conse-
quence, since there is a girl by the name of Carrie
in the world ; fourth, I am not happy here, and
sigh for a fire and dry garments on terra-firma ;
fifth, I dislike inaction, and unless I act now I
shall not have strength to act at all ; sixth, if I
go this minute I can explore and return for you ;
and seventh, I hope by the glimpse of a light on
shore, there may be a house near and comfortable
lodgings for two. Are my reasons satisfactory ?"

"Amply so, my dear Captain, especially the
seventh, which is the ancient number for com-
pleteness, as it would seem to be yours. At any
rate, it is complete enough for me, and almost
warms me to think of it."

"Then, like Simon Peter, I go a-fishing—not,
however, as a fisher of fish, or of men, but for the
sake of one little woman and yourself. Au revoir!"

"Nay, I go also. Let us not be over-anxious
to get on fast. Many people needlessly drown
by not keeping cool."

"We shall be cool anyway!" said he, slipping
into the water. I followed, and, reaching under
the boat, found to my joy, a board seat, which,

as a precaution, I drew under me, and, holding it
there with one hand, swam with the other. To
our great relief we reached the shore in a few
minutes. It was now raining hard. We climbed
the bank with some difficulty, and at once set out
through the murk and mud towards a light, which
glimmered faintly in the distance.

CHAPTER XXXVI.

CHARLEY IS RECOGNIZED.

AS the silhouette of a house appeared on our approach, nearly at the same time the light disappeared; but we found a door, and I said to Charley, "I am only a high private; it is your knock." We were both shaking with the cold so that our articulation was very imperfect, yet, though the preliminaries to a fire might be prolonged, I could not resist so unique an opportunity of enjoying his odd way of doing things. He knocked gently at first, and then banged the door till a man's head was thrust out of an upper window, when a hoarse voice started the following dialogue :

"Who's there ? "

"It is I."

"Well, who is I ? "

"Don't you know me ? "

"No."

"Well, I don't wonder. I scarcely know myself this dark night, wet and dripping like a drowned rat ! "

"Do you know *me*? "

"Know you ! Do you suppose a man of your generous hospitality can hide under a bushel? "

336

" But who the devil are you anyway ? "

" Please don't introduce me to your friend, till I am more presentable."

" What friend ? "

" Why, the one you just spoke of—Devil, I think you called him."

" Te, he! I guess you don't need no interduction ter him. Yer voice sounds 'ef he'd got ther upper hands on ye ready."

" Well, my good friend, you must remember that your river-water is intoxicating when taken continuously, of a cold night, by an immersion of two hours' duration ; and, so, we want you to warm and lodge two of the best fellows you ever saw—sort of angels unawares, you know."

" Where's t'other feller ? "

" There he is under that tree, tongue-tied with the cold, waiting for the glow of your hospitable fire."

" Did you say you are wet ? "

" Perhaps you have the knack of soaking two hours in the water and keeping dry, but we haven't learned the knack in Massachusetts."

" Where did you say you came from ? "

" From the bottom of the river, of course; where do you suppose we came from ? "

" Lost anything there."

" Everything."

" Why didn't ye tell that before ? "

He took in his bushy head, and then thrust it out with the following result :—

" Have you a lantern ? "

22

" Lantern! How can a man from the bottom of the river be supposed to have a lantern?"

"Oh!" And the head disappeared, when, after a small cyclone, evinced by tumbling chairs and tables, a slender shaft of light shot through the small window-panes, the door was unbarred, and, in nocturnal habit, our bushy friend stood enframed before us.

"Come ter think on't," he said, "my boat's unfit ter use, and lantern's broke, and ye might as well come in, I reckin, and let yer stuff wait till mornin'."

We entered a large and disorderly-looking room, which served for kitchen, dining-room and parlor combined. An ancient cook-stove stood in a large old-fashioned fire-place, with one length of funnel up chimney.

"We're just settlin," said our host, commencing at once to build a roaring fire, "but I reckin I can make ye as much ter hum as ye was in the river—te, he!" The tea-kettle was soon singing, and, pouring us out two cups of hot water, he declared, "That's as stimerlatin as brandy. I found that out at Saratog where I worked a spell rubbin' down the dudes arter a hot bath, in Dr. Bedortha's water-cure. Ye orter seen um dance when they came out the hot tub and I throwed three or four pails of cold water on um as tight as I could throw! I can see um hop now—te, he, he! ho, ho, ho—o! I'm the feller to tend to ye."

As the heat began to creep satisfactorily into

our nerves, he placed us, denuded of our clothing, one after the other, into a washtub, and turned warm water on our shoulders, and then, throwing over us a sheet previously warmed, rubbed us until we glowed and cried enough. He then rolled us up in warm blankets and quilts, till we looked like mummies, and laid us on a cot-bed in front of the stove. Wringing out our clothes, and hanging them over the stove well filled with wood, (in the meantime solving the stone-wall mystery), he went up to bed, assuring us, with a " te, he!" that we would come out " chic and peert in the mornin'."

By hugging the shore too closely we had, it seems, got into a recently formed arm of the river, across which had been built a wall previous to the washing away of an embankment and the resulting overflow.

We slept a little, and dreamed, and tossed much, until the morning hours warned us that the family would soon be down. To our joy our clothes were quite dry, and we were hastily getting into them, when our host appeared. Something in Charley's incomplete toilet seemed to remind him of the past; for he stared at him, and then, coming nearer, bent forward with his hands on his knees, and, looking him straight in the eye, began to grin.

"Golly, and by jiminy!" he burst out, "ef ye don't look like the ghost what raised the price of my mule! Say, did ye ever ride a vicious white mule? —te, he, he! I'll be dogonned ter hokey

ef you ain't the same chap! Jimminy-crack-corn!
It's you just like a mice! Ef this ain't a treat,
the demnition bowwows take me!"

He began to see-saw with laughter, holding his
sides, when (and just as Charley had got enveloped in pantaloons) the hostess came down, and
he exclaimed :

" Marm, this is the feller that frightened me so
like the devil, a settin' on the barnyard post in
his white clothes!—Hi, hi! ho, ho! oh! ho, ho,
ho—o! You are a little the beatenest, queerest
cuss I ever seed, and I tell ye, I'm eely most
tickled ter death ter see ye. Ef ye ain't welcome
to my bed and board, then take me ter heaven
this minute!"

" You did us a good turn, mister," said " marm,"
a masculine, but good-natured looking woman,
" and paw has been mighty tickled about it ever
since."

" Tickled! Well, I never!" ejaculated the host.
" Why, it split me every time I thought on't, and
it does seem as ef I'd never git the idee out o'
my ticklin, spot, the hull thing was that queer—
the queerest in all my born days. And what
makes the laugh on the right side o' my mouth
is, that that ar mule is as do-cile as a lamb, and I
could git a big price for him. I put him ter work
that very day a movin' down here, and now
(slapping his knee) I'm pretty well fixed for a
rise in the world, as the dough said, with the
emptins under it. You see, t'other farm I worked
ter halves; but this ere one is mine, when I finish

payin for it ; and I shall pay for it much quicker
for the boost you've gin me."

We were congratulating him on his improved
prospects, and ourselves especially for having
fallen into so good hands, when "marm" said,
"Breakfast is ready, paw." We sat down to a
much better meal than we expected; and when
we took out our wallets, our host and hostess
flatly refused to allow any of our money to be left
at their house, not even with the young hopeful,
their only son. It was broad daylight, and our
host said we must be off looking for our plunder.
He led the way to the river, and soon discovered
the boat near shore, and wading in, hauled it to
land, and emptied out the water. The seats, oars,
tent, food and housekeeping conveniences were
all gone, and no trace of them could be found.

"Don't spose yer wanter sell this ere craft, do
ye?" said he, examining the boat with care.

"Shall we turn landlubbers?" I asked Charley.

"It looks like Hobson's choice," he answered,
at the same time scribbling his resignation as
captain on a scrap of paper, and handing it to
me with a polite bow.

"It is reluctantly accepted," I said, "and though
your captaincy ends, your genius as navigator,
and especially the wonderful skill with which you
jumped our vessel over a stone wall will always be
admiringly remembered."

"Te, he! That's a good un!" laughed our
would-be purchaser, looking up in time to hear
the last remark. "I swanny, ef you ain't the

very fust pious fellers that ever made me wanter go ter Heaven! Most o' them kind o' chaps allus seem ter feel so bad 'cause they expected ter go up thar, that I made up my mind I should have ter go down t'other way ter have a good time, and feel ter hum!"

"I hope you will change your mind," I said, grasping him by the hand; "for a Christian is the only one who has the right to be brimful and running over with fun and good cheer; and, unless suffering, he ought to feel it a sin to wear a long face, or be anything less than thankfully, joyously, happy. It is ungrateful to be otherwise."

"Wall, the pious dumps I've met mostly, allus seem ter me ter have somethin' in um that hurt um, and, as I don't want that kind o' stuff in me, I've ginerally managed ter shun their chin music. They act as ef they were tryin' ter please ther Lord by bein' miserable; and either they've got the Lord and Devil, and Heaven and Hell awfully mixed up, or my idees of common-sense are mightily twisted outer jint—one or t'other."

"Narrow Christians do their cause much harm, my good friend, and I hope you will become a thoroughly converted, whole-hearted, joy-beaming and love-o'erflowing Christian, and set the misguided an example. And now, to come back to business, what can you afford to give for the boat?"

"I hain't tin enough about my trowsers ter mor'n half pay for her; but I think I can make her pay for herself this Summer a-lettin' her, ef ye can trust me for the balance."

" Well, let me have what you can spare, and I will leave it to you when to send the rest, and how much." I took his money, giving him my address, and, being unencumbered with luggage, we were ready to start for the railroad station, which, we learned, was much nearer across fields than by road ; and, preferring to walk, we refused our host's proffered " wagin," accepting, instead, his pump-handle grip, as we took his rough hand, and said good-bye. We left him, happy in his new possessions, scratching his head and grinning, looking alternately at the boat and at us, as if there must be some doubt about his identity and great good-luck. " By jimminy ! " were the last words we heard him say, and, when we turned and waved our hands at him, he threw his hat high into the air like a school-boy.

" That fellow is a phenomenon, and, in by-words, a cosmopolitan," observed Charley, laughing. " Do you expect a remittance ? "

" If the boat earns it. At any rate he is happy, and, since he has, perhaps, saved us from illness, I am satisfied."

" I think he intends now to pay it, and may, if he earns it before the story becomes old; but I doubt if you get another penny, Elbert."

" Well, Charley, let us wait, and see which of us has read the deepest into this man's character. He is uneducated and in the rough more than any New Englander I ever met : but if he has not a homely honesty, which will put to shame the polished exterior of many a city gentleman, I am greatly deceived."

We were now crossing an old pasture, and, picking up a stone which attracted my attention, and, finding it light for its size, I broke it open carefully, and, as I anticipated, found it hollow and lined with beautiful crystals. This geode, which we divided between us as a souvenir of our journey, quickened our mutual taste for geologizing, and we entered the station reluctantly, our walk and studies having been so delightfully recreative and inspiring.

" Did you ever see two happier fellows than we are?" Charley asked, as we sat down in a cool corner—"just as happy without a boat, as with one ; when facing an advancing robber, as when he ignominiously retreats ; on the slippery bottom of an upturned boat, as on dry land ; with teeth chattering before a stranger's door, as when rubbed down and warmed and fed by—by—our bushy-headed bath-man !"

" Well, well ! " I exclaimed ; " neither of us can tell that man's name ! "

" His name is Paw," said Charley, and this, suggesting a panorama too vivid for anything more than interjections, we lost our dignity, and laughed immoderately, unreasonably, till the natives stared.

"You'd be too tired to laf like that, if you'd broke up a quarter of an acre of sward ground, as I have this morning," declared an old farmer, rather enviously, as he halted in the door, goad-stick in hand.

" We broke up more than that several hours ago," Charley controlled himself to say.

" How much did you break up, I wonder?" asked the incredulous farmer.

" We broke up all our calculations," Charley replied soberly, and that made the laugh unani-mous, the tired farmer being as much pleased as anybody, and he turned to go out, guessing he could plough the next quarter acre easier for that pun.

" You can do everything easier," Charley as-serted, " if you will adopt our creed."

" What might that be?" the farmer asked, ex-pecting another joke.

" It is the belief, and living up to the level of your belief, that there is no such thing as mis-fortune, except, as my friend here says, doing wrong."

" That's a short creed; but it's mighty hard packed with meat!—mor'n the teeth in my poor brain can gnaw just yet. No use tryin' to catch a weasel asleep. Good-bye, Mr. Weasel!" This compliment brought down the house, and the good old farmer left for his plough, with a help-ful thought in his heart, amid cheers and explosive laughter.

CHAPTER XXXVII.

THE WILLIAMSBURG FLOOD.*

WE had not got enough of rustic life and were wishing ourselves among the Berkshire hills, or that we had some other than a public conveyance, when a couple of Yale boys from New Haven walked into the station, one of whom proving to be Charley's classmate who played the guitar at the Negro dance I had witnessed near Dr. Blentwood's, and who was now studying for the degree of LL.B. As we have not introduced him to the reader, we will not do so now, only remarking that he is to-day one of the most useful men of New England, and has solemnly promised not to reveal our identity. They had come in a two-seated carriage, and were expecting two classmates on the next train to join them at this station; but as they kindly failed to appear, we were gladly offered and as gladly accepted, their places, and were soon a merry party of four young men on our way north over the most unfrequented roads along the hill towns of Connecticut and Massachusetts.

As the incidents of this most enjoyable trip

* The flood occurred Saturday, May 16; but the slight anachronism must be forgiven for reasons best known to the author.

346

are not necessary to our story, suffice it to say that, after sufficient wanderings, we found our selves at an evening party in a little village, the home of Charley's friend. Here the people were greatly excited over the Mill River flood, caused by the bursting of the Williamsburg dam, of which the daily papers had been full for many days. They read over and over the early as well as the latest details, which the " Springfield Republican " and " Springfield Union " had shown great enterprise in giving, and eagerly sought the more distant Boston and New York papers for what additional accounts and illustrations they might contain.

Some idea of the wide-spread sympathy aroused by this disaster may be formed from the fact that George Bliss, a wealthy merchant of New York, subscribed $60,000, and the Connecticut Legislature voted $10,000 for the sufferers, whose affliction was declared to be unparalleled in history. A mountain reservoir had broken away about eight o'clock in the morning, and a few minutes later, Williamsburg, Skinnerville, Haydenville, and Leeds, four manufacturing villages, which, the day previous, were the abode of industry, peace and plenty, were almost wholly wiped out of existence, and 138 human lives lost, to say nothing of domestic animals. An appeal had been made for volunteers, provided with shovels, crowbars, etc., and it was estimated that a thousand men were at work one day, recovering the dead bodies of men, women and children, buried in the sand and other débris, and it was this appeal, though several days old, which changed our plans, perhaps the whole course of our lives.

It was now Thursday, and, leaving our friends, who had other duties, Charley and I reached Florence that night, which had suffered only in loss of property, and the next morning, with one spade between us and a try-stick, we started early for the scene of sad activity, and found that a once fertile valley had, indeed, become a desert. The broad meadow lands above Florence were covered with sand two or three feet deep and with thousands of cords of timber and building material, some of which was crushed and ground to splinters.

Farther on towards Leeds appeared household furniture, becoming more and more abundant as we advanced, and then mingled with this, as we went on, and half buried in sand and gravel were large quantities of wearing apparel of both sexes, portions of Bibles, hymn-books, photograph albums, mantel ornaments, every step carrying our thoughts away from things, and closer and closer to persons — away from the loss of property to the loss of human life. Parts of cradles and their bedding were strewn everywhere, and when, in addition to these, we came upon broken dolls and children's playthings and babies' shoes and socks and dresses, and thought of the music of pattering feet and innocent voices stilled forever, and happy homes so suddenly, and apparently so needlessly, swept out of existence, it was enough to make the heart ache and tears to flow from eyes unaccustomed to weep.

It being early, we met no one to give us specific directions, and so travelled on, examining every pile of sand not already dug over, especially where protruded any human garments. Something in one of these mounds yielded suspiciously to the pressure of my stick, regaining its original position when the pressure was removed. I called to Charley, who came with his spade, and, after much labor, we extricated from the limbs of an overturned and completely buried tree, denuded of its bark by the rough scrapings of the torrent, sand and rubbish, a much-torn plush sacque, empty, however, of any human body, but protruding from one of the pockets was a letter which I took out, thinking it might be of value to some one. It was much stained, but the superscription was sufficiently plain, it seemed to me—too plain for my peace of mind, and yet I could not believe my eyes. My hands trembled so I could not hold the letter.

"Take it Charley," I said, "read the address carefully, and make no mistake."

I walked about while he examined it, until at length, getting better control of myself, I stopped in front of him. His blanched countenance told me that I was right. I turned away.

"Yes," he said, "the name is certainly Ethel Blentwood, but this does not prove anything."

"That is so," I responded, catching at a faint hope. "To what town is it directed?"

" Williamsburg," was the answer.

My spirits fell again. Still there was no proof that Ethel Blentwood was drowned, only a fearful presumption.

" I will not believe it," I said. "God would not allow it ; for she has a mission yet. But I must know the worst. Let us go to Williamsburg at once."

We made a sand-pile to mark the place and started. We passed Leeds and Haydenville, or rather where they had stood, almost unheeding, though destruction, wreck and ruin, and desolation were everywhere. Not a road or bridge could be seen, though of the latter there had been some fine structures of iron and stone. Not a particle of soil or green thing was left anywhere, nothing but stones and gravel and sand, and it did not seem credible that there ever was such a thing as a grass plot in all that valley.

At Skinnerville, which was completely wiped out except the main part of Mr. Skinner's mansion, not even a cellar remained visible. On the outer edge of the flood-track were a few houses not demolished, but standing on their ends, sides, roofs, and even cornerwise, supported in these positions by sand, gravel and rubbish piled up about them. At Williamsburg, which was struck in the lower part of the village, we were told by eye-witnesses that the flood, like a hill or wall of water thirty to forty feet high, and preceded by a cloud of dust and mist, came down the gulch seething, boiling, thundering, like the rapids of Niagara, scattering and destroying everything in its way. Mammoth trees bowed down before it, or snapped like a reed shaken in the wind. There was no time for reflection. Within fifteen minutes the flood had passed, and the saved came down from high places to find their families, or other near and dear ones, dead and gone.

But these things were incidental to our search, and forced upon us. We did not seek to learn of anything except the one object we had in view. People were now fast gathering, and moving about with sad countenances. We met the Reverend E. R. Thorndike, pastor of the M. E. Church, who had officiated on a previous day at twenty-eight burial services, and was familiar with the names of many of the lost, but none bearing the name on our letter was among them. We secured the latest list of the dead and missing; but the object of our search was not there. This, however reassuring, did not relieve our anxiety. We went to the post-office; no one there remembered delivering the letter.

"Charley," I said, "you are an old acquaintance of the family; it will be proper for you to telegraph an inquiry whether Ethel is at home."

"Yes," he replied, "but the lines are not yet repaired, I think."

I caught a glimpse of a familiar form through the window, and rushed out, followed by Charley.

"Doctor Blentwood!" we both exclaimed in one breath.

"Well, well!" he responded, as much surprised as we, cordially grasping and holding a hand of each of us, ✝this is sunlight on a dark picture. You look as good as new, Brother Bloomfield, and you, Charley, never had any rain fall into your life, Longfellow notwithstanding."

"Are you all well at home?" I broke in, wishing to end the suspense at once.

"They were when I left. I have been on the wing since, and so have not heard from them. The sad scenes here enacted make me long for the good old home which Ethel has saved to me, and made so bright and cheerful since the death of my dear wife. She is all I have now, and the family separations by this flood are brought home to me with great force. I have come here on my return to learn what God has to say in this great disaster; for I must preach on it Sunday."

"I wish I could hear you, doctor," I said, not yet daring to make known our discovery.

"Come home with me, and help voice this terrible event to my people. I have a feeling that we should not differ in, the meaning of it; but, however that may be, I am only anxious that this lesson may not go unheeded, and that God be as fully heard and understood as possible. Besides, I should like to have you take my place one or two Sundays, so that Ethel and I may go on a little journey. My library and home shall be at your service, and you may rule monarch of all you survey."

"I cannot *fill* your place, but shall be glad to

try," I replied, but with a voice a little unsteady, and, as I had betrayed myself, and not knowing how else to proceed, I handed him the letter addressed to his daughter, at the same time explaining how it came into our possession.

He took it with trembling hands; tears came into his eyes, and, with a voice choked with emotion, he said :

" I left Ethel with her cousin at Northampton, and they were to visit Florence, I believe, but were not coming to Williamsburg so far as I know. Let us take the next train ; for we are not needed here, and should only fill the places of better men. Besides, your company is a necessity to me now, though I am quite confident that Ethel is safe at home ; for she did not wear a plush sacque, and, moreover, I think God will not kill me just yet. When I can see her well provided for, I may then look for the great summons any time ; but——"

He did not finish the sentence, and, taking him between us, Charley and I supported his trembling steps to the station where we took the train for Graynoble. When we arrived, the house was well lighted, and, to our immense relief, Ethel was there to receive us, and a delicious supper was in waiting, for she was expecting her father. The doctor embraced his daughter with unwonted affection and tenderness, and she explained the wave-washed letter by the fact that her cousin had addressed her at Williamsburg the very day the doctor had left her at Northampton, supposing her to be there with an old schoolmate, who was

23

to have had a class reunion. It seemed that the servant girl who went for the mail that fatal Saturday morning, got caught someway in the flood, and was carried away. Her body was found entirely denuded of clothing, which accounts for the separate finding of the tattered sacque containing the letter.

It would be difficult to describe my feelings on taking once more the hand of Ethel Blentwood. As I held it and looked into her lovely eyes, the same thrill I had felt before swept through me ; but I could not tell how far the cry of my heart awakened a responsive answer in hers. Inclined to be self-depreciating, I felt uncertain, and so unreasonably disappointed.

As I retired that night I called to mind Theodocia Thornton and her great love for some one, so confidingly revealed to me, and thought how blessed it would be to have such love ! Constituted as I was, it would be more to me than all the wealth of the world. I could not bear to think of mere prudential ideas entering into the motives which weld the bonds of wedlock. I trembled at the very idea of a home in which entered anything short of the purest devotion and the most complete abandonment of self.

As much as I loved Ethel, I could not wish her to become my wife so long as there was a doubt of her returning my affection in full. I must love, if at all, with my whole being, and I saw no hope of making her life a happy one, if I could not express myself strongly without the consciousness

of a check, however slight. I could not be satisfied
with that general sort of love which is so common
among married people. To wake up after marriage to find I was only receiving a fraction in return
for the whole I had given, would be a horrid revelation too terrible to contemplate. The wreck of
my happiness might involve the wreck of hers also
and others; for I felt sure I should fail to make
her life round and full, unless her heart was unreservedly mine. If her life could be fuller of
meaning with another than with me, it were better
to see her wedded to that other; but how it would
tear me to see her tied to one incapable of appreciating her! O, I must win her love, I thought,
to save her from that cunning, heartless Stockmire —"that pampered, oversated, stall-fed beast
of selfishness!" At least, I must protect her, and
if my mission ends there, God's will be done!

In all these musings I did not entertain a single
suspicion, that Ethel would not deal honestly
with me, or that her ideal of love and home was
not as high as mine. I was only reassuring myself of the folly of wishing to marry her, unless
her heart could repose blissfully in mine, and never
wish for another home. That she was above me
need not in itself separate us; for Jesus was above
his disciples.

Charley Lightheart, who slept with me, had also
his thoughts, which, however, were most pleasing
and satisfactory to him, judging from their expression, in his morning dreams, as I awoke. It
should be stated that he had spent the previous

evening with Carrie until a late hour. Some of his words were muttered; but I had no difficulty in divining their import.

"Carrie Horton," he said, "you love me, of course; for how could you help it! The only question now is, will you wait till I climb the hill of destiny? or will you climb with me? The only danger of waiting is, that being a very susceptible young man, with so many pretty girls dying for me, I might slip away from you. While star-gazing with some charming belle, and being lifted on the wings of poetic fancy, by the magnetism of a charming night, and the still greater magnetism of a glowing cheek close to mine—occasioned by the focalization of our minds on some bright, particular star, and the intensity of our desire to study that star from the same standpoint, who knows but that in the stealthy, delicious enchantment of the hour, I might be borne away into a new love, and your Charley be lost to you forever! It is a fearful risk! Dare you wait, Carrie? Of course you'll not wait. Well, we'll commence together at the foot, and enjoy the climb all the way up; and, when the prospect is sufficiently bright, we will build a wigwam, and in due time a palace."

I burst out laughing. Charley opened his eyes with, "What's the matter now, old fellow? Glad because you are back again where you left your heart?"

"I am laughing, Charley because you are so sure of your game, and are so happy over it."

"YOU LOVE ME, OF COURSE?"   page 356.

"Sure of my game and happy! Art thou dreaming of the chase, young man?"

I only laughed the more. He turned towards me with a stare, and, apparently guessing the source of my merriment, said:

"Dear old shipmate, you may laugh; for I am happy as a clam in high water. I am swelled, lifted, exported with happiness—an emigrant from infelicity and an immigrant to bliss perpetual. My soul is as full of song and sweetness as a lark just up from a bed of rosebuds! The fact is I am in the swim, on the topmost wave of good fortune, floating on it, deliciously basking in the glad sunshine of a peace most serene! In short, I am rocked, rapturously rocked, in the cradle of an accepted lover! Wonder not at the neophyte's happy mood!"

"How and when did you get on so amazing fast?" I asked.

"The climax was capped last night," he answered.

"Then what you said in your dream this morning was not all a dream."

"What was it?"

I told him. His laugh was a sufficient answer; but he would neither affirm nor deny, that the closing sentences were distinguished by any unnecessary punctuation marks.

The tones of the rising bell now reached us, and we dressed for breakfast. Charley's happy mood seemed to be catching; for, when we went down, we were cheerfully greeted, and it was a

chatty group that gathered about the family-
table. A feeling of gladness seemed to pervade
all hearts that we were together again safe and
well. We talked and laughed of our first meeting, of Charley's and my experiences down the
river, and up among the hill-towns, of parish incidents, and other light relaxing themes. It was
in part a reaction from the sad sights and thoughts
of the previous day. Ethel was as bright and
sparkling as the dewdrops, which were seen
dancing in the sunlight through the eastern window. It was a glad morning indoors and out, and
after breakfast, Dr. Blentwood led in a prayer of
great tenderness and thanksgiving for God's pre-
serving mercies to us all. Then Charley hurried
me off to his brother's office.

Dr. Lightheart was much pleased with my improved condition, and expressed his satisfaction
that I was to give in Dr. Blentwood's pulpit the
first draft of a course of lectures, which I had
promised the Thorntons more formally to give
later; but he stipulated that I should shut down
the mental mill each day at noon, and roam the
woods and hills. This I could do, as no pastoral
work was expected of me.

Leaving Charley with his brother, I came back
via the river, spending most of the remaining
forenoon arranging my thoughts on the Williamsburg disaster, sitting under a wide-spreading elm,
and on the very seat occupied by Ethel and me
the evening I first met Stockmire.

Fortunately I broke away from that enchanted

"THEY WERE TOO HAPPY FOR INDOORS."—*page 359.*

spot in season for dinner; and, after that necessary repast, who should call but Charley and his
Carrie!

They were too happy to contain themselves indoors on so pleasant an afternoon, and so, Dr.
Blentwood being engaged in his study, we four
took a long stroll into the woods, and up the
mountain, so called, to a peculiar formation of
ledge, known as the "poet's seat," overlooking a
very pretty landscape. The weather was just
right for comfort, and we sat there for an hour or
two, chatting, laughing, and singing gospel
hymns.

Occasionally Ethel's eyes met mine, setting in
motion an electric current, which caused my pulse
to beat faster. There was so much depth and
meaning in those orbs of hers! They fascinated
and drew me like a magnet. I wondered if they
had so much for others as for me. They were
windows indeed, through which her very soul
seemed to look. Was there not something more
than kindness there? And would that something
ever be transmuted by my great passion into the
glow of an ardent love? Time would tell, and I
must be patient.

On our way home, when I might have had an
opportunity for a little private conversation with
Ethel, who should cross our path but Stockmire,
the man for whom I felt an unexplained repulsion,
as from a creeping thing! A change came over
Ethel's countenance; but what that change meant
I could not decipher. With a bland smile and

that innocent drawl of his, he welcomed Charley and myself back, as if he honestly meant it.

He invited himself to walk with us, and so spoiled my enjoyment for the return home, though I tried prayerfully to free myself from prejudice, and to appreciate him at the value accorded to him by others. I even punished myself by trying to be affable to the man, whom, in thought, I had perhaps injured. I wished to think well of him, as others did: but in all my attempts to charitably analyze him, I could not escape the conviction that at heart he was deceptive and utterly selfish. So unaccountably did he affect me, that, when he had shaken my hand at parting, I went at once to my room and washed off the slime, which seemed to have gathered there, before I realized what I was doing.

CHAPTER XXXVIII.

AT CHURCH.

SUNDAY morning we all went to Church, even to Tom and Tot and their unruly Pomp; for no cooking, and therefore no excuse for absence, was allowed on Sunday. Dr. Blentwood's text was from Amos iii. 8—"The Lord God hath spoken, who can but prophesy?" He could recall no period of American history in modern times, where it seemed to him God had spoken so loudly and so plainly as in the Williamsburg flood ; and that person, he thought, would be remiss in duty, who did not study to know the meaning of the message and profit by it. He graphically described what he saw and heard and felt, relating many touching incidents and providential escapes, and then asked the meaning of all this?

"Some tell us," he said in substance, "that God caused all this destruction and sorrow as a direct punishment of the people for their sins; but I prefer to say what we know to be true, that the cause was a broken law of nature and of nature's God. God did not break one of His own laws to punish anybody. That law was broken by

361

man. The fact is, the Williamsburg dam, professing to protect the people from one hundred and eleven acres of water, forty feet deep in the centre, with an average depth of twenty-six feet, was a builded lie. Had it been built in harmony with God's laws, it would have stood, and that beautiful valley would not have been turned into the valley and shadow of death.

"Who does not know that sand will wash and clay slip, and water seek a level? These laws have not changed since the foundation of the world, and are, therefore, familiar to everybody; and yet that dam, which might have had the permanent support of the law of gravitation, was built and maintained in defiance of it, and, slipping from its insecure foundation, a wall of water forty feet high rolled down on unsuspecting villagers, some of them asleep in their beds; and, were it not for the warning cry of the flying horseman, 'The dam has burst, flee to the banks,' the loss of life would have been much greater. Shall we blame God for this disaster? or shall we learn the lesson that God's laws are eternal and cannot be broken with impunity?"

He then spoke of the majesty and beauty of God's laws, the loss we sustain in neglecting them, and the injury we inflict on ourselves and others in disobeying them, dwelling, at the close, upon the help to obedience from Him, who came to build up, and not tear down, our manhood and womanhood.

He was very eloquent. Never before was I so

impressed with the perfection and beneficence of God's laws, both natural and spiritual. I dropped my pencil and notebook, and listened spellbound to the end of the discourse. It would be useless to attempt a portrayal. Enough has been indicated to define his position, which is all that is essential to this story. Suffice it to say, the audience went away with tear-dimmed eyes, except a few carping critics, whose hearts were too dry to weep, among whom I recognized the voice of Mrs. Lightheart, declaring emphatically:

"I wish Dr. Blentwood would preach to sinners, and let us Christians enjoy our religion. Just as though I have anything to do with law, when Jesus paid it all, all the debt I owe! God drowned those people for their sins, and it's rank heresy to deny it."

I made no reply, concluding to adopt the plan of the Autocrat of the Breakfast Table, and wait. That evening, when the hour came for me to speak, according to announcement, I said in support of the doctor's position, in the course of my address:

"I am afraid some Christians will not learn anything from this disaster, and that is the most fearful thing about it. The Lord God has spoken in plain, unequivocal terms, declaring that those who disobey, or even neglect, His laws, incur the risk of a terrible penalty; and this is as true of spiritual as well as of physical laws. And yet, so-called Christians tell us they have nothing to do with law!—that Jesus relieves them from any

and all obligation to law; whereas He expressly
declares He came, not to destroy, but to fulfill;
in other words, to bring His followers into harmony with law, and help them obey it. The real
Christian loves the law of God, because it is the
expression, the very transcript of the Divine
Mind. He thankfully sings with the psalmist,
'Oh, how love I Thy law! Great peace have
they who love Thy law.' It is the man who loves
not God, that hates His laws; for he is out of
harmony with them, and has no help to obey
them.

"It is a sham Christianity that would be relieved from the responsibility of doing right. If
this disaster teaches anything, it teaches that
God's face is eternally set against shams and all
forms of hypocrisy, and that the only way to be
safe in our walks among the laws of God, is to be
honest and true and square-dealing, not only in
building dams, but in all our business and social
relations—in other words, to wear our religion
every day in the week, and not merely on Sunday
and in the prayer-room.

"If this doctrine prevents any one from enjoying his religion, then, I fear, he does not know
God or Christ, and is crying Peace, peace, when
there is no peace. His sham Christianity, like
the Williamsburg dam, may deceive for a while,
but detection and disaster must eventually overtake it. Let those, who are misled by false in-
terpretations, remember that those, who trusted
a false dam, suffered the penalty of their unwis-

dom as much as if they had been participants in
its construction; and let them not rest, till they
have worked their feet down through the rubbish
of error, and felt them firmly planted on the rock
of eternal truth."

"Amen," cried several voices, but Mrs. Lightheart only groaned, and looked upon me as a
heretic to the established faith. Stockmire, in
the after-meeting, was profuse in his praise of
the morning sermon and of the evening address; but we afterwards remembered that he sat
down glancing at Ethel to see what impression
his remarks had made upon her. He went home
with her from church, while her father and I
conversed together, arm-in-arm, a little behind
them. Stockmire seemed to be urging something
with great earnestness, but what she said in return
seemed to be monosyllabic. At the next street
corner they went home another way, and the
doctor and I went at once to his study to consult
a Greek verb, and I did not see her again that
night.

CHAPTER XXXIX.

STOCKMIRE HAS DESIGNS.

THE next morning Ethel Blentwood appeared pale and worn, as if she had passed a sleepless night. Her hands trembled, as she officiated at the breakfast-table, and she was so perturbed and absent-minded, that she made some awkward mistakes. I was sure that her condition had some relation to Stockmire; but her father, if he noticed anything unusual, only felt the urgency of getting her away from excessive church cares, and tales of sorrow poured into her sympathetic ear by those who had lost intimate friends in the Williamsburg flood—one of those bereaved ones being a sister of the girl in whose sacque I had found Ethel's letter. These things, undoubtedly, had something to do in rendering her susceptible of agitation, but they were not the direct cause, I was certain.

I drove them to the station, and as Ethel gave me her hand and said good-bye, I pressed it with both hands, and felt its trembling, but could not see her eyes, which were cast down, and, therefore, could not read what I wanted to find there.

366

Without turning towards me again, she entered
the car, and disappeared, though the doctor lifted
his hat, and waved me a final adieu from the car
platform.

"That trouble," I said, as I drove back, "is
something more than physical."

While Tom was taking care of the horse, I got
from him the exasperating fact, that Stockmire
had called very often during my absence, and that
it looked to him "as if he were done gone on
Miss Ethel, sure."

"He proposed to her last night," I said to myself, as I went to the doctor's study, which was
now to be mine for at least two weeks, "and who
knows what poison he has poured into her unsuspecting ear! I was tortured with vague guesses
and fears all day, and sleep brought no surcease
to my anxieties; for I only slept at intervals to
dream of horrid plots by Stockmire to secure the
hand of Ethel. His oily tongue would make
everything smooth to her, and yet, under the
cover of that smoothness, he would stop at nothing to compass his personal aims. I felt sure of
it, though he was popular, and held one of the
highest local offices. I did not then know the
questionable methods by which he had defeated
a much better man; but I felt what I could not
explain, that, beneath his humble exterior, he was
hard and unscrupulous at heart—not of the Uriah
Heap sort exactly, but more like the polished,
yet equally hypocritical, Pecksniff.

I met him during the day, and he was unusually

cordial and adroitly flattering towards me, if not to everybody. " Is his politeness due to his acceptance by Ethel?" I queried. It looked like it, and a momentary wave of despair rolled over me, engulfing all my bright hopes. Is it possible that one with the delicate sensitiveness and spiritual insight of Ethel Blentwood, could fail to see through the false pretences of Wilson Stock- mire? I thought not, and yet what made him so apparently happy? On the other hand, what made Ethel so nervous and shaken! If she has accepted him, it must be from a painful sense of duty, and not from love. There must be some dia- bolical plot beneath this fair exterior of Stockmire, which is tearing the heart of that dear girl, and which he is counting on as ultimately succeeding if not already victorious, with her.

" It must not, shall not succeed," I said, with every nerve and muscle in full tension. It was with difficulty I could contain myself in my anx- iety to fly at once to her rescue. I hurried back to the library, or study, in a state of frenzy, and, throwing my hat on the lounge, walked the room repeating, " It must not, shall not be. I will ferret out this wickedness.—O, diabolism itself! to deceive an innocent girl, and lead her to sacrifice her happiness under a false sense of duty! for that is the trick I expect to unearth. If it be right to ask help from above for anything, it is right to ask it in saving this beautiful and accom- plished girl from the letter of a loveless marriage and a lifelong regret."

That night, as I read my Greek Testament and sank on my knees, my prayer was that her happiness and usefulness might be subserved, whatever the loss to me. If I was self-deceived and was seeking my own happiness more than hers, I wanted my selfishness revealed to me. At the bedside I knelt again, repeating the same prayer, and asked to be guided aright. At length the shadow of heavenly wings seemed to brood above me, and, comforted and refreshed, I fell asleep, and in my dreams, heard angelic voices singing, " I will guide thee with mine eye."

The next morning Tom informed me that Mr. Stockmire wanted him to help about the store, as one of his clerks was absent.

" Go by all means, Tom, and act as my diplomat," I said.

" What's dat ? "

" Keep your eyes and ears open to everything Stockmire says and does, but do not let him discover that you are watching him."

" I larned to do dat down Souf, where all de slaves were dipplemats, peers like. We knowed eberyting de white folks did, but we nebber let on," and Tom pumped his shoulders in high glee over his astuteness.

When Tom returned from his day's work at Stockmire's, he brought me a note from the Elisons, inviting me to tea the following day, and reported.

" I haint much plomacy to tell, but dare be somfin goin on under a mighty mystification, sa'

24

for Boss Stockmire tuk mose eberyone to where
I couldn't hear, and talked bery spiciously; and
once I heered him say, 'It's too bad dare be such
a feelin' 'ginst Dr. Blentwood.'"

"Feeling against Dr. Blentwood!" I exclaimed
in amazement. "Everybody loves him."

"Dat be true, sah, as I allus heerd so; but I
tells ye de truf perzactly what Boss Stockmire
said, and I is mystified, sah, I may say discom-
boberated, sah. But Ize gwine to keep my plo-
matic eye open, till I fine de debbled at be snuffin'
round here like a roarin' lion seekin' whom he
may devour somebody, and hep you drive him
out before he git us all inter de quagmire, Perfessor Boomfield."

As I had two lectures to prepare for Sunday,
and to arrange whatever side thoughts, which
might be awakened, for an address to the young
people, I had no time to mingle much with the
members of the church, taking my exercise
through unfrequented streets into the fields and
woods, in obedience to Dr. Lightheart; and if
sometimes condensing needed stretch of. muscle
and expansion of lungs into as short space of
time as possible, it was only to gain time for
study in the afternoon. I hoped, however, by
accepting a few invitations to tea, to learn something of the status of the parish mind, and Stockmire's relation thereto.

The supper at Mr. Elison's passed off pleasantly, Mr. and Mrs. Elison and daughter proving
agreeable and even intelligent people; but Stock-

mire was there to prevent any too confidential relations, and the consequent attainment of the object I had in view, by engaging me in conversation for his own purposes. He surprised me by asking if I agreed with Dr. Blentwood in denying that God caused the Mill River flood, explaining that the pastor's position had produced a good deal of commotion among some of the church members.

"God permitted it," I answered, "because it was the natural result, or penalty, of His broken law, or laws."

"What laws?" he asked.

"The laws that water will press in proportion to its height, and that an unstable foundation will wash away. Both of these laws were violated in the building and maintaining of the Williamsburg dam, and God did not suspend the penalty naturally following such violation; but His loving providence was seen in the saving of hundreds of innocent lives, as their marvelous escapes plainly indicate."

I felt chagrined to have to explain so simple a matter, and for the second time, to an intelligent man at this late day; for I suspected he was feeling for a new wire to pull against Dr. Blentwood or me, with some ulterior design on Ethel's hand, though just the game he was playing, I could not then fathom. He was very attentive to Miss Elison, the heir to a considerable fortune on the death of her parents. "If he can't get Ethel, he is preparing the way to secure Miss Elison," I thought. I went home puzzled, and got little light from Tom.

The next day Charley Lightheart called, and I unfolded to him my suspicions. He had engaged as a reporter on a Boston daily, and had but little time to look up the matter; but he learned that Stockmire had been quoting others against the pastor, always refraining, however, from giving his own opinion. Finally Charley called at his store, and Stockmire told him, with apparent regret, of a general desire for a change in the pastorate, and that it was too bad, since there had been such a good feeling in the church. Charley tried to get him to name individuals, who were dissatisfied ; but he would not come down from generalities, repeating, that come thought him not sound in doctrine, and others that he was too old, and that a young man with new methods would better build up the church.

"If the feeling is so general," said Charley, " I should think you might name one of the malcontents."

Under hard pressure he finally named Mrs. Smithers, an old lady and a widow. Charley went to her direct, and found her greatly grieved that she, or any one, could be supposed in opposition to Pastor Blentwood.

"Then you have expressed no dissatisfaction?" he asked.

"Indeed not," was her earnest answer. " We are very fortunate if we can keep him, he is so able and such a comforter to the worn spirit, such a feeder to the hungry soul!"

"What did Stockmire say to you, Mrs. Smithers?"

"He asked me if I should want a man for my pastor, who held that God took no interest in such disasters as the bursting of the Williamsburg dam, and I answered no, for such a pastor could not preach the God I needed and believed in."

"Did Stockmire claim that Dr. Blentwood holds such views?"

"He told me that church members so interpreted his sermon on the Mill River flood, and were demanding a change in the pastorate."

"When I heard that," said Charley, in giving an account of the affair to me, "I did not have to hunt round after the ancient Adam in me in order to get mad. I was furious, or righteously indignant, as the ministers might say, and presumably shocked the old lady by calling Stockmire a creeping, crawling serpent, fit only for crocodile swamps and the demnition bow-wows! He knows that the majority of people are not independent thinkers, but are unconsciously led by the opinion of others; and, so, he is endeavoring to create public opinion by misrepresenting it—announcing that to be public sentiment, which, originally at least, existed only in his own lying heart.

"It is true, my sister-in-law, and those like her, disapproved of the sermon, because it touched their selfishness; but even they would not originate a movement to get rid of the pastor."

CHAPTER XL.

THE next Sunday, among other notices I read from the pulpit, was one announcing the annual meeting of the Church and Society to be held the following Friday evening.

Of the two lectures given that day it need only be said that they awakened a good deal of interest among the thinking portion of my audience.

The only dissent from the views expressed came from the Mrs. Lightheart class of minds, whose opinions, though having some influence, were of no value to a scholar.

At the annual meeting there was a large attendance of Mr. Stockmire's friends, who were unaccustomed to attend such meetings, and a strong under-current of feeling pervaded the assembly. The appropriations for music and other expenses of the church were made without much opposition; but when the question of the pastor's salary was reached, Mr. Stockmire moved to adjourn, thinking, no doubt, that would be the best way to lead the pastor to resign. Charley Lightheart, who was present and still a member of the Society, moved that two hundred dollars

374

be added to the salary. This Stockmire opposed in the interest, he pretended, of Dr. Blentwood, for whom he professed great friendship. It would be misleading, and might prevent the pastor, under a mistaken sense of duty, from accepting a more desirable call elsewhere ; and for one he thought it the pastor's privilege and duty to go where he could retrieve his fortunes lost by bad investments.

Charley answered, if the pastor had lost money through the advice and agency of Mr. Stockmire, he should be the first to put his hand down deep into his own pocket, and not plan to send him to strangers. That was not the way to discharge an honest obligation.

I had supposed until this moment that Dr. Blentwood was financially well off, if not wealthy ; but Ethel's sorrow came into my mind, and it flashed upon me instantly that Charlie's quick inspiration had hit the real cause of any loss the doctor had sustained, and, therefore, that Stockmire's covert fling had only recoiled upon himself, where it belonged. Stockmire turned red and green and then blue ; but Charley held the floor, and, stepping into the aisle, said :

" I have heard a good deal about dissatisfaction with the pastor, but in every instance I have traced the rumor to one source. It has also been extensively reported that the young people desire a young pastor, but as one of them I wish to correct that report. Though a young man, when it comes to food I prefer beef-steak to veal—in other words, a pastor who knows more than I do, a man of experience and thought, and no mere gabbler.

"It is said (Mr. Stockmire is my authority) that a young man would be more emotional; but what does emotion amount to unless distended with thought? We want something better than assertions and everlasting gabble. With some people skim-milk is as good as cream, if only kept stirring. They are attracted by noise, and he that makes the most noise is the best fellow with them. Goldsmith's noisy geese that gabbled o'er the pool, would highly entertain them, if said geese only wore the human form. Gabble seems to be the fashion just now. The pulpit gabbles; the bar gabbles; the bench gabbles; the rostrum gabbles; office-seekers gabble; everybody that is anything gabbles, and he who can't gabble, or won't gabble, better go to sea, or so command bayonets and bullets as to make the enemy gabble, as Grant did, and then all the people will gabble for him, and he can sit in his presidential chair, and gabble back or not as he pleases.

"Give me a man of mature thought, who has outgrown the gabble age of his development, for my pastor. And you men of experience, I must believe, want no greenhorn, fresh from the gospel mills, who thinks he knows everything, and yet knows nothing except what books and theological seminaries have taught him. As to orthodoxy, there can be no heterodoxy so dangerous as the infinite fear some people have of ever learning anything. They eat, and would make everybody else eat mouldy bread, made in the early periods of the race, whereas we can have it at the hands of wiser cooks, fresh from new wheat growing in the fields of to-day.

"Dr. Blentwood is abreast of the times, and preaches a gospel, which appeals to every man's nineteenth century common sense. If I have learned that there is a grand truth in Christianity, which wins me, it is owing to the eminently reasonable views of Dr. Blentwood and Professor Bloomfield."

Charley's speech called forth hearty laughter, and when he sat down there was a general clapping of hands and calls for Professor Bloomfield. I arose, and simply said:

"It does not become me to speak at your business meeting, not being a member of your society. I may properly say, however, that I have been very strongly impressed with the great worth of Dr. Blentwood. I esteem him as a man of rare ability and goodness; and no people, in my opinion can be more fortunate than those privileged to listen to the grand and helpful truths, to which he gives utterance in his pulpit ministrations.

"Like my friend Lightheart, I am a young man, but I bow with profound respect and reverence to age. Indeed, I never get quite so near Heaven, as when I take an old man by one hand and a little child by the other, the one fresh from the portals of Eternal Morn and the other just entering there."

Hearty cheering followed these brief remarks, indicating that the friends of the pastor were largely in the majority ; but Stockmire jumped up, and tried to feel the pulse of the opposition by making a Pecksniffian speech ending with the following question :

" I would like to ask Professor Bloomfield, with reference to Mr. Lightheart's nineteenth century common sense, if we have not the truth once delivered to the saints, and if there is any progress in truth?"

" I certainly believe," I replied, " that we have the truth, as we have the earth, once delivered to the saints ; but I should be very sorry to think man so stationary that he cannot have, and enjoy a progressive interpretation of both the earth and the Bible."

Stockmire reefed his sails, and started again :

" Church members complain that the pastor preaches righteousness too much, and against hypocrisy, dishonesty, social exclusiveness and unbrotherliness, and thus disturbs their devotional feelings and peace of mind, instead of giving them their needed Sabbath rest by having their hearts flooded with love."

Charley was on his feet before Stockmire was fairly seated, and said :

" The last speaker's remarks remind me of Robert Colyer's Chicago man, who spent much of his life in prison, but in the intervals of freedom had blessed seasons of hymn singing and prayer in religious meetings, where nothing was said to disturb his conscience."

Dr. Lightheart, who was standing at the door, having just come in, added :

"When I was South, I learned of a colored preacher who had great power with his audiences, and was asked to preach against theft and other dishonest practices, of which his church was guilty ; but he replied, ' Dat will nebber do, brodder, it would frow such a coolness ober de meetin'.' I don't know that *all* of you church members can stand honest preaching, but those of us outside believe in it."

During the laughter which followed, I noticed Charley tucking a dollar bill into Tom's hand, who rose rather falteringly, but spoke with all the more effect because it took the audience by surprise :

"Dear Brederen, Misser Stockmire have said dat he wish ter so lib as ter leab de world better dan he fine it ; and I wish ter say for his couragement, and de comfort ob us all, dat de signs am pooty clare dat he'll hab his wish ; for it peers like as if de world will be better off when he's gone."

This brought down the house, metaphorically speaking. The audience fairly roared with laughter, occasionally bursting out afresh after they had determined to control their risibles. Had a vote been taken, it would have been carried overwhelmingly in favor of the pastor ; but Mr. Stockmire gave a very plausible, and apparently very honest, but, as it afterwards proved, trumped-up excuse for adjournment at the call of the chairman to be given Sunday from the pulpit, and the meeting was so adjourned.

As the chairman was Stockmire's tool, the latter was very complacent and full of honeyed words for everybody. Indeed, so excessive was his warmth that Charley declared it would require an extra watering-cart to lay the dust occasioned by his over abundant sunshine.

" I fear," he whispered, " I shall be out of pocket to the extent of a sun-umbrella, or out of health to the extent of a sunstroke, if that smile becomes any more sultry and scorching ! "

At that instant I happened to look at Stockmire, who was watching us, and was startled at the almost fiendish spirit, which, in a moment of forgetfulness, had come to the surface and made ugly his Jewish features. The smile, then, was only a veneer to cover up something fierce and grim, which, in an unguarded moment, had darkened forth from the whole man !

From that time on, Stockmire went diligently to work, poisoning the minds of church members, not in open warfare, but in true Pecksniff style, quoting everybody in general and nobody in particular, except where he knew the lie would not be detected. Where he could, he made the most of what he declared to be a universally accepted fact, that the pastor did not believe in Divine Providence, and was otherwise theologically unsound, and consequently an unsafe teacher.

It is needless to cumber these pages with the

falsehoods and half-truths, worse than falsehoods, with which he effected his purpose, all the while attitudinizing as an aggrieved friend of Dr. Blentwood. Suffice it to say, no notice of the adjourned meeting was handed me to read the following Sunday. This aroused the friends of Dr. Blentwood, comprising all the thinking and wealthy members of the society, and a paper was circulated, giving a very cordial and urgent invitation to Dr. Blentwood to take charge of an independent body to be known as the Church of Christian Endeavor, with pledges amounting to $2,500,00 for his yearly salary—$500 more than he was then receiving. This paper was to be presented by an influential committee on the doctor's return from his vacation trip.

CHAPTER XLI.

THE maiden aunt of Miss Elison died suddenly, and Mr. Elison, who felt her loss keenly, was taken ill a few days later, and sent for me. I went at once to his bedside, and found him much agitated. Drawing me towards him, and eyeing Mr. Stockmire, who had become a boarder in the family and very officious in his attentions to all the inmates, he said in a half whisper, " I am being poisoned." Whether Mr. Stockmire heard these fearful words or not, he must have divined their import; for, on my departure, he followed me to the door, and soberly asked:

"You will not think anything of what he said ? "

"Certainly not," I answered, "Mr. Elison is evidently a little out, and not responsible for all he says."

In three days Mr. Elison was dead; and from that hour Mrs. Elison became a changed woman. At the funeral her pale, haggard face moved my sympathies deeply, and I tried in vain to lead her to rest her burden at the feet of the

382

Burden-bearer, and to remember that she had not lost her husband, but that he had only gone a few days in advance to eventually welcome her to a better mansion on high. I called the next day, and reminded her that she had now a loved daughter to live for, hoping, by centering her thoughts and affections on the living, to bring her back to the duties of the present; but she was uncommunicative, and her eyes were fevered and wild, like one surprised and stunned by a blow from a friend, and had no one left to trust. She seemed frightened at times and to pant for words to express something, and would then make some commonplace remark, all the more pathetic from the effort made to conceal, rather than reveal, her thoughts.

I found it impossible to comfort her, and she grew paler every day, until she became ghostly, and almost transparent in appearance. Taking her bed soon, she gradually, but steadily, wasted away, her physician, as he explained it, finding in her system no leverage of strength, against which his medicine could pry.

But before her demise the city was thrown into excitement by the news of a railroad accident, and that among the dead and wounded were Dr. Blentwood and daughter. From the description given, I concluded that the accident occurred not far from the Thorntons, and I took the next train for the scene of sorrow.

I will not burden the reader with any details of the sickening horror, of which the papers were full. Suffice it to say that the names of my loved friends were not among the dead. Hearing that Thornton was early on the scene of action, and that he and his sister had thrown open their house to the wounded, I crossed the newly-made gully, bridged by an overturned car, and was quickly at their door. Mr. Thornton met me cordially, and, to my earnest question, answered that the parties I desired to see were there, all the others having been removed by their friends, and he took me at once to Dr. Blentwood's bedside. He looked up, as we approached, with a pleased surprise, and returned my greeting with all the warmth of his friendly nature.

" Providence has sent you to me a second time," he said with a grateful smile, " once on your account and now on my account. We are friends by providential arrangement, and may be destined to some pleasant duties together hereafter, differences of age and strength notwithstanding."

" Yes," I answered, venturing at what I thought to be his meaning, " neither extent of space nor duration of time, nor the loss of what is merely foreign and of no further use to us, can touch our souls or our friendship."

He pressed my hand, which still enclosed his, as he added, " You and I know—and what a comfort it is!—that real life is not dependent on fortune or misfortune. It is beyond the reach of accident or bodily disaster."

As he paused, I looked about the room, and

seeing the question in my eyes, he explained the absent one by saying:

" Ethel, dear girl, I hope is fast asleep. She has been an angel of mercy, watching by my side, anticipating every want, heroically covering every sign of fatigue, till I became conscious enough to know she was almost completely exhausted, and then I had to plead our mutual love before she would go willingly to seek rest in sleep. She is like her mother, all devotion, self-sacrifice itself. God bless her ! " and the tears moistened his eyes. " For her sake only I would like to live a little longer, until——"

He did not finish, and I said enthusiastically, " You will ; you must ! "

He smiled faintly, and, noting his weakness, and promising to see him after he rested, I retired to the adjoining room. Thornton was waiting for me, and I asked :

" Where is your sister? "

" Theo," he answered, " is in bed. I left her a few moments ago resting beautifully."

" What ! Is she ill? Was she hurt ? " I asked eagerly.

" No, not hurt," he answered, " but she over-worked in the excitement of the disaster, and, being delicate, she was quickly prostrated. I hope to see her up in a day or two ; but she is not so strong as when you were here before, and every unfavorable circumstance, like this, worries me, though, in the end, I think, through Miss Blentwood, it may be a God-send to her ; for they

25

fell in love with each other at once, and it was Miss Blentwood who put Theo to bed, and has run to her whenever she could leave her father even for a moment. She seems a charming girl, and a very worthy daughter of a very worthy man. Old acquaintances of yours, I infer?"

"Yes," I answered, thinking of heart-throbs rather than clock-time, "and very dear friends of mine; but when can I see Miss Thornton?"

"She will wish to see you as soon as she learns you are here."

"Has she really been failing in health?"

"Yes, rapidly."

"Can nothing be done to arrest the disease?"

"Everything apparently has been tried; but it is a case physicians cannot control."

I looked at him inquiringly, and he proceeded.

"There is one man, and only one, who can prolong her life, and he is not a physician."

"And he will not?" I asked in surprise, and then recalling my last interview with her, I added, "Does not the man she admires and loves yet know?"

He eyed me closely, and, it seemed to me, almost suspiciously, as he answered, "She has told you all, and yet you ask such a question?"

"Nay, not all. I only know she worships some one, and my advice to her was to let the man know the treasures of heart and brain in store for him."

"I believe you," he said, thrusting his hands through his hair in great perplexity.

"Believe me! Did you say believe me? That implies a previous doubt. Explain yourself," I said with great earnestness.

"I—I thought," he stammered,—"I mean I had special reasons for wishing that you did not know, and my words were in the nature of a glad assurance to myself, and yet, I thought—I naturally inferred that you knew. I see now how it is. I suppose sister Theo confided in you to get your advice. Do you still advise that he be informed?"

"Yes; for he may be a modest, self-depreciating person, who could not believe, unless actually told, that he is the subject of so much good fortune; and such a love, from so noble a woman, is certainly no common prize in this world of superficial attachments, and one too valuable to be lost. It is above all price to any man worthy of her. It is such love that redeems the world; for it is akin to that which saves the soul from sin."

"It ought not to be difficult to tell one who appreciates her, and yet I hesitate; for it will be against her will. I came into her secret through a transaction requiring my approval and signature. I have not her delicacy of feeling, and think I ought to tell, and yet I would not have her know —O, for God's sake save me this hard duty! Theo is my only sister and almost my only relative. Why need I say more? God forgive me, if I have wrongly interfered in this matter, and done more harm than good."

" What do you mean? You cannot mean——? No, impossible ! "

" I'm rough, sir, and unused to such matters ; but remember it is hard to see her wasting away. Her life is in your hands. Oh ! this is terrible to you, I fear, and in me a grave mistake ! "

He rushed from the room, and left me in dumb amazement. A thunderbolt from a clear sky would not have startled me more. What was there in me to call forth such love ? I asked my-self over and over. The idea seemed absurd, and yet absurdities had developed in the world before, and though I repeated, " Impossible, impossible," and declared, " There must be some mistake," the clearer I recalled my last conversation with Theo, the clearer came the conviction that I was the man. But what had I done to evoke her love ? and what was I to do about it ? Here was a dilemma.

I began to chastize myself for being thoughtless in my deportment towards her ; and yet I could not recall one word or act, which could lead her to regard me other than a friend. I had fre-quently said to my mates, that it was of the nature of murder to deliberately win a girl's affections only to blast them ; and here I was where I must save or blight the future of a very dear friend. I thought I had realized before how careful a young man should be of giving a wrong impression, but the danger was greater than I supposed ; and I record this maze into which I had fallen as a warning to others, who may read these pages.

Here I was with all my hopes, and perhaps those of another, in one hand, and the very life of a most estimable young lady in the other. Which should I choose? It was a terrible ordeal for weak human nature. No one, who has not stood where I stood, can have any adequate idea of the perplexity, the self-accusation and torture I suffered. The perspiration stood beaded upon my forehead. I clutched a chair, not for support merely, but that by some expression I might clear my brain for more thorough and exact thought. What if Ethel Blentwood, to whom I had probably revealed something of my feelings, had begun to regard me as my heart had so ardently craved! What if the future of two persons depended on me! Where then would lie the path of duty? For duty and right, I was clear, should be consulted, and not my own happiness.

But how could I know what injury I might be doing Ethel by turning to Theo? Ethel must know something of my feelings for her, and Theo must remember that I told her plainly of my love for another, though she knows not that that other is Ethel. If I knew Ethel would reject me, the line of duty would be plain, and, furthermore, I could not be unhappy in the great love of so noble a girl as Theodocia Thornton; but, and here was the rub, if the discovery should ever overtake me when too late to remedy it, that Ethel's life was being shortened on account of my apparent treachery, the thought would kill me.

"O, God!" I cried in my heart, as I sank on my knees, "why am I in this seemingly wicked position, where I may do harm whichever way I turn? Forgive me if the fault be mine, and lead me through whatever punishment, if only I may undo any possible harm I have done. Wherever Thou leadest, I will go." In that surrender I felt that I should be guided.

I had arisen and was resting my head in my right hand, my elbow against the window-casing, when I heard the rustle of a lady's dress, and knew that Ethel was in the room. I turned, and, true to my heart's divination, there she was in all her grace and beauty advancing towards me, pale but calm. I took her extended hand tremblingly into mine, and held it while she said:

"It is very kind of you, Professor Bloomfield, to come to us in this hour of our great anxiety."

I wished to remind her that she was to call me Elbert, but the thought of Theo deterred me, and I tried to appear only as a sincere and grateful friend. I was congratulating her on her providential escape from the railroad catastrophe, when Dr. Lightheart was announced. Although the local doctors had done nobly, no one could take the place of the old family physician, in whose friendly skill and knowledge of the patient's power of endurance we all had confidence. His coming was a great relief to Ethel; for she felt sure that the very best that was in him, of brain and heart and untiring study of the case, would be given her father; and so felt we all.

He was soon at Dr. Blentwood's side, and we awaited his diagnosis as patiently as we could, and when he returned to us we looked to him eagerly for the verdict. He tried to look cheerful for Ethel's sake and said:

" Dr. Blentwood is hurt internally, but how seriously I cannot at present determine. I am going to take the whole care of him to-night, and watch every symptom. There is no immediate danger, but I will not leave him until I know what I can do for him."

A conscientious physician, who will not prescribe until he knows the condition of the patient he is prescribing for, is a great blessing to the world; and this thought, awakened by Dr. Lightheart, has never left me.

He ordered us all to bed, assuring us he could watch the patient better alone with nothing to distract his attention. " I must look through that man," he said, " and so must need concentrate every faculty and power I possess."

This was hardly a hyperbolic expression. He had cultivated his powers of perception to such a degree of intensity that, with his scientific knowledge, it was almost literally true, that he could see into the human system. Every faculty we possess, is susceptible of improvement, and mental sight is no exception. It is a part of our heritage, if we will take it, to think more, feel more, see more, and be more as time wears on.

We do not know the alphabet of our powers yet.
It seems miraculous to talk with a person a thousand miles away by means of the telephonic wire;
but it is not nonsense to say that the time may
come, by living up to our privileges, when mind
will communicate with mind without the aid of
telephonic appliances, or perhaps of even physical
speech. Were we sufficiently spiritual, we might
not need to wait the end of the world to be
" caught up " into celestial society; we could see
through the veil, and be literally with the Lord
now.

Miss Blentwood retired that night, as we all
did, feeling comforted and confident, knowing
that her father was in safe hands. Poor girl! she
needed that night's rest to prepare her for what
was to be revealed the next morning, when she
and I reached the door of the room adjoining
that of her father, which we did at the same moment. It was ajar, and there, opposite, sat Dr.
Lightheart, so deeply absorbed that he did not
notice us, the tears rolling down his kindly, sympathetic face.

We stood still for a minute, till he looked up,
and then Ethel advanced tremblingly, fell down
at his knee, and wept silently. The good doctor
bowed his head to hers, and, with one hand gently
resting on her head, whispered softly:

" He will not suffer much, his mind will be
clear, and you will have him perhaps a week
longer, and, when he goes, you will not feel that
you have lost your father."

She struggled with her tears a little longer, and then raised a victorious face, the most spiritual I ever beheld, and, with a grateful look at the faithful doctor, she passed into the sick room. What thoughts were there exchanged with her father, and the greater Father above, we knew not ; for we felt that one room in that house was, at that time, too sacred for us to enter.

CHAPTER XLII.

"BLOODY NIGGER."

I FOUND it impossible to sit, and so, passing down into the parlor, I was pacing up and down the long room, my image reflected by mirrors from every side, giving the impression that there were many others as excited as myself, when, hearing a scream, I opened the dining-room door. As I did so, Polly Durgin, whom I had almost forgotten, came rushing in from the kitchen, wildly gesticulating and exclaiming, " Bloody nigger! O—oh!"

Sure enough, there lay a negro on the kitchen-floor with evident traces of blood on his forehead; and what was my surprise to recognize in the prostrate form, Tom, the faithful servant of the Blentwoods!

"Are you hurt, Tom?" I asked, feeling his pulse; and, ascertaining that he had probably fainted, I gave directions to Polly, and then went quietly for Dr. Lightheart, who soon had him restored to consciousness.

Taking him by the hand, I said:

" Tom, my good fellow, what brought you here in such a plight?"

"Seems like I dunno perzackly. Please gimme sumfin ter chaw. Cup-er-tea'd feel mighty ticklish. I's clean plumb gone wid vacancy."

Polly brought him a lunch, and, soon after, a cup of smoking tea, and then I impatiently renewed my inquiry.

"Do tell us, Tom, what has happened to you?"

"It happen' las' night, sah, and it seem long time since de las' meal got away from me, and de smell ob dis yere beckfus make me feel powerful glad dat I has room for it. I is empty's er gun barrel arter de charge am fired off."

He ate voraciously as if starved, but, after swallowing two or three cups of strong tea, his tongue was loosed, and his eyes opened wide.

"I bigin to 'cognize whar I be and de concatenation ob events. I's powerful exercise wid pleasure to seen you faces once mo', Perfessor Boomfield and Dr. Lightheart. Peerd like I'd nebber git heyah nohow; but de Lord am too much for de debble ebery time," and Tom began to grin and lift his shoulders in high glee over the way he outwitted the devil.

Dropping his knife and fork, as if struck with a sudden recollection, he put his hand into his breast pocket, and then into one still more interior, when, wild with excitement, he exclaimed, "De letter am gone sure, and I is no mo' worthy to be called a messenger ob de Lord. De debble smarter den I tuk him, or, may be—I mus' go right back whar I had de squabble wid 'im."

He rose to go, groaning under his sense of un-
faithfulness, but I detained him.

"Tom, did any one entrust you with a letter
to me?"

"She did, sah; she trusted me, and I——"

"Who trusted you?"

"Missus Elison, and she charge me mos' on
her dyin' bed to gib it to nobody but you, and
when she'd got one foot on de golden stair, I
started wid the letter in heyah," striking his
breast.

"What became of that letter?"

"Dat be jes' zakly what bustifies my compre-
hension, sah. When I travel a good smart piece,
and it were mos' dark, a team obertuk me, and
went by like Jehu. De man's face were covered
up wid him coat collar and hat, and I thunked
by myself, What if dat be Stockmire? Ob cose
it ain't though, and yet I was afeared, for I spi-
cioned de letter had sumfin to do wid 'im.

"Wall, de road tuk me fro' some woods, and,
when furd nuf in to be dark, I seed what peered
like a horse and wagin side de road, and fore I
knowed it I tuk to my heels, but sumfin hit me
on de head, and I din know no mo' for a spell.
When I wake up, man say way down him froat,
like bullfrog, if I stir he blow my brain out. I
axed him what for he want me, and he say money.
Dat ar' revive me; for I fort ef he doan want de
letter, he be welcome to de fifty cents; and so I
comed away mighty tickled. But now I's tetotlum obfuscated whudder de letter drop out some

way, or whudder de debble tuk it for to punish
me fer—fer my sin."

" What sin, Tom ? "

" Dunno, 'less cause I look too smilin' for a
married man on a purty yaller gal I met on de
road. Yaller be my special takin' color, and she
look so peert and cheery ! But I come right
away, sah, and din't roll de sweet morsel ober in
my heart."

" It was Stockmire, and not the devil, who took
your letter," broke in Dr. Lightheart.

" Wall, doctor, if Stockmire got de letter, and
de debble got Stockmire, peers like all de same,
don't it ? "

" Not much difference, Tom ; but I withdraw
my assertion. I don't say who the scamp is, that
robbed you."

" Perhaps I were puffed up wid pride, and de
Lord wanted ter spank de wind outer me. What
kin I do, gemmen ? "

" You can watch and search wherever you
have any suspicions," I said guardedly, " and
here is five dollars for what you have tried to do
thus far."

He took the money with widely dilating eyes ;
but before he could express his emotions, Miss
Blentwood came into the kitchen, and exclaimed,
" Is that you, Tom ? and what is the matter ? "

" It is I, Miss Ethel, and tank de Lord you is
safe. We were mighty skeered at fus, dat you
bof were smash up ; but de report wer conter-
dicted."

" Father was hurt, and you shall see him presently." She got a basin of water, and washed the blood from his forehead with her own hands, and, covering the bruise with courtplaster, she took him to her father's bedside. We did not follow, but as he left the kitchen, we caught the murmured words, " angel ob de Lord," and when he returned he was weeping sadly. He had prayed with the doctor at the latter's request, and now, heart-broken with fear, like the elders in separating from Paul, that he should see his face no more, he burst out in his grief:

" I doan see how de Lord kin stan' de dear pleadin' face ob Miss Ethel! Ef I were on de frone, peers like, I'd raise de good man up quicker'n lightnin', ef it busted me, and I had ter pick up de plaguy splinters and build my calkerlations all ober agin! I say, it peers like; but I is a poor fool before de Lord, and I 'spects He laugh at my heterdoxy, and will sometime make us all laugh when we discubber how much wiser He lub us den we lub ourselves. He knows I is a po' silly coot; but He pity me, 'cause I feels so bad in my ignorance. De dear doctor! De dear Miss Ethel!"

His voice choked, and he could say no more. As he was not needed, he could not be prevailed upon to even wait for a more hearty breakfast; but, provided with a generous lunch, he started homeward, declaring if he could not find the letter on the way back, he would follow his "spici-ons unde: de eye ob de Lord widout fear."

CHAPTER XLIII.

A SUPPOSED ENGAGEMENT.

AFTER breakfast Theodore Thornton or Thede, as he was called, whispered that his sister was sitting up and would see me. I went to my room, and in silent prayer, asked to be guided aright in all I should do or say.

On my way to Theo, I managed to get one more look at Ethel, while my heart was hers, and before it might be bound to another. I would have given worlds, I thought, had I them to give, could I know what her feelings were towards me.

"Does she see how I have silently loved her? and does she expect me to avow it? and will she be disappointed and suffer if I do not?" These and other burning questions surged through my brain, and stirred my heart, as I looked longingly after her for some sign or token for my guidance, ere it should be too late. My destiny seemed to me to be hanging in the balance, which a few minutes would decide irrevocably and forever. She looked pale, doubtless thinking of her father, but no less beautiful on that account. Indeed, her pathetic, spiritual face seemed all the more glorified as if it had caught something of the light which illumines the immortal fields beyond.

399

"She would never suffer on my account like Theo," I thought; for she is stronger to conquer disappointment, but more especially because she could never love me like Theo. She is too supremely lovely to find sufficient attractions in me," and I turned away with a sigh and a benumbing pain in my heart, which words cannot describe.

"God, help me to do just right," was my prayer, as I stopped at Theo's door, which was slightly ajar, and entered in answer to her voice. She certainly looked very attractive, even angelic, and it seemed to me there must be some mistake in Thede's intimation that I was the ideal object of her devotion. If Thede was right, she must have got too high an impression of me, and it was my first duty to undeceive her if possible.

As I have elsewhere explained, Theo and Ethel had attractive qualities very much in common. Their points of resemblance in disposition and in their innocent, winsome ways were wonderful; and I was conscious that I liked Theo immensely, and that had I not met Ethel, that liking might easily ripen into love, especially under the warmth of her own great affection.

After we had exchanged greetings and little mutual confidences, in which she revealed some traits strikingly reminding me of Ethel, I exclaimed in a burst of frankness, "Were there ever before in this world two such delightful creatures as you and Miss Blentwood!"

"Is she the one? Is Ethel the one?" Theo

repeated eagerly, her face all aglow with interest.
She raised her hand trembling with excitement, as
if to wrest the truth from me. "If she is the one
I am the happiest person alive."

She does not love me after all, I thought, and
strange to say, I felt a twinge of disappointment.
If Theo did not, then Ethel could not, and I felt
myself rejected by both.

"Are you then so eager to get rid of me?" I
asked unreasonably, forgetting for the moment
that I was supposed to be ignorant of her love for
me.

"I?" she asked, looking at me greatly puzzled.
"Have you forgotten the conversation we had on
a former occasion?"

"No."

"You then loved one to whom you had not proposed?"

"Yes."

"Well, now my question was simply this, Is
Ethel Blentwood the one? I call her Ethel, for
we have become the most intimate and dearest of
friends."

"If you two could not love each other," I said,
trying to smile, "I should think the world was
going back to chaos, and that such propositions
in Euclid as, 'Things equal to the same thing are
equal to each other,' are fundamentally wrong, and
that there is no such thing as a self-evident truth."

"That does not answer my question, please,"
she urged, half smiling, yet with an anxious, wistful look.

26

"Well, what if I did have the hardihood to love Ethel Blentwood——"

"Did? Do you not love her still?"

"Well, what if I do? A cat can look at a king; but that does not imply that the king takes any notice of the cat. My love, however, is not an impertinence so long as I do not trouble her with it."

"Why not trouble her with it, pray?"

"It would be foolish to expect her to respond favorably, and I fear it would be wrong to ask it of one so superior to me every way—so worthy of the wealthiest as well as the wisest and best."

"You do not estimate yourself at your proper value, unlike most young men I know."

"Do you mean to imply that Ethel Blentwood could love me?"

"I don't see how she could help it, if she felt sure of you. Why do you doubt?"

"Because—because I think if—if you do not, she cannot; for you two are strangely blended in my ideal. You belong together. It is hard to separate you."

She looked up at me amazed, and yet pleased, as she saw I was not trifling. The color came and went, the golden clasp on her bosom rose and fell, and visibly shook with the conflict of her emotions. She dropped her eyes, but at length growing calm, looked up at me so frankly, so completely unreserved, and withal so affectionately, that I wanted to clasp her in my arms, and call her my—dear sister. I refrained, how-

ever, from the fear that I should use stronger
terms, and, thus, perhaps, go beyond the leadings
or requirements of Providence.

"I see," she said, "you wish me to interpret
Ethel's feelings towards you. You are right in
this, that our tastes are alike, and our hearts beat
as one. What she loves I love, and, therefore,
only one of us can marry, and that one cannot be
myself."

Not knowing what I ought to say, but thinking
of Thede's implication that her very life depended
on me, I arose and walked the room. Stopping
at length near her chair, and placing my left hand
on her shoulder, I asked:

"If it be true that you two must love only the
same person, why should you yield the wedding-
ring to Ethel? Why not accept it yourself?"

"If I could, you mean;" and she smiled
tenderly up at me. Closing her eyes for a
moment, either to think or to hide them from
me, she continued, "I think I can put my answer
into three reasons: First, Ethel has the prospect
of a long and helpful life, while my days are
numbered; second, she could make the man of
her choice more useful, and therefore, perhaps,
more blessed than I could; and third, I should
feel happier in her happiness, as well as more
content with myself in the consciousness of doing
right, than I otherwise could."

"You are an unselfish girl," I said warmly.
"You will occupy a higher place in heaven than
I. You deserve it. You are qualified for it.

Yes, you have the qualities that make heaven on the earth. Why not live, and make it?"

"I would if I could," she answered, sweetly puzzled. "Where and how shall I begin?"

"Begin with me, here and now," I replied, led on by great admiration and sympathy, by a desire to discharge my whole duty, by the luxury of self-sacrifice for another's welfare, by gratitude for her affection, and by a feeling closely akin to love. "You must not think of dying. The world needs you. Your friends need you. I need you. Live for me, if for no one else. Will you? Promise you will live for my sake." I took both of her hands in mine, and the consciousness that I was doing right thrilled me with content and happiness, as I waited her answer.

"May I not live for another's sake?" she asked, with a roguish twinkle in her moist eyes, referring to Ethel, though I did not then catch her meaning.

"Yes, for your sake and mine," was my answer.

"I feel as if I must cry a little," she said, with a trembling voice. "Will you let me cry on your shoulder?"

"Certainly," I replied, drawing her to me; "cry all you wish. When she at last dried her eyes, and looked up, she asked:

"Do you think me childish?"

"No," I answered, "it is even noble to cry. The shedding of tears is something the lower animals cannot do. Jesus wept, and He was the highest ideal of humanity. I should be afraid of a woman who could not cry, and I hope you will cry in the same place whenever you feel like it."

She laughed a happy, bird-like little laugh, and said gratefully, " I thought men did not like to see women cry. I thank you for bearing with me. I appreciate your kindness, and am myself again now."

" I hope you will have no cause for weeping, except for joy on your own account, or in sympathy for others. But you have not answered my question. Will you start a heaven on the earth, and live for my sake?"

" Does that depend on my own volition?" she asked, smiling.

"Yes."

" Then I will accomplish my mission, if you will let me have my own way about it."

" You shall follow your own sweet will fully and freely. Gladden us all by getting well, and I will be obedient to your every wish."

"I thank you," she said simply, though affectionately, " and now let us talk of another matter?"

Not appearing to notice my surprise at this anti-romantic climax, she asked, " Do you know one of Dr. Blentwood's parishioners by the name of Stockmire?"

" Somewhat."

" What kind of a man is he?"

" I do not know."

" You doubt him?"

" Perhaps unjustly."

" Well, Ethel has showed me a letter from him, on which I wish your opinion, as she wished mine. Mr. Stockmire writes he cannot take as final Ethel's refusal of her hand in marriage, and urges her to consider well her father's lost fortune, and his precarious pastorate, which may terminate any day, should he withhold his aid, but which, supported as it always would be, by him as his son-in-law, might be prolonged indefinitely. He closes by trusting, that, for her sake as well as that of her father, who losing his present pastor-ate, would be too old and feeble to command another, she would respond favorably to this, his last appeal. He would give her two days to decide, and then, if not heard from, he should let things take their course."

" The rascal ! " I said, springing up from Theo's chair, on which I was sitting. " She must loathe the reptile. What does she say ! What——"

" Please be not so excited,'' interrupted Theo, with a meaning smile and a still more meaning little shake of her head. " Your judgment may not be disinterested ; but I think you are right. A man, who would bring a girl's father into his plea for her hand the way Mr. Stockmire does, is— is all you pronounce him to be. Ethel asked me if duty to her father required her to make such a sacrifice. She trembled as she asked it ; for she loves her father, and would do everything she deemed right to save him pain or add to his happiness."

" And what *did* you tell her ? " I asked, unable

to wait longer, and not realizing that Theo might
be testing my feelings for Ethel.

"Ah! you are interested, I see," she answered,
looking at me slyly, and yet sympathetically. "I
admire your impatience. Well, I told her I would
help remove the sense of duty, and then she could
let her heart decide. I went—for my sympathies
made me strong—I went to the safe where Thede
and I keep some of our valuables, and, taking
three thousand dollars in Government bonds, I
placed them in her hands."

"Noble soul!" I cried, taking my seat again
on the arm of her chair, and looking at her
admiringly. "How can the world spare such a
blessing as you are to everybody?"

"Oh! that was not a noble act," she answered,
deprecatingly. "I fear it was one of the most
selfish things I ever did."

"I would like to know how you figure that
out," I interjected.

"For," she went on as if I had not spoken,
"I loved her from the very first, thoroughly, ex-
haustively, if you know what that means, and
craved her love in return—craved it with almost
a death hunger, and I wished to bind her to me
forever, as well as to save her for her own sake."

"I do not wonder," I said, enthusiastically,
" for——"

She put her hand on my mouth with, "Tell
that to Ethel."

"Well," I said, patting her flushed cheek, "do
let me wish the world were full of just such self-

ish creatures as you are. And now tell me how Ethel received your kindness, or selfishness, if you so term it."

" O, she refused it until she saw she was making me unhappy, when she accepted ; and then we embraced and kissed each other, and cried and laughed, and finally thanked God together, she for the rescue as she called it, and both of us for a God-given friend. I do believe Ethel Blent-wood is the best girl that ever lived ; and I feel so exalted by her love—so happy in it ! And—and then there is your own, good, kind, noble, generous self ! I have both of you, the very best of your kind. I have abundant reason to be grateful. And Oh! I am in ecstasies of delight at the prospect of a goodly mission before my promotion to a higher service, where, at the proper time, I will wait and watch at the gate for Ethel and for you. And now, good-by for a while ; for I think I can rest with pleasant dreams, day-dreams though they be."

CHAPTER XLIV.

CHARLEY AND I.

AS I left the room, Theodore Thornton met me in the hall, and announced that Dr. Lightheart's brother had arrived and wished to see me. I found Charley in the parlor walking the floor impatiently, and he sprang to me with his old-time, delightful greeting.

"I have seen Ethel and her father," he said, "and I fear she will soon have to find in you a father as well as a friend."

A groan escaped me at the thought of being debarred from that privilege. Charley took it only as a token of sympathy, and went on:

"You need not fear Stockmire; he has married Miss Elison, and, with her parents dead, he is now in the coveted management of all the Elison estate."

"Well, well!" I exclaimed, "When did that take place?"

"Last evening, and he has sold his business and is to go west at once, doubtless full of dreams of coming millions on a cattle ranch, which is the promising business just now."

"You surprise me. The movement is so sudden, so extraordinary!"

"It is high time he's off. His popularity is on
the wane. People are putting together his con-
troversy with Deacon Toper, in which it is now
believed Stockmire lied; his taking pay fraudu-
lently out of the proceeds of a church fair for his
own dishes, which he, himself broke by his own
carelessness; his selling bonds, which he must
have known to be worthless, though it cannot be
proved; his dishonest stand against Dr. Blentwood, pretending to be his friend, when he was
at the bottom of all the mischief; and finally, his
obtaining money under false pretences, to say
nothing of whisperings and suspicions of something too dark to be believed——"

"I cannot think he committed murder," I
broke in, "though the three deaths naturally
raise a suspicion. Stockmire had two gods,
money and position, and his object with the
pastor was to line his own pockets, and, at the
same time, reduce Dr. Blentwood to penury and
dependence, and secure the hand of Ethel through
her sense of duty to her father." I related what
the reader already knows.

"He is a worse knave than I supposed!"
Charley exclaimed. "And that reminds me,
there may be something worth studying in these
bits of a letter Tom made me promise to deliver
to you."

He poured the contents of an envelope on a
table, and we worked on the pieces for over an

hour, arranging and rearranging ; but so many
bits being gone, we could make out only parts of
sentences. On one piece was " Mrs. E.," which,
we inferred, might be the signature to a letter
from Mrs. Elison. Other pieces indicated a
financial statement by Mr. Stockmire, in which
the names of Elison and Blentwood appear with
the selling to them of Vt. C. bonds, at a net
profit of $10,000 ; but we could not make out a
statement sufficiently clear to prove a fraudulent
transaction, however morally convinced of his
rascality. Miss Blentwood was called in and
asked how many bonds her father bought of Mr.
Stockmire. She only knew that nearly all his
means were invested in them, even to a large
mortgage on their house, probably all the house
would sell for in the present financial depression.

"When did you learn they were worthless ?" I
asked.

"The evening before we left home," was her
answer.

"Ah !" I said, " that accounts for your agitated condition the next morning at breakfast."

"You noticed it, then! Well, it was wholly
on father's account I was troubled. He does not
yet know his loss, and I do not wish him to know.
I prefer Mr. Stockmire should go unpunished
rather than disturb father's few remaining days
by the thought that I am left penniless. I am
not destitute, however, thanks to a very dear
friend," referring to Theo.

Cut off from the only source of information available, and as Stockmire was about to leave the state, we felt forced to drop the whole matter, and leave him in the hands of Providence, believing that in time his real character would be revealed.

"And now, Elbert, my boy," said Charley brightening, and placing a hand on my knee familiarly, as we were alone again, "let us talk about a matter, where I am living mostly these days. Congratulate me on my forthcoming promotion on the paper. It is a worldly fact, I know ; but it stands in the outer court of my soul, prophetic of paradise ; for promotion means more money, and more money means housekeeping! As soon as I am advanced in pay, I shall run for the steam cars pointing towards wedded bliss. You know Carrie has consented to begin at the foot of the hill, and climb up with me ; and when the little more pay comes, I shall fly to my Carrie, and then to you. Have the noose ready to slip over our heads at once."

"No immediate danger of a promotion?" I asked, smiling at his half-earnest and half-mock enthusiasm.

"It may come to-morrow, and if it does, steam-power will be too slow in taking me to Carrie, the first and only real Carrie of the ages ; the town clerk will be too slow in writing out the certificate, and the distance thence to you will seem leagues too long!"

"Carrie's folk will wish to give her a home wedding and reception, will they not, Charley?"

"A reception is all right. I can issue 'At Homes' after my happiness is secured; but a wedding party implies delay, and delay is suspended life. What! do you suppose I am going to dally outside of domestic felicity after the only hinderance to our marriage is removed? I am not the boy to rush headlong, panting for breath, in my hurry to reach heaven's door, and then stand shivering on the step with my hand on the door knob! No sir! The moment my hand is on the knob, the knob turns, the door to double blessedness flies open, and I am within! Every second of felicity in this world is worth saving that's my motto; and, whenever and wherever I see any particles of bliss lying round loose, I am going to pick them up, if I have a right to them."

"An excellent motto, Charley, if rightly apprehended," I said, after getting control of myself. "It enfolds a whole volume of sermons. If people would appreciate and use every opportunity of giving and receiving pleasure, this world would quickly become a paradise. The world has advanced in science and the arts, and general intelligence, much faster than it has in learning how to be happy. Sympathy and spirituality lag behind; and half the cruelty and half the unhappiness of the world comes from sheer, stupid incapacity to put one's self in another's place."

"Good, my dear Elbert! Now put yourself in

Ethel's place. Her father is about to take a long journey never to return, and then she will be lonely indeed. Make her and that anxious father both happy by marrying her before he goes."

" Your application isn't the logical sequence to my comment on your motto, I think; but if it is, you forget, Charley, that it takes two, and in this case three, to make a bargain, and that the standard of excellence with Ethel Blentwood and her father is very, very high—too high for me to reach."

" I forget nothing. They are both great and good, I know, and so are you. Oh, don't interrupt me with that deprecating look and gesture. I'll take your opinion on everything except yourself. Don't you suppose I know the estimation in which you are held? If you wasn't as blind as a bat, you would see that Ethel loves you, and that nothing would please her father more——"

" Oh, don't, Charley!" I interrupted, "you are cutting me as with a knife."

" I am only trying to cut away the films from your eyes to give you a glimpse, and then a walk-over, straight into heaven—a heaven below, I mean. Is it a torture to take a peep into unlimited happiness?"

"You know not what you are saying," I said, rising and walking the room, trembling with emotion. " The subject is too painful, too sacred to trifle with. Let us talk of something to our profit."

" For once, at least, I am serious," he replied,

coming forward and placing both hands on my shoulders. "Mark my words: Ethel loves you, and expects you to propose. You have given her reason to expect it, and if you do not, the first sin of your life, I believe, lies at your door."

"Charley Lightheart!" I cried, grasping his arms in the intensity of my feelings, "you and I are near and dear friends, and I charge you, if merely surmising, to take back those words, and save me from a life-long sorrow."

"What can you mean, old friend? Don't I know how you have loved her? And now do you not welcome her love in return? Are you not the same Elbert? How can I recall words truly spoken? And why should they not make you glad?"

"Charley," I answered, slowly and solemnly, "what if duty calls in another direction, and the very life of a noble girl hangs on my willingness to put the wedding-ring on her finger?"

"Is it possible you could give another girl reason?"

"No, no, Charley; not knowingly. Indeed, I expressly told her (when she was extolling some-one I had no reason to infer was myself) that I loved another. It has always been a matter of sacred honor with me to give no false impression. I speak in confidence, because you require an explanation, and I trust in your honor not to repeat it. Remember, I am not to be commiserated. Theo is worth a dozen of me, and will make me abundantly happy, if ·I can be assured

I have done no harm to Ethel, to whom I may have unconsciously revealed my heart. God bless them both."

" Ah! it is Theo, is it? She is indeed a noble girl ; but I do want you to marry Ethel for her sake, for her father's sake, for your sake and mine, and for the sake of the infinite fitness of things; and I do not think she can forget you any easier than Theo, though, being stronger, she may more easily conquer and control her outward appearance. I believe she can love as truly, as tenaciously, and even more heroically."

" Her equal she may doubtless so love, but I am not her equal; besides, what can I do, Charley? I do not deserve either of these girls. God help me to know and to do exactly what is right. I see no way but to go right on as Providence seems to direct, hoping for the best."

We were silent for a few minutes, when Mr. Thornton came in to take us to dinner. He had looked in upon Theo, and his face was beaming with gladness. Casting a grateful glance at me, he said, " The day of miracles is not passed! Theo says she is to dine with us to-day, and is more like her old self than for a long time."

CHAPTER XLV.

THEO IMPARTS A SECRET.

THEDE had hardly finished, when Theo entered the room with a pleasant greeting, and a cordial welcome to Charley, and walked to the dining-room with as firm a step, apparently, as if she had not been ill. She took my offered arm, she said, "as an ornament, and not for use." She was very chatty at table, and entertained us with her varied and pleasing conversation.

As we rose from dinner, and lingered a little behind the others, she squeezed my arm, and, looking up at me archly, remarked in a low voice :

"I have a surprise for you, and am so happy over it, I don't know what to do with myself, or when and how to tell you. I think I must roll it as a precious morsel under my tongue, and enjoy its sweetness as long as possible."

"Will the sweetness exhale as soon as you have parted with the secret?"

"No, indeed! but the surprise will."

"Well, now you have warned me, I shall be fortified against surprise."

"Against the fact, but not against the kind. I have taken Ethel and her father into my con-

fidence somewhat—just a little bit, to make sure
it would not kill them!—did it when you and
Charley were entertaining each other. And I
shall break the news to you—oh, sometime!"

"Is it something dreadful, Theo? Had I
better take chloroform as a preparation? Is it
something that will come suddenly or gradually?
And will it last long?"

"Ah! how much will you give to know?"
with a tantalizing look and a pretty shake of the
head. "Oh—Oh! I am afraid I shall have to
tell right off. It is too great happiness to keep
from you any longer. You are too good a boy.
After Charley leaves, come into my sitting-room."

We had now reached the long parlor, where
Ethel excused herself, and, bidding Charley good-
bye, went to her father. Charley left soon on
"urgent business" for his paper, and Theo, in-
forming her brother she had something to tell
him by and bye, went to her room, leaving Thede
and me alone together.

"I think I can guess what she has to communicate," said he, rising with his big hand
extended; "for no one but you could have
wrought such a miracle in my sister's condition,
and I wish to give you a brother's grip of thanks.
Have I not a brother in you?"

"You have," I answered, returning his warm
grasp, "and I will do all in my power to make
Theo's life a happy one as long as Heaven loans
her to earth, and, should I outlive her, I shall ever
honor and cherish her memory."

"May the God you serve bless you both," he said earnestly, and left the room. At the door, he managed to add, "I leave you both to better company than I can furnish."

I remained alone a few minutes, lost in my own reflections, and then, recalling Theo's command, I tapped at her door. She came forward as I entered, and, taking me by the hand, led me to the sofa, and seating herself by my side, looked up into my face with that charming confidence and sweetness, which she and Ethel both had in common, and beaming with pleasure at what she was about to communicate, said:

"I have good news for you—awfully good news."

"Awful and yet good! So good I shall stand in awe of it, I suppose?"

"Yes, bordering on the sublime, you know. At any rate, it is tremendous, stupendous, magnificent, perfectly lovely!—just what ought to be."

"I am afraid you are raising my expectations too high. Do divide your secret with me before I burst with curiosity."

"Well, first I must exact a promise that you will not fly up through the roof never to come down again!"

"I promise."

"Prepare yourself for the shock, then. Here it is—Ethel Blentwood loves you and you only!" And she looked into my face as if to read my every emotion.

"How do you know that? I asked.

"O, not from her own lips; but I saw it in her eyes."

"And you are jealous, and are going to shoot somebody?"

"Do you see the green-eyed monster in my eyes? It would be there if you were not loved by her." She scanned my face more closely.

"What! do you wish her to love me? Aren't you afraid that will make me love her?"

"You do love her already."

"That is past tense. Let the dead bury their dead."

"Yes, if dead; but this happens to be a corpse a little too lively to submit to burial."

"I thought it understood between us, that that particular past should be buried and forgotten; and here you are raking off the ashes from an old fire to see if there are any live coals, and fanning them into a flame by telling me that Ethel loves me. Are you testing me to see if I can——"

"No, no! You would be as true as steel wherever you had set your promise. I know that. But I want you to love Ethel Blentwood with all your heart—with all the intensity of your being."

"And not love you?"

"I want a place in both of your hearts—a loving and trusted sister's place."

"And that is all?

"All."

"Then it is true, is it, that you do not love me?"

"O, no! That is not true. I must be frank with you. I really believe I could immolate my body on an altar of fire, if thereby I could add to your happiness, and at the same time, please the Master. Your blessedness would take away all the pain of physical torture."

"My God! What am I to receive such love? And yet you are willing and anxious to give me up to another?"

"I would give you up to no one but Ethel."

"And why even to her?"

"Because I love you better than I do myself, and want to see you make the most of yourself in the line of usefulness as well as happiness; and Ethel is the angel sent down from Heaven expressly to meet all your requirements, and help you accomplish your mission."

I took both of her hands. "Do you think I can so easily give you up and lose so great a love, the like of which I could never hope to see again? I am too selfish for that."

"Too generous, you mean. You would be equal to any sacrifice for my welfare, and I know you would love me dearly, were there no Ethel; but there is an Ethel, my ideal, my nobler self, the perfect expression, like you, of what I would be, but am not, and, knowing her to be so much better fitted to bring out the affection, the glory —all that is highest and deepest in you for your own good as well as others', I want you to marry her. In so doing you will marry my true self Theo at her best."

"And neither retain, nor gain, a Theo's love."

"Yes, you will retain my love cleansed and purified from all earthly dross, and you will gain a love equal, if not superior, to mine. I have sounded the depths of her noble nature far enough to believe that she may be yours with all the wealth of her being, so abundantly, so richly endowed—yours for the asking."

"Theo, the very sacrifice you would make only reveals what a treasure you are, and draws me closer to you. You are too good to lose."

"You will not lose me. I shall look upon you as the husband of my spiritualized and better self, and I want the privilege of being a trusted, confidential friend to both of you. Ethel reads me, and knows me, too well to be jealous of the sister's love I propose to give you both henceforth."

"Theo," I said, looking earnestly into her eyes, "do you mean it? Do you really and truly wish me to marry Ethel Blentwood? And would you live just as long, and just as happily? Speak out freely, frankly, right from the centre of your great, good, true heart. To ever know that you vary now a hair's breadth from the truth in your answer, would kill me. I cannot see you sacrificed, and be myself happy."

"Call it not sacrifice; for I can be happy only in seing you the happy husband of happy, confiding, tenderly loving and glorious Ethel Blentwood. I speak the truth."

Her face seemed transfigured, as she looked at me, her very soul shining through it clear, pure, translucent and transparent as the sunlight which fell at that moment on her brow, as if to crown her for the victory she had attained over self. It was a marvelous exhibition of the higher nature over the lower.

How did she reach a state of unselfishness so beautiful and so commanding? The Darwinian might answer, that she had thrown off the brute-inheritance, which is always selfish, by developing the kindly, sympathetic side of her nature, and, thereby, risen above the animal into a spiritual life. The Christian could answer, that the secret of her victory was something, which, in the language of Jesus to Peter, "flesh and blood" had not revealed unto her, and that her attainment was clearly the fruit of the Spirit, which, Paul tells us, is "love, joy, peace, long-suffering, gentleness, goodness, faith, meekness, temperance," or self-control.

But the question forces itself upon us, Why should such goodness, great and glorious as it is, be so exceptional? Is it not within the possible reach of every human being? Is it not rather marvelous that in these last days of the nineteenth century, since the planting of Christianity on the earth, that, instead of one person, there are not hundreds exhibiting the full fruit of the Spirit? I venture the assertion, that when Christianity, as portrayed in the person of Jesus, shall be better studied and appreciated, there will be a great revolution in Christian methods, and in the personnel of the Christian church.

Then the dispositional man, or beauty of character, will be looked upon as the safest exponent of his creed, as a follower of Jesus, the Nazarene. Creed-worshippers doubtless believe they are following Him; but are they, except from afar? Do they exhibit his love, his self-sacrificing spirit, his sweet temper, his considerate attention and condescension? Faith in a creed may not be faith in Him. Jesus says, Follow Me, and to follow Him is to pattern after Him.

But to our story. Can the reader imagine my feelings, as I looked upon Theo's glowing face? Her assurance that my first and real love was reciprocated, made me long to fly to Ethel and tell her, in her hour of sorrow, how dearly I loved her, and would lift the burdens of life from her; and then, again, it seemed awful to forsake Theo, who had revealed such devotion—such exalted traits of character. How would her self-denial affect her health and happiness in the future, if I acquiesced in it? Would there be no reaction to her enthusiasm, no coming regret?

"How can I leave you?" I asked, "or be happy in the thought of having left you, however blissful my union with Ethel might otherwise be?"

"Oh! you need not, must not pity me. Know you not that the happier you and Ethel are in each other's love, the happier I shall be? Ever since learning that Ethel was the one, I have been satisfied and glad in the thought of your union. Everything is just as it should be, and we shall all be happy, gloriously happy. Remember you promised to let me have my own way, and the only way I can start the little heaven you asked for is to bring you and Ethel together. Any other course would be misery, and, therefore, foolish, suicidal, wicked."

The rising tides within me overflowed my eyes, and Theo, pulling my head down, said sympathetically, "There is no reason why a brother should not weep on his sister's shoulder!" and I did weep and felt better for it; and let no one think to blame me, or to belittle the act, until able to put himself or herself in my place. The trial to a sensitive moral nature was tremendous.

CHAPTER XLVI.

AT length the mists of doubt and uncertainty cleared away, revealing the path of right and duty for me to tread, though I felt none of the assurance Theo possessed, that I should be accepted by Ethel.

Theo, in raptures of anticipation, exclaimed, " I can hardly wait for the joyous consummation. Delays are dangerous. You must see Ethel this very afternoon. She must not know, certainly at present, that I have ever had anything but a sister's love for you, or she would refuse you for my sake, which would be a disaster all round. My hopes of a satisfactory life depend now on realizing the happy and useful home you and she can create, together with what I may be able to contribute. I will go at once and take her place at her father's bedside, and send her to the garden, where she may enjoy the fragrant air and sunshine. She needs them, and she needs you. There is an arbor there, if the sun is too hot ! "

There was a pleased, a joyous look in her sparkling eyes, as she raised them to mine, and then Theo Thornton went on her errand of exalted love.

426

I took my hat and went out, not knowing whither I went, and scarcely knowing whether in the body or out, my spirit flitting, now into the past and now into the future, leaving my body to guide itself as best it could, with little more than the mechanism of animal life. I walked on the front piazza, and then on the lawn, and finally gravitated towards a little grotto leading, unexpectedly, through a covered way, to the flower-garden. I was not yet fully conscious where I was, being in a day-dream or visionary mood, lost to everything but the world in which lived Ethel and Theo.

I came to myself on entering the grotto, its stones, its mosses, its shells and ferns, kept cool from the slow dripping of a concealed water pipe, attracting me to its refreshing shade and beauty. At what appeared to be the end of the cavern, and artfully hidden by rock-work, was an opening into a long grape arbor; and here a sight met my eyes, which made me feel for an instant that I was in the presence of a supernatural visitant; and I could only wonder whether Heaven held anything more beautiful.

At the other end of the grapery, into which I was looking, where a golden ray of sunlight rested on her head and brow, stood Ethel Blentwood in a snow-white dress, with one arm raised above her head; the sleeve, made for comfort, falling back and displaying a round, white arm; her graceful figure framed in beautiful contrast with the surrounding green; her head and neck splendidly poised ; the resplendent color seeming to mount and play over her finely-cut features, as if delighted to do duty there ; her large, lustrous eyes raised, and her ruby lips slightly parted, as if in prayer, or as if seeing a vision which surprised and delighted her ; all combining to make a picture supremely lovely—so lovely that I felt like falling at her feet in worship. She seemed too angelic to be of this world.

"Is it possible," I queried, "that she can love a poor mortal like me, of so much coarser clay ? "

It staggered belief, and I felt the weight of great misgivings. I had walked so softly she did not hear my approach. I stood irresolute for a moment, whether to retreat or go on ; but finally, unable to control myself any longer, I stepped heavily to call her attention and then exclaimed :

"O, Miss Blentwood ! Stay just as you are— don't stir, please, and let me look at you a little nearer."

Though somewhat startled at first, she obeyed, and as I drew near, smilingly asked, in her effort to conquer her blushes, " Was I statuesque ? "

"You must let me bring a photographer and have you taken in that position," I replied. " The picture ought to be permanently preserved. I should value it so much, Miss Blentwood."

" Why do you call me Miss Blentwood ? " she asked demurely. " I thought you were to call me Ethel."

" You looked so spiritual, so far above and

beyond me, I could not feel worthy to use that familiar title."

"I cannot think you would seriously banter me in just this way," she said, dropping her eyes more perplexed than annoyed; and yet, how can you, from whom I have learned so much that is noble and spiritually uplifting, feel as your language inditates?"

"Dear Miss Blentwood!—Miss Ethel, I mean— you have no idea how heavenly you looked. I felt like John on the isle of Patmos, when he fell down at the feet of his angelic guide to worship him. And this is not the first time I have felt so in your presence, though never so much as now. Oh! if I were higher, nobler, more worthy if my spirit shone as purely, as beautifully through all my features and acts, as does yours, I would not only dare to call you Ethel, but dear Ethel, and even ask you to be my Ethel--and and —selfish and bold as it seems in me, I must ask it any way." Grasping her hands impulsively, and looking earnestly and pleadingly into her face, I added, "Can you—will you be my own dear Ethel?"

I waited, the spirit of compelling love pervading me, and speaking more powerfully than words. She did not speak, but two tears gathered, and I asked, "Are these the tears of pity and refusal?"

I felt certain that a nature so transparent would speak frankly the exact truth as far as she could interpret it, from the very center of her being. When she found her voice, she answered:

"They are only tears of gratitude. I have loved

you from the very first, and love has only been
growing deeper, broader, purer ever since; and
now it seems a part of my very life, inseparable
from it, and had you not spoken, how could I
have lived?"

"Thank God! My own, precious, darling
wife!" I ejaculated, stretching out my arms as
she came to the heart that claimed her. "I had
seen you with my mind's eye, and known and
loved you before we ever met, and this is only the
outward acknowledgment of a long, long love,
which was yours as soon as I first saw you.
Counting time by heart-throbs, I have known you
years, where I have known others only moments."

That there was music in our hearts and on our
lips, the divinest that mortals ever hear, need not
be told; for our love was real, grounded in the
spirit, and sustained by all the laws of perfect,
mutual affinity.

The new, strange thrill of heart meeting heart
may be imagined, but not described. Suffice it
to say, we were as blissfully forgetful of the world,
and as luxuriously grateful and content, as two
mortals could well be. It seemed to me that there
could not be, on this whole earth, so perfect and
felicitous a union of head, heart and soul, as was
ours. We who had been separate and incomplete, because wanting each other, were now one
in thought, purpose and feeling, each supplying
and completing, in the other, what was lacking to
a full, rounded-out, human entity. May not such
a perfect, complemental union, such a satisfying

"I SHOULD BE SO HAPPY, FATHER, IF YOU WERE NOT HURT." —*page 451.*

sense of wholeness as we enjoyed, give some slight hint of the united qualities in the   and personality of Jesus, the perfect Man! In Him there was no lack. All His faculties and powers were in perfect proportion, perfect harmony, perfect union.

How long we stood, or when we sat down on a rustic seat in the arbor, I know not. It is enough to say that we went with glowing countenances and happy hearts into the presence of her father whom I now looked upon as my father. Theo had that moment stepped out of the room, designedly I think, and hand in hand we approached his bedside. He looked up inquiringly into first one face and then the other, and then a bright smile broke over his face like a wave of light.

"You need not say a word," he said. "I understand. It is all written in your faces; and may the light kindled there never lessen, but rather grow brighter and brighter as long as you live!"

"It is all right, then, is it? You give your full consent, Doctor Blentwood?"

"I do unreservedly. I cannot leave my beloved daughter in safer and more trusted hands. I shall now die content."

A great sob burst from Ethel's heart despite her efforts to control herself.

"I should be so happy, father," she said, bowing her head on his face, "if you were not hurt!"

"You must get well," I added, "and live with us. What a happy home we will create!"

"I have no doubt of it," he replied, stroking Ethel's head tenderly, and with moist eyes, "and it would be pleasant to spend there my declining years in Christian-literary work. But you must neither of you let my little illness interfere with your joys. I do not suffer, and am getting well fast, and shall soon have perfect health, never again to be impaired. I am to live as never before. You are not going to lose me, nor I you. A few days of separation, and we come together again."

Placing Ethel's hand in mine, and pressing them in both of his, he added:

"This is one of the most sacred and blessed moments of my life; for I can almost see my angel wife making one of this group, joyfully giving her consent, and saying in her old sweet way, 'They will be just as happy as we have been; so you have nothing to hinder you from coming home to me and Heaven.'"

Something in his cheerful mood and words comforted Ethel, and she raised her head and looked upon him, and then upon me, with a sweetness which seemed seraphic. Heaven seemed so near to her father that he murmured, as if talking to his wife, "Not quite yet. I have one more duty." Then turning to me he said:

"It would be very pleasant to me to see you married before I go. I can then leave the old home unbroken in number, and with its ideal blessedness preserved."

"It would be a source of great satisfaction all

my life to remember that you performed that ceremony for us," I answered, looking to Ethel for her consent.

She pressed my hand gently, and bowing, hid her face in her father's neck, and amid kisses and little sobs, whispered something in his ear which caused a sympathetic smile to ripple over his kindly face, as he said, —

" I am very, very thankful that I can leave you so happily matched. It is a union, I believe, sanctioned by Heaven, as was that of your mother and myself. I could not ask anything different. There is nothing in this world more beautiful than a perfect union. When shall it be legally consummated ?"

" Whenever you and Ethel shall decide," I made answer, as I retired into another room, leaving them to consult together.

When I returned, it was decided that it was not safe to delay longer than necessary for the preparatory steps to be taken.

Looking at my watch, I remarked, " We have time, before my train starts, to acquaint Theo, our kind hostess, with the news of the day."

" Yes," the doctor interjected, thoughtful only of others, " go with him, and I will rest awhile ; but first humor my weakness, if you call it such, by each taking my hand and joining your own. Now kiss each other as a pledge of eternal union. Now, Ethel, give that mutual kiss to me. It will be a comfort to carry the remembrance of it to Heaven and your mother, should anything happen

28

to prevent my seeing you united in marriage. There! Now go, and God bless you, my dear children. I cannot hold any more happiness just now."

Profoundly grateful for his cordial assent to our union, I turned as we were leaving his room, and waved back my adieus laden with emotions not to be expressed in words. He signaled an answering joy, and looked, as his words indicated, a very happy man, to be envied rather than pitied.

We found Theo in a restless state of expectancy. As soon as she saw our approach through the partially opened door, she flew to us like a bird, embracing us enthusiastically and exclaiming, " Do tell us what has happened ! You both look as if you had reached the seventh heaven of bliss! Marvelous transformation! I scarcely know you ! Your faces shine as Moses' must have done, when he came down from the mount ! O, do keep on looking just as happy always! It glorifies you! It spiritualizes you! But please don't vanish out of my sight !"

She danced about us in raptures of delight, so unlike her quiet self, that I began to fear the recent strain had been too much for her. She drew us into the room, and, seating us on the sofa, looked at each of us alternately with eyes sparkling and cheeks aglow with excitement, as if she expected a " a feast of fat things."

" What is it ?" she urged. " I must know all about it, you know,"

As I did not speak immediately, she pressed Ethel's head close and lovingly to her shoulder, and, looking down into her eyes steadily for a moment, said softly:

" I see the whole, tell-tale affair in these beautiful soul-windows of yours, unobscured by even a curtain. I can look right into the living room, and see a throne erected, and love on the throne. He has conquered your two kingdoms and made them one, and that is why the signals of joy are hung out so plainly on your faces. I pray you, let me have a sister's place in this new kingdom, or I shall be lonely indeed."

"We cannot reign satisfactorily without you," I said, and Ethel added:

"You have been an angel of goodness to me ever since I have known you, and to sustain such a relation to you, in reality and not in name merely, will be a source of great comfort and satisfaction to me. I need just such a dear sister as you can be; and I want you to be a sister to Elbert, too."

"O, you precious, darling Ethel! What a dear prize you are!" Theo burst out, clasping and kissing her passionately.

They remained for some time locked in each other's embrace, mingling their tears of mutual joy and sympathy, when I remarked dolefully:

"I seem to be left out of all this good fellowship!"

They both laughed, and Theo asked Ethel, "Shall I kiss my new brother?"

" Nothing would please me more, unless—unless it would be to kiss him myself also," and Ethel hid her blushes in Theo's lap.

Something approaching a gentle little frolic followed, which was a necessary relaxation of our overstrained nerves, and helped prepare us for the ordeal throught which we were so soon to pass. It was mutually agreed and pledged, that Theo should regard herself, and be ever loved, esteemed, and confided in, by us, as a sister tried and true.

CHAPTER XLVII.

PREPARATORY.

THE next train found me whirling towards Graynoble, where I had first met Ethel. Thede drove me to the station, and on the way I explained to him the situation of affairs, as best I could. He was disappointed, but somewhat reconciled when he learned that the new arrangement was Theo's wish, and that the happiness and usefulness of all concerned would be subserved by it.

Arriving at Graynoble, I found Tom suffering from a slight attack of pneumonia, and he and Tot overwhelmed me with protestations of pleasure at seeing me, and with earnest questions about Dr. Blentwood and Ethel. Since I had come from under " de holy shadow ob de Blentwoods," Tom wished me to pray with him.

" It may please de great Oberseer," he said, with tears of joy glistening on his glad face, " dat I climb de golden stair jes, when good massa Blentwood do, so I kin hep him all de way up to glory. He be so use to me I kin sarve him better den any udder spirit, and if de soul ob my ole fiddle go wid me, I knows jes what ter play for to

437

chirrup him up on de long journey. An'—an' if he wanster rest on one ob dem steps, and take anudder' look down hyyah at you and Ethel, I knows jes how ter hole 'im, for dese hands hab done it when he had de newrollogy and spinal megintis. Please tell de Lord 'bout dis, an' ax Him ef I mount be foun' worthy to go wid 'im. 'Twould happify my soul bery much."

I complied with his request, and read to him some comforting passages of Scripture, though neither I, nor Dr. Lightheart, whom I consulted, considered him critically ill at that time. As I shook hands with him, and bade him good-bye, he said :

"De prophetic vision am now sure to come to pass. Please tell Miss Ethel Ize gwine to take keer ob her father, and so she needn't worry 'bout him."

I had only time, as I supposed, to catch the train, and so hurried away, examining my note-book and pockets, as I went, to make sure that I had done all my errands ; but when seated in the car I began to wonder what Tom meant by "prophetic vision." After long and persistent retrospect I recalled the fact that on my first walk with the family at Dr. Blentwood's, Tom, whom we met, had hinted of a vision, which I might know would come to pass if I prayed at his dying bedside. "Tom evidently thinks he is going to die," I mused, "and so wishes me to understand that his vision of my bright future is to be realized." Did he mean *with* Ethel ? The more I recalled his language, the more I was satisfied that that was what he meant. It did not seem at all probable that I had come from Tom's death-bed, and so I dismissed the subject.

Seeing Miss Elison through the car window, I went out and learned that she had become Mrs. Stockmire the day previous. She expressed great regret that Dr. Blentwood, or myself, or both of us, as was her wish, could not have officiated at her wedding.

" Poor girl," I thought, " she will soon regret she ever married at all," and this feeling was confirmed as I caught a malicious glance from Stockmire, who had been watching us, and at that moment turned towards the ticket-office, and pretended not to see me. That look was a revelation. In an unguarded moment the hard, cold, hideous selfishness of the man had come to the surface, and his hating, revengeful spirit stood bare before me. His resumption of the soft veil of hypocrisy would now be of no avail to blind me, since I had seen the guilt in his heart reddening forth like the miraculous blood-stain of a murder.

The thought of what that man might do, in an evil hour of temptation, made me shudder. And yet, a man like Stockmire, living in externals, seldom or never looking within, doubtless took no note in his daily life of his ability to do evil, so effectually covered and polished over, as it was, by ornamental disguises and ostentatious humility.

On my journey back to the Thornton home, which contained what was most dear to me in life, I was tortured by the fear that some untoward event might occur to cut off the prize apparently so near at hand. It seemed too great and too good to be mine. My anticipations also were tempered and shadowed by the certain demise of Ethel's father, both because he was her father, and because he was a man after my own heart. "How can I fill the place of so grand a man, and relieve her from a life-long sadness?" I asked myself over and over. O, how I prayed that his nobility of mind, heart, and disposition might be mine!

The train did not move half fast enough, but as all things must come to an end, I alighted at last at the desired station, and, to my surprise and great satisfaction, found Thede in waiting.

He did not much expect me, he said, but Theo had insisted on his coming, and somehow he had fallen into the habit of obeying her, as she had a "knack of being pretty generally right."

Ethel was the first to greet me, telling me with tears how her father had failed, and how she had longed for my return, and how thoughtful and self-sacrificing Theo had been; and then stopping suddenly, and looking earnestly in my face, added pathetically:

"Do you know, Theo watched for you, and when she saw you and Thede far off, she hurried to me, and, taking my place, made me leave the sick room, that I might be the first to greet you,

though the dear girl was almost as impatient as I
myself! Isn't she lovely? And aren't we fortunate in having such a friend, such a sister?
Her frequent companionship will be so delightful! She will help me make home pleasant for
you. Oh! we must have a home just as near
heaven as we can make it, for dear father's sake,
for your sake and for everybody's sake, and that
means for the Master's sake."

"Yes, darling," I answered, clasping her in my
arms; "but it will be heaven wherever you are;
for, with my love for you there is always blended
something above the human, something divine,
an uplifting gratitude to the Master, which is an
inspiration. I am so grateful for you I am filled
with worship. We will make home-life a study,
a loved science, the noblest art.

"Without you," she replied, "how could I bear
up under the dreadful thought of separation from
my dear, dear father! He says he shall go away
without an anxious thought for me, so confident
is he that you will more than fill his place. His
restful faith in you, and trustful reliance on you,
help me bear the thought of his loss."

"And it pledges me," I affirmed, drawing her
closer to me, "most sacredly and irrevocably to a
life-long endeavor to do, and to be, all that he
believes me, and what the Master would have me;
but, dearest, remember that I am very faulty, and
do not expect me to fill your ideal, until you have
patiently taught me."

Holding up a finger of warning, she darted off,

saying, "Sister Theo must now have the pleasure of seeing you, and directing your supper."

She had scarcely gone, when Theo came tripping softly through the open door, and greeted me as a sister should, in accordance with our tripartite agreement ; and, escorting me to the dining-room, she presided at the table as cheerful and happy as thoughts of the near dissolution of Dr. Blentwood would allow.

I found the latter considerably changed during my absence, but still bright, and much gratified to see me safely returned. As he was stronger in the morning, it was thought best to defer the intended ceremony till the next day.

That night, as I was sitting up with the doctor, the others having just retired, a telegram came to me in care of Theodore Thornton from Charley Lightheart, stating that he had been promoted, and would be ready for my services to-morrow morning.

" That means a wedding," I said to Thede, who brought the telegram. " He is probably on the night Pullman, and is proving what he said about marriage following promotion was not all a joke."

" That is the funniest fellow I ever saw," said Thede,—" full of it, boiling over with it, but an upright, downright, and all-through, royal good fellow, and I hope he will find in Carrie Horton the wife he deserves. The medical fraternity could not get much practice where he is. I almost think even Theo might get well in the constant sunshine of his hopeful, fun-loving disposition.

Next to you I would like him for a brother-in-law. But something has worked a miracle in Theo, and I laid the improvement to you. I don't quite understand her. I know she loved you, and yet she seems to take as much interest in your approaching marriage to Miss Blentwood, as if it were her own wedding. What does it mean, friend Bloomfield?"

"It means,' I replied, taking Thede's hand warmly, " that your sister is a wise and thoroughly unselfish girl, taking infinitely more delight in making others happy than in any thought of good which might accrue to herself. She is a practical illustration of the joys of self-sacrifice made for the noblest ends. Ethel and I are very happy in each other, so much so we cannot conceive how we could be happier, and yet I believe Theo's joy is even keener and more glorious in the sight of Heaven than ours. I look upon her sometimes almost with envy for the divine quality, which glows and glistens through all her acts of self-renunciation. I know she is more delighted and more thankful in what she has done to bring Ethel and me together, than she ever was in the thought of marrying me; and so I feel I am only carrying out her wishes. She knew I loved Ethel before Ethel knew it, and it was her woman's intuition that discovered Ethel's love for me. She feels that it would be wickedly contending against the divine plan to hinder in the least, or even fail to help on, **my marriage** with Ethel. She believes in it with all her heart. In fact, her happiness, as our friend, is bound up in it.

" I need not say how high Theo stands in my esteem. I admire and love her greatly as a sister, and so does Ethel, and we hope for the closest friendship with her and yourself through life. We owe much to you both, and as she is to let us regard her as a sister, will not you be to us a brother? The ties of a common friendship are not sufficient ; we crave a closer relation, that we may share with you the esteem, the trust, the confidence, the freedom of a family united in the strongest bonds of attachment."

He was visibly moved. His big hand closed about mine with a grip which made my hand ache, and with that he left me alone.

This conversation had been carried on almost in a whisper in the room off from the sick chamber, and as soon as left to myself, I carefully looked in on the patient, when he opened his eyes. He beckoned to me, and, as I went to his bedside, he said :

" Heaven is beginning to open to me, and I am so thankful for this and for the sweet satisfaction I have in the thought that Ethel's future is safe in your hands, that I cannot sleep for very joy. I know not how to express my gratitude in words, and need your help. Will you not offer thanks for me ? "

I slowly took his hand in both of mine, and, with a silent petition that I might meet his wants, I knelt by his side and poured out my heart to

Him, who can hear with answering grace when all earthly helps and sympathies fail. Though grieved to lose the father of my espoused wife, I caught something of his gratitude that the way from earth to Heaven was made for him so smooth and bright. When I arose, the good man pressed my hand and said:

" You have told the Lord just what I wanted to tell Him, and now, with my feelings so adequately expressed, I think I can sleep. I thank you."

He closed his eyes, and I retired to the adjoining room to think, and I thought deeper into life that night than ever before, and when morning came, much of earthly dross had passed from me, forever. Henceforth Heaven seemed nearer, clearer, dearer, as a real, actual advanced condition, and the opportunities of life more valuable as means to an end.

In the early hours of the morning, before anyone else was stirring, Ethel came and insisted that I take some sleep. She wished also to be alone with her father awhile ; and as the nuptial hour was fast approaching, when she would become a wife as well as daughter, I felt rather than reasoned out, the appropriateness and beauty of her wish. She was about to take the most momentous step in life ; and, as her father, until within a few short weeks, had absorbed all her love and confidence, her act was a thoughtful consideration, in perfect keeping with the absolute trust which had been mutual between them, especially since the death of the mother, which threw upon him the tender watchfulness and care inhering in both parental offices.

But why should not every father be as tenderly sympathetic, and delicately appreciative, towards his children as the mother? And why should not a daughter, or son, be as free to confer with one parent as with the other? The frivolous and shallow-brained have marred society and retarded human progress too long. It is time that a deeper, broader, holier view of the sacred obligations involved in all the relations of life, pertaining to human welfare, should prevail.

These reflections, however, are the result of years of study, and not those occupying my mind on that supposed last morning of single blessedness. What were then my thoughts and feelings may, perhaps, be better imagined than described. My increasing veneration and love for Dr. Blentwood, the transcendent delicacy and tenderness of father and daughter in their attitude towards each other, my desire to minister to them both in all possible ways, together with questions of future happiness and usefulness with Ethel as the mistress of my home and my companion through life, were among the thoughts which kept me awake, and even invaded my dreams, when I at last fell asleep on that eventful morn—a morn which was to settle the destiny of at least two loving hearts for time, and, perhaps, in some respects, for eternity—who knows?

CHAPTER XLVIII.

WEDDINGS AND REUNIONS.

CHARLEY Lightheart and Carrie Horton arrived about eight A.M., and insisted on my marrying them at once. "Dear old chum," Charley exclaimed, unable wholly to suppress his quaint love of fun, "I am to be metamorphosed, transmogrified into a staid old married man, and the transformation must be associated with you."

"I don't think," said Theo, "that you will lose your identity easily. I hope, at least, your effervescent spirits will stand the test of time and change; for society, and especially we invalids, need persons like you to drive off the blues. You are better than medicine, Mr. Lightheart. If you were only a physician, you could prescribe bread pills and cure your patients by means of social visits."

"I thank you," Charlie responded, bowing low, "Your suggestion is a revelation of a possible new profession, which I may adopt, if I lose my position on the editorial staff."

At this juncture Dr. Lightheart was announced, and, as Dr. Blentwood was asleep, he came into the long parlor, and in his presence and that of

the household, I united in holy wedlock my
friend Charley Lightheart and Carrie Horton.
Charley had secured seats in the next Pullman
train for New York, and so, scarcely touching
coffee and cake, which Theo, in her usual thoughtfulness for everybody, had provided, they departed, full of hope and bright anticipations,
leaving us with our immediate future clouded by
thoughts of bereavement and mourning.

Dr. Blentwood awoke at ten o'clock, and was
ministered unto by Dr. Lightheart, when, bol-
stered up in bed, he received Ethel and me with
a smile of satisfaction, as we went arm in arm to
his bedside.

The marriage ceremony was unique. I have
often said it would be worth a year's labor, could
I recall, word for word, all that dropped from his
lips, so entirely new and helpful were his ideas,
falling sweet and sacred, and with healing balm
on our waiting, sorrowing hearts. He seemed to
stand, and as the sequel proved, did actually stand,
at the open door of Heaven, and was as much inspired as any prophet old or new ; and when he
had finished, without premeditation, we instinctively knelt and received from him, with his hands
on our bowed heads, a fervent " God bless you,
my dear children."

His countenance was so radiant with spiritual
light, he seemed like one talking to us from the
very gate of glory, and to come down to earth
only when he placed his signature to our marriage
certificate. Then followed another scene, at the

very thought of which, tears unbidden blind my
eyes, so that I can scarcely see to write—tears,
however, not of vain regret, or unillumined
sorrow, not even of sorrow of any kind, but on
account of the very sublimity of what occurred,
so full of the realities of the unseen world.

He spoke of his near departure, as if he was
only to move from one good room into a better
one, and a little in advance of us—that was all.
"She is waiting for me," he said, pointing upwards, "and we will wait for you. What difference who goes first, since all must go? Time
passes quickly even with the longest life. I have
finished my course, and now have nothing really
to detain me. School is out. I leave you happy
in each other's love to complete your earthly
schooling, and I have no anxiety for your future.
A few more days of study and toil, of joy and
perhaps of sorrow, and then we shall all be together again. It is as certain as that we are
together now. I begin to know. Faith is changing to sight. This ceiling is not real. It lifts.
It dissolves. I see through it. It is all open
above me. There are flittings of angels' wings.
They are hovering round. They have come to
take me from this fleshly prison. Oh, what ex-
panding freedom! Listen! What strains of en-
trancing melody! It comes nearer. It is a
welcome. Life and Heaven! Oh, how beautiful! Yes, dear wife, I am coming. Glorious!
glorious!—glo—rious!"

The last word was a whisper. His eyes became
29

fixed heavenward, and, with one finger pointing up, he passed away, leaving a smile behind, as a farewell benediction.

" He is with mother now," Ethel whispered, a gleam of comfort lighting up her tearful face.

" And what a blissful reunion is theirs ! " I answered, " I thank God I have known Dr. Blentwood. His memory will be a sweet and helpful presence as long as I live."

Ethel looked to me gratefully, and as she bowed her head on my shoulder, as if to say, " I have only you to cling to now," I whispered, " We have each other, and my whole heart is yours, Ethel, and let us thank God for this revelation we have witnessed, proving that your father, and my father also henceforth, still lives in the enjoyment of a blissful immortality, there to await and welcome us, when we have finished our course, as he has finished his."

Theo, with the peaceful smile of one who had seen a vision, came up and kissing us both, said simply, but joyfully, " He is not dead."

All this time Dr. Lightheart stood gazing at the silent form as if he would look through him into eternity, and, at last exclaimed, as he turned away, " Would to God I had that man's experience ! "

I dwell a little on this scene, for I value the memory of it beyond all price, because it is an ever vivid proof of immediate blessedness, not only after, but at death, of a soul that has developed spiritually, and come up into harmony

with the higher life. I do not mean to say that
every such soul will exhibit at death so manifest
a revelation, but that the spirit-land cannot be
wholly hid from the spiritually minded, whether
making it known to others or not.

We had not expected Dr. Blentwood would
leave us so soon, and his sudden demise was a
great surprise to us; and yet his going was so
divinely illumined, we did not seem to stand in the
presence of death. There was nothing forbidding
about it. We could not feel that he had really
gone far—that we had in any true sense lost him.
He was still Ethel's father and mine, only just
now invisible to us—that was all. Sometimes,
even to this day, Ethel and I, when sitting together, become conscious of his presence, and
speak of it. If it be imagination, it is God-given
imagination, and a great comfort to us. Whether
he comes in any other sense than through
memory or not, we know that he LIVES.

www.ingramcontent.com/pod-product-compliance
Lightning Source LLC
Chambersburg PA
CBHW022028120726
47901CB00006BA/1484